I0577336

MENDING LOST DREAMS AT THE HIGHLAND REPAIR SHOP

KILEY DUNBAR

Boldwood

First published in Great Britain in 2025 by Boldwood Books Ltd.

Copyright © Kiley Dunbar, 2025

Cover Design by Lizzie Gardiner

Cover Images: Shutterstock and Adobe Stock

The moral right of Kiley Dunbar to be identified as the author of this work has been asserted in accordance with the Copyright, Designs and Patents Act 1988.

All rights reserved. No part of this book may be reproduced in any form or by any electronic or mechanical means, including information storage and retrieval systems, without written permission from the author, except for the use of brief quotations in a book review. This book is a work of fiction and, except in the case of historical fact, any resemblance to actual persons, living or dead, is purely coincidental.

Every effort has been made to obtain the necessary permissions with reference to copyright material, both illustrative and quoted. We apologise for any omissions in this respect and will be pleased to make the appropriate acknowledgements in any future edition.

A CIP catalogue record for this book is available from the British Library.

Paperback ISBN 978-1-83656-678-6

Large Print ISBN 978-1-83656-677-9

Hardback ISBN 978-1-83656-676-2

Trade Paperback ISBN 978-1-80656-079-0

Ebook ISBN 978-1-83656-679-3

Kindle ISBN 978-1-83656-680-9

Audio CD ISBN 978-1-83656-671-7

MP3 CD ISBN 978-1-83656-672-4

Digital audio download ISBN 978-1-83656-674-8

This book is printed on certified sustainable paper. Boldwood Books is dedicated to putting sustainability at the heart of our business. For more information please visit https://www.boldwoodbooks.com/about-us/sustainability/

Boldwood Books Ltd, 23 Bowerdean Street, London, SW6 3TN

www.boldwoodbooks.com

This one is for Lisa who always knows what to do. I am so grateful to you.

A WORD FROM KILEY

Hello, there!

Welcome to the Cairn Dhu Repair Shop and Café! Some of you have hastened back for a return visit, but for many this will be your first time stepping through the doors of the big repair barn on the western edge of the Cairngorms National Park up here in the beautiful Scottish Highlands. You don't need to know anything special about this area, I'll show you around soon, but if you're not familiar with the idea of a community repair project, let me fill you in.

Charlie McIntyre – who is in charge of the whole thing – won't mind me saying that, once upon a time, he was a hoarder of materials, tools, machinery and gadgets of all kinds. All he wanted was to be left in peace to tinker away the second half of his life in his massive, lonely shed. Unfortunately for him, he had sticky beak pals and a loving (if a wee bit direction-less) family encouraging him (read 'nagging') to put his collection (and his amazing fixing skills) to good use.

Following the ethos of 'remake, reuse, recycle' and inspired by the 'Repair Café' model – initially established in 2009 in Amsterdam by environmentalist Martine Postma – McIntyre decided to turn his shed over to the community so folks would have a place to come when their worn-out belongings were in need of expert repair.

Cairn Dhu's Repair Shop takes its place amongst the planet's many community fixing factories, tool, toy and equipment-rental projects, skills share ventures, clothes swaps and sewing circles, staffed by volunteers and expert fixers, and all for free.

You can search online for your nearest repair workshop, and (just in case you're craftily inclined) they may well be on the lookout for extra helpers!

The Cairn Dhu community know that taking care of their belongings and refusing to bin them and buy new is one in the eye for planet-polluting con-sumerism, while the town's repair specialists know *never* to take broken for an answer, and that goes for broken hearts too.

With the right mix of creativity and expertise, everything can be given new life, and that is why folks in need of hope and comfort (and maybe even a wee bit of romance) are today finding their way through the wild landscape and wintry weather to the Highland Repair Shop and Café. In fact, that's where new doctor, Alice Hargreave, is on her way to, right this second, and although she doesn't know it yet, there's no place on earth she needs more.

Happy reading, and happy repairing,

Love, Kiley, x

1

Why was the train going so slowly? Alice wondered, peering through the window into the late-afternoon pitch darkness, using her hands to block out the glare from the carriage lights overhead. All she could make out was a vague sense of big black mountains against a big black sky.

'Next stop, Kingussie. Next stop, Kingussie,' came the woman's voice over the speaker.

It was the same voice that had asked her if she'd wanted to buy, 'A wee cup of tea?' a few stops back as the trolley wheeled down the aisle. The woman had smiled so concernedly at her, Alice wondered if she looked as ghostly as she felt. She'd picked a tartan-labelled bottle of water and tried to smile reassuringly as she paid, hoping to convince the stranger (like she always wanted to convince everyone) that she was absolutely fine and totally in control.

Sleety January rain cast horizontal dots and dashes along the pane. A wet weather Morse code. Alice imagined each line an SOS. That's what this race north was: an emergency. One last effort to save herself and prove she was cut out for the medical life after all, and that her years of expensive, wearying training hadn't been for nothing.

The train rolled on through the dark, a few pinpricks of light suggesting farm buildings or tiny villages out in the gloom.

Until now, she'd thought of her hometown of Manchester as 'North', where everyone joked it was 'grim', where you needed your 'big coat' well into March or sometimes even late April. But this? This was north of North, and yet the train kept rattling up the track with as long as forty minutes between stops.

They'd called at so many tiny villages since leaving... what was it called? Something beginning with B? Birnam? Blair Atholl? The place names announced over the speakers had become a wash of sonorous Scottish vowels and rolled, rhotic consonants, the words growing stranger as the landscape grew less familiar the further she ventured from home.

By now, her suitcase was the only one in the luggage rack and so heavy she doubted anyone could nick it even if they tried. She didn't have to keep an eye on it now. Her stop was somewhere called Aviemore at the very end of the line so she wasn't going to accidentally end up at the North Pole or anything. She should try to get some sleep.

Sleep didn't come, however, even after that chilly, dark departure from Manchester long before dawn. Even after changing trains at Carstairs, then again at Edinburgh, she'd stayed alert, fighting every instinct to jump out at the very next station and turn for home.

It was way too late for that now. She was down the rabbit hole. This was where curiosity got you.

She really should close her eyes and rest. The other doctors she'd trained with seemed to have a knack of being able to sleep anywhere they could grab a rare break: across the mess sofas with the lights on and the telly blaring, slumped on armchairs in the on-call room, even on the floor in the supply cupboards or laundry store, or out in the hospital carpark after the night shift, reclined behind the steering wheel because it was safer to nap there than risk the bleary-eyed drive home only to have to come back a few hours later.

Alice hadn't the knack of switching off, even when exhausted, and she *knew* she was exhausted now. The glimpses of her reflection told her so: sallow white skin, dark-circled eyes, her fringe needing a trim, and the little lines at the edges of her mouth that wouldn't go away no matter how much she spent on miracle cure moisturiser.

The train had stopped and started again while she'd been looking at her rain-streaked reflection. She had the vaguest sense of her carriage having emptied and being left alone.

Whenever the carriage doors opened, a gust of air, unfathomably fresh and clean-smelling, had swept in. Compared to what she was used to on her cross-Manchester commute (petrol fumes and foody smells, fruity vapes and great clouds of weed smoked on the streets) this may as well be the high Himalayas.

She checked her phone: 16.37.

She fidgeted with her settings. No signal.

The mountains must dampen noise because all she could hear now was the heavy rumbling of the carriages over the tracks. No sirens. No voices. No distractions.

Alice didn't do well when left alone with her thoughts. Her brain liked to play tricks on her.

Within minutes of sitting slumped, staring out the window, her eyes glazing, her brain was already showing her a scene-by-scene derailment, her body thrown from her seat, glass smashing, bodies spilling on the track, fire and smoke everywhere. Alice as the lone survivor, desperately dragging the nice lady with the trolley out from beneath the twisted metal wreckage, performing CPR all by herself in the dark out on the rails, barely able to see straight, each burning lungful blown into the woman's strange, cold mouth sending her dizzy...

No. She shook her head to dispel the horror she'd conjured. Not here. She wasn't going to succumb to her brain's worst behaviour here.

Be present, she told herself. *Mindful*. Thinking fast, she reached into her bag and drew out the two envelopes she'd found yesterday on the mat while she was packing up her room in her trainees' flatshare.

Tomorrow, Saturday, the third of January, would be her birthday. She'd open her parents' cards now; separate cards, now that they were getting divorced. Inside, there were separate cheques, both made out for the same amount. They'd consulted one another. Like they had with all aspects of their painfully recent separation. They prided themselves on how amicable it had been. Meanwhile, Alice had felt like a frightened child witnessing them calmly divvying up the belongings they'd bought together over the last thirty years.

'We simply... fell out of love,' her father had explained at Boxing Day lunch, as he stood by her mother's side at the Aga; a smiling united front, breaking the news to their youngest child. Si and Rich, her brothers – both surgeons and living in London and Melbourne respectively – had been on shift and far away over Christmas. Si led a cardiothoracic team and Rich was in vascular surgery. She assumed they already knew about the separation; that was how things usually went in the Hargreave sibling pecking order.

'But we still love each other *very much*,' her mother had put in, gripping her wine glass a little too tightly.

Then they'd all eaten cold turkey salad at the kitchen table and pretended there wasn't a great seismic shift taking place while Alice wondered (but couldn't bring herself to ask) how long they'd been pretending to be happily married. Had she missed them falling apart since she'd been living away?

The next day her dad had moved into a house fifteen miles from her childhood home, where, it emerged, he had already installed a beautiful young surgical registrar.

Alice hadn't had a chance to speak to either of her parents since the Boxing Day bombshell. She tried not to feel too bad about it; it was only a week ago, and her parents were busy people. Consultant cardiologists always are. Cue as many jokes as you like about being the ideal couple to heal their own broken hearts. Her dad had cracked them all over that last family lunch.

'Twenty-eight years old!' her mother's card said inside, and, 'Good luck in Scotland, my darling.'

'Stiff upper lip,' her dad's read.

Nothing from Bastian, of course. She wondered if he'd text her tomorrow to wish her many happy returns. She hadn't heard from him since the day, a few weeks ago, she told him she was taking this GP training post and he'd sulked, saying she'd 'blindsided' him, before lecturing her about how she simply wasn't cut out for being so far away from him. How would she cope?

'You know how you've been lately,' he'd said. 'Do you have it in you? What if... you know, *it* happens again? Another episode? In a place where nobody knows you like I do?'

She couldn't tell him that was precisely the reason she'd accepted a job three hundred miles away, where nobody would know her secret. Besides, with a change of scenery and a change of pace, maybe she could get out of the habit?

That's what Bastian had described her vivid daydreaming as, a bad habit, and he only knew about the stuff she'd let him in on. Once she realised he thought it was a failing of hers, she kept the worst details secret, worried one day she might come close to losing her grip on reality entirely.

The textbooks hadn't helped reassure her either, or that one phone call with the consultant psychiatrist, a friend of her dad's, who'd told her it was possible she was 'exhibiting some of the traits of maladaptive daydreaming', her brief clinical experience of the condition frightening her so much she'd cancelled her second appointment and not dared to investigate his theory further.

After the big argument, back when she thought Bastian was simply taking some time alone to regulate his emotions, she'd texted him her train departure time, but he hadn't replied. That's when she realised they probably weren't going to recover from this.

Nevertheless, that hadn't stopped her from looking for him in the crowds at the station this morning, or imagining spotting him frantically searching for her at all the carriage windows, and when he found her, his face a picture of torment and relief, he'd run to her, his white clinician's coat flapping, telling her he was sorry, he'd overreacted, *of course* he'd wait for her. Then he'd lifted her in his arms, spinning her, laughing up into her face, kissing her like in the movies.

That daydream had been powerfully real too. So much so, as the vision evaporated she'd dropped into her seat, shaking and breathless. After a while, as the train pulled away, she'd waved goodbye to no one but the gammy Manchester pigeons.

'A dreamy child,' her teachers had called her. 'In her own little world.' It hadn't mattered so much when she was tiny and it was still cute.

Sometimes, when she was getting lost in her visions when they were supposed to be watching a movie together or when he was regaling her with gory tales from his wound care clinic that day, Bastian would snap his fingers near her ear and call her name like she was a patient on a resus trolley. 'Stay with me, Alice,' he'd say.

'Aviemore station in ten minutes,' the tannoy voice announced, bringing her round. Alice had been tracing a fingernail over the gilt figure-of-eight on her mother's birthday card like a race car on a track.

She stuffed the cards and cheques away in their envelopes before pulling free from her handbag the leaflet Dr Millen had sent her. She'd read it many times already.

Cairn Dhu General Practice looked recently built, if absolutely tiny, with only two consulting rooms, currently staffed by the ageing Millen and one part-time nurse practitioner.

Fiona, the Health and Social Care Partnership's HR exec for Cairn Dhu and its surrounding villages, had travelled to Dr Millen's surgery especially to conduct the interview, and Alice had joined them online. They'd been seeking to fill the post for some time, according to Fiona. Dr Millen's retirement was looming and they needed someone to take over from him, once they'd learned the ropes and 'got used to certain...' Dr Millen had cleared his throat, '...*eccentricities* of the area.'

Alice hadn't given much thought to what that might mean, only remarking that after half a decade of studying and two hair-raising stretches split across Geriatrics and Accident and Emergency, with some palliative care and hospice rounds too, there was absolutely nothing that could surprise her about medicine. Fiona had cast a sideways look at Dr Millen, who'd feigned composure, but Alice still caught the stifled, amused snorts.

They'd taken a long time to get back to her after that and she'd assumed it was a non-starter, but then suddenly it was all happening. Dr Millen himself had offered her the job over the phone. How quickly could she get to the Highlands? It would be an immediate start. 'In at the deep end, eh?' he'd said, something wry but grandfatherly in his voice.

She had bought a one-way ticket there and then, found a flat from a letting agency online, and broken the news to Bastian that night that she was leaving Manchester for eighteen to twenty-four months of on-job training, she couldn't be sure how long exactly. She'd be back as soon as her stint was over. She had zero plans to stay on in Cairn Dhu at the end of her placement and there was literally no way she wanted to take over from a country GP at the top end of nowhere, although at her interview she'd made sure to give the impression she'd love nothing more.

All she needed was a chance to forget the toll her training had taken, to get unstuck. Then she could return to England and show everyone the stern stuff she was made of.

Maybe then she'd be back in her own good books

after all the times she'd let herself come untethered from the here and now, not to mention that one mistake she'd made, when it all came to a head at the hospital; the one Bastian had covered up for her, knowing it could have been enough to end her career. Even though she hated to admit it, and Bastian never let her forget it, she owed him big time. In her mind's eye she saw herself now with the blue bloods tray, filling in the transfusion form, preparing that IV, all while she'd been in one of her dreamy stupors... She shook the image away, thanking her lucky stars Bastian had been there.

'Aviemore station! This is Aviemore,' the voice announced. 'All change. All change, please. Minibuses to Cairn Dhu, Stranruthie and onwards to the Garten valley estate leave from the stand opposite the station exit... if you're lucky.'

Alice jumped up even as the train rocked and rumbled, pulling on woolly gloves and gathered her belongings.

If you're lucky? Was this the beginning of the regional 'eccentricities' she'd been promised? Whatever it was, she'd take it all in her stride, like she handled everything else in life, head down and business as usual, and she'd mostly been fine. Right?

Besides, how bad could it be, doctoring in a small

practice, compared to the gritty relentlessness of the city hospitals? And in a Highland town in the middle of winter where probably nothing much ever happened?

'I feel better already,' she reassured herself, breathing through her nerves as she hauled her suitcase onto its wheels and the train pulled in alongside the rainy platform.

2

'I don't mind taking the teas through to the builders, cheers, Senga,' said Murray McIntyre, hurrying to relieve her of the tray and ignoring the pointed look the woman threw her sister, Rhona.

He knew what that look meant. It meant the Gifford women who ran his family's repair shop's café corner thought him *very* hospitable to the workmen who'd descended upon the big fixing barn shortly before Hogmanay. It meant they'd noticed him trying not to get flustered over that youngest one, the one sleeved in colourful tattoos, the one who'd clocked Murray the day they arrived with their scaffolding and who'd been trying to make him blush ever since.

'Chuck on a few of your iced biscuits an' all,' said Murray.

'Coming out of your pocket, are they?'

Senga, the retired GP's receptionist, talented baker and general busybody, positively vibrated with the urge to jump to conclusions. She'd have the pair wed by lunchtime if she could.

Cairn Dhu, you see, despite being remote and a wee bit lost in time, doesn't labour under cruel prejudices the way some places do. Pairings of every kind sent the old gossips into fits of matchmaking glee. Everyone here was looking out for love, it seemed, especially in the hungry, cold days of winter when salacious interest was thin on the ground.

Rhona, the quieter, put-upon Gifford sister, hastily worked her biscuit tongs and sent Murray on his way.

He straightened his spine as he made his way through the flap of plastic separating the floor of the repair shop and its café nook from the construction area at the shed's deepest point where the massive new eco-extension was taking shape, picking his way between the cables and power tools, piles of plasterboard and wool insulation rolls.

The repair shop hadn't been the same since Murray won the community development grant for the extension back in the early autumn. There'd been a sudden invasion of surveyors and architects and sustainable construction advisors, not to mention, more recently, the Cairn Dhu nosey parkers who wanted to have a keek (which, in Scotland, is an especially meddlesome kind of peep) at the transformation work.

'Teas up,' he called as flatly as he could, lifting his face to the temporary platform up in the apex of the old barn's roof. Three heads appeared over the parapet. The gaffer, oldest of the bunch, told him to, 'just leave 'em doon there,' but another voice, punchy and amused, shouted that he'd be straight down.

Descending on a pulley like the Nativity angel, the man appeared before Murray's eyes. Plaster-splattered boots slid past first, followed by two lengths of faded denim tight over sculpted calves and thick thighs. The scaffolder's pelvic harness gripped in a way that made Murray gulp and avert his eyes, and then came the t-shirt that suggested gym-sculpted pecs alongside rainbow flashes of ink on muscled arms, followed by a beautiful neck, a squared jaw and the palest blue eyes that put Murray in mind of that time he saw a kingfisher diving beneath the cool blue of the Nithy river in summer. All of this was delivered up with a smirk on pillowy lips that hid behind them a cocky Dutch accent. Deadly.

'Good morning, Murray. Are you joining us today?' said the builder, pointing to the heavens through a leather workman's glove.

Murray had to laugh. 'Again, no. But thanks for asking, *umm...*'

'Kurt,' the builder said, his maddening tooth gap on show, white and pink.

Murray ignored the alarm bells that smile set off within him, determining to act like he encountered flirty European construction experts every day of the week and he was completely chilled about it and in control of his blushes.

'Kurt,' Murray repeated, not sure why he'd pretended not to remember his name. 'Anyway... repair Saturdays are always busy busy busy. I'd better...' He fought the urge to wince at his awkwardness, hiking a thumb back towards the workshop beyond the café nook.

'Go fix things?' Kurt tried, still dangling hotly from the rope pulley, his steel toecaps grazing the floorboards. He reached for one of the takeout cups on Murray's tray and sipped through the steam without breaking eye contact.

'Aye. I'd better go fix things.' Murray set the tray hastily down on top of a circular saw case. 'Not that I'm good at fixing things. Not like you... I imagine. I mean obviously you can fix things, you're a builder.'

Kurt's eyes sparkled with humour. 'You work in a community repair shop and cannot fix?'

Murray cursed himself for giving away the fact that he was the obstinate underdog around here.

'I can do *some* stuff,' he said, feeling stupider by the second.

'OK.' Kurt nodded slowly. 'Go and do some stuff.' He was mimicking Murray's Highland accent, enjoying himself immensely. 'Catch you later.'

Murray turned to leave, masking a hard swallow.

Kurt shouted something in Dutch to the men up above and, still holding his cup, he ascended again.

Murray could feel Kurt's amused eyes burning upon his back as he hastened through to the shop floor, leaving the iced biscuits untouched on their plate like a votive offering on the steps of a temple.

Safely through the plastic sheeting, Murray fought the urge to pat himself down, straightening his shirt, checking his cargo pockets, his chest. For what, he wasn't sure. Scorch marks? The few encounters he'd had with Kurt had all left him feeling this same way.

Murray hid his discomfort as best he could while passing the café nook, resolutely *not* meeting the Gifford sisters' inquisitive glances as he went. He focused on hitting the light switches at each workstation as he walked around the repair barn.

In turn, he illuminated: the sewing area – where his mum, Roz McIntyre, would soon preside over the textile repairs and alterations with her fashion student proteges, Willie and Peaches; the woodworking bench and tool-sharpening station where carpenter, Cary Anderson, was already setting up (a man of few words, Cary gave him a friendly nod); next was Murray's father's bench, the messiest of the lot, where Charlie McIntyre – who everyone referred to simply as 'McIntyre' – would undertake all kinds of general repairs, there was nothing he couldn't fix. Next, Murray lit up Sachin Roy's triage counter where repair clients would arrive with their treasured belongings; and opposite this was Murray's spot, the tech repair desk. He glumly made his way there now.

Technically it was Ally's spot. She was Murray's twin sister, but she was still in Switzerland temping at her dream IT technician job for Future Proof Planet, the global environmental charity where, until a few months ago, Murray had also worked, heading up international donor relations.

Now, somehow, they'd traded countries and workplaces, and Ally's repair bench had passed to Murray.

He was the first to admit he was no repair expert, and certainly no tech guru like Ally was.

He watched his dad arriving through the big sliding doors having ambled down the garden path from the McIntyre family home, the old mill house next door.

'Morning, a'body!' McIntyre said cheerily, stopping to turn on the pink neon sign with its steaming teacup and threaded needle passing artfully through the handle. Underneath the logo, also in pink fluoro, glowed the words *Cairn Dhu Repair Shop and Café*.

The glow reached the depths of the huge barn, its gaudy pink reminiscent of the decadent nightclubs Murray frequented not so long ago in Zurich, back when he had to pretend he wasn't his boss's secret live-in boyfriend and he'd been content to sneak around in the glamorous wake of Andreas Favre. Back then, he'd wilfully confused Andreas's fear of gossip for some exciting clandestine affair of the heart. *Ugh!*

Andreas, it transpired, had a billionaire boyfriend all along and Murray had been little more than his Scottish side piece, a convenience, devoted as a lapdog.

A drill started up behind the plastic dust sheeting just as he was suppressing a shudder of shame. Then came a lot of hammering from the workmen too, intruding on his memories.

Livvie Cooper, the repair shop's new events manager and general administrator, was just arriving too, her little girl, Shell, in tow behind her.

'You all right?' Livvie asked in the brusque, prickly way Murray had chosen to put down to the tough times she'd gone through recently before she found her way to the repair shed. He'd determined not to take any of it personally, even if she seemed permanently irritated with him. What mattered was that she was a great worker, and it meant he didn't have to do as much of the paperwork side of things, especially now the build was underway.

'I'm absolutely fine,' he assured her, not that Livvie was waiting around for an answer. She was pointing Shell towards the beanbag chairs in the kids' corner and telling her to settle down to her homework while she made a start on her admin.

Murray was just making sure the little girl (who, painfully shy as usual, hadn't even tried to protest about the homework) had her favourite pink milkshake from the café counter, with extra cream and sprinkles, when he caught sight of shapes moving in silhouette behind the big plastic screen. He couldn't help watching the shadows shifting as Senga shoved a straw in the glass and handed it over in exchange for the two-pound coin from Murray's pocket.

As he delivered Shell's drink, and received a barely audible thank you, Murray caught the rich bravado of Kurt's lovely accent mixing with the Scottish voices of his workmates. Even this reminder of the Dutch man's proximity made Murray thrill and quail in equal measure.

Kurt was nothing like cool, suave Andreas Favre. Yet somehow the builder could prod painfully at the burning embers of what had happened in Switzerland last summer, threatening to reignite a self-sabotaging impulse that Murray had fought long and hard to dampen.

Even so, his brain whispered intrusive little things. It told him that at least Kurt made it clear he liked him. In fact, Kurt seemed incapable of hiding anything. Getting to know him better could prove to be fun? It had, after all, been six months since things with his boss had imploded and he'd fled home to the Cairngorms having drunk a great big draught of Andreas-flavoured antidote to his lifelong assertion that 'keen blokes give me the ick'.

He'd confessed it a million times to his twin sister, Ally. He would run for the hills if a guy ever asked for a second date, cringe at the gift of chocolates, block the overly invested texter after a one-night thing.

Ally would tell him it was a defence mechanism to stop himself getting hurt but he couldn't help scolding himself now. Look where it had got him: sneaking down the fire escape stairs of Andreas's apartment building, 'just in case you're spotted in the elevator'.

Murray rearranged the screwdrivers on the bench before him. His workstation was the only one in the entire shed that was immaculately organised.

Another movement caught his eye, a ripple of suddenly shifting opacity. The plastic sheet parted and Kurt's gappy smile and ice-blue eyes searched him out. He was biting into one of the iced biscuits. Murray smiled weakly back.

If he had indeed learned his lesson about giving up on unavailable men, why was it still the case that the joyful, flirty, multilingual, good-with-his-hands, hot-in-a-harness, totally uncomplicated Kurt sent a shy, cowardly impulse through him? He couldn't account for it.

Kurt would be leaving when spring came and his contractor job was up. Would it be *so* risky if they, for instance, shared an innocent drink under the strobe lights at the Ptarmigan – the only club within a fifty-mile radius? Or spent some time getting to know each other better at the hotel where Kurt was lodging for the winter? Someone enthusiastic and fun, someone who sought Murray out just to smile at him? He should be jumping at the chance.

The first repair clients of the day were clustering around Sachin's triage desk with their bags and boxes of broken bits and bobs. For once, Murray found himself wishing Sachin would direct them across the room towards his bench. Anything to distract him from Kurt's gaze and these duelling feelings of retreat and temptation.

His desire for distraction died within him when he noticed Reverend Meikle coming over. The Minister was clutching a mobile phone in his hands and a pair of old-school white wire headphones and he wanted to know why he couldn't 'plug them in'.

'Into your phone?' Murray asked.

'That's right. For the podcasts, you see?' replied Meikle, in his white dog collar and grey shirt even while running his Saturday errands.

'Uh, well...' Murray took the phone from him. 'Is this your new phone, Minister?'

'That it is, latest model. The chap in the phone shop said it was the best there is.'

'Right.'

'But there's no holes.' Meikle's bushy white brows were crumpled in consternation.

'Well, there wouldn't be. New phones tend not to have headphone sockets. You need to connect your headphones with Bluetooth.'

'Go on then.' The Reverend nodded encouragement.

'Oh, uh? No. You need Bluetooth earbuds. These wired ones are...' He gulped, fearing what was coming. He'd been the bearer of bad news too often this year as the town elders brought in their new Christmas gadgets. '...These are obsolete.'

'You're kidding!'

'Sorry to say it, but... it's true.'

'Why would the phone people do that to us?' the Reverend asked in innocence.

'So that you spend even more money buying new headphones, I guess?' Murray knew not to shrug. Being flippant about these things made people mad.

'No holes, eh?' the Minister was saying, shaking his head, turning to leave. 'So I have to spend more money.'

'Fact of consumer life, I'm afraid,' Murray said. 'Inbuilt obsolescence. Companies know that the worst kind of customer is a happy one who only comes into their store once every ten years.'

This was met with a sorry eyeroll at the state of the world and the Minister let himself out of the shed.

Murray didn't dare call after him to let him know the phone itself would be phased out in only a few years and he'd find himself queuing for an upgrade. Instead he let himself wonder exactly which podcasts a Highland minister might enjoy.

This was cut short by the sight of a queue forming before him, each hopeful person clutching bits of tech he more than likely couldn't service for them, at least not without a lot of trial and error and watching video demos or searching up online manuals (thank goodness, he thought, for iFixit dot com), but even with their help he'd probably still have to sneakily ring his sister for repair advice.

He rolled up his sleeves, hoping he wouldn't have to be the bearer of bad tech news *all* day. 'Who's next, please?'

Post Office Pauline carefully set down on the workbench her mother's turn-of-the-century iPod; a solid state, practically unopenable sleek metal casket with its inaccessible, and very dead, battery sealed within it.

'Oh, for the love of Pete...' Murray had to bite back his frustration, trying to fix his face in a sympathetic smile, yet still unprepared to ask himself whether hiding in here pretending to be a repairman really was preferable to facing up to the real world out there.

3

Finlay Morlich cast sharp eyes over the wintry mountain vista below him, where, fifty yards away, ears and tiny antler stubs poked up from the bracken that almost concealed the lone stag who was resting, sending up a haze of vapour from his warm body. During the autumn rut the stag had carried his eight-pointer headdress like a crown. Now he was hiding away, bareheaded and embarrassed, in the damp fern thatch.

Finlay and the stag had caught sight of one another many times out on the straths and glens of the Cairngorm range, when they'd momentarily freeze and stare at one another before passing peacefully by. Theirs was by far the easiest friendship of Finlay's thirty-one years. He related more to the stag (and the other creatures of the mountains) than to any of the humans he encountered as they clambered past his cruive (that's a wee Scottish cabin to you and me, fit mainly for sheltering shepherds and their lambs, or crotchety hermits like Finlay). The cruive sat amidst a tiny patch of ancient forest beneath the lower slope of Cairn Dhu mountain's western face.

To Finlay it was paradise. Or it would be, if it weren't for the hillwalking parties who'd stop, wanting to chit chat on their way to the snow-capped summit, so many of them with the attitude of Disney day-trippers visiting a big pink plastic castle. Not that Finlay had ever been to Disneyland to see if it really was pink, or made of plastic.

'Couldnae think of anything worse,' he huffed now, sending white vapour spiralling in the frigid air.

Solitary, still, watchful. Just like the stag; it was the only way Finlay Morlich knew how to be.

Cairn Dhu mountain, in the westernmost reach of the Cairngorms National Park, rises like a great split tooth above the populous valley. Even from up here on the boulder pass, where he liked to take his morning coffee, Finlay could make out the strung lights on the high street, the last of the Christmas display, now that the council had taken down the big tree by the police station. The bulbs twinkled through air thick with white dampness as if to say *why not take a wee wander down and see what's on offer? January's the time for cultivating new, sociable habits.*

'*Pfft!*' Finlay snatched his eyes away, taking a swig from his steaming enamel mug with the chip on the handle. 'Nonsense.' He rarely ventured into town, preferring it up here where he had everything he needed.

The weak morning light worked upon him, recharging him like a battery. Breathing in, he tasted the sweet scent of lichen and moss, wringing wet after the recent downpours, the clean, resinous smell of the pines, and the reassuring earthiness of the cold granite and dirt beneath his feet. More than enough sustenance for him.

Through binoculars, he witnessed his colleagues' van pulling up at the Rangers' Station all the way down on the scrap of tarmac where the visitors would soon be arriving, wanting to scramble up the mountain; far too many of them turning up ill-prepared and ignorant of the dangers they'd face: from scree slippage to avalanches and hidden crevasses, or the threat of suddenly descending fog or winter darkness leaving folks stranded.

He'd seen grown men felled by something as simple as bad boots and wet socks. He'd followed rescue teams on the search for city lads on 'team-building' outings who'd badly miscalculated their water supply, thinking a hike up a four-thousand-foot incline nothing but a jolly jaunt, and they'd come down on stretchers, jittering like tadpoles in their jelly and hallucinating with thirst.

God knows, if there were dunderheids with perilously thin rain macs and a death wish, or microspikes instead of mountain crampons, they'd make a beeline for *his* mountain. So far, he'd helped save every one he'd been called out to, meaning that, for Finlay Morlich, the worst day was yet to come.

Every ranger, every rescue unit, has their story of the one they couldn't get to on time, the one who hid so well in the snow they couldn't be found until the spring thaw, the one who couldn't have seen the black tarn at their feet until they'd fallen headlong into the breath-stealing slush.

The waiting for that awful day, looming darkly inevitable somewhere on the horizon of his life, had long ago turned Finlay's heart bitter with anxious fear. Yet all that the carefree day-trippers and picnickers registered as they sallied by on the tourist paths was a crabbit man in camo gear with a ranger badge and an attitude problem.

'*Hmph!*' He shook off the notion. Who cared what people thought?

The stag's ears twitched to attention and Finlay apologised soundlessly for disturbing him.

A light went off down at the edge of Cairn Dhu town, drawing his attention – it was that garish new floodlight that had been installed in the autumn to illuminate the carpark of the community repair shop. Finlay's eyes settled on the old mill house and its huge shed that housed the repairers, currently with its back end under scaffolding. The floodlight's glare wouldn't be needed now that the morning sun was trying to cast watery rays through the wet white fog that sat inside the bowl of the valley. Still, it irritated him that the floodlight existed at all. It confused the migrating birds and frazzled the moths. He'd have to mention it when he was next down there. Not that he had any reason to go down, yet.

He checked his rations tin by his side on the low storm shelter wall where he breakfasted. There were two squares of Senga Gifford's walnut tablet left, smelling deliciously of condensed milk and caramelised sugar, one of her chocolate-dipped rock buns, and one wee piece of her clementine short-bread. Not enough to send him panicking yet, even if his sweet tooth was telling him to get back down there and stock up right this instant.

Senga sold her goodies from her café inside the repair shed, and Senga was an old nuisance, always questioning him about his life on the mountain, telling him, 'But you *must* be so lonely up there, and such a handsome laddie as you! What a waste,' and she'd tut and shake her head like she knew what was good for him. Unfortunately for Finlay, Senga also made the best biscuits and buns, traybakes and sweeties this side of Hadrian's Wall, so he was bound to suffer her again soon. The fact she often slipped a few extra chunks of cinder toffee or coconut macaroon into his tin didn't make him inclined to forgive her intrusions, but he wasn't about to ask her to stop.

He checked the lid was sealed shut on his treats, and with a gruff word to himself, he rose, picked the crumbs from his weatherproof fleece, downed the last of his coffee, and went about his day patrolling the mountain and saving daft folk from themselves, trying to ignore the gnawing feeling in his belly. It was probably only sweet-hunger and almost definitely not a yearning for something he couldn't quite pinpoint, something that had been threatening to get the better of him recently whenever he stared down into the sparkling valley and imagined the lives lived down there beneath the bright lights.

4

The new arrival was getting very tired waiting for the bank to open. What is the use of a high-street bank, thought Alice, if it doesn't open on a Saturday morning?

She clutched her two birthday cheques ready to pay in to her account, money she'd need to tide her over until her first wage from the surgery came in at the end of the month. There was no sign of life inside the bank's tall arched windows and the wooden door was shut and barred like a castle keep.

All the buildings along Cairn Dhu high street, it seemed, had turrets like in fairytales, even the ones that were clearly just flats over the chip shop (also closed) or, she read the signs, Ozan's barbers, the mountain rescue charity shop, or Bernice McAdam's Accountancy Office. Did these people know they were living in a fairytale town? Well, a very overcast, drizzly sort of fairytale where the wind cut like icy daggers and was at that moment threatening to blow the postman off his bicycle as he cut his way through the slow-moving traffic.

There were no actual castles in sight, where an evil queen might reside, but there were brooding, craggy snow-covered mountains lining the valley, and smoking chimneys poking out of hobbledehoy slate roofs, and everything everywhere was strangely old-timey and quaint, if she ignored the tourist tat shops and the traffic lights.

She'd have stopped the passing policeman on his beat to ask him the bank opening hours if he hadn't been intent on cautioning a tractor driver for parking on the pavement. Yes, on the pavement! A little ancient-looking red tractor with a scruffy, indifferent little driver who was waving away the policeman's concerns like they were no big deal.

This certainly wasn't the Manchester Oxford Road Corridor, that's for sure, with its signs everywhere and congested bus lanes, and hordes of students heading this way and that, takeaway coffee cups in every hand.

Thinking of coffee shops, she'd have killed for a matcha latte and avo smash on toast right about now, but there was only the stuffy hotel on the corner advertising its famous Scottish fried breakfast with haggis and black pudding, not her sort of thing at all. She'd seen with her own eyes what that stuff did to arteries.

Her apartment fridge was still empty, however. Grocery shopping was high on her 'to do' list today, but so far all she'd spotted was the corner shop that doubled as a Post Office with their pricey canned food and refrigerated, pre-packed processed hams and cheddars.

Where was the fresh food? Weren't towns like this supposed to have picturesque farmers' markets and allotments and orchards on every corner? She'd ask someone, if she could be sure they weren't a tourist and unlikely to know.

That's when she saw something even more out of place than herself.

A great grandfather clock was sailing down the street, bobbing and weaving through the crowds, right past the steps of the bank and away. The man pushing it along (it was partially swaddled in blankets and strapped onto a wheelbarrow) seemed to have stepped right out of the pages of a vintage catalogue or knitting pattern book. Tall and handsome, tan-waistcoated and in shiny nut-brown shoes, he scurried along, his coat and baggy brown trousers all coordinating with a dapper herringbone baker boy sort of cap on his head.

She followed him. In the moment it felt quite natural to stop him and ask about the bank, even though he was clearly busy; there was something curious and trustworthy in his busy, jaunty manner that told her he'd help.

'Excuse me?' she called at his back and he stopped, turning dark brown eyes upon her under the brim of his cap. He was younger than she'd expected from his outfit, still older than her though, and handsome with brown skin and overlapping constellations of lovely freckles.

He wasn't saying anything, only waiting expectantly, holding the handles of the barrow, ready to hurry off again.

'Sorry,' she began, not sure why she was apologising. 'I only arrived yesterday and I was wondering...' The man cast a glance in the direction he'd been travelling. 'Sorry, that looks heavy, you should probably keep...'

'No, no,' the man said, lowering the wheelbarrow and straightening up in front of her. 'I've got time.'

'I can see that.' She tipped her head towards the clock, peeping out of its blanket wrapping.

He only smiled placidly, making her regret herself.

'Sorry, uh, I was wondering when the bank opened?'

He caught sight of the cheques in her gloved hands. 'Ah, OK. That'd be Thursday.'

'Hmm?' She couldn't be hearing him right.

'Yeah, I know, it's a pain. It's only open on Thursdays now. There's a branch near Garten if it's urgent.'

She had no idea where that might be and no intention of finding out. The cheques went back in her wallet. 'Never mind,' she said, feeling herself even more deflated than she'd been when she finally got on that minibus from the train station last night after fifty minutes' rainy waiting and it had carried her all of three stops and fifteen minutes down the road and into the high street, and in all that while her map had refused to load on her phone.

When she'd stepped off at the town's only bus stop she'd asked the driver if he happened to know where number eighteen, Cairn Dhu High Street might be and he'd turned a bony finger towards a gap between two buildings and he'd said, 'doon the vennel' and shut the bus door upon her before puttering away again.

It turned out a 'vennel' was a scary, unlit, un-sign-posted passage that led to a block of low-rise seventies flats, nothing like the auspicious, gothic buildings along the main street.

There'd been no elevator to take her up to flat 3A, no automatic lighting, and no switch to be found, so she'd dragged her belongings up the stairs in the dark using the torch setting on her phone, draining the last of the battery, and after two trips up and down, she at last let herself inside, clammy and panting, only to find herself under a glaring bare light bulb in a sparsely furnished white box of a flat that smelled of cheap disinfectant and the effects of being left un-heated for weeks in winter, and which looked exactly like every student accommodation she'd ever rented back in England.

It had not been a good start. Now that she was here and actually meeting a real local, things showed no signs of improving, and on her birthday too.

'What about shops?' she said, stopping the man lifting his barrow handles again, not even thinking to ask him why he was wheeling a grandfather clock through the town. Of course that was the sort of thing people would get up to in a lost-in-time place like this.

He pointed back towards the Post Office like she knew he would.

'No, I mean, a supermarket? Or health-food shop?'

The man scratched the cropped black waves behind his ear, his cap lifting a little. 'There's always Laura's deli,' he offered, hopefully.

'Great, where's that?'

'It's not a place, as such. It's a delivery business. You just ring her and say what you want.'

The disappointment must have shown on her face as the man reached into his waistcoat pocket and drew out a phone, which surprised her as he didn't look like he came from a time where phones existed, let alone like he'd know how to use face recognition to unlock it, like he was doing now. He smiled for the screen like he was having his photo taken. It was wonderfully odd, and a tiny bit endearing.

'I'll send you the deli number, if you like?' His voice was gentle, nothing pushy or brash, and again she found herself following along, pulling her own phone free and reciting her number for him, something she'd never, *ever* dream of doing back home with a complete stranger, but this wasn't back home. Far from it. And this man was like no stranger she'd ever met.

He dutifully typed in her number, scrolled and tapped until the notification sounded on her phone.

'There,' he said, and after hesitating as though he

had more to say but didn't quite know how, he nodded and went on his way with his barrow.

'Thank you,' she called after him. 'You're a lifesaver.'

He didn't reply, only smiled over his shoulder, hurrying like he was late for something important, leaving Alice watching in his wake, feeling very much like running alongside him, asking him where he might be going, and couldn't she go along too? He was the only person she'd spoken to in hours and there'd been something appealing in his unstudied gentle-manliness, nothing like the Manchester thrift-store hipsters who'd kill for his vintage gear or an ounce of his quiet charm.

She stopped herself dreaming up a story for him, placing him in a woodland burrow of a home, turning him fully into the White Rabbit he'd reminded her of. He was nothing but a helpful stranger. She let him go and peered at the message he'd sent, a phone number with the words 'Laura Mercer's deli' and, under the number, what she assumed must be his name: Cary Anderson.

She rang the deli immediately as she turned back for her flat where at least the heating was on now. When the call connected, a bubbly Scottish woman greeted her with, 'Good mornin', what's your order, please?'

Alice resisted the urge to ask if they happened to sell birthday cake by the slice and enquired about their fresh fruit and veg instead.

5

The traffic lights glared in the Saturday afternoon gloom. Sleety drizzle slashed sideways. Beats blared from slowly passing cars. Dirty slush gathered in the gutters. Compared to the silent wilderness of the bare mountain slopes with their dusting of pristine snow, Cairn Dhu town was a nightmare.

The green man flashed. Walk Now. An orange countdown of seven seconds hastened Finlay Morlich across the street as though this were a sprawling urban metropolis and not, in fact, a valley gouged by retreating ice millennia ago, leaving a pewter-coloured river and a spot ripe for the nineteenth-century development of a hundred or so granite houses in the frumpy Scottish gothic style. Their chimneys choked out smuts and sweet pine-resin smoke for the winds to whip away.

A minibus carrying adrenaline junkies in ski gear rumbled past on its way to the mountain resort on the other side of Aviemore – much bigger than Cairn Dhu's offering – as Finlay tramped along, his arms crossed over his body. Headlights glared. Some vehicles were hazardously double parked outside the animal feed store and the Post Office, their owners unfazed by the presence of the police station just yards away.

Light spilled from every shop window as well as from the streetlights overhead and the phone screens of teenagers too absorbed to drag their eyes upwards as they passed him on the pavement.

'Mind yersel'!' he warned, as a group of teens in black hooded jackets barged past. 'You'll be needing reflector patches on those jaikets!'

A brief silence followed before the lads burst out cackling behind him.

'Suit yourselves,' he muttered as he walked on, scanning the street for fresh dangers.

Ahead, the floodlight above the repair shed further spoiled Finlay's afternoon.

With a resigned sigh, he made his way towards it, with his rations tin in his coat pocket, its contents scoffed by the group he'd escorted down the mountain no more than an hour ago.

He'd been alerted to the news that three office workers from Kilmarnock had lost sight of the community path somewhere to the south of Gillie Fell and he'd stormed out with his rescue gear on his back. It had taken him all of thirty minutes to locate them in the early-afternoon gloaming, their (useless) GPS glowing on their phone screens and giving them away.

He'd taken no pleasure in showing them the way back through the scrubby low heath and onto the path, only a few metres from where they'd wandered off it only to discover that, in the winter dusk, it was impossible for them to retrace their steps.

They'd been all apologies and pasty faces, promising that next year they'd book a bowling alley for their team-building outing. Finlay had agreed that'd suit them much better than an amateur survivalist adventure in one of the most dangerous environments in the world.

He hadn't really registered the smirks two of the lads exchanged as he marched them down to the rangers' station and sent them on their way armed with the *Staying Safe in the Cairngorms* leaflets he carried with him always.

One of the men, however, was shakier than the others, and hadn't said much since Finlay discovered him, further off from the other two and staring into space, muttering about how he'd seen a huge shadowy figure of a 'yeti man' coming out of a bank of low cloud.

'It even waved to me!' the lad had said, his voice trembling, and his friends had found the whole thing hilarious.

'That was nae yeti,' Finlay snapped, silencing their laughter. 'You saw the Brocken spectre.'

One of his pals made a ghostly '*wooo*' sound at this, which Finlay nipped in the bud with a scowl.

'It's no' a ghost of any kind. It was your own shadow cast against the low cloud as the very last of the sun set behind you. It's a well-known phe-nomenon amongst mountaineers. Never seen it my-self, mind you.'

'But it had sort of rainbow rings all around it, and it held its arms out to me,' the man confessed in a low voice only for Finlay's hearing. 'Near aboot shit myself.'

'Trick of the light,' Finlay told him. 'The pair go hand in hand, glory they call the coloured rings, and your shadow projected onto the mist. Brocken spec-tre.' He shrugged like that should be more than enough to make the lad understand, but from his haunted eyes, Finlay saw he thought he'd met his maker.

If he was any other man, Finlay might have patted him on the back or offered some soothing words, but despite knowing that's what he *should* do, Finlay couldn't help but maintain his usual irritated stiffness and formality.

'Here,' he had said begrudgingly, taking his ration tin from his backpack. The man would never know this was the most caring thing Finlay could ever do.

He'd surrendered his provisions to the shaken young man, then watched in horror as the other lads fell upon the goodies too.

Finlay had tried not to watch as they made short work of his clementine shortbread, his very last chocolate-dipped rock bun, and the sweet scraps of tablet. They'd barely chewed them.

So now here he was, underprepared for an expedition to town, passing through the wide gap in the high wall that enclosed the McIntyres' historic mill house, where the old water wheel churned the clear, reedy burn that flowed through McIntyre land. He shielded his eyes from that awful floodlight overhead, crunching across the gravel towards the big barn.

Banging sounds increased as he made his way

closer. He wanted to shove his fingers in his ears. 'Noise pollution *and* light pollution,' he grumped, as he hauled one of the double doors aside and stepped into the pink glow of the workroom.

The warmth hit him first, followed by the good smell of – *Sweet Scottish Jesus, preserve me!* – cranberry jam tarts, and was that – he sniffed – marzipan? Could there be Battenberg cake?

Senga Gifford was at his arm in an instant – *dang her!* – pulling him inside, fussing, commenting on 'those mucky boots', but not allowing him time to wipe his feet on the mat. She'd all but dragged him towards her café at the back of the shed.

'Well, well! More sweeties!' Senga clucked, sweeping behind the counter where the glass domes covered the last of the Saturday offerings. 'There's no' much left, mind, but what's here, you can have. Half price for you.'

'Right, thanks,' he said, keeping his eyes on the goodies. 'What's that thing?' he couldn't help asking, lifting a finger to the glass protecting a glossy red orb with a diamond of something crystalised and sugar-sparkly on top.

'*That* is my chocolate and cherry mousse bauble.' Senga's chest swelled with pride under her pinny.

He nodded in gruff acquiescence.

'Oh, you'll deign to try it, will you?' Senga sounded fierce but her eyes were gentle, reminiscent of Finlay's Great-Aunty Shelagh. She'd been a good baker too.

'And some Battenberg slices, please. And any walnut tablet you've got back there.'

She'd already set two of her cranberry jam tarts in the bottom of his provisions tin without him having to ask. He held it out in both hands for her while she worked, feeling like Oliver Twist.

Rhona, who wasn't permitted to do very much in her sister's café dominion, rang it all up on the till, making sure to apply the discount.

'How's things on the mountain?' she asked gently.

'Treacherous,' Finlay replied, quick as a flash, trying to put them off attempting a visit. Though they didn't look much like hikers. Senga was shuffling about in her furry slipper-boots; safely a town-dweller.

'Nine fifty, please,' Rhona said, reaching for his ten-pound note.

'Are you going along to this meeting at the GP's surgery on Monday?' Senga said, eyeing him.

'Eh?' he replied, distractedly snapping the lid down securely upon his goodies and wondering where the paper-wrapped tablet block had got to, scanning the shelves behind the women.

He forbade himself from asking what this meeting was. He wasn't interested. And he'd learned not to ask questions. That's how they inveigle you in their schemes. Or they try to.

'Tablet! Right enough,' said Senga, jumping to attention and passing him the package. 'That's the last of the tablet till I make some more. It's about... what's it about, Rhona? The meeting?'

'Oh.' The younger sister thought hard while counting the change out of the till as slowly as she could. Both sisters knew he'd flee as soon as the coins hit his pocket. 'Sociable prescriptions, is it?'

'Social prescribing,' corrected Cary Anderson in his unassuming way as he washed his empty cup at the sink behind the women's counter. 'A new thing we're trying, with the doctor's surgery.' Having registered Finlay's utter disinterest, Cary went back to sanding the runners on a child's snow sled at his carpentry bench.

Seeing there was no hope of piquing the interest of the mountain man, Senga too gave up, and pointed to her chalkboard.

'Pay it forward?' she said, indicating the chalked sketch of coins dropping into a teacup.

'Eh?'

'Do you wish to buy a future customer a cuppa?' she clarified. 'Paying forward your own good fortune to benefit someone else who maybe can't afford a coffee that day for whatever reason.'

Finlay thought about this. 'My good fortune?'

The Gifford sisters nodded in unison.

He looked at his sweetie tin, thought of his cruive cottage up in the hills with its patch of ancient woodland, the wagtails and snow buntings that pecked around him as he ate his breakfast every morning. He thought of the deer and his fireside, his stars, and his wildflowers in summer.

He stuck his hand in his pocket and fished out another tenner. 'Go on then.'

Rhona, satisfied in the knowledge that he was a sweet fellow beneath all the growling, swapped the note for the last of his change.

He gave a guarded grunt, just in case they tried to detain him further, and turned, pocketing the coins and making an awkward attempt at pulling free his grandfather's compass so he could slip the brown-paper-wrapped parcel of tablet safely inside his pocket, thinking only of how he'd have a wee taste of it on his way back up to the cruive. 'Thank you, then. Cheerio.'

Head down, boots shifting. He was stocked up and

he was *offski* (which is the Highland version of *outta here*).

Only... *Ooft!* He'd hit a pillar or something. Smack bang! Ploughed straight into it in his haste to get away.

Only the pillar was turning on him, apologising, gripping at Finlay's coat to steady itself from falling. '*Whoops*, sorry!' the obstruction was saying, a warm hand gripped over Finlay's cold one, the initial impact having shoved the delicate old compass hard into Finlay's chest while something chilly and solid scraped his knuckles; a mobile phone, Finlay guessed. These hillfooters are addicted to their mobile phones.

It was all Finlay could do to keep his compass protected in his palm while clinging to his ration box in case his precious goodies fell to the floor.

The apologising man – who had tufty red hair like a woodland squirrel and eyes just as wide – was asking him if he was OK.

'Absolutely fine,' Finlay said, attempting to step away.

The man was still on high alert and wildly staring, his hand *still* pressing against Finlay's.

The redhead's eyes flitted down to where their skin touched before yanking his hand away. 'God, sorry. I...'

'Nae damage,' Finlay assured him, though that metallic phone case would likely have left a graze over his knuckles, but he wasn't thinking about that right at this moment. Instead, he was thinking about this pair of green eyes. All the greener against the man's auburn hair. Red and green. The colours of the mountains in autumn. Odd, Finlay never normally noticed these things.

He was suddenly aware of the Gifford sisters looking on and nudging each other. Finlay determined to get away all the faster.

He tried to dodge around the man, but they both stepped aside at exactly the same time, leaving them chest to chest like they were dancing 'Strip the Willow' at a Hogmanay ceilidh.

''Scuse me,' Finlay tried, close to losing his patience.

'You're the one joining us for the meeting at the surgery, aren't you?' the man was saying.

Not you an' all! Finlay wanted to say.

Why? *Why* would he be here to meet people? He did everything he could to avoid meeting anyone. Didn't they know that about him down here?

'On Monday, at half five?' the man was saying. 'Senga's going to make us her chocolate digestive squares specially.'

Dangling a carrot like that wasn't going to work either. Finlay glowered harder to get the message across: he was *not* one to chat.

'You're a mountain ranger, aren't you? The rangers' station manager told us they were providing a nature expert from their team. We've already got Cary the carpenter helping build the raised beds and drafting a design plan for us. I'll be sorting the funding streams. Livvie Cooper's our new events manager. She'll be managing the press side of things and...'

Finlay stopped trying to escape and looked at the man – handsome, slender – and smiling as he wittered on, hopeful for something Finlay couldn't give.

'I've nae idea what you're on about, but whatever it is, it's not my thing.'

Undeterred, the man was unlocking his phone, reading something from his planner. 'Are you not Finlay Morlich?'

Hearing his name from those lips made the earth rattle below his feet like that day in June when there'd been one of the range's rare earthquakes and he'd stood at the door of his cruive while the whole mountain roiled for all of five seconds and the birds had instinctively stopped singing.

'That's me. What of it?'

'I'm Murray... Murray McIntyre?'

Finlay shrugged. This guy clearly didn't see there'd been a misunderstanding of some kind.

'You see, the thing is, the surgery approached us here at the shed about a social prescribing scheme where patients can join in with the building of a garden just out there.' Murray pointed through the wall of the shed. 'It'll be made using recycled and repurposed stuff, fully organic, zero waste. It's for the patients' mental wellbeing. To get outside, meet new folk. You're being loaned to us, to help with the native wildflower and tree planting, aren't you? Our wildlife expert.'

Finlay held up a hand, shielding himself. 'Not me.' He attempted another escape.

Too bad for one of the other rangers, getting saddled with that. Though, from what he'd observed of his ranger colleagues, they'd be pretty well cut out for this kind of thing. Chattering, eager, sociable. Sure, Finlay knew wild plants and trees and the names and habitats of all the wee sneaking creatures, but so would the others. 'I'll be off.'

He took steady strides towards the doors and it seemed he really was going to make it outside to freedom this time.

He ignored the startled silence and the feeling of eyes at his back as he escaped into the floodlit carpark, lurching away from the old mill house, feet crunching hard on the gravel. That had been a close scrape, and way too much idle chattering for his liking.

There was just enough time to collect his book reservations at the library before it closed, and so that's where he headed, planning a speedy in and out with zero chit-chat, even though there was one librarian who always made reading recommendations for him, and, admittedly, she was usually bang on with ideas for stories he'd enjoy, but when he got there he found the library closed and so died the tiny light that had been burning within him for a backpack heavy with new reads. So, he gripped at his rations tin and worked his legs, left right, left right, along the last bit of the high street towards the turning he'd take for the mountain path, unsatisfied.

The sign for Cairn Dhu doctor's surgery at the edge of town flickered with a dodgy bulb. He couldn't account for it catching his eye otherwise.

There'd be no community project meetings for him. Definitely not. No getting involved with repair shop folk, even red-haired men with spiked auburn lashes.

He was relieved to be getting away with his peace

(and his precious block of sweet tablet) safely preserved.

He stalked away from the lights, slowing only to tear at the paper around the tablet, taking a hungry bite, working his jaw, sweetness bursting on his tongue. Comfort in a crumbly block. Only, something was off, and the sensory hit he'd been seeking didn't quite satisfy him.

Had Finlay been capable of interpreting the clamorous urges warring within him, he'd know the delicacies he guarded like a dragon with its treasure hoard wouldn't be able to placate the fresh pang of need surging within him.

On he stomped, back to the mountain and his solitude. It was going to take a hard lesson before Finlay Morlich could slake his long-neglected appetites. For now, his sweet treats had to suffice.

6

Two vexatious things were about to shake up Finlay's peace.

The first came in the shape of a note found on his doormat when he let himself inside his cottage cruive after his encounter down in the town. It was hand-written, and signed by Jemmy, his boss, the rangers' station manager for this part of the region, the one who'd given him the job in the first place almost four years ago, when he'd said he could see Finlay wanted to be in the mountains and how impressed he was with his knowledge about wild Scotland and that he had every hope the work would 'bring him out of himself a wee bit more'. Jemmy had held onto that hope ever since, no matter how patently Finlay had failed in that regard.

Finlay glowered over the note as he read, stomping his way to the fireplace with its grate already set for a fresh evening blaze. He'd switched on the one overhead bulb to better see the words, powered from his cruive's solar panel.

SORRY TO MISS YOU. HOPE YOU DON'T MIND, WE VOLUNTEERED YOU TO HELP OUT WITH THE SOCIAL PRESCRIBING GARDEN. A PITY YOU DIDN'T MANAGE TO ATTEND THE INITIAL MEETINGS ABOUT THE SCHEME, IN SPITE OF ALL THE EMAILS, BUT YOU ARE SURELY THE EXPERT IN CAIRNGORMS FLORA AND FAUNA OUT OF ALL OF US. I TOOK YOU OFF THE ROTA FOR SUNDAYS SO YOU'RE FREE TO HELP OUT. REPORT TO THE SURGERY FOR FIVE-THIRTY ON MONDAY AFTERNOON FOR MORE DETAILS.
　　BEST OF LUCK,
　　JEMMY

There'd been a deal of mumping and moaning after reading this (which is an especially Scottish kind of grumbling, and a good deal more sweary than the English sort), ending only in the crumpling of the note and the striking of a match.

There'd be no peace though, he knew, as he watched the note catch light amongst the kindling and balled-up newspaper sheets. There was no way out of it. What Jemmy said went, and not because his boss was a tyrant, but because Finlay owed him big time.

'*Dammit!*'

A white curl of smoke rose as the kindling caught. Sundays in the town, helping make a new garden? And at the repair shed, of all places.

Though why this one place was any worse than any other, Finlay's brain wouldn't enquire more deeply. Yet there was no forgetting the feeling of what had happened down there earlier this afternoon.

Adding the smallest of the dry logs from the hearth pile to the fire and swinging the black kettle on its metal hook over the flames, he mulled it over now.

He'd almost gone and done it again; lost his rag with a stranger. As his mum always reminded him, he wasn't properly cut out for dealing with people. He got folks' backs up.

Only, Murray McIntyre hadn't looked at him like

he'd encountered a mountain yeti, a faerie-dog or forest bogle that had accidentally stumbled into Cairn Dhu, the way that townsfolk sometimes regarded him. On the contrary, his lips had curled up at the corners. A sparkle had lit his green eyes. He'd seemed – Finlay tried hard to fathom what that reaction had been – impressed, somehow? *Delighted*, even?

Mulling over recent altercations like this was nothing new for Finlay. He could spend hours decrypting exchanges after a visit to town: like that GP's receptionist who wanted to know what exactly was wrong with him before she'd give him an appointment ('That'll be nane o' your business,' he'd told her, while the whole waiting room's ears were flapping, before he'd stalked out of the surgery), or that ditsy woman, Laura Mercer, from the bicycle delivery deli who he'd meet every Tuesday at noon down at the rangers' station to hand over his loaves, salad stuff and fresh fruit and to refill his tea caddy and his canisters of rice, pasta, and scotch broth mix.

She'd say suggestive things to him about how she was still single and 'just waiting for the right fella to come along and sweep her off her feet', and she'd simper in ways that made him wonder how she could possibly think he liked her in *that* way, or in any way, really, when in fact he'd be happy to buy his messages (that's 'groceries' for those outside of Scotland) from literally anyone else if there was a more convenient way. Mind you, Laura didn't bring everything wrapped in polythene like the big shops would. That was one big point in her favour, he supposed, and he always made sure to tip her on top of her delivery charge because, goodness knows, the rangers' station carpark was a fair bike ride out of town for her and she never once missed a meeting.

As much as he'd muse over town conversations when he was alone again (before letting himself forget all about them) he couldn't quite forget Murray's voice, not that the man had said anything particularly noteworthy. Maybe it was how Murray's voice had *felt* that he was having difficulty shrugging off? That hand upon his as he'd steadied himself after their clash had also left a sensation inside Finlay's bones that had made him check and recheck his fingers ever since, flexing his hand, peering closely at his skin. No damage. So why the burning feeling?

It was true, no one had touched Finlay for a long time. The last had been that pharmacist giving him his booster shot right in the middle of the chemist shop and telling him not to be 'such a big bairn and kindly mind your language'. All he'd said was 'dammit' at the scratch, and there'd been nobody but a few families in the queue waiting for their jabs. Granted, one of the wee kids had burst into tears and he'd thought he heard their mother muttering something about 'the Grinch', but she could have been talking about anyone.

'No,' he told himself now, pouring the steaming water from the kettle into his chipped old teapot, watching the tea leaves drown in the dark chamber. He had to put Murray McIntyre, and all the rest of them, far from his mind.

He sat back, cross-legged on the rug, pulling his woollen blanket around his shoulders and reaching for his textbook.

A bit of Gaelic was what was needed. He'd been teaching himself for well over a year, fancying that it was the language these mountains spoke and that they would understand him all the better when he wanted to tell them things if he said them in the old tongue.

He had never mentioned these self-directed lessons to his recently departed mother. The Gaelic was probably another of his 'notions', the likes of which she used to tut about, like the time long ago he'd learned the name of every British native tree and made a notebook with their leaves and buds drawn in pencil, instead of doing the chemistry or maths revi-

sion for his exams. Maybe the Gaelic *was* just a notion, but he knew full well the mountains didn't
whisper *anything* to him in English.

He flipped to the correct page, poured his tea into
his mug, lifted the chocolate and cherry bauble from
his tin, and settled in to revise his colours and shapes
vocabulary – he was still just a beginner.

Rich, glossy chocolate gave way to smooth deep
pink mousse as he bit. There was cherry syrup and a
satisfyingly soft biscuit base, so good he momentarily
closed his eyes to chew.

Another bite. The warmth, the solitude, the sweet-
ness. It was enough to make him think generously of
good old Senga Gifford. Another bite. A slurp of hot
black tea stirred with sugar. The fire crackled and he
turned a page. The steam from his chipped mug may
as well have spelled out *There's No Place Like Home
Alone* in the air as he tried to relax into his evening.

'Red. *Dearg* or *ruadh*. Green. *Uaine*. Pink. *Ban-
dhearg* or simply *pinc*.' He rehearsed the vocabulary,
while his slippery, troublesome brain conjured up
Murray's ruddy hair, shining green eyes, rosy cheeks.

'*Dammit!*'

He licked his fingers clean now the bauble cake
had disappeared, then downed the last of his tea in a
gulp.

His hand strayed to his chest. The hand that still bore the residual sensation of Murray's touch where he'd crushed against him. There was only the faintest white graze over his knuckles where the metallic thing Murray had been holding had scuffed him. It hadn't hurt at all. On the contrary...

Finlay's hand happened to settle on the compass in his breast pocket. He pulled it free now and stared down at it. Its familiar dial might help orientate him, drag him out of this strange brain fog he was in danger of getting lost in since bumping into Murray McIntyre.

'*Whit?* Aw, naw!'

He shook the compass, then turned it over, briefly sighting the engraving on the nickel casing, his grandfather's name, Fredrick Morlich. 'You've got to be kidding me!'

He shook the compass again. The dial, a slender Cupid's arrow of aluminium, jumped a few degrees before smoothly pinging back to the wrong cardinal point once more.

Finlay knew his cruive and its fireplace wall faced due south. The compass arrow now directed itself right at his chest and the north. The dial was lying to him.

North had become south and south had become north.

'Broken!' he said, giving the device another little jolt.

He ran through how it was possible the poles had switched places.

Then it hit him. It happened when Murray ran into him with that sleek brushed-metal thing in his hand. Now he knew it had to have been a phone case. He was the very type of man who was chronically online, never separated from the internet and would own a magnetised phone case which had grazed Finlay as he shielded his compass. That metal had demagnetised the sensitive compass, turning Finlay's world on its head.

'*Dammit!*' he yelled again, throwing off the blanket from his shoulders, leaving the warmth of the fire and his books and tea. He crossed the cold stones and well-worn rugs, grabbing a box from a shadowy alcove. The room was chilly even this short distance from the hearth. He rummaged among the odds and ends, confirming what he already knew. He didn't have a strong magnet with which to repolarise the compass; the only way he knew of fixing the thing and getting his life realigned once more.

The awful, irritating realisation seeped in. He'd

have to go back down to the town on Monday and ask for help.

Even through the thick stone walls of the croft, even through the heavy droplets in the damp night air, Finlay's friend the mountain stag flinched at the sound of the shout that echoed along the pass.

'Dammit to hell!'

7

Her first morning in her new job and Alice had slept badly. Typical.

She'd jolted awake just after six that Monday morning in the pitch darkness of her strange new surroundings, having dreamt she was stuck on the Friday night on-call shift with six wards and a hundred and fifty patients to oversee. Dream-Alice had been hunching over a desk with a phone pressed to each ear while colleagues barked orders at her or begged for her help, and all the while her bleeper was going off non-stop. She'd been one sweaty, breathless second away from snapping and running screaming from the hospital when she had jolted awake. Not the most auspicious beginning to her first day.

Now, however, she was standing staring at her name on her very own consulting room door.

Dr Alice Hargreave

She'd never had a name plate before. She couldn't resist the temptation to take a few pictures with her phone, making sure to get a selfie pointing at the letters inset in brass. She immediately sent the picture to her dad, and then to her mother, remembering with a twinge how they weren't sharing a home now so, wherever they were, they wouldn't be discussing the photo together. She fired pictures off to her brothers too, knowing they'd be too busy for much more than a thumbs-up emoji in response. She wouldn't hold her breath for actual replies. When you're the youngest in a family of super-achievers a name plate probably isn't all that special.

The sound of footsteps behind her made her start.

'Right! That's your ID, lanyard, and...' the surgery receptionist, Gracie, was saying, handing her the items, '...your morning tea.' She didn't look much older than thirty and her dominant traits seemed to swing between a helpful, if clipped, efficiency and a slightly scatty interfering nature that might, Alice worried, become annoying.

Alice slipped her phone into her blazer's deep pocket and took the steaming cup which was fashioned in crooked ceramic with a lustrous brown glaze and hand-painted letters. 'Oh, my name's on the mug as well?'

'I bought a pottery wheel cheap off Amazon and now we've all got matching mugs,' Gracie told her. 'Well, sort of matching. It's hard to get them all the exact same.'

'Wow!' Alice didn't know what else to say as she turned it in her hands, pondered how she'd safely drink from the wrinkly lip without spilling on her clothes.

'I knew you'd be pleased! Anyway, I plumped for skimmed milk, no sugar, correct?'

'How did you know?' Alice passed her new lanyard over her head.

Gracie only raised an eyebrow as if to suggest all general practitioners took their tea the same way. 'Passcode for your office is one two three four. Got that?'

'Uh, OK. Great.' Alice wondered if she should be affronted or relieved that Gracie clearly understood the pressures of remembering these things. She suppressed a shudder as the memories returned of all those hospital door codes and floor codes and elevator codes she'd been made to memorise over the years and how painfully often she'd found herself on an urgent store-cupboard run and utterly unable to recall the digits and she'd have to find someone to ask, slowing her shift down when she had so much important stuff to be getting on with.

'Dr Millen's is four three two one, and the records room is zero nine nine nine. If you forget, tell me.'

'Should be easy enough.'

Gracie was looking at her expectantly. 'Are you planning on seeing your patients oot here in the waiting room?'

'Oh, right.' Alice jumped to it and input her door code, letting herself inside.

Everything in the office was new, much like the rest of the surgery building, which had been renovated only a few years ago. Desk, computer, phone, swing chair, examination bench and lamp. Nothing seemed to have been used before, and there was that familiar warm plastic smell combined with the sting of hospital detergent.

Gracie flicked the overhead lights on and Alice found herself drawing to a halt, wanting to scrunch her eyes closed at the familiar flickering and throbbing of institutional strip lighting, barely perceptible to some but, for the sensitive Alice at least, ever present in whatever setting she worked. It made her want to pull the office blinds open and rely on the weak winter morning light, but with the entire building on ground level and people walking past in the carpark outside, that wasn't going to be an option when she had patients to see.

'Do you think anyone will mind if I buy a couple of floor lamps, and a desk lamp, maybe?' she asked Gracie, who told her she could do whatever she liked, it was her room, and Dr Millen wouldn't even notice, frankly.

A tiny flicker of excitement accompanied the thought of this place flooded with soft light. Light on her own terms. A luxury in this job. It would have to wait for pay day, though.

'Where is Dr Millen?' asked Alice. 'I was hoping to meet him properly before work started.'

Gracie was arranging folders on Alice's desk and pulling out her chair, indicating for her to sit, which she did. 'House call in the Garten valley estate. Won't be long.'

That meant she was on her own, for now at least. Probably for the best, so she could familiarise herself with all the new systems without being observed. Not that Gracie showed any signs of leaving.

'Drink up,' the receptionist told her, leaning over

the desk to turn the computer on. 'Login's on your lanyard. So, how's your flat? Settled in OK?'

Alice obediently sipped from her mug before having a go at getting into the surgery system. 'Yeah, it's OK, I suppose.'

'You're in number eighteen, along the vennel, aren't you?'

Alice nodded, a little thrown by the screen denying her access, as well as the creeping realisation that Gracie might be the eyes and ears of this town. Gracie had to intervene, re-typing Alice's details for her. This time it worked, no problem.

Alice rolled her eyes. 'Ugh, sorry.'

'You're renting through Carenza McDowell's property agency, aren't you? Have you met her yet?'

'Uh, no, I haven't,' Alice said, not sure why this was important, and trying to concentrate on the appointments calendar that was populating on screen.

'That woman's a martyr to her hammer toes.' This was said with a tap at the side of her nose as if that somehow erased the rules on patient confidentiality. 'But if there's anything even remotely wrong with that flat, you go straight to Carenza. Don't bother with her minions at her office. OK?'

'Got it.'

'And don't mind if she seems a wee bit fear-

some; so would you be if you owned half the prop-
erties in town and had to cram feet like that into
three hundred quid Louboutins every day. Toes
like plaited pastry, that one. And you live alone,
don't you? Didn't move up here with... anyone
special?'

Alice felt intuitively that making eye contact
would only greenlight more of Gracie's prying. She
moved the mouse cursor around the screen. 'I live
alone, yeah. Are these all my appointments?' she
tried, hoping to divert the woman away from the topic
of her living arrangements.

'Just the six patients. To break you in.'

Six still seemed an awful lot for a first day, even
though Alice had worked in A&E and could triage
and admit that many people in an hour.

'I might also have to send your way any emergency appointments that crop up as the morning goes
on. And there's a meeting at half five you have to go to,
about the social prescribing project? Dr Millen mentioned it in your interview?'

Alice shook her head. She hadn't heard a thing
about any project.

'Ach, he'll fill you in about it soon enough. And
I've put together some notes about your stroke clinic,'
Gracie added briskly. 'You'll need to read them in ad-

vance. That's on the second Tuesday of the month. Three o'clock.'

'I'm in charge of that?'

'Uh-huh.'

'All right.' The beating in her chest now seemed amplified in her ears but Alice smiled through it.

'If you need anything in clinic, ask Dr Millen. He's your supervisor and won't mind being called in for second opinions or to run something by him. Just ring through to his room.' Gracie pointed a stiletto nail in a fiery orange gel finish at the number two button on the desk phone's keypad. 'Or you could just knock on the wall.' Gracie didn't laugh so Alice wasn't sure if this was really a joke. 'Did you bring your lunch?'

Alice felt herself at risk of conversational whiplash. 'Just brought a salad. I had to ring the deli to have them bring me some shopping and...' She faltered to a stop, unsure why she hadn't just said yes.

'The staff fridge is under my desk in reception.' Gracie had her hand out. Alice surrendered her bento box to her.

'Laura's deli, was it? That one's a devil for other women's boyfriends. Keep an eye on her if you're ever winchin' a local lad.' This was said with absolute matter-of-fact seriousness, and as if she'd know what 'winchin' even meant. 'She isn't registered here, mind.

Goes to some surgery in another town. Skerrybridge, I think. No idea why, when we're so conveniently on her doorstep.'

Alice had an inkling why Laura (who'd seemed perfectly nice when she'd arrived at her flat with her bike basket filled with her fresh fruit and veg) might prefer a surgery where she could be safe from gossip, but she didn't say as much. Gracie was pressing on with her orientation anyway.

'Your first patient's at half nine, as you can see. Ten minutes each. You know the drill. You'll see their appointment notes here.' Gracie tapped the computer screen, indicating the first patient. Alice clicked the mouse and some words appeared.

Itchy rash on underboob area and upper back since three weeks, tested allergic to cocoa eight years ago but that hasn't stopped her wolfing the chocolate buttons!!

'These are your notes?' Alice asked, a little queasy at the intrusion. She imagined they were all like that.

There was something preening and proud in Gracie's look. 'If I happen to have helpful intel, I'll add it to your appointment notes, since you don't know the locals.'

'I'm not sure that's entirely...'

'Practice Nurse comes in on Fridays and Saturday mornings.'

Gracie was turning to leave, carrying Alice's lunch away with her, only stopping at the doorway to add, 'And Pigeon Fergus is your ten o'clock. He's to sit on paper at all times, even in the waiting room. I'll bring in the vacuum cleaner when he leaves.'

'Uh... Sorry?'

'Pigeon fancier,' Gracie said as though the rest should be obvious to Alice. It wasn't. 'Mites. It's all in my appointment notes.'

'Ah, OK. Got it.' Alice had already made a mental note to tell this woman absolutely nothing about herself from now on.

'And your ten past eleven, Mrs McAlpine, will try smuggling that chihuahua in in her handbag, but don't you mind about that. I'll make sure to head her and her dog off at the reception doors. Her precious wee Bo-Jangles is to stay tied to the bike racks outside.'

'Right.' Alice tapped a finger to her fringe, throwing her a goodbye salute, wishing she could be alone again with her sinking feelings. 'Thank you.'

Gracie was pulling the door closed, announcing to a waiting room growing with chatter, 'The new doctor will be ready for you soon. Mind it's only *one* medical issue per appointment. No sneaking in any acne or dry scalp problems, just because she's new. I'm looking at you, Niall McNeil!'

The door sealed closed.

Left alone at her desk, Alice sat back and blew out a long breath. What kind of a place had she come to?

8

Some winter Mondays at the repair shop just happen to be like this: quiet, focused and cosy.

McIntyre was carefully re-painting the newly re-paired wood of a nutcracker doll that had split in a fall from a Cairn Dhu mantelpiece at Christmas, as he hummed along to his wife's choice of music, her favourite, Enya.

Roz, tranquil in a fluffy mohair handknit, darned the holes in a client's cashmere jumper with colourful threads, stitching over each one with the decorative shape of a tiny rainbow moth.

Peaches and Willie, her helpers, were away at their Highland fashion college now that the semester had begun again.

Sachin Roy wasn't here either because his repair triage desk was rarely busy on weekdays and any one of the regular repairers could handle the occasional clients who dropped in with their broken or worn-out treasures through the week.

There were a small number of new mums in, clustered in a half-moon on the café-corner armchairs around the shed's new real-flame fire (a bioethanol eco-stove, for the curious, another of Murray's clever installations). They were making the most of the chance to chat and enjoying the Gifford sisters' iced spiced buns while their babies napped in their prams.

Livvie Cooper had this morning helped Cary set out the children's woodworking benches for the primary school group who'd be on their way later, and now Cary was silently sorting bundles of goggles, aprons and sandpaper-wrapped blocks in readiness for their lesson, while Livvie settled down to the shed's accounts with a steaming mug of tea.

Senga and Rhona had put away the ingredients delivery and, having exhausted their supply of Cairn Dhu gossip for the day, were peacefully mixing up chocolate cornflake cakes for the kids.

Even the building site behind the plastic sheeting had fallen quiet, the whole team having taken their truck to the sawmill for supplies.

Glad to escape the feeling of always being on guard for Kurt's provoking presence, Murray sat at the café counter putting his signature to the risk assessment for the repair shop social prescribing garden project. There were a fair number of faulty laptops and games consoles still to work on, but he was only too happy to have an excuse to put those off for now.

Everyone in the repair shop and café pottered on, while those who could, kept to their houses, taking their ease, avoiding the icy chill of the foggy winter's day outside where the chimneys smoked, moisture droplets hung suspended in the still white air and there was nary a driver to witness the traffic lights moving through their sequences at the crossroads on the edge of town.

Murray expected the quiet would only be shattered by the arrival of the schoolkids with their teacher later, so he kept his head down and made the most of knowing nobody was going to ask anything of him for a while, and no one was flirting with him.

Last night he'd given the first of his talks at the shed. It had gone well enough. Nine locals had turned up in addition to his mum and dad and the repair café fixers, and they'd all nodded and stroked their chins as he'd explained how the repair shed would soon be a net-zero, fully renewable establishment. Murray had been astonished to find Kurt had given up his evening just to hear him speak.

At the end of his talk, when Murray had asked if there were any questions, there'd been a clamour amongst the locals to understand the difference between the terms 'net zero' and 'carbon neutral' and it had all got a bit fractious when Peaches's mother, the local property mogul, had wondered aloud if they weren't 'the same thing as carbon positive' and Murray's dad had interjected with, 'I think that's the same thing as climate neutral, is it no'?' and at this, the whole audience broke out into grumbling about how they couldn't keep up with the lingo and Murray had wanted to pack up his laptop and slide deck and go home, all the while he'd been saying a silent prayer that Kurt wasn't going to raise his hand and probe him with a silly query, full of smirking self-assurance, just to make him blush in front of the crowd.

He hadn't, thankfully, and when their eyes met at the end over the applause, Kurt smiled at him in such a way that told Murray he'd had no intention of joining in the confused grilling. Kind, as well as keen.

Murray had given him a grateful nod and, making excuses about a Zoom call with his sister (there wasn't one), left his parents to see the audience out into the floodlight's glare.

Back in his childhood bedroom afterwards, he'd had a stern word with himself about not being afraid of Kurt liking him, and that if the builder ever did ask him out he was going to say, 'Aye, why not?' because that's what single guys do.

Murray should really be focusing on the risk assessment and not going over the promise he'd made himself, but Kurt's smile was playing on his mind again, making it hard to concentrate. Well, that and the sudden commotion of the shed door slamming open, followed by heavy footsteps and heavier breaths advancing upon him. Murray snapped his head up to find Finlay Morlich, his rugged features pinched and thorny, holding out a silvery disc.

'*You!*' he cried. 'You broke my compass!'

9

'You broke my compass!'

'How?' Murray said, on his feet.

Finlay didn't know how he could make it any clearer.

'When you bumped into me. You had something magnetic in your hand. Your phone?'

He was drawing the attention of everyone in the repair shop. A startled-awake baby had begun mewling and there was tutting and angry muttering coming from the group of mums around the cosy stove but Finlay didn't pay much attention to any of this.

He was focused on making Murray take responsibility for his actions. 'Things get damaged when people charge around carelessly,' he said. *People can get hurt*, he thought.

'I can take a look at it for you,' McIntyre was saying in an affable way, approaching the pair, having put down his paintbrush.

'Something magnetic?' Murray was saying, still way behind.

'Ah-hah,' said McIntyre, now peering at the faulty needle under the gently domed glass. 'You're right enough. It's depolarised.'

'That's what I said.' If Finlay had any patience left, that would have torn it entirely. 'I havenae a strong magnet up at the cruive to fix it with.'

'I can see to this,' McIntyre offered.

'No,' Murray said firmly. 'If he says I broke it, I'll happily fix it.'

This was just what Finlay wanted. An admission. Action. So why did he still feel so riled?

'Will you?' McIntyre was asking his son, a dubious note in his voice.

'Aye, I will. It just needs a...'

'Strong magnet,' Finlay and McIntyre said in dry chorus.

'Precisely.'

Finlay looked down at Murray's outstretched palm

awaiting his precious compass. It suddenly felt very hard indeed to part with the thing.

He had to hold in his feelings as he watched Murray carrying it off to a workbench and muttering, 'How hard can it be?'

'Careful with it now!' Finlay followed close behind, not wanting to take his eyes off his compass. 'It was my grandfather's. Never had a problem with it before now.' *Before you!* Finlay thought. 'What's that you're doing now?'

Murray turned to show him his phone screen. 'It's a YouTube tutorial.'

Finlay had to run a hand down his face, stopping at his mouth to prevent the words coming out. If Murray would just hand the magnet over he'd do it himself in an instant and be on his way. Instead he stood next to the man, watching the demonstration too.

'Seems easy enough,' Murray remarked as the video ended. 'I just need to find...'

McIntyre, who'd been rummaging in one of the many storage tubs around the shed, had returned, bringing the metallic block with him.

'...Thanks, Dad. Right...'

Finlay watched on as Murray positioned the magnet in his left hand, the compass in his right, shifting his weight, flexing his neck like a magician building up to a big trick.

'What are you waiting for?' Finlay urged, wanting to get on, and simultaneously unable to draw his eyes from Murray's hands. Desk job hands. Indoor hands.

'All right, all right,' he was saying, taking his time, bringing the magnet to the face of the compass with slow caution, passing it over the face in a controlled glide. The needle juddered and resisted, jumped and shifted, until ever so slowly it submitted to the lodestone's pull, swinging the one hundred and eighty degrees into obeyance and staying there.

'There!' Murray said, Finlay reckoned more in amazement than in satisfaction. 'I did it!'

He reached for it immediately. The way the compass fit his palm settled his agitation a little. He ran a thumb over the glass. The needle pointed directly towards Murray's chest. North.

'Right, well. Very good.' He wished he could be less grudging, but this whole needless exercise was one huge inconvenience.

Murray was looking at him with those green eyes shining like he was waiting for something.

'Uh, thank you,' Finlay tried.

'I'll just need your number.'

'My number?' Finlay had to look down to where

his boots met the ground. Was the earth shifting again? What was going on?

'Or an address?' Murray said as he dashed to the triage desk, bringing back a printed pad. 'For the repair docket?'

'Oh, uh, right. Of course.' Finlay took the pad and hurriedly filled in his details. 'I've got a phone,' he felt compelled to say. 'For rescues and mountain alerts.'

The awareness of Murray's eyes upon the pen, watching as Finlay wrote the address of the cruive, deeply conscious of his poor handwriting, made him strive to do it nicely for once. All the while he could hear his mother complaining, 'Oh, Finlay! What a scrawl!'

Murray was saying something. 'You live in that tiny lower slope cottage on the edge of the auld wood, don't you?'

Finlay returned the pad and pen. 'That's nae secret.' He wasn't sure why he was answering in this way. He just wanted to escape. To run, right out the door.

'I always think how idyllic it looks.'

Finlay held in a scoffing laugh. 'Idyllic?' he repeated, weighing up the idea.

'From down here, I mean,' Murray was quick to

add. 'I imagine it can be a bit hairy up there, some days.'

Hairy was a highlander's way of calling something wild and dangerous. Finlay had never thought of his cruive in that way. If anything, those four walls were his only safe place. He was always fine once the mountain was safely swept of silly tourists and his door was locked.

Finlay nodded, faking agreement to be polite and pocketing his compass. The way it slid in next to his heart settled him further.

'I, uh, I'm happiest up along the tree line, in the green,' Finlay said, wondering why he was explaining himself to this man.

He'd been raised in the Scottish Kirk by his Reverend father, but if you asked Finlay Morlich what God meant, he'd answer that it was another word for nature.

Whatever this was affecting Finlay, he was clearly the only one fighting the urge to run away, and now he risked overstaying his welcome, just to see more red curls and green irises.

'What, eh, what do I owe you?'

'It's donations only. Entirely at your discretion.' Murray was taking a step back, like he didn't want to seem overbearing, a little embarrassed about the matter of money, perhaps?

Finlay had no awkwardness about money talk, not like some Scots. He pulled a twenty-pound note from his pocket and handed it over. What was money to him? He was rich beyond compare, if only he could get back to his mountain to enjoy his wealth of sky and granite in peace.

'Anything else you need fixing, bring it down to us,' Murray said, adding the donated amount to the form in a flowy, easy script, nothing like Finlay's own, and making to move away.

'You've no' broken anything else of mine, have yi?' Finlay heard himself saying, attempting a joke.

'I don't think so.' Murray was returning the magnet to his father who was busy running a delicate paintbrush over a gaudy Christmas decoration. Something in Murray's wake yanked Finlay from his spot, compelling him to follow, like a moon dragged by its planet.

Just in time, before Murray turned, the ranger managed to break away and divert himself towards the door. 'Thank you, then,' Finlay called out.

'I'll get the door for you,' Murray said suddenly, coming for him.

Finlay caught the sound of Senga Gifford re-marking to that sister of hers, 'Save him nearly yanking it off its runners again!'

He suddenly wanted to shrink and drop through the gaps in the floorboards. Had he banged the doors when he came in? Another thing his mum had always picked at him about, charging around like a herd of elephants.

'See you at the surgery meeting tonight?' Murray said as he slid the doors apart for him.

'Oh, I dinnae ken.'

Sitting in a stuffy room trying not to spill from a teacup, sharing talk about gardening and all that touchy-feely wellbeing stuff with the ancient Dr Millen and who knew how many local do-gooders and gossips? He shuddered.

'Not interested in the environment and your carbon footprint?' Murray said, with a maddening little grin.

This made Finlay's feet stop upon the threshold. A spark of indignation fired within him, not something he could prevent. 'Not interested? Not *interested*?'

Murray drew his neck back, his eyes rounding in alarm.

That's more like it, thought Finlay. The man was finally looking at him the way everyone else in the town looked at him. Affronted. Dubious. Critical. And safely from a distance. It felt, not *good* exactly, but familiar. Better than the closeness of before.

'*I* live almost entirely off grid,' he began, determined to further widen the gulf between them. 'My *carbon footprint*' – Finlay tried to inject as much ridicule into the words as he could – 'is next to nothing. I hike myself aboot on foot. I pick up a'body's litter and tramp it doon the mountain to the recycling centre. I forage the tree line for wood sorrel and chanterelles, berries and nuts. I sleep when it gets dark, burn my own store of fallen firewood, and it's a rare occasion I buy anything new. Anyway, *you* cannae talk to *me* aboot feetprints...' He wasn't sure that was a real word, but it was too late now, he'd said it, and when he'd been building up to his big finale too, '... while this place is runnin' that godawful floodlight for hours at a time as though your carpark is flamin' Hampden Park Stadium!'

There. He'd done it. Roared out the only fellow that had ever regarded him with anything other than amused disdain or polite disinterest.

Only, there was that light returning to Murray's eyes. That same look he'd had the other day, as though Finlay were somehow impressive.

'Ah-hah! So you're an authentic sustainability life-

style guru? Walking the walk!' Murray said, relent-
lessly cheerful.

Was he *looking* for things to praise about him? He
couldn't account for this level of interest.

'As in...' the redhead went on, 'you're all hashtag
underconsumption core.' He was making ridiculous
air quotes with his fingers. 'That's very on trend.'

Finlay felt his brain turn blank. 'Hashtag *whit*?'

'You're actually living and breathing the way of life
we're trying to engage with down here at the repair
shop.'

'Aye.' Finlay bit the word out as resignedly as he
could and turned on his boot heel to go. 'That I am.'
He stepped out from the warm reach of the shed, the
bitter cold of the courtyard hitting him.

Too right he was living sustainably. There was no
other thing for it. So many times he'd taken his
morning coffee to his spot on the low wall of the
storm shelter and sat there squinting down at the delivery vans clogging up Cairn Dhu high street,
bringing who knew what plastic rubbish from the
other side of the globe to his wee corner of it. He'd
seen the bins on the community paths stuffed with
packaging and unnecessary junk every day since he
moved here. Single-use snappable light sticks. Self-

heating hand-warmers (also single-use and disposed of like they were paper hankies). Countless plastic-lidded cardboard coffee cups shoved in the gorse, as though out-of-their-sight meant this stuff dissolved into nothing.

It brought a wild rage to his belly to see the people of the world wasting its precious resources, and it looked all the more ridiculous, no, it looked all the more callous and greedy, from his vantage point up amongst the rocks and shrubs where he tried to keep peace with nature and leave no trace of himself, harming no creature, destroying nothing, taking only the barest of what he needed. These town folk hadn't a clue.

'It's wind powered, you know?' the voice called from behind him.

'Eh?' Finlay glanced back.

'The floodlight? Wind powered.' Murray was grinning from the shed doorway and pointing to the sky, in case Finlay didn't know that was where the wind was kept.

'*Ach!*' He swept a dismissive hand, stomping away, wishing there was some way of turning back the clock hands and having that meeting all over again.

'The other children won't play with you if you must be

so gruff, Finlay Morlich!' came his mother's voice as though carried on the icy gusts.

He tried his best to step lightly along the pavement after that, but knowing full well it was too late for softness now.

10

In another ten minutes Alice would have finished her very first day of consultations in her new post. She was already dreaming of a bubble bath, steaming and full to the brim, even if it would be taken in the little white tub back at her new temporary accommodation along that windy high street. Even with the white plastic shower curtain, yellowing grout and the fan that didn't work properly. She'd learned not to wish for more, not with her student debts to pay off.

There was still this one consult left and already the room was charged with strong emotions.

'You say Jolyon doesn't speak at all?' Alice enquired, looking at the little boy playing on the consulting room rug.

'Jolyon laughs and makes sounds. He can make his feelings known,' the boy's mother, Mhairi Sears, began, 'and he screams too.'

The circles under the woman's eyes told Alice that, lately, there'd been rather a lot more screaming than laughing.

Alice looked again at the boy, not a toddler at all, but a big boy of reception class age, busy with a toy car clasped in his sweet, if a little sticky-looking, fist.

Like she'd told all her other patients today, Alice had also explained to Mhairi Sears that this was her first day and that although she'd completed her medical training at uni and on placement in hospitals, today was her very first day of specialist GP training. She'd even asked whether Mrs Sears wanted her to call in Dr Millen, currently hunched over admin in his messy office next door.

The woman had said no. In fact, she was 'glad to be seen by a young woman doctor, after everything...' Then she'd tailed off and left Alice to guess what the 'everything' was that this woman had gone through.

Alice had only ten minutes and a long list of questions to ask; partly following the diagnostic guide on her screen, partly intuiting her way. All she had to do was recall her training and hope she didn't miss anything major. Not so easy after what had been a long day, especially not now her head was full of conditions she wanted to revise and referrals she needed to make and patient queries that needed following up.

Concentrate, Alice. Concentrate.

'And Jolyon sleeps all right?' she asked.

'Uh-huh,' the mum answered. 'Mostly during the day in cat naps. You love to stay awake at night, don't you, Jolly?'

The boy looked up at this but quickly returned to driving his car along the floor.

'We've had a lot of late-night *Bluey* marathons in the living room while Dan sleeps.' Mhairi's lips twitched ever so slightly and her eyes narrowed in a way that suggested she was picturing her husband snoring, oblivious, in a big comfy bed.

Alice didn't know what to do with this sign of parental discord. Nor did she know what *Bluey* might be. She focused on the list on her screen, taking notes, hoping she was doing this right. For now, she wasn't sure which of the two was actually unwell or what she was expected to do.

'Would you like me to check on Jolyon's referral to the Speech and Language team?' she said, searching for the correct system on her computer.

'If you can, please. We had one session with a lady

at the Repair Shop Café. You know how they do drop-ins with experts now and again?'

Alice had to admit she didn't know anything about that.

'She was great. I'd hoped we'd be getting to the top of her referrals list by now though.'

Alice's computer screen didn't have much in the way of good news in that regard. 'Tell you what, I'll send them a note letting them know we've seen you both again, see if we can hurry them along,' she said, not feeling hopeful.

'All right, so I noticed Jolyon arrived in a pushchair today,' Alice continued when she finished typing. 'Is that typical?'

'He doesn't tend to walk far,' the woman explained. 'He often just drops to the ground and cries. Life's easier with the buggy.'

Alice typed this into the little boy's notes while the woman talked on.

'It's not as though there's some kind of discipline issue, if that's what you're typing.'

Alice let her hands fall from the keys. 'I wasn't...'

'"Mum gives in to tantrums too easily",' Mhairi said in air quotes, turning red-faced. 'I've heard that one before, sometimes from my own sisters-in-law, to make it worse.'

'No, no... I'm just recording our consultation.'

The mum sat back, hands clasped between her knees, giving her the same look she'd seen many times on the wards. Was she thinking how young Alice seemed? How inexperienced? Unready for this kind of responsibility, and certainly way too unworldly to know much about parenting?

Alice reached for her water bottle and took a swig to hide the lump in her throat.

No, there was something kind about Mrs Sears, and even though she was married with a kid, she was only a little older than Alice. Plus, she seemed too weary to go interrogating Alice like some of the patients had back in Manchester as she followed the consultants on their rounds. *'How old are you then?'* they'd ask while she nervously changed catheters and fitted cannulas and the nurses tried not to roll their eyes (the nurses were always a million times better at those things and not afraid of anything at all).

She needed to focus. *'Where is your head, Alice in Wonderland?'* she heard Bastian saying.

'And... he likes to eat?' Alice said. 'Is he putting on weight?'

'I've tried him with different solids for years now. Spag bol, steamed veg, fish fingers...'

Alice tapped softly at the keys, hoping not to spook the woman again.

'...but he only really eats plain pasta, breadsticks and Greek yoghurt. The occasional iced biscuit.' Mhairi's shoulders slumped in defeat.

'Doesn't like fish fingers?' Alice repeated, still typing. Her nephews adored them. She thought all kids did. Though, looking at Jolyon now, he wasn't all that much like her boisterous, chatterbox nephews; boys who, if anything, could do with a lesson in self-contained peacefulness from Jolyon Sears.

'I know what you're thinking,' Mhairi said, the words tumbling out in self-defence. 'I've seen that look before.'

Alice wiped her face blank.

'I've seen it over and over, since he was about six months old and that Baby Tambourine Jamboree leader mentioned Jolly wasn't meeting expected milestones.' The mother's eyes stayed fixed on the boy, who was very busy straightening out a paperclip he'd found on the floor.

Alice tried a sympathetic smile. If she could only read minds, she thought – and not for the first time.

If Alice could have dug inside Mhairi Sears's brain at that moment, she'd have been confronted with a big angry, messy knot of memories and indignation

She'd uncover how the young mum had stopped going to the stupid Baby Tambourine Jamboree classes after that. She'd know what it felt like when the nursery assistants had said the exact same things about Jolly's milestones and how it had become increasingly hard to dismiss their concerns the older he got. She'd feel the burning anxiety when half the mums at the Health Visitor's weigh-in mornings had made similar remarks. She'd hear the endless crowing chorus of, *'Has he not moved on to baby rice yet?' 'Not even crawling? Goodness!' 'My Skye was on the move at nine months, she was into everything!' 'Of course, my Henry's taking swimming classes now!'*

'Have you tried introducing a multivitamin?' Alice tried, shut out on the other side of the wall.

'He gets liquid vitamins added to his bottle,' Mhairi said.

'His... bottle?'

There they were. The big round eyes of a patient feeling judged. Alice quailed. She'd have said something consoling if Mhairi wasn't now hurriedly defending herself.

'He doesn't get his mouth round a cup, somehow. It spills everywhere... I tried giving him cups, hundreds of pounds worth of fancy toddler cups off the internet, all shapes and sizes, he didn't get to grips with any of them. It's not as easy as just giving him a cup and making him drink… and I can't let him go thirsty, can I? What mum would do that? So he still has his bottle…'

'That's OK,' Alice put in quickly, typing up a referral for the paediatric occupational therapist as well. This had been a prickly issue, clearly. 'Adding some ice lollies would be fine too,' Alice added. 'If he likes those?'

This stopped Mhairi. 'He likes some of them, actually.'

'And those sucky frozen yoghurt sticks, and there's jelly sweets you can buy with fruit juice centres.' Alice remembered those from the palliative care ward and all those shifts when she'd followed the bedside rounds at the hospice.

'What about the sugar? His teeth?' Mhairi asked, like she'd been warned about this before.

Does it really matter right now? Alice wanted to say, remembering the parched lips of some of her patients. 'You can buy low or zero sugar ones, and so long as he's hydrated, it doesn't matter too much. I'm sure you do your best with teeth-brushing.'

Mhairi's face suggested teeth-brushing wasn't entirely successful either but she wasn't about to admit it here.

There was only one minute left on the clock. That's when she saw the tears welling in the mother's eyes and the fight to hold them back.

'Would you... describe yourself as depressed at all?' Alice said tentatively, reaching for the sheet with the tick boxes that she'd learned to give out in situations like this. 'How many of these would you say apply to you?'

Cautiously, Mhairi took the sheet.

Alice knew the symptom check boxes by heart. Tearful? Low mood? Low libido? Intrusive thoughts? Difficulty sleeping? Loss of appetite?

'I'm not here to talk about me,' Mhairi said. 'I'm here for Jolly. And I'm not *depressed* depressed,' she said.

Jolyon, who'd wobbled to his feet and came over to his mum, sensing her getting upset, took the sheet from her hands. The women watched him crumpling it into a ball and bowling it along the rug. She sensed Mhairi feeling embarrassed but also wanting to smile. So Alice made sure to smile first.

'Nice bowling, Jolyon!' she told the boy. She placed another sheet on the desk, but Mhairi didn't take this one.

'Dan, my husband,' said Mhairi, clearing her

throat, '…said I might be suffering from an imbalance of some kind, but I'm fine. I'm just tired.'

If Alice could have glanced into their marriage she'd have seen Dan saying this on his way out to work while Mhairi struggled to rip open the lid of the supermarket savers mega tub of Greek yoghurt after Jolyon had turned down yet another attempt at mashed banana on toast.

'Do you have any friends in a similar situation?' Alice tried.

Mhairi explained her best friend was away in Switzerland for a while, and she didn't have any kids, though she had two other mum friends who were also lovely and always offering to help, but they were super busy like everyone else was and she didn't like to burden them.

'It might help you to meet other parent carers,' Alice suggested. 'Does Jolyon have many friends to play with, because play is so important, isn't it?'

Alice registered the way the woman's face froze. Had she made another mistake? Did Mhairi not think of herself as a parent carer? Or are they more isolated than she was letting on? Maybe Jolyon didn't have many little buddies to play with? She wished she hadn't said anything about it now. She wished there was longer to talk. Mhairi was looking down at her hands in her lap. Alice had to think fast.

'I wonder whether we should begin a referral to the educational psychologist. It'll be a very long wait, probably, but they can help with things like school and education plans. He'll be starting school soon, won't he?' She was aware of not trying to promise too much. Resources were so thin on the ground.

'I've deferred his place for a year,' the mum said. 'The idea of school terrifies me. How can he be ready for it?'

Alice didn't know what to say about this, and she found herself wondering why Dr Millen hadn't made these same referrals. What had he been waiting for?

'What else does Jolyon need, do you think?' Alice faced Mhairi now, her hands in prayer between her knees.

'I... I thought you could tell me that.'

Alice blinked, at a loss.

Time was up. She should be showing Mrs Sears and her son out, their worries gone, or at least on their way to being gone.

She let her eyes fall to Jolyon who was now happily sitting in a splayed-ankle kneel, picking fluffy bits from the rug. He beamed up at her, then at his mummy.

Mhairi smiled tenderly back at her son, and a little conspiratorially too, like they were the only two who understood each other in the whole world, and like she was very, very glad when her son was affectionate with her in public. Maybe because it stopped people thinking the worst about her and her parenting?

'You look happy to me,' Alice tried, addressing Jolyon. 'And you're growing, and playing.' She indicated the little cairn of rug fluff that the boy had piled on the toe of Mhairi's trainer. 'And you communicate very well, given the way you scrunched up that questionnaire for your mummy.'

Jolyon, seeing his mother smiling, smiled too.

'I... I don't have children myself.' Alice let this tail away to a shrug, turning back to Mhairi. 'But if he's loved, and clothed and growing and happy, and making his feelings felt, that seems *great* to me.'

Mhairi's face fell as though she didn't know whether to thank her for the vote of confidence or throw herself on the floor and have a fit of rage at this brushing-off.

'Great?' Mhairi echoed.

'Really, *really* great!' Alice's double thumbs-up detracted from the reassurance she was desperately trying to offer.

'Right, well, thank you.' The woman was shrinking before her eyes.

Oh no! Alice could see it all now. Dr Millen had been the practice GP for decades now, and he could be fusty and set in his ways, if Alice's first encounters with him this morning were indicative of how he was all the time. He'd shaken Alice's hand in greeting with the relieved look of a man who ought to have retired years ago and who was now in the presence of his ticket out of here and onto his final-salary pension. He was literally the only doctor for miles, experienced and wise, yes, but overburdened and, Alice sensed, rapidly losing interest in new medical developments, if the conversation they had about a training initiative he was required to attend soon was anything to go by.

He'd grumbled about how the surgery had been chosen to trial 'some new ambient voice technology thing, supposed to transcribe consultations for us and keep medical notes without us having to do a thing. I don't know, what is the point of doctoring if I can't write my own medical notes and draft my own patient letters?' Then he'd shut himself in his office and left her to her patients. Plus, Alice hadn't failed to notice, he'd expected Gracie to make his tea and take in his lunch to him, treating her more like his secretary than the surgery's receptionist.

Yet, now here she was, the 'young woman doctor', a fresh new presence in the staid old surgery. She *had* to be up on childhood developmental stuff, right? And if Mhairi Sears had been looking to her as a lifeline at last, other patients would too.

Queasiness spread from her stomach to her throat. She looked at the little boy again.

Just because Jolyon seemed happy enough right this second didn't mean he didn't still deserve the very best support and understanding possible, and just because his mum had coped until now didn't mean she wasn't worried sick about the future.

'What was it you wanted to get from today?' Alice asked softly, because she'd been trained to ask this, feeling herself being pulled out on the tide, way beyond her depth. She'd experienced this feeling on many occasions at the hospital, but still, it was dreadful, because it wasn't her who was at risk of going under. It was Mhairi and her little boy.

Silence bloomed between the three of them. Mhairi's face set into a dignified, placid mask. She hauled her bag onto her shoulder and reached for Jolyon's hand.

'Thank you for seeing us, Doctor,' she said, unable to answer the question. 'Come on, Jolly. Let's go home.'

Alice watched him get into his stroller without complaint and Mhairi pushed her beautiful son right out of the room.

Alice had jumped up, obligingly holding the door. 'If it's any help, I don't think it's you or Jolyon who needs to adapt? It's the rest of the world that needs to be more understanding and accom-modating.'

Mhairi's tears welled and she put a hand to Alice's wrist. 'That's what I think too, but the world is the way it is...' She heaved a sigh. 'There's just never enough time at these things.' Mhairi gestured back towards the empty chairs where they'd just sat. 'People often say a lot, promise a lot, but nothing much seems to materialise, unless I'm willing to fight to the point of exhaustion, you know?'

Alice didn't know exactly, but her heart cracked all the same. 'Let's see how we get on with those referrals, eh? Come back in three months for a review and we'll talk again. Or sooner, if you want.'

Mhairi crossed the now empty waiting room, keeping her head down and only replying with a hasty 'Cheerio' to a concerned Gracie behind the re-ception desk asking if she was all right.

Alice shut her consulting room door and pressed her forehead to the cool frame, trying not to cry.

'Dr Hargreave?' a voice called from the other side after a few moments.

She dabbed her eyes dry before pulling the handle, showing her face, hoping she wasn't as pale as she felt.

'Ah, there you are. Time for the social prescription project meeting,' said Dr Millen, his bushy brows slanting, lending him a slightly puzzled-looking expression which, Alice was beginning to suspect, he wore much of the time.

Behind him stood a ramshackle group of strangers, all staring expectantly at her, getting their first eyeful of the new doctor in town.

'Right away,' she said, putting on a practised smile.

11

Cary Anderson's life was all about balance.

He had his one-man carpentry business which brought him a great deal of professional satisfaction. He'd spend his Saturdays sharing his skills at the big fixing shed and now he ran the schoolkids' carpentry session during the week as well.

Volunteering at the repair shop was his way of giving back to the town that sustained him, even while he maintained a shy, almost silent, mystique amongst its people.

The carpentry meant he had enough money for the things he needed to live as well as a few of the things he simply wanted, which included any number of dapper vintage waistcoats, crisp white or tan work shirts, the brown, sandy or khaki 'Oxford bags' trousers that he favoured and wore sometimes with leather belts, sometimes with braces. His style was unostentatious, a little shabby and understated but certainly distinctive, and now that everyone in town was used to seeing him cutting about in his classic, preppy gear, nobody batted an eyelid.

He didn't buy vast amounts in the way of vintage clothing, but what he did buy, he looked after, extending its useable life by decades, one of the central principles of repair shop life.

Because his draughtsman dad had worked away in the city till all hours, it had been his grandfather, once a Fellow at the Glasgow College of Art, who'd taught him about style, showed him how to tie a tie and pomade his curls and how to shine his boots to a nut-brown sheen – which he still did to this day. Like his grandfather, Cary was the sort of methodical man that revelled in a job well done. That went for his personal care as well as his craftsmanship.

His mother often repeated the story that young Cary hadn't uttered a word until he was seven years old and that this had been a source of some wonder amongst the Glasgow health workers and nurses of the 1990s. Then one day he had simply replied, 'No ta, Glo Glo,' to the offer of a mug of his grandma Gloria's favourite milky Mellow Birds and that was that. He talked. Nobody really knew what had happened, but his mum, a nursery teacher, always maintained that 'children must be allowed to do, or not do, things in their own sweet time,' and he'd held on to that as a motto for his adult life too.

However, Cary Anderson remained a man who wouldn't speak just to hear the sound of his own voice. If it was vital, he found the words to express it; if it was chatter or small talk, he rarely felt compelled to pitch in. This was how he practised contentment, never getting too involved in discussions that didn't require him.

His balance of work and community life and the way he never wasted anything, including time and words, meant he was contented in ways few folks are, and that balance brought him stability and an un-studied calm which was written upon his fine upright body and fixed in his handsome, placid expression.

Unfortunately for Cary Anderson, today his tried and true system for steadiness and simplicity was about to be sent careering loop-the-loop, and he had no idea whatsoever what was about to hit him.

'This is Dr Alice Hargreave,' old Dr Millen was saying, making the introductions while the repair shop regulars filed into the messy consulting room cluttered with old books and papers, the corners stacked with dead printers and old disconnected telephones strangled with their cords.

The old doctor presented the woman Cary had met outside the bank, the one whose number he'd deleted from his phone out of respect for her privacy. The woman who he'd barely been able to string a coherent sentence together for, when she'd been lost and asking him for help. He'd probably scared her when he blurted out that he'd text her the deli's details, and he'd mentally kicked himself over it afterwards. It had been a dick move and not like him at all.

It was just she was so befuddled that day on the street with her hair rain-spotted and clinging to her face. That, and she was almost certainly the most beautiful person Cary Anderson had ever encountered in his thirty-five years.

Cary didn't want to push himself forward so he hung back now, allowing Murray McIntyre, who headed up the repair shop party, to greet the new doctor first. Then Livvie Cooper, who he introduced as the repair shop admin, shook her hand, welcoming her to Cairn Dhu.

A little girl in school uniform, a small blanket clasped in her hands, revealed her face from behind Livvie's long Afghan coat, gazing up at the new doctor.

Livvie introduced her as her daughter, Shell, saying they went everywhere together when she wasn't in school.

Alice greeted the little girl warmly but it only made the child withdraw.

There followed a search for coloured markers and Alice tore a few pages from her notebook so the shy girl with deep-set eyes and skewwhiff pigtails could hide herself away behind their backs and draw while the adults talked.

At last, it was Cary's turn to say hello.

Something within him quavered at the sight of Alice, so slight and tentative, her eyes scrunched into tight smile lines, the tips of her white teeth bared, her lips a little parched. She was smiling, yes, but there was apprehension behind it. She looked fit to drop, or to flee.

'We've already met,' Cary said.

'You're the man with the clock.'

He was glad to know she remembered him. He hoped the detachment in her demeanour wasn't down to her remembering him as the creep who'd taken liberties asking for her phone number.

She hadn't offered him her hand, so he didn't reach out his own. Instead he nodded and took his seat, and something in her face loosened as if with relief. Everyone was claiming chairs now amongst the untidiness of the elderly medical man's office, the formalities dispensed with.

'Survived your first day?' Dr Millen asked Alice. 'I see you got to grips with the referral system, anyway. You've really gone to town on them today, eh?'

Cary knew this was the old doc's way, paternal, a little ironic perhaps, but generally kindly and well-meaning. Alice, however, looked like she thought she was in trouble.

'Shouldn't I have?' she was saying.

Cary averted his eyes, fussed with his bag, shifted his chair.

'You know what's best for your patients,' Millen said with a crumpled brow, and he sat too, seemingly forgetting the matter.

Cary couldn't help picking up on the defeated way Alice folded into the low armchair. It couldn't be easy for her heading into a meeting after a long first day at work in a new place. She was crossing one leg over the other, her notepad and pen poised over her thigh. She was pretending to be fine.

All of this was from the corner of his eye. He didn't dare stare, but something about her was sounding a strange alarm within his body.

She had chosen the chair by his side, which was

oddly lower than his. All the furniture was mis-matched so no one in here was meeting eye to eye.

Murray McIntyre sat next to Millen and looked uncomfortable on a wheely office chair he was fiddling with, trying to lower it, and failing.

Livvie perched on a stool like a nervous bird poised to take flight. Shell scribbled away, shielded behind her.

The old doctor lounged on his consulting chair and cleared his throat, his once-sharp eyes over-shelved with bushy brows that moved in a comical way, putting Cary in mind of the bedraggled dog from *Fraggle Rock*, one of his favourite childhood shows. His heart lifted, noting the similarity.

The new doctor beside him sat dead still, nothing but tiredness and shrinking heaviness pulsing out of her like signals from a dying star.

Gracie the receptionist appeared at the door with a tray of oddly homespun ceramic mugs and a milk jug with a lopsided, pouting lip. She poured tea for everyone except Shell, who was passed a wonky mug of milk which she only stared at before shaking her head in refusal.

'That's me away home, then, if that's everything, Dr Millen?' the receptionist asked. 'I'm throwing my first vase tonight!'

'Best of luck with that, Gracie.' The old doctor was of an age where he didn't even try to hide his wry amusement. 'Cheery-bye now.'

'Senga's made us some of her chocolate digestive squares,' Murray said as the receptionist left, and he pulled the lid from a tub to release a sweet scent of milk chocolate over buttery, bashed biscuits cooked with condensed milk, soft brown sugar and golden syrup. He made sure Shell was offered the first tasty piece.

When he offered the tub to the new doctor she looked sorely tempted but after hesitating over them, she scrunched her nose. 'I don't really like to eat re-fined sugar.'

This elicited a shared glance between Murray and Livvie as Dr Millen dived his hand into the tub and claimed the biggest piece.

'As you know,' he said, biting into the treat, still cool from the repair shop fridge, 'we've been asked to provide a new community service. An initiative to combat the mental-health crisis and loneliness epi-demic we know all too much of in this part of the world.'

'The weather isn't helping,' Murray put in. 'Can't remember a rainier winter.' He too bit into his bis-cuity square, careful to catch the crumbs.

'Tell me about it,' interjected Alice, only realising once the words were out that everyone had turned to face her. 'I... I, uh, thought Manchester was dark and grey in the wintertime, but this is something else.'

Cary caught the shake in her voice that told of her sudden discomfort, and he remembered a time when he was the new arrival in town. Cairn Dhu certainly took a little getting used to. It must be harder for the young doctor, landing in the depths of January when she'd been used to the shelter and fun of a big, towering English city.

'You get used to the long dark nights,' he wanted to tell her, 'and the people.' Cary wished he could ask the new doctor if she'd had a chance to observe the stars over the mountaintops since her arrival; the brightest in the British Isles, the air was so clean here. The sight of them could cheer anyone and help get them through the winter. But he said none of this because Dr Millen evidently had his dinner waiting for him at home and was intent on pressing on with this meeting.

'Social prescribing is all about supplementing health care with social solutions,' droned Millen. 'The idea is to tackle the things that often accompany health issues; loneliness, barriers to social mobility, panic and anxiety, for instance, *before* they compound into larger health concerns. Thanks to Murray's funding bid talents we've been gifted a few hundred pounds to begin a community garden to be created and run by volunteers for the benefit of patients in the community, where they can grow their own food, learn about plants...'

Out of the corner of Cary's eye he noticed Alice wasn't note-taking at all, but circling her Biro in black loops the way children draw curly hair on the head of a stick figure. Her pen travelled in tight rings along the margin.

'Come to think of it...' Dr Millen was saying. Alice's pen froze. 'Where's the laddie they were sending from the mountain rangers' station? Jemmy promised us a man, did he no'?'

Murray McIntyre knew the answer. 'Oh, yeah, uh... the guy called in at the shed earlier, said there'd been a mix-up? Finlay, his name was. Finlay Morlich. He wasn't much interested in helping out.' Murray shrugged. 'Sorry 'bout that.'

'Maybe they'll send someone else?' Livvie offered. 'We might be better off without Morlich, anyway, bringing everyone down with his grumpy patter.'

'Oh, I dunno,' Murray tried, generously, 'he seemed all right, just a bit... harassed.'

Cary had seen the ranger around the town, recognising within him another reticent soul, but Finlay was surely someone with no time at all for others. A shame really, as a few days in town with his hands in the earth would probably do him good. Some people, he'd come to learn, didn't take much of an interest in the world, or in themselves for that matter, and without knowing it, they cut themselves off from everything good. Until they had the awareness or the courage to ask for help, they often couldn't be helped.

Livvie had more to say about him, clearly not a fan. 'I doubt Morlich will lumber into town again any-time soon, not until he wants more of his precious snacks, anyway.' This elicited a tiny giggle from be-hind her where Shell concealed herself.

'No matter,' Murray said. '*We're* all here, and fully committed to helping. Cary had some thoughts on where to start, didn't you, Cary?'

This pulled him from his position as quiet ob-server. 'Ah, right enough.'

Drawing the plans from his dad's leather satchel that was probably as old as he was and, also like him, soft as butter, he shared the blueprints he'd inked up on his drawing board at home. The papers brought with them an apple from his bag that he caught in a quick hand before it could tumble to the floor.

'Shell?' Cary said, softly, knowing the little girl was prone to getting startled. 'Apple?'

The child's face appeared around her mother's side, looking to her for approval before she spread her hands to catch the fruit. Cary passed it to Livvie first, instead of chucking it. With the red fruit delivered into her hands, Shell went back to drawing, trying to silence her bites. Cary's heart ached a little to see her still so shy, in spite of all the time she spent at the repair shed on Saturdays and after school, sticking so close to her mother there was rarely a gap between them.

Although nobody really knew for sure, Cary had a rough gist of what Livvie and Shell Cooper had been through in recent months. The local police had uncovered a crime gang operating across the region. They'd been using Livvie's house as a kind of ad hoc HQ, and using Livvie as... he dared not think.

Ally McIntyre, who'd left town for Switzerland in the summer, had a policeman boyfriend, Jamie Beaton, and he'd had something to do with the raid that saw the gang's ringleaders jailed and, as far as Cary had gathered from the scant facts published in the papers and what Ally had been allowed to tell the repair shop volunteers, Jamie had put his life at risk in the process.

Livvie and Shell were never mentioned in the papers, of course, and for four months they'd been rehoused somewhere out of sight for their safety. Now they were free of the tyrant man who'd controlled them. The gang had been put away for years, and little Shell was re-enrolled in the primary school down the road.

Livvie had been unable to resist the welcoming gravity of the repair shop (something Cary Anderson knew a little about too), and she'd quickly found herself drawn into its schemes. Murray's clever funding bidding had made sure she was salaried, their official events manager and overseer of the various community groups who met at the shed, including Cary's children's woodworking group. Cary couldn't count her as a friend exactly, she was too self-contained for that, but he admired her organisational skills and competence.

'Get on with it then,' Livvie snapped, rather testing his sympathy for her.

Cary spread the papers across his legs and softly cleared his throat. 'This is the land to the south of the repair shed,' he began. 'Generously surrendered to public use by the McIntyre family.'

'Thanks, Mum and Dad,' threw in Murray.

'It's laid to lawn at the moment,' Cary went on.

'There's room for four large raised planting beds at each point of the compass, like this. One for fruits, one for veg, one for herbs and medicinal plants, and one for cut flowers. I'll help to build the raised beds.'

'And I'll oversee the rotas and liaise with the surgery about patient access and safeguarding,' Livvie said.

'And the surgery will refer patients to the scheme,' said the doc. 'Although anyone can join in with the planting and upkeep. This garden's for the whole community, yes? And, in fact, that's where young Dr Hargreave comes in.'

Cary felt the tension sharply rising from the woman to his right.

'Me?' she said, her pen hovering.

'Patient engagement officer,' said Millen, with what passed as a smile for him. 'It's only social pre-scribing if the surgery sends a medical presence to the site to talk with the locals, do a bit of mental-health first-aiding where needed and generally facilitate en-gagement with the garden, so patients can fully access its benefits.'

'But I don't know anything about gardening,' she said. 'I've never looked after so much as a window box!'

'You know about patients.' Millen's smile grew weaker still.

'I'll be there to help you,' Cary told her softly.

'We all will,' Murray added in his easy way. 'My role is general dogsbody, so if there's anything you don't know, or anything you need, you can tell me.'

None of this seemed to reassure the woman, if the waves of panicked energy coming from her were anything to go by. Cary was surprised to realise they'd set off an unusual response within him too.

Not a man who had to scrabble around to label his feelings correctly, he knew exactly what it was. It was a careful kind of tender attentiveness.

Without having to think too deeply about it, he'd already subconsciously committed to making Dr Hargreave happy in her work at the garden, and if that couldn't be achieved, he'd strive to make her, at least, feel comfortable.

He didn't enjoy witnessing anyone out of sorts, but this woman was something else. To Cary she appeared as out of her element as a planet in retrograde, a lost soul. Her whole demeanour was an unhappy one, her pallor sickly, as though she'd spent the last decade under fluorescent lighting. Maybe she had? A young doctor at the end of her training, at last released into the real world, and a Manchester girl too?

Cairn Dhu had to be a far cry from home. He'd experienced the culture shock himself, a few years back, and he'd only moved from Glasgow.

'We'll need a naturalist's expertise when choosing and sourcing the plants and trees,' Murray was saying.

'The trees?' Millen asked.

'Yes. Here, here, here and here.' Cary pointed to equidistant points between each of the raised beds on his drawing. 'I'd hoped we'd plant alder trees, if no one minds? They're an indigenous species to Scotland, not to mention wonderful for woodworking.'

The others agreed they had zero objection to the idea, and Murray said it sounded 'braw'. Alice Hargreave, however, was staring into space, her gravity turning heavier, like a black hole, emitting exhausted dark energy.

Cary heard her sighing softly more than once, and her posture slumped inch by inch. She was fighting the weight of existence, that much was obvious. It made his heart soften all the more for her.

The meeting went on for some time, and because Cary had said his piece, he had nothing more to add, other than nods of agreement. Murray and Livvie went over the flow of funding and the release of monies for the initial materials. There was some discussion of safeguarding and protecting vulnerable groups and criminal disclosure checks for all volunteers, as well as some words on patient confidentiality.

Dr Millen made sure that Alice, who had accepted her gardening fate, understood her role, telling her she'd only be required on site on some Sundays, or the occasional errand early on a Saturday. He'd see to it this was taken into account in her surgery workloading, remarking pointedly how some time outdoors would do her good. She was smiling in weak agreement when the consulting room door banged open and little Shell screamed and ran to her mother's arms.

'Uh, I'm sorry, I didnae mean to...' said the gruff, hulk-like figure in the doorframe, his fists tightly curled by his sides.

'Good grief, man!' Dr Millen shouted, jumping to his feet. 'What's all this in aid of?'

Cary, always observant, noticed multiple things happening at once.

First, he saw the quailing shame in Finlay Morlich's expression as he apologised and stomped inside, asking pointlessly if he was too late. He also registered the bright flash of something victorious in Murray McIntyre's looks as he directed the unfortunate, clumsy ranger to the only spare chair, piled with books and next to Alice, and Cary couldn't miss Murray's gaze following the mountain man as he knocked every chair and table leg and stumbled over his own boots on his way to his seat.

'Sorry, lassie. I didnae mean to frighten you,' Finlay was saying to Shell, who didn't look inclined to forgive him during her lifetime.

'You've missed the lot,' Millen scowled, hoiking up his trousers at the knees to sit again.

Finlay shiftily eyed the biscuit tub and did nothing to hide his dismay at finding it empty other than crumbs.

Murray seemingly couldn't help smiling in sympathy at Finlay, but the ranger put his head down, clasping his two hands tightly together like a man steeling himself to suffer through a public meeting with no refreshments of any kind.

The meeting soon concluded with plans to start the landscaping and bed-building while the patients were referred by Alice to the project. She was to pick suitable participants, said the old doctor with a sly cheerfulness, since she'd proven herself 'so good at firing off referrals'.

There would be an official tree planting to launch the scheme on the morning of Sunday the twenty-fifth, the very first time the participants would be invited onto the site, and the local paper would be invited to take everyone's picture, so the organising committee would have to crack on if they were going to break ground, prepare the beds and make the place safe and ready for them to start gardening in. Finlay was asked if he'd mind accompanying Murray to the plant nurseries on the tenth before the repair shed opened for the day.

'On Saturday?' confirmed Finlay. 'I didnae ken we'd be startin' so soon!'

Not one to indulge moaning, Livvie ignored this and asked, 'We need to get the plants and trees ordered. Can you borrow the ranger truck, do you think? Pick Murray up at eight?'

As soon as he was released, Finlay stormed out with barely a word of farewell, even more out of sorts than when he'd arrived. Murray, who the ranger hadn't even said goodbye to, didn't appear quite as smirking and self-assured as he had earlier.

Then, suddenly, Alice was pulling herself from the chair, hauling on her coat, and lifting her bag of textbooks onto her shoulder.

At the door, Cary managed to stop her.

'To tide you over till tea,' he said in the hubbub of everybody taking their leave, handing the new doctor a second apple he'd had in his bag. He stored them for winter in his attics, having picked them from his own apple trees in his little woodworking yard behind his cottage where the wood shavings blew around his ankles and accumulated in cobwebby corners.

She looked with apprehension at the red fruit cradled on his fingertips, but she accepted it with a nod, as though she had not a word left in her head.

'Mind how you go,' he said, though she didn't seem to hear.

Cary purposely didn't watch after her from the surgery ramp as she left, as, unknown to her, she took away a piece of him he'd never get back, a soft portion of his heart that wanted her to be glad she'd travelled all the way here from England. He'd do everything he could to see to that.

12

Alice rushed onto the high street, head down against the wind. The streetlamps and strings of lights garlanded between them glowed overhead. There was a queue of cars trying to pull in at the chippy. The shops were closing. The bank was still resolutely shut.

All she had to do was get indoors, take her bath, chop some carrots and crack open the red pepper and chilli hummus she'd had delivered from Laura's deli.

A few stars peeped out between dark cloud up above, the first glimpse she'd had of unobscured sky since she got here. Maybe the clouds were lifting? *Something*, she felt, was changing. And now she had fourteen hours all to herself. She pondered watching a K-Drama on her laptop while she ate. That's the kind of thing restful people did.

She'd completed her first day at work and it hadn't been all bad. She'd held it together. Sure, she was in a whole new place with new systems and new people, some more alarming than others, but the stakes were lower. There was no one screaming on trolleys out in the corridor. No nightshifts where she'd be left in charge of three hundred patients with half the agency staff busy elsewhere, and... No! She wasn't going to get drawn in to remembering, not now she was turning over a new leaf.

She slowed her pace, noticing for the first time the red 'SALE' signs in the kilt shop window and all those gorgeous tartans. She stopped to look at them.

She'd made it through her first day unscathed, even if the image of Mhairi Sears, compliant but on the verge of tears, haunted her now. There had to be more she could do for her and her little boy. She'd have to do some more research on local services. She wondered if Mhairi would enjoy getting involved at the social prescribing garden. She'd ask the surgery to send an invitation first thing, letting the mum decide for herself whether or not she accepted.

'There'll always be outliers,' she heard Bastian's voice saying. 'The ones that the systems can't really help.' That was how he'd comfort her when she got home after a hard day, feeling inadequate and over-whelmed, worried she'd not done enough to help a patient with a complex presentation, someone re-quiring multi-agency collaborative support, and knowing that, for all kinds of reasons, they were un-likely to receive it, at least not right away and in a joined-up, streamlined manner. She herself knew no-body should be considered beyond support.

Jolyon and Mhairi aren't outliers; he's a sweet little boy and she's an under-supported mother, she answered back in her head, surprising the spectral Bastian who was *tut-tutting* in her imagination. This too made her feel lighter. The feeling of being able to separate herself from the way he was so confident in his opinions. The longer she spent away from him, the more sympathet-ically she seemed to see the world.

She turned once more for home, having not really taken in much of the shop window display. There were crowds around the bus stop ahead of her, shop workers leaving town for the night. She could see the minibus was on its way down the high street towards them and people were hauling huge hiking packs onto their backs in readiness.

It was a squeeze, getting past them on the narrow pavement, and there was a big red phone box in the way, and, as she pressed against a stone window frame to allow other pedestrians to pass, her eyes flew to the sight of a head bobbing, only partially glimpsed through the milling people. It was a person in side profile, their shoulders working, kneeling over someone in the street, a serious set to their face. They were doing chest compressions! *One, two, three, four, one, two, three, four...* and in an instant she was spirited into an instinctive battle between fight, flight or freeze. She'd be the only medic on the street, surely, the only person trained to help.

'I'm a doctor!' she called over the throng, trying to get through the bus stop crowd and bulky luggage. All eyes turned on her, questioning.

The person hunching over the prone figure on the ground looked up too.

How long had the patient been without oxygen? What were the chances of bringing them round? She knew from experience the chances were slim. Cold sweat ran down her spine.

'Don't stop with the compressions!' she yelled. 'Can you let me through, please!'

Why were these stupid locals gawping at her? Why were the tourists not shifting?

'Excuse me!' she shouted, pushing someone's snowboard out of the way and revealing... *oh, shit*! Not a member of the public performing lifesaving CPR and in desperate need of help, but a hiker trying to force a puffy winter jacket into an overstuffed backpack.

'Oh!'

Over her own panting breaths she heard a mocking laugh behind her, and there was a child asking, 'What's wrong with that lady, Mummy?' followed by a sharp, '*Shoosh*, she'll hear.'

'Oh,' said Alice again, the burn of shame lighting up her cheeks. 'Sorry, I thought...' She didn't want to say out loud what she'd thought she'd seen. Everyone was already staring at her like she was raving mad. The man with the backpack was now getting to his feet and looking at her.

'You all right?' he asked, and not without judgement.

Head down, clutching her coat lapels, she picked her way as quickly and lightly as she could through the crowd, before breaking into a run for home.

* * *

Oh no, oh no, oh no, Alice's brain looped as she climbed the stairs to her flat, feeling as though she were trying to clamber up a downward escalator.

She fumbled for the apartment key in the deep pockets of her big woollen coat, perfect for winter in Manchester, nowhere near warm enough up here.

Running away to the Highlands had been futile. She was still getting carried away here just the same, still seeing and imagining the worst. 'Catastrophising,' the psychiatrist had told her. 'A common after-effect of complex or cumulative trauma.'

She was still trapped in that state of always being on high alert, waiting for her bleeper to go off on the wards and having to run this way and that, pulled by priority patients in every direction and being the only doctor on staff for all those overnight patients, everyone wanting her at the same time, not under-standing she was spread too thin, and just wanting to run away from it all, screaming in surrender.

The ordeal of being thrown in at the doctoral deep end had seeped into her neural tissue forever, it seemed; her amygdala now misjudging everyday situations and sending out panicked messages to her body, turning her guts inside out, making her sweat and see things all wrong, and her hippocampus had lost its way too and couldn't help her regulate. Once again, she'd ended up drowned in adrenaline and stress cortisol when there was no need for it.

Back in Manchester the comedown after a shift

was always so sharp, it felt like being lifted off her feet, losing the thing that tethered her to the ground, and she'd float home from hospital in a daze, seeing nothing, processing nothing from her day, leaving everything that had happened queued up like a traffic jam, unresolved at the back of her brain: all the patients she hadn't been able to help, all the ones she had, and yet they'd still have such tough recoveries ahead of them, all the mistakes she'd made, the patients who'd cried, the ones who'd shouted, all the times she'd been slapped or body-slammed by people too ill to know better, or the furious ones who knew full well what they were doing but did it anyway and the police had to be called. These were stored up alongside the difficult conversations in the hospital's family room, or next to the vending machines when the family room was in use. She could still hear the scream of that one bereft mother when she let herself think about it, all these years later. Her head was abuzz with it all, but there seemed never to be any time to explore it properly, to come to understand any of it, or to let some of it go.

She slammed her door shut. The flat was dark and overheated. She poured a glass of water from the tap, downed the whole thing.

It seemed that even after her GP surgery shifts she

was fated to feel the same way; trapped in the awful unreality of exhaustion.

All she'd needed was a change of pace, she'd told herself when applying for this job. A change of scenery. Cairn Dhu surgery had offered both. Or she'd hoped it would.

Maybe she needed to run her bloods again? No, she'd done that just before Christmas and all her levels were good, though her cortisol was high and according to the charts her BMI had fallen again, not that she set much store in those, but the numbers could tell her one thing; she certainly wasn't getting better.

A holiday might sort her out? Two weeks, or a month, on a lounger on a beach, eating barbeque and tropical fruits, not talking to anyone, drinking coconut water and sleeping whenever she wanted to, washing in warm saltwater, soaking up vitamin D and slowly reading a long novel that had nothing to do with real life or her textbooks.

She pulled her shoes off, shucked off her coat, shuffled her feet across the floor to the bathroom re-membering as she did so the patients endlessly drag-ging portable IV stands along hospital corridors.

A holiday wasn't going to happen, of course. Her bank account knew that. Student debt meant a good ten or even twenty years ahead of solid work before she shifted what she owed.

But this work was the thing she'd trained for. The thing she should be happy to have. She'd just about made it out of the trainee trenches. Things were supposed to be getting easier now.

When she'd asked her mother how she coped with it all – and *she'd* had an actual baby by her age – she'd shrugged and said, 'Well, you just get on with things, don't you?'

She hadn't dared ask her father the same thing. He'd only have given her that look, the *Toughen up, Buttercup* look, the *School of Hard Knocks* look. His father had been a consultant too. Resilience and hard work ran through this family. Alice's brothers didn't seem to share her problems, and they'd far outshone her in their clinical practice. She was the only one like this.

The bathroom light hurt her tired eyes.

She ran the toothbrush over her teeth without paste then made her way straight to bed and climbed in. The dizziness was back.

She wondered vaguely if she'd remembered to bolt the door to her flat and tried to remember where she'd even thrown her keys. The light switch by her bed, only just distinct in the green glow from the fire escape sign, seemed to be stretching and melting down the wall.

She felt nothing.

Bastian would tell her she should eat something. She knew she should shower, ring her mother, see if she could work out how to tune in the telly, try to self-regulate. But the shock of seeing someone prone on the street, needing CPR, or so she'd imagined, had been enough to immobilise her again and all she could do was keep her head on her pillow.

Something hard in her palm drew her attention even though she was tied up in the black knot of the familiar panic and exhaustion cycle.

It was an apple. Given to her by that man. Cary. The one with the quiet voice, the clothes from another time, the kind eyes.

The fruit wasn't glossy and waxed like the supermarket Pink Ladies she lived off back home. Its skin was rougher and it released a mellow orchard scent that put her in mind of a misty autumn ramble in the Bridgewater garden that day after med school registration with her new flatmates, before they'd really understood what they'd signed up for. That September day there'd been dragonflies over the river and a young orchard laden with fruit.

Still lying on her side, she brought the apple to

her mouth, sinking her teeth into the subtle flesh, per-fume meeting her senses.

It was a small thing, but it was a good thing. She bit again and again until it was gone before curling up like balled laundry, her body softening as the sweet-ness and acidity raced through her system. Sleep was coming for her and she offered no resistance to the great wave of nothing.

In the morning she would jolt awake before her alarm and find herself still gripping the browning core of the fruit she didn't remember eating, black pips spilled on her white sheets, and she'd promise herself, again, that today would be different.

Today she'd be well, because this was supposed to be her re-set Highland hideaway.

13

Murray could think of better things to do with his Saturday morning, like sleeping until the very last minute before the repair shop opened, for instance. Or, if he was really letting himself dream, and since the clouds had cleared and the sky was a bright, cold blue, he could take a train to Aberdeen or Inverness, find some good coffee, browse the higher-end stores, check out the new tech – which he was hopelessly out of touch with since leaving Zurich. He may not know a lot about fixing the latest devices but he sure missed treating himself to them.

He blew out a long sigh which turned to white vapour in the crisp morning air. It was probably for the best he was stuck with this errand, given the way his savings were dwindling after paying his share of the bills and groceries at the mill house these last six months. He couldn't have his parents paying for everything, even if they told him they didn't mind and – this they'd said especially pointedly – he really should save his money to buy his ticket back to Switzerland.

Volunteering was all very well as a way of helping out his parents but it didn't pay a penny, and in truth there was very little for him to actually do now that his funding bids were secured and the shed extension was well underway. He knew he couldn't hide behind that desk every repair Saturday forever.

He stamped the warmth back into his feet, waiting, not all that patiently, at the roadside for his ride.

Even this garden project he'd been lumbered with – which hadn't been his idea but the surgery's – felt like a pastime and not his real purpose in life, whatever that might be now that his career in the global environmental charity sector had hit a wall.

Murray could really do with a day to himself for some sort-out-your-life admin, but here he was waiting for a lift to the garden centre, of all places, and he'd have to make small talk for at least a couple of hours with Finlay Morlich. Not a prospect he relished.

He stepped onto the road so he could peer down

the high street. Barely any cars were on the move yet, despite the dry clear morning, and none of them were heading towards the dead-end of the high street where the semi-scaffolded repair shed rose above the McIntyre mill house plot. Theirs was the very last building on this side of town and, with the shed yet to open for the day, Saturday strollers would turn down the leafy riverside path before even coming within sight of their walled boundary. People only came to the repair shed if they wanted something, or someone.

'*Goedemorgan!*' called a deep, heart-stalling voice accompanied by approaching footsteps. Kurt came into view. He was wearing an orange and black patterned jacket which only he could possibly look good in.

'There you are!' he said, stopping before Murray who was trying to feign absolute coolness at his unexpected appearance.

'You're not working already, are you?' was the best Murray could come up with, and it was met with a laugh and those blue eyes shining.

'No, silly. I am here early to ask you out. Do you want to go out?'

How can anyone on the planet be this direct or

this confident? It was bewildering. It was faintly terri-
fying too.

'You mean *out* out? With me?'

Kurt's smile only broadened. 'Of course. Why not?'

'Well...' Murray couldn't think of a reason to say
no. 'Where?'

'Anywhere you like.'

Nothing he said would put Kurt off now. They
were going out and that was that.

'There's not a lot of places to go around here, except the ski slope bar. It's a sort of nightclub.'

'The Ptarmigan? I know it. Tonight?'

'Oh!' That felt alarmingly soon. 'I'm busy,' he lied.

'Next Saturday?' Kurt was nothing if not determined. 'At nine?'

Murray felt his face heating. 'Sure.'

Suddenly, there was the ranger truck pulling up,
its electric engine totally silent, while Kurt was
pressing his hands into his pockets, winging his arms
in a happy shrug. 'Good. So, see you.'

Out of nowhere, and before Murray knew what
was happening, Kurt swooped a pillowy kiss directly
onto his cheekbone. The effect was alarmingly, melt-
ingly incredible.

The builder was gone in an instant, bouncing

along the pavement, all tallness and warmth, leaving Murray face to face through the driver's side window with a stone-faced Finlay staring hard at him.

Murray fought hard to regain his balance from the impact of being enthusiastically, unexpectedly kissed in public. Any soul-soaring feelings would have to wait until he could unpack them later over a call with his sister.

Finlay didn't return Murray's half-hearted wave; his hands looked clamped to the steering wheel with white-knuckle tightness.

Murray made his way to the passenger door, more out of duty than desire. It was going to be a long morning, and now that he had a date to prepare for in a week, time was going to go even slower.

14

'Why aren't you stopping?' Murray said as Finlay stuck to the sixty-mile limit and not a bit over.

'Eh?' He hadn't a clue what Murray was on about.

'That was the entrance to the garden centre back there. You'll have to turn around.'

Again, Finlay didn't get it. 'Fillbarrows Garden Centre? Who said we were going there?'

'You did!'

Murray had seemed agitated since getting in the truck, but now he simply wasn't making sense. Maybe it had something to do with that lanky fellow kissing him. It had turned him stupid. Finlay had been given all of one second to disguise the shock of seeing it happening right in front of his eyes. A kiss that they'd probably have preferred to go unwitnessed.

He had felt their kiss like it was his own mouth warm against Murray's chilled cheek, aimed right at the spot below the wide cuff of his black Swiss flag beanie where auburn curls spilled out in every direction. Finlay had felt that kiss in his gut, had wanted it – in the simplest, most primal way – to be his, and yes, he'd immediately added that tall, handsome fellow in orange to his long list of people he would not get along with.

He'd sort of guessed Murray was gay or, at least, deep down, he'd hoped he was, but why hadn't he considered the possibility that he would already be with someone? Stupid, really, considering. Not that Finlay had any plans of actually *trying* anything, obviously, and as this morning proved, he'd been completely correct in that decision. He wouldn't have stood a chance. Naturally.

'Where are we going, then?' There was a note of alarm in Murray's voice.

'Right enough, I never said.' This was his way of yielding. He was being generous because Murray had assumed when he'd mentioned picking up plants he meant the giant commercial place with all the imported bedding and ornamentals that had travelled further than Finlay himself had in his whole lifetime. 'I booked us in for a visit to the Snow Road Native Plant Nursery.'

Murray pulled a face. Clearly he'd never heard of the place.

'Nae reason you should know it. It's the only place round here that grows Cairngorm montane trees and species on the rare plant register.'

'Montane?'

'You know? Upland species?' Murray really did need his help if he didn't know something as simple as that. 'I thought you wanted this garden to reflect the botany of the region?'

'I'd assumed we were going to turn up at the garden centre and put in an order for a few trays of...' Murray paused.

Finlay simply *had to* tear his eyes away from the road, just for a second, not something he'd usually do, just so he could see Murray flailing, searching his brain for the name of literally any plant. Sure enough, he was puffing his cheeks, eyes screwed in meditation.

A tiny glow sparked into life inside Finlay's chest. Regardless, he wasn't about to help the guy out. 'Go on,' he prompted, actually at risk of enjoying himself.

'Petunias!' Murray announced in triumph.

Finlay sniffed a laugh, but soon after, silence fell

and Murray took to adjusting the cuffs of his sporty white jacket with the expensive European logo that Finlay, of course, hadn't recognised.

Murray seemed put out. Was he? The regret flooded in. He hadn't been trying to upset him. He'd assumed they were participating in the kind of 'banter' these town folk went in for, but which, more often than not, left Finlay wondering what exactly was required of him.

He resolved not to say anything else. Stupid of him to think he could compete with... well, with anyone, in the flirty patter stakes. What had come over him? *No more getting carried away*, he told himself.

Finlay carefully mirror, signal, manoeuvred on the deserted stretch of road and turned slowly into the nursery carpark, empty save for an ancient Collie dog with grizzled white chops who was bouncing with excitement all of one centimetre off the hardened mud yard where he seemed to roam freely.

'Is this it?' Murray said, peering through the windscreen at the polytunnels behind fencing. 'Bet they don't have a coffee shop or houseplants or nice cookware stuff here.'

Finlay yanked at the handbrake. He didn't know if Murray's petulance was in jest or serious.

'We're no' here for galivanting,' he snapped.

Murray's face snapped into a look of irritation. Good.

Sticking to his old tried and true defences was by far the safest way of navigating this excursion, and yet the pinch at Finlay's heart made him regret his charmless ways, and, not for the first time, he wished himself a different, easier-to-like person altogether.

* * *

Murray could at least help haul the trolley. That, and having possession of the project's credit card, would be his only contribution to today's trip. Finlay had the rest under control.

The owners, a youngish couple in matching green fleeces and wellies, had let them in, handing them plastic luggage tags and black marker pens so they could claim the larger items they wanted delivered to the project site. Then they left the pair to it, and Finlay led the way up and down the rows of plants, with the resident soppy dog following at his side.

He'd been surprised to see Finlay greet the mutt as soon as it ambushed him getting out of the driver's side door. He'd not gone so far as to talk to the dog in a baby voice, but he'd crouched before the animal and scratched behind its ears and asked permission to take a look around.

It shouldn't have surprised him that Finlay liked animals, hiding away with them up on that mountain of his. Still, the sight had softened Murray's opinion of the curmudgeon.

Seeing him picking through the pots of plants in their winter dormancy surprised him even more. To Murray, most of the plants looked like nothing but un-promising stumps caked in earth, but to Finlay they seemed to be something else, a whole magical forest he could conjure in his mind just by reading the labels.

'Ah, we'll need a few of these!' Finlay said, lifting a tray of tiny rosettes of wet green. This really was a ter-rible time of year for buying plants, if Finlay hoped to enthuse Murray about them.

'Really?'

'Aye! Creepin' lady's tresses. These'll make a braw green carpet around the trees and they'll encourage the bumblebees. Unless,' he said, looking worried, 'you're planning on keeping the grass as a pristine mowed lawn with the stripes and all that?'

Murray shrugged. 'That doesn't sound anything like as much fun as a load of creepy ladies dresses, or whatever it was you said.'

A light flared behind Finlay's eyes but seemed to extinguish itself as quickly as it appeared. 'They're evergreen and throw up green spikes with wee white orchid flowers in summer. We'll take twenty to be getting on with, knowing they'll spread themselves aboot.'

'Right, right.' Murray tried to follow Finlay's business-like lead, writing 'McIntyre x 20' on a label and attaching it to the tray.

Finlay moved quickly onward to something else. 'Twinflowers! These are rare in Scotland now. We'd better have some. They've two wee pinky-white pixie hats hanging like bells from a double stalk. Hence, twinflower. Can we have twenty of these too?'

He was like a child at the cinema Pick 'n' Mix.

'I'm a twin,' Murray blurted, out of habit whenever the topic came up, but also trying to get in Finlay's good books, if such a thing was possible.

Finlay stopped to observe him. 'There's *two* of you?'

'A sister, so unidentical, obviously, and she's not much like me, really.'

'*Hmm.*' Finlay turned back to the plants. 'Label, please.'

'Oops, sorry.' Murray hastily labelled the twinflowers, feeling every bit like Finlay's secretary and as far from making friends as you can get.

The ranger stepped along the row, making sure to scratch the dog's head to keep it by his side. 'I'm an only child myself,' he said in a begrudging way.

Murray ignored the urge to say something jokey and overfamiliar about how that explained a few things, and chose to ask instead, 'Are your family from around here?'

This was clearly a question too far. 'Cuckoo flower. Four trays?'

Murray poised the pen with a sigh. 'How'd you spell cuckoo?'

'Just put lady's smock. The caterpillars love them in the spring.'

'Not sure we want caterpillars eating...' Murray checked the price sticker. 'About thirty quid's worth of flowers.'

'Have you ever seen a cloud of orange-tip butter-flies?' Finlay challenged. 'Or a green-veined white, for that matter?' He asked this like he already knew the answer. The smartarse.

'Four trays it is,' Murray conceded, writing on the label.

'Did you ken that a long time ago our ancient Caledonian woodland was an Eden of wildlife and plant species, before it was decimated for game hunting and logging?'

Murray had the feeling a lecture was coming, like the one this guy had given his sister when she'd got caught in the fog up Mount Cairn Dhu last summer and she'd found a fun way to keep herself and her policeman boyfriend entertained while she was stuck there.

Ally had hinted as much, swearing her brother to secrecy. It didn't require a detective to put two and two together and deduce it was Finlay Morlich she'd described as the 'misery-guts ranger' that'd lectured them all the way down the mountain about how being irresponsible even at lower altitudes cost lives and he had made them both take home leaflets about staying safe in the Cairngorms.

Finlay was still talking, lifting plants and examining them, putting them down again, anything to avoid eye contact, Murray guessed. 'We've a responsibility with this garden to encourage missing or threatened species, don't you think? If we plant strategically we could see new populations of mining-bees, pine hoverfly, aspen hoverfly...'

'Aspen? That's the trees Cary wanted us to buy, wasn't it?'

'That's right. We'll look at those afore we leave.'

Murray actually felt proud for remembering in front of Finlay.

'Here.' Finlay drew out his phone. 'Have you ever seen a dark bordered beauty before?'

Murray had to admit he had not, and joining him by his side, separated safely by the tail-wagging Collie, Finlay opened up the oldest smartphone Murray had seen in ages, housed in a wrinkled plastic protective cover, and searched for a picture.

'Wait till you see this!' he was saying, scrolling through a gallery of nothing but landscapes and close-ups of insects and greenery of all kinds. A hot glow of enthusiasm was flowing from him, no matter how much he might begrudge Murray sensing it.

Murray couldn't help being warmed by it too, and for the first time in his life he could, hand on heart, say he wouldn't mind learning a wee bit more about the mountain bugs and beasties when there was a teacher as passionate as this.

'See?' Finlay was saying, enlarging a photo of what seemed to Murray an unremarkable brown leaf-like winged thing. 'These moths are found in only two sites in Scotland at the minute...'

'Fascinating,' Murray said, looking not at the moth but at the rosy glow in Finlay's cheeks – and truly, that was no lie. Murray was finding himself a tiny bit fascinated.

* * *

If the plant nursery had represented a small breakthrough in their relationship, the drive home had well and truly undone any advances made.

Murray had merely mentioned that his mum had told him to 'please be sure and get some bonny red roses' (they were her favourite), as well as plenty of colourful winter bedding, packets of herbs and perennial seeds. Murray had risked showing Finlay the list she'd made him write early that morning over croissants and coffee. Finlay had refused to look, keeping his eyes fixed on the road.

'She suggested...' he read, 'tomatoes, cucumber, sunflower, basil, calendula, whatever they are, borage, again, no clue, and something called love-in-a-mist. Ring any bells?'

'Not one of them are Highland natives.'

'Listen, Finlay. You don't mind if I say this...' Murray had begun, steeling himself for a difficult conversation the way he'd learned at work when someone was being belligerent or not pulling their weight. There were ways of going about these things and he was this project's manager after all, sort of. 'We all appreciate having you on board. Your expertise is, honestly, really quite something, and we'd be royally screwed without you.'

Finlay stared dead ahead.

'But this isn't some individual's rewilding passion project. It's a community garden, to make people happy and give them something to do. It's about rehabilitating patients and healing broken community ties just as much as it is about establishing a garden. And yes, we do have to consider the site's aesthetic.'

'Och!' Finlay's brows knitted tight. 'There you go again.'

'What?'

'Consider *the aesthetic*.' He was mocking him. 'Hashtag lifestyle guru, or whatever it was you blethered on about. Getting consumption core.'

'Underconsumption core,' Murray corrected. 'And yes, these things matter too. But they're not *just* trends for me, or for any of us at the repair shed. We care about the town and about trying to help people. So can we *please* just pull in to Fillbarrows and buy a tonne of brightly coloured blousy things, or else you'll have my mother to answer to?'

Murray had pulled out the big guns, not that Roz

McIntyre was a scary sort of mum, quite the opposite actually, she was more handknits and nineties grunge vibes than fire and brimstone, but the very idea of upsetting a mother worked its magic on the sulking ranger.

'Well, if we must, but I *absolutely* draw the line at those unholy dyed heather plants. There'll be nane o' them in our garden. Got it?'

Murray played nice. 'OK, I promise, no dyed heather,' he replied, just as seriously.

Finlay flicked on the indicator and made a (for him) speedy turn into the garden centre's giant parking lot. Granted, he was grumbling under his breath as he did it, but Murray thanked him all the same.

Finlay hadn't seemed at all inspired, in amongst the plastic trugs and garden statuary with the piped music playing and the slow-moving Saturday morning shoppers filling their baskets with imported decorative rubbish that had crossed the world in container ships and would break in a few months, and when Murray suggested they grab a quick bite because it was ages since breakfast, Finlay had barked back that it was only ten to ten and he had his job to get back to.

So they'd shopped and left. Finlay carried the bare

root rose bushes in a cardboard crate back to the truck. Murray had shoved the seed packets in his pockets and swung from his wrist the bag of gardening gloves in all different sizes, from kids to XL grown-ups, which hadn't been on the list but seemed a good idea. He was happily munching on the bag of foamy pink shrimps he'd impulse bought at the tills, and when he offered one to Finlay it had elicited a flicker of interest, though he clearly hated to declare it.

'I got you a bag of your own,' Murray admitted, throwing an unopened pack into Finlay's lap after they'd climbed back into the truck.

'Happy now you've trailed me round that hellish place?' Finlay asked, refusing to acknowledge the gift, even though the scent of soft chewy shrimp sweets was tempting in the extreme. Murray had chowed down almost his entire bagful before they'd hit the Cairn Dhu town limits.

After a long silence, Murray had felt the need to speak. Finlay really wished he wouldn't.

'Do you mind if I ask... the other day, you were late for the meeting at the surgery. What kept you? I thought you might have decided not to come, then changed your mind at the last second.'

This needled Finlay, who didn't enjoy explaining himself, having been asked all his life why he did things the way he chose to. 'I'd nae intention of being late. If you must know, I was on my way when I came across a daft lad who'd crashed his drone into the top branches of a Scots pine at the foot of the western face. Had to go for ma ladders and retrieve the thing.'

The truth was Finlay had educated the offending boy on the reasons why drones were not permitted in the area and how the next time he was caught disturbing raptors with his flying camera, he'd be reported to the wildlife police. He'd let him have one of his safety leaflets and sent him on his way, only to realise he'd wasted a full forty minutes on the delinquent. Then he'd run cursing the whole way into town, not that Murray needed to hear about any of that.

Murray McIntyre had evidently made up his mind to think the worst of him, just like all the others. Something Finlay was used to.

Better to let them think what they wanted than stoop to explaining himself and begging for understanding when people so rarely wanted to think of him as what he was: generally well-intentioned if a little 'unfortunate', as his mother would have said.

'Go on. Oot you get. I've no' got all day to waste,' he'd said when they pulled up outside the mill house, and Murray hopped out, not thanking him, then spending an annoyingly long time retrieving their purchases from the back of the truck.

When he was done, he'd come back to the window and, peering inside, looking at the bag of shrimps that still lay untouched on Finlay's lap. Murray shouted through the glass, 'A wee birdy told me you liked sweet things.' He'd been grinning smugly, knowing he'd pinpointed Finlay's weakness.

Finlay had shaken his head in dismissal and set the truck in motion, turning it round as Murray waved him off from the pavement.

As he hit the mountain road, glad to be alone again, Finlay found his lips wanting to twitch into a smile.

When he got safely back inside his cruive, he bolted the door shut and tore open the bag, devouring the soft pink sweeties without even tasting them, re-playing the conversations of the entire bizarre morn-ing. He was startled to realise he had actually referred to the project as 'our garden', his and Murray's. What had possessed him? He'd said it while complaining about those ridiculous garden centre heathers artifi-cially dyed with lime green and gaudy red colouring.

He let his shoulders slump at the memory, wondering why he'd said it, only glad that Murray hadn't seemed to notice. Dejectedly, he crumpled the sweetie bag, somehow already empty, as though he could also crush the memory.

15

That same Saturday it was Alice's first day off after a busy first week. A sign read 'triage', just like a hospital. Unlike a hospital, though, the Cairn Dhu Repair Shop smelled amazing: wood shavings, oil and metal, like the garage at Alice's grandad's house where, having retired young, everything was orderly and clean and he'd sand down old furniture and shine his vintage Jaguar XJ for hours at a time.

In addition, this place also smelled of warmth, coffee and baking. It was shortly before lunchtime and there was a good smell of toasties in the air too. She glanced with a little pang of longing at a group of women huddled on sofas, chatting around the stove fire, clutching steaming mugs. It would be so nice to sit there with a friend and hear the ordinary little details of their life, a friend who knew nothing whatsoever about medicine so couldn't talk about it. She didn't really have any of those back home, let alone here.

'You're the new doctor,' said a man, and without waiting for confirmation, he extended a hand. 'I'm Sachin.'

'Alice,' she told him. 'I was wondering if the repair shop fixes medical equipment?'

'I cannae say we have in the past.' Sachin scratched his head. 'But there's nothing McIntyre cannae fix, in my experience.'

She looked along the rows of repairers at their desks in the big shed. 'Which one's McIntyre?'

'Oh, he's no' in right now. Let's see...' Sachin scanned the room, eyes landing on the guy from the meeting. Murray, was it? The one who'd been in charge of the funding side of the garden project. Murray was watching a loud repair demo on his phone and occasionally looking worriedly at a set of electronic kitchen scales on his desk. 'I maybe wouldnae look to Murray for help...' Sachin said. 'You can try Cary?'

Alice's eyes followed Sachin's towards the man who'd given her the apple, and there it was again, the great big grandfather clock with the door in its long chest opened up, its pendulum and chains showing, and Cary's head practically inside the cavity. An older woman stood next to him, peering inside as well.

'Go on,' encouraged Sachin with a jolly burst of mischievous laughter. 'The doctor will see you now.'

Alice thanked him and tentatively stepped deeper into the darker recesses of the shed where Cary remained in deep conversation with the woman, or rather the woman was talking *at* him, saying, 'The case was *certainly* made at a later date and in a style influenced by the Glasgow Art School and Charles Rennie Mackintosh but...'

Cary stood straight as a sentry when he noticed her approaching.

'We meet again,' Alice said awkwardly.

'*Hmm?*' The spectacled woman turned to observe her through startlingly thick lenses. Cary only smiled apologetically for what was to come.

'The, uh, grandfather clock,' explained Alice. 'I've seen it before, I was just saying...'

'Ah, now that's a common misnomer,' the woman said, lifting one large pair of spectacles to the top of her head to reveal a second pair underneath. 'This is in fact a long case clock and rather an intriguing one at that, the mechanism being of Barbadian origin, possibly mid-nineteenth century. Its being manufactured in the Caribbean is in itself noteworthy.' She turned back to admiring the inner workings of the thing.

'It looks nice,' Alice tried, unsure what else to say. 'Got a nice... face.'

'Dial, you mean,' the woman corrected, without even a glance over her shoulder.

'Are you repairing it?' Alice asked Cary.

'Hoping to. The clock itself belonged to my grandmother, and my granddad built the case. He was a carpenter too, like me.'

Alice looked at it with a stronger interest than a moment before. It was a lovely thing, with a brassy dial in the shape of a twelve-rayed sun and a smart long body of polished wood carved simply with lines, knots and stylised roses.

'Rather naïve woodcarving,' the woman said in a voice that echoed inside the case, 'but with its own charm, I suppose.'

'Oh, uh, let me introduce Dr Bonnet,' Cary said, seeming to remember himself. 'And this is the town's new GP, Dr Alice Hargreave.'

The older woman barely drew her face from the clock's insides. 'Very good.'

Unperturbed, Cary pressed on, explaining to Alice

that, 'Dr Bonnet is the repair shop's new volunteer horologist.'

Not that the clock doctor was paying much attention. She had her hands inside the cavity now, fiddling about, pulling at chains and putting Alice in mind of the emergency intestinal laparotomy she'd sat in on in her third week of training which had confirmed the surgical route was definitely not for her.

'Poor old thing's got a dicky ticker!' Dr Bonnet guffawed at her own joke, while inspecting the pendulum.

'Maybe Alice can help with that?' replied Cary, indicating the stethoscope around Alice's neck.

Bonnet, however, didn't think this was an amusing suggestion.

'Oh, that's right,' said Alice, snapping back to the reason she was here. 'I was wondering if this was fixable? It seems to be broken after my train journey.'

'May I?'

He waited until she handed over the stethoscope, putting it in his own ears, checking if any sounds could be heard from his wrist.

'It's just a cheap one,' Alice told him.

He asked how long she'd had it and she told him less than a year. 'I lost my other one, cost Dad a fortune.'

That day, her mum, dad and Bastian had pulled her up front at her graduation party in the big marquee in the back garden – her superstar surgeon brothers, Si and Rich, hadn't made it home for the celebrations – and a hush had fallen as she'd opened the gift box. She'd hung the stethoscope around her neck to a burst of applause and a cry of 'three cheers for the Doctors Hargreave!' Her parents had waved away the chants of *hip hip hooray* as the music started up again and Bastian had looked delighted, as though he was somehow included in the chorus. Sometimes she wondered whether he wanted to be her father's son-in-law more than he wanted to be her boyfriend, he'd admired her dad so much.

While everyone at her party had fallen to chatting, her dad had pointed out where he'd had her name engraved on the stethoscope's metal stem and he'd glowed like summer sun upon her. His approval meant everything to her at the time, and on that day, at that party, in front of all of her parents' friends, she had enjoyed a rare chance to bask in it.

'I'm pretty sure it got cleared away with a bunch of medical waste after a messy night on call in F1 general med,' Alice said, regretting her lost gift. 'Never saw it again anyway.'

'There's no sound at all through these earpieces?' Cary said, still attempting to listen to his own pulse.

'Not much.'

'Let's take a closer look,' he said, leading her to his repair desk, leaving Dr Bonnet to appraise the clock alone.

'Shall I scrub in?' Alice said, and incredibly, Cary laughed.

With Cary's lovely, generous, easy laughter ringing in her ears, she came to a fresh realisation. If she ever attempted a joke with Bastian, he'd either ignore her or – if he found it irresistibly funny in spite of himself – he'd stifle his laughter by adopting an ironic, superior look, as though she was such a silly thing. *Why not just laugh along?* she used to think.

She'd seen Bastian do it with other women too, and he'd one-up anyone who told a joke in front of him, adding his own, determined to get the last word and the last laugh, and it usually worked. People generally found him hilarious, rarely seeming to recognise the trait as domineering. It had been, she'd only just this second come to realise, something that had irritated her.

Cary's eyes were sparkling, his cheeks staying sweetly rounded, having formed little gleaming pinch points under his eyes. Maybe Cary didn't feel the need to be the funniest, smartest person in the room and was content to acknowledge humour in her? Whatever it was, she liked how it felt. She wanted him to do it again.

'Your tubing's not airtight,' he said, cutting short her thoughts.

'Huh?'

'See here?' He was pointing to the tiniest fracture in the rubber. 'I'm assuming that for sounds to travel along the tube it needs to form an airtight seal?'

'I guess so.'

Cary was examining the shelves behind him, pulling out boxes, peering inside.

'I think the rubber's gone brittle from wearing it next to your skin,' he was saying, immersed in his task, finding a small box and opening it, perching on the stool, pulling the lamp down to illuminate his hands.

It took all of five minutes for him to make the repair using a quick-drying flexible adhesive smoothed thinly over the perforation. While he worked she explained how she'd also lost the little holster that had held her stethoscope safely at her hip, having not been allowed to wear it around her neck in training, blathering about it being a safely thing.

Satisfied the seal was dry, he handed it back. 'If

you write down the model number, I can order you a replacement tube and fit it, but will this do for now?'

She fitted the earpieces.

'Here.' Cary offered his wrist.

'Oh!' She'd meant to check upon her own body, but since she had a willing volunteer, why not? 'Thanks. It's actually easier if I first feel for a pulse manually...' She pinched the wrist he had offered her. '...And then I do this.' She lifted the round resonator to his chest, pausing to get his permission before touching it to the linen of his shirt front exposed between the two lengths of a muted plaid waistcoat, finding the correct auscultatory spots, the way she'd learned from hours of practice.

She listened hard, closing her eyes, paying attention to the pulse beneath her fingertips where she held his wrist, using the feel of those beats to locate the sometimes elusive *lub dub* sound in her earpieces.

Nothing came through at first, maybe because she'd normally do this without a layer of clothing getting in the way. Was there something else interfering with her ability to hear?

At this proximity she couldn't help detecting the fresh laundry scent, and the glimpse of smooth throat at his open collar. Where the side of her pinkie was grazing his shirt fabric, she could tell it had been laundered a million times into the slubby cotton softness only vintage textiles have. This, combined with his woody, lavender cologne and a buttery, nutty lotion scent, meant she had to force herself to listen, distinguishing her own heartbeat loud in her ears from his. *No wedding ring,* her intrusive inner voice told her, and she shoved this away.

Then it came to her through the sounds of waves on a shore. Zoning in, it grew louder. *Lub dub, lub dub, lub dub,* only... She lifted her eyes to Cary's. His heart was beating *awfully* fast.

'Did you arrive here just before I did?' she asked. 'Were you running?'

She heard Cary's throat move in a loud swallow. 'No. Been here all morning.'

She counted, closing her eyes. 'It's a little too fast.' That was putting it mildly. It had to be around a hundred and fifty beats per minute, and at resting that was not good. 'No swishing sounds or murmurs,' she said. That was good, but he was definitely tachycardic. 'But it is faltering a little too. Do you suffer from iatrophobia?'

Cary was unsure what that was.

'Fear of doctors?'

He shook his head.

'Any light-headedness? Chest flutters?'

He hesitated this time before shaking his head.

Pulling back, she removed the earpieces. 'It's probably nothing,' she said, for the thousandth time in her career when she had absolutely no reason to be sure it was probably nothing. 'But I think you should pop in to the surgery so we can take a proper reading. Your heart's working awfully hard right now for a man standing still.' It was hard to tell with the background noise of the repair shop, but she'd want to rule out A-Fib or STV, but he didn't need to know that.

Cary nodded and took a step away, smoothing his waistcoat, not that she'd rumpled it, returning to the shy, reserved man she'd met out on the street.

'Nothing to worry about, of course,' she said.

Cary wasn't speaking at all now.

'So, uh, thank you for fixing this.'

'You're welcome.'

After the briefest of goodbyes, Cary made his way back to the clock doctor, and Alice made reluctantly for the exit.

Had she overstepped? Upset him? It was hard to know with such a quiet, unassuming person what they were thinking.

'Dr H?' Sachin at the triage desk stopped her, handing her a form on a clipboard.

Paperwork. The story of her life.

'Just your name and contact details for the repair docket,' he said, and she dutifully filled them in.

She watched Sachin take back her signed sheet and use her spelling to write the word 'stethoscope' as he chalked up the repair on the blackboard behind the triage counter. She'd been fix number five today and it was still only early.

There was a donation jar on his desk, she noticed, to which she added a twenty-pound note and Sachin told her to come back any time.

Something about leaving felt like an anticlimax, and the warmth and comfort of the shed told her to stay, but what happened next made her wish she'd hurried straight out into the cold weather.

'Doctor?'

A woman, her mum's age, maybe a little older, but a lot more glam, commandeered her out of nowhere. Usually when people did this it was friends' partners or non-clinical or facilities staff looking for a quick word of advice without going to the bother of seeing their own doctor, but this woman introduced herself as, 'Carenza McDowell, property management', in an accent that spoke of the posher English home counties almost as much as it had a soft Highland ring. 'I'm sure you'll recognise me from the "LET" signs all over town?'

The woman struck an imperious pose, recreating her own posters.

'Oh, yeah,' Alice agreed. There'd been one outside her own flat the day she arrived. 'You're my landlady.' The memory of Gracie gossiping about this woman's hallux valgus condition came back to her and she couldn't help sneaking a glance to her feet where, if she really did suffer from bunions, they were crushed into a pair of towering designer stilettos. 'Was there... something you needed?' she said quickly.

'I tried your flat but you weren't home. Enquiries along the high street directed me towards you here.' Carenza smiled a red lipstick smile.

How on earth did anyone know she was here? Was the whole town keeping an eye on her, tracking her every movement? This place!

The woman was talking all over Alice's indignant thoughts. 'You're new in town, but you'll soon come to know that, as well as being treasurer of the Women in Business Association *and*...' she was bobbing her blonde head in faux modesty, 'three times winner of Property Manager of the Year, Cairngorm region, I'm *also* president of the Burns Club.'

'Oh!' Alice's interest was piqued. 'You're in dermatology?' It didn't occur to her to think this might be a bit strange for a rental property mogul.

The woman almost laughed, taken aback. Something unpleasant and a little bit sneering was happening in her features. Alice had evidently made a mistake.

'Oh, are you a burns *patient*?' She lowered her voice. 'Sorry, I shouldn't have leapt to...'

'Robert Burns,' the woman interrupted, her eyes narrow.

Nope. Alice was none the wiser.

'Rabbie Burns? The ploughman poet? The Scottish National Bard? No?'

Alice shook her head. 'Sorry.'

Carenza observed her with a look of absolute disbelief. 'Goodness! What are they teaching you at medical school?'

Mainly how to save lives, Alice didn't say, however much she'd have liked to.

'Well, don't let on to folks around here that you haven't a clue who their national poet is, honestly. They simply won't forgive you.'

Alice absorbed this advice without saying anything; not that this Carenza was giving her the chance to say much.

'As I was saying, I'm in charge of the Burns Club, now that they've had to allow women members. In fact, as soon as I took up my post, half the committee stepped down and I've had the run of things for these last three years.' She shrugged primly, clearly seeing this as some kind of triumph and waiting for Alice's reaction. 'Breath of fresh air and all that.'

'Wow?' Alice tried.

'Indeed. And each year we celebrate Burns Night with our traditional Burns supper and ceilidh, at which the town doctor traditionally delivers the "Address to the Haggis".'

'*Riii-ght?*' Alice had a horrible sinking feeling.

'And since Dr Millen is, let's say, *disinclined* this year...'

'*Hah!*' came a loud laugh from the café counter where two women in aprons had been earwigging this whole time. '*We* heard he told you and the rest of your Burns cronies to get knotted, did he no'?' one of the women called out with wicked glee.

Carenza gritted her teeth, clearly used to tolerating this sort of thing from the townspeople. 'Since the outgoing doctor declined our invitation to read this year,' she trilled, rising above the mockery, 'and since you're here now, ready to take over his duties...'

Alice wanted to speak up and tell this woman that wasn't the case at all, and *please* don't involve her in local things concerning haggises – she could barely cope with her workload and finding her way in a new country as it was – but Carenza was in full sail and not to be stopped.

'...On behalf of the Cairn Dhu Burns Club Committee, I have the pleasure of extending a formal invitation to you to attend the supper as our guest of honour and deliver the Address. You'll take it, yes?' Carenza said this as though she was generously gifting Alice a complimentary, no-strings, champagne spa day, not roping her in to whatever nonsense this was.

'I, uh, I don't know. I'm not much into poetry...' Alice began.

'And you don't have to wear the traditional ceilidh dress,' Carenza cajoled, ignoring her protest completely. 'Only, wear something nice. Evening attire?' She asked this like Alice might not know what she meant. 'Your best frock will do.' She eyed Alice's sweater, jeans and winter boots: her Saturday comfies. 'Probably.'

'I might be busy that night,' Alice tried. 'When is it?'

'What? When's Burns Night?' This was accompanied by another look of pained disbelief. 'The twenty-fifth of January, of course. His birthday.'

Alice searched her brain for anything that could prevent her from taking part, but the truth was she had her evenings completely to herself. Already, she'd fallen into a routine of finishing up at the surgery by seven, seeing to the last of the patient phone calls and pharmacy sign-offs, and she'd head back to her flat for a bite to eat and a bath, before hitting her text-books again, brushing up on symptoms and conditions she'd come across during consultations that day and had found herself hazy on their finer points, or which she'd never learned about in the first place. Old study habits died hard and she'd often worked on until midnight this first week.

'Super!' Carenza crowed, seizing her victory. 'Seven for seven thirty at the Cairn Dhu Hotel ballroom. I've already taken the liberty of emailing the surgery with your lines. See that you practise them. Cheerio for now. Oh, and...' She stopped in her tracks. 'The kilt hire shop also has a range of perfectly serviceable ceilidh frocks, not that we insist on you wearing one, but... well, I'll leave that with you.'

In a swirl of blonde hair and expensive perfume, she was gone, off to pin down her next victim, no doubt, leaving Alice aware of the grumbles of, 'That Carenza's a blinkin' menace,' from one of the women in the café corner, and the look of sympathy from Sachin (who'd practically hidden under his triage desk when Carenza appeared).

Alice staggered the few feet to the exit, surprised to find herself wondering if Cary Anderson had seen her being ensnared. Would he be watching her now? Why did she care if he was?

She fixed her eyes on the world beyond the repair shop doors and hurried away.

16

Gracie had prepared the tea and the orange juice, and Alice had re-read the NHS guidance on stroke rehabilitation in adults, and the chairs were set out in her consulting room in readiness, but still, Alice was apprehensive, even as she sat under the warm glow of the new floor lamp she'd bought with her birthday cheques.

'Don't worry,' Gracie was saying. She evidently knew everything, even Alice's secret reservations about hosting this clinic. 'The patients you're seeing have all been transferred to community care or early supported discharge from hospital and have been meeting with Dr Millen for months. They're used to coming here now.'

'Remind me why Dr Millen can't continue with the stroke care group?' Alice said, flicking through her session plan one last time before everyone arrived.

'Handover has to begin somewhere,' Gracie said, and because Alice didn't want anyone to wheedle out of her that she had no intentions of staying here until she was in her seventies like Millen, she kept her eyes fixed on her notes.

'So you know who everyone is today, aye?' Gracie was saying, not even trying to hide her lack of confidence in Alice.

'I've read all their notes.'

Gracie thought for all of a second before sighing and closing the door, swiftly coming to sit down in front of Alice. 'It's not for me to talk about patients, but...'

Alice couldn't help but feel relieved. She fixed her attention on Gracie. 'Spill.'

'So, there's Mr Forte. Clyde.'

Alice found him in her notes. 'Uh-huh?'

'He had a big seventieth birthday do at the hotel in the summer. Next day, bosh! A stroke.'

Alice read from her papers. He'd been left with dysphagia, impaired swallowing function, which made taking his medication difficult. He'd also struggled with post-stroke fatigue. 'I know about him,' Alice said.

'Did you know his wife passed away in September?'

Alice lifted her eyes. 'I didn't.'

'Rosie Forte. It was unexpected, and his recovery took a nosedive, as you'd expect. He must have dropped two stone since then and only really leaves his house to get his messages and to come here once a month.'

'Oh.'

'He likes custard creams best.' Gracie bobbed her head towards the refreshments table and a plateful of his favourites.

'Got it.'

'It's the wee things that matter.'

Alice nodded. She'd sat in on rehab clinics before but they'd been largely impersonal, and not a regular thing at all, so she hadn't got to know any of the patients. 'I suppose in Cairn Dhu you come to learn these things about the community?'

Gracie was in full delivery mode, so didn't pause. 'And then there's Kellie Timmony.' She was leaning forwards now. 'Poor lassie got the fright of her life a year ago when a stroke struck her at thirty. She's only a few months older than me; same class at the school.

She was working away in Kirkaldy at the time, and nobody at her office job wanted to believe somebody so young could possibly be having a stroke, so they delayed calling an ambulance.'

'Oh dear.' Alice knew too well what that could mean. A speedy response was imperative in preventing the spread of a stroke. She'd read the woman's notes. Kellie's had been a hard road to recovery, going through months of treatment to help with her aphasia as well as intensive physio to improve her mobility. She'd only recently stopped using her wrist splints and foot orthoses and was currently prescribed supervised circuits which the group would complete together today as part of Alice's clinic.

'The hurdles she's facing now,' said Gracie, 'are mostly mental ones. Lost her confidence, as well as her job and her flat in Kirkaldy. She's back at her mum and dad's in Cairn Dhu.'

'Got it,' Alice said, with the familiar twinge of sympathy in her chest.

'Who else have we got?' Gracie was saying, standing now so she could see Alice's patient list.

'Don't expect to see *him* today,' she said, pointing a long blue acrylic nail at one of the names. 'He's one week into a fortnight's holiday in Malaga, and I happen to know this one's got a Baltic cruise lined up, so you won't be seeing him for a while.' She ran her nail down the list. 'And *she's* got her sister from Arbroath visiting so she'll be a no-show, and *this one's* already installed in the members' bar at the hotel watching the curling championship qualifiers. Saw him queuing up for opening time.'

'Sorry?'

'His brother's a professional curler, and he never misses a match.'

'Got it. So... only two patients today?'

'Probably for the best that your first one's not too crowded.'

There was a knock at the door.

'Are you inviting them in, or no'?' the secretary said.

'Oh yes, of course.' Alice bounded to her feet. 'Come in!'

The door opened and a face appeared. Grizzled cheeks, shaven hair on top with straggly lengths at the back and with sad eyes. Gracie went to the door and held it open for the gaunt man.

'Mr Forte?' she asked. Somehow, from Gracie's description, she'd expected a sweet old grandfatherly fellow, but this man was in ancient biker gear and a Harley-Davidson t-shirt that had seen better days. He smelled of cigarette smoke and his skin was sallow.

'You're not Dr Millen,' he said.

'No, I'm Alice,' she said, offering him her hand which he didn't take.

'A nurse?'

'GP.'

He didn't look like he believed her.

'I've only ever had Dr Millen. Is he here?'

Alice knew she had to get this handled swiftly. She'd experienced it on the wards; it went with the job as a young female medic, but in her own clinic it could be a bigger problem. 'He's handed the group on to me, but I assure you, I've read all your notes and...'

Mr Forte was scanning the room, looking for something, his eyes landing on the plate of custard creams. 'Did *you* bring those?' he interrupted.

'Uh...'

Gracie, behind his back, was nodding vehemently.

'Yes. Yes, I did. Your favourites, aren't they?' Alice said with a smile.

He made a disgruntled sound that said he'd be no pushover.

'Have a seat, Mr Forte.' Gracie hustled him into a chair, his teacup at the ready – a real teacup, not a Gracie special, Alice noticed. As soon as he was sitting, she set it – along with the biscuits – on the low table before him. 'Dr Hargreave's come from a hospital in Manchester,' Gracie was telling him. 'Top of her class, too.'

Alice might have wondered if Gracie had peeped at her CV, if only for the fact that she absolutely hadn't ever been top of any class. Gracie was just trying to help her gain his trust, which, given his mutterings and scowling, wouldn't be easy.

Over his knuckles in faded ink Alice saw tattooed the name Rosie. He was in mourning for his wife and recovering from a stroke. She had to go gently.

'You're not going to make us kick that around, are you?' he said, spotting the sponge ball on her desk.

'I definitely am.'

He sighed and dunked a biscuit in his tea.

Next through the door was Kellie Timmony, in sharp contrast to Mr Forte, she appeared to be in good health, but appearances, Alice knew, meant nothing.

'Come in,' she said, aware of Gracie pouring an orange juice for the new arrival, before leaving Alice alone with a thumbs-up from the doorway.

'Dr Millen's not taking the group any more,' Mr Forte said before Kellie had even taken her seat.

'Oh! Right.' Kellie brightened considerably.

'Since it's just going to be the three of us today,' Alice said, which made Mr Forte glance to the door, probably still hoping for Millen to appear and say this had all been a prank, 'Let's get started. I've got your exercise regimes here in my notes.' She reached for the ball, and Mr Forte rolled his eyes.

After a slow kick around the room while the three remained seated, a word-search exercise which Mr Forte found a good deal easier than Kellie, and a series of chin tucks and head manoeuvres, Alice had performed nearly all of the activities on her list and taken notes to send back to the stroke team at the hospital.

'Before we make our circuits,' Alice said, and Kellie audibly groaned at the prospect, 'it says here we need to update our long-term goals. Goal setting is an important part of recovery, as you know.'

Mr Forte cut in. 'Mine's not changed. I want the sign off so I can get back on my motorbike.'

Alice nodded, writing this down.

'And what do *you* want, Kellie?' she asked, worrying immediately that she sounded patronising like a Santa's grotto elf.

Kellie didn't speak.

'Go on, lass. Tell her what you told Dr Millen,' encouraged Clyde Forte, who wasn't grouchy with everyone, it seemed.

Kellie appeared unsure but she cleared her throat before speaking. 'I just... I just want my spark back.'

Mr Forte nodded sadly at this, as though he'd given up hope of rediscovering his own.

'I just want to feel like me again, but... will walking round the surgery carpark do that? Or kicking that bloody ball? Or...' Kellie stopped, shame-faced. 'Sorry, I just...'

'I know,' said Alice. 'I know.'

Alice thought of their lives put on hold while they recovered, thought of the frustration and the pain, and the fear these two had been through, and there'd be their family's shock and worry to deal with too, or – she wondered about Mr Forte – dealing with this by themselves. Progress in stroke recovery, Alice had read, was often accompanied by setbacks, emotional and physical. All of this seemed written as plain as day on Mr Forte's face and in Kellie's downcast eyes.

Alice spoke on. 'Listen. I know I've just appeared in your lives as if from nowhere, but I do want to help, and I'm qualified to help you...'

'You're no Dr Millen,' grunted Mr Forte.

'Thank God,' whispered Kellie.

'I think I *can* help...' Alice went on.

Mr Forte sniffed a sharp little laugh. '*Dr Millen* was helping. He's been in our lives since Kellie was born, since my Rosie was in the surgery's mother and baby group...' A wash of emotion stoppered his voice and he, just like Kellie, looked on the verge of tears.

Alice, not knowing what to do, reached for the referral letters on her desk. 'I do have something I can offer you, something new.'

Mr Forte fixed her with a look that said he already wasn't interested. Kellie didn't look up at all.

'It's a community gardening project, actually,' she began, and even though she knew she was fighting a losing battle, she went on to sing the project's praises to the people she at least hoped would be her first two recruits.

17

Mid-week and the children taking part in the woodwork class were not from Shell Cooper's class – *she* was in primary three; these were the *babies* from primary one. But her mum, Livvie, had spoken with Mrs Hendry, her teacher, who'd then spoken with the Head, to ask if Shell could be allowed to join the little ones in their high-viz vests, tramping in pairs along the road to the repair shed for their weekly wood-working lessons.

Shell wasn't supposed to have overheard their conversation about it at home time but since all the grown-ups insisted on talking about her like she wasn't standing *right there*, she'd heard everyone agree that Shell would benefit from frequent sightings of her mother while she was 'reintegrating' and being 'brought back out of herself'. What she *hadn't* been privy to was her mum's idea that it didn't hurt to expose her to nice, gentle men like Cary Anderson.

Shell generally didn't trust men, taking pains to avoid them and, if they were loud and grumpy (like that scruffy mountain monster, Finlay Morlich), she'd cower from them, visibly trembling. The builders behind the big plastic sheet at the back of the shed weren't her favourites either, always shouting to each other over their radio and whistling along to the music, spoiling Sachin's choice of jangly, happy music (he'd called it Scottish Bhangra; all she knew was that she loved it). She wouldn't even *look* at the builders.

Cary Anderson, however, was universally known to be sensible and mild, and not at all frightening, not like Francie Beaumont, who everyone hoped Shell had no memory of.

Shell didn't let on to anyone that she could remember absolutely everything about Francie Beaumont, not even to that lady who'd asked her all those questions that night at her granny's house and who'd pretended she wasn't a police lady but most definitely *was*. She remembered his gold tooth and his scuffed, peeling knuckles, and his aftershave stink. Most of all she remembered his simmeringly threatening, angry-under-the-surface feeling that she couldn't put into words but it had filled up the whole room those few times she'd been near him.

She'd also never forget when her mum didn't come back for her at Granny's that time and she'd missed her and cried for her and asked her gran over and over when her mum was coming for her, and then one morning, on her way to school, she'd caught a glimpse of her on the street corner with a big dark circle around one eye like a panda bear and her mum had suddenly hidden her face and walked quickly away even though Shell was shouting for her.

Nobody in the world could understand the things Shell had seen. Some of it she had hidden even from herself, but she could always feel something dark and troubling in the back of her mind, something that gave her nightmares and made her hands shake all the time. She'd taken to clasping her old baby doll's blanket to stop people noticing and now she couldn't be without it.

One day, shortly after she had returned to school, having lived in that faraway hotel room with the broken blinds where the wall lit up all night, *red, orange, green, orange, red*, Mrs Hendry had tried to coax the blanket out of her hands and into her desk drawer where she promised, 'it would be safe until home time', and Shell had screamed and shaken so much her mum had to be phoned and after that she was allowed to have her blanket without anyone interfering.

It had all been enough to put the fear of men into her at the age of seven, and meant that, for now, she was allowed to tag along on days like today as the little ones' 'special helper'. So far, she hadn't felt inclined to help much, and she'd huddled on the beanbags near the Duplo box to keep a close eye on Livvie working.

Shell liked the repair shop better than anywhere, especially because the nice policeman, Jamie Beaton, who'd put Francie in the jail, called in sometimes, and Sachin Roy stopped everyone at the shed doors and sussed them out before letting them come inside. She wasn't afraid of either of them, so long as they kept their distance.

Shell eyed the other kids now, all tiny, boisterous, happy things. She was much more grown-up than them, she thought with a burning streak of resentment. That resentment was just one more thing she had to hide from the adults, especially from her mum, who she knew worried about her. Her mum had told her so, almost as often as she'd told her she was sorry she'd let her down.

Shell didn't blame her mum for anything: not for

leaving her at Granny's, not for being afraid of Francie Beaumont and his horrible friends, and not for the long time they had to leave Cairn Dhu 'to stay safe', away from her classmates and all her toys.

When she got back it was like she didn't know any of the children in her class any more and all they wanted to do was ask why she'd been gone so long. One had asked if she had done something naughty and been sent to prison, and when she'd made the mistake of telling her mum this, she had shouted about 'all those bloody gossiping parents', so she wouldn't be doing that again. She mostly ignored the other kids now. They were silly and bad, and she'd watch Mrs Hendry in sympathy as she had to deal with their babyish behaviour in the classroom.

Shell kept an eye on her mother now as she flitted around the little circle of child-size workbenches, three kids to a bench, offering encouraging words as they practised planing the wooden blocks clamped in little red vices.

Cary Anderson sat on the floor behind his own mini bench demonstrating how to do it, speaking in a voice so soft Livvie had to repeat almost every utterance for the benefit of the little group who were only delighted to be taken out of school for a while.

Shell hoped there was another pink wafer biscuit

coming her way, but didn't have the nerve to try and catch Murray McIntyre's attention. She looked at him now, behind the desk nearest the beanbags and toy area, sighing and scratching his head and making a right song and dance over a broken radio she'd heard he'd been trying to fix since Saturday. He didn't look like he knew what he was doing. Shell settled upon wordlessly willing him to notice she was peckish and had no wafers left, all while sitting stock-still. Maybe if she put on an especially hungry face, he'd take pity on her?

That was when she noticed the buggy coming through the doors with a big boy dozing inside it. His legs were so long his shoes skimmed the ground, making light-up trainers flash blue and red.

'Hello, Shell,' the boy's mum said, even though Shell didn't know how the woman knew her name.

The feeling of being seen, of being known, gave her a tingly, shrinking feeling in her belly.

'Can I leave Jolyon here beside you while I grab a cup of tea?' the woman continued. She was nodding encouragingly like she was going to leave him there whether Shell liked it or not. 'I'll only be over there for two seconds.'

Shell's mum answered for her. 'I'll keep an eye on him too,' Livvie told the woman, who'd parked the buggy right by Shell's side and hurried away to the café counter, not even asking her if there was anything she wanted, such as a pink wafer or another pink milkshake or anything.

Shell took the opportunity to study the dozing boy who was blinking himself awake in the buggy. He was red cheeked and had wild bushy hair. She hoped he wasn't going to wake up and want to play with her! She didn't like boys. They were loud and made up nasty names, and the ones in her class always swung back on their chairs when they'd been told not to, and she'd seen Stevie Mason wipe his nose on his school jumper during phonics and thought she might actually throw up.

The boy's eyes turned from faraway and glassy to alert and blinking. He was looking right back at her, staring, saying nothing.

Shell considered sticking her tongue out. Instead she looked away.

He was *still* staring. Stupid boys. Getting in everywhere and spoiling things.

'Ah, Jolly's woken up,' his mum said, on her way back with a tray. She had a sing-song voice that Shell didn't think should be coming out of a grown-up woman's mouth. 'Here you go, Jolly. I got you a milkshake to try.' The lady's voice was wobbly like her mum's used to be.

'And I got you one as well, Shell,' the woman said. 'Your mum said it was OK.'

Shell checked this wasn't lies by meerkat-peering at her mother across the room, and Livvie – who could always read her mind – winked at her to say she could have it.

The boy had slipped himself out of his pushchair straps and onto the floor where he inspected the milk-shake glass with its red and white stripey straw like a helter-skelter in a picture book.

That's when Shell noticed his drink came with *two* pink wafers. The boy clutched one of the delicious biscuits in his hand. Shell could see he was gripping it so hard bits were falling off and making a mess. Why wasn't his mum telling him to be more careful? In-stead she was holding onto a teacup and staring into the steam like she wasn't even in the room.

The injustice of him having two wafers which he'd smash to smithereens while she had *none* at all was still washing over her when, all of a sudden, the boy very slowly shoved the saucer with the second wafer over the floor towards her with his foot.

'Aww, that's so nice of you, Jolly. Good sharing!' the

mother said, overdoing it a bit, but still, Shell wasn't about to say no.

She reached out a hand and took his gift.

The boy's eyes followed the pink biscuit from the plate to her mouth and as she sank her teeth into it, he copied her, biting into his own.

Shell couldn't stop the smile forming as the boy's eyes shone. Sure, he was making crumbs all down his front, but at least he too seemed to appreciate the brilliance of a pink wafer biscuit. Not everyone got it.

Shell had no idea when Livvie had joined the boy's mum in staring in smiling amazement at him while he sucked on the biscuit. The mum had a hand over her mouth as though the boy had done something completely amazing. Mums were so confusing. She'd never, ever understand them.

'I think you've made a friend there, Shell,' said her mother, patting at the other woman's shoulder.

Shell didn't like this at all, and turned her back so she could try her milkshake, which really was completely delicious and had the swirly cream on top and raspberry sauce and everything. After a while, Shell realised her mum had gone back to watching the woodworkers while the boy's mum was just sitting there stirring her tea like she was half-asleep. Shell decided she probably should keep an eye on that boy, since no one else could be bothered.

He was turning the pages of the shed's big bumper colouring book. She supposed it might be very nice of her if she helped a bit. So she dislodged her best yellow crayon from her pencil case and, just as he'd done with his saucer, she rolled it across the rug towards him with the toe of her school shoe.

He grabbed the crayon and started scribbling immediately, making a little happy giggly sound, and his mum, looking between Shell and her boy, seemed like she was going to explode with happiness or something.

Mums are so weird.

18

Kurt greeted Big Kenneth, the Ptarmigan nightclub's doorman, like they were old buddies, and led the way through the entrance and up the stairs with the authority of a man who frequented this place regularly.

Murray followed, a little unsteady on his feet but trying to pretend he was some easy-breezy first dater. Kurt couldn't know how long he'd spent practising his smile in the bathroom mirror earlier, miming a handshake greeting, deciding against it, telling himself he needed to 'just breathe' before rehearsing meeting him with a casual kiss. This time, he'd told himself, *he* might try to be the one putting a peck on Kurt's cheek while maintaining a hands in pockets, *hey I'm cool about this* stance and saying something along the lines of a cheery, 'Hiya, good seeing you.'

The bathroom mirror version of Murray would be very disappointed to learn that all his planning had gone out the window when real-life Kurt bounded up to real-life Murray at the foot of the nightclub steps and went in immediately for a hug, leaving Murray with his hands trapped stupidly in his coat pockets, unable to hug back.

'You ready for this?' Kurt was saying now, smiling over one shoulder, standing before the double doors that would lead to the bar and dancefloor.

Murray returned what he hoped came over as an enthusiastic smile.

* * *

Only an hour before, his sister had done her best to convince him everything would turn out all right while he'd tried on every one of his favourite jumpers and hooded tops for her to rate over videocall.

'Honestly, the first one was fine,' she'd said dryly, as he sported look number five.

'But this one's new season Loewe. Kurt might appreciate good design?'

'From what you've told me, he'll like you even if

you wore that Christmas jumper Mum knitted for you.'

'Don't remind me.' From the wardrobe behind him, a jarringly lime green cuff of loopy, loose knitting showed itself over the open top of a snowman giftbag.

He'd pulled the black sweater off and retrieved the first one he'd modelled for his sister. Ally might not care about luxury gear but he trusted her judgement on dating, which was another huge turn-up for the books, considering the mess her love life had been in only a year ago. Yet only recently she'd shared a cosy Swiss chalet Christmas break with Jamie, her policeman boyfriend, and she still wore a loved-up glow of self-assurance as a souvenir.

'Just throw something on and go. See if there's really a spark there, and let the evening take you... wherever.'

'It's not the spark I'm worried about, it's the *wherever*,' Murray had said, holding up two pairs of boots and letting Ally choose.

'The black ones,' she'd said with a shrug.

'These are Kurt Geiger sloanes!' he'd told her, mock offended at her ignorance.

Ally rolled her eyes. They did this when he was nervous. It was comforting.

'Just let him ask *you* some questions, OK? Be sure

he's interested in getting to know you. If he doesn't ask you anything at all, run.'

'Got it.' There'd be no problems there. Kurt had made no secret of the fact he found Murray fascinating. He was anticipating a barrage of interested questions; the dreaded, 'so why *are* you single?' coming top of the list. 'It'll be too loud in the Ptarmigan to talk all that much anyway,' Murray said, glad this wasn't going to be a chatty kind of date.

'And text me if you're staying out all night, OK?'

'Well, *that's* not going to happen,' he'd said, fixing his hair for the tenth time, checking his teeth on the screen, not enjoying the feeling of lying to his sister, not sure why he was. He was fully prepped for a long night.

'Murs. Just go, will you!'

'Since when did you get so assertive?' he'd said, pulling on his second-favourite winter coat, a chic darkest blue Moncler, pointedly ignoring the camel cashmere on the next hanger, which had been a 'moving in' gift from Andreas Favre. The sight of it made him want to pull it over his head and curl up in the bottom of his wardrobe, hibernating until Kurt left Scotland in a few weeks, but he hadn't confessed any of that to his sister, though she must have picked up on his mood shifting.

'He's not here, you know?' she said.

'Who?' They both knew he was faking nonchalance. Ally let it slide for the sake of her brother's dignity. 'He hasn't set foot in the building for weeks. I daren't ask, I'm just the tech intern, but I reckon he's relocated to the California hub.'

Murray had wanted all this time to ask if Andreas had enquired after him. Wasn't the guy even a little bit curious about how he was doing? Was there any guilt on his part? Any regrets? But now Ally was telling him he's not even in the country?

'Your office is still empty,' his sister went on. 'They haven't readvertised your job. I'm sure if you talk to Barbara—'

He cut her off. 'I'm not asking for my job back. I'm happy here, honestly. And I'm still needed at the repair shop.'

Ally let that lie slide too. 'Promise me you'll think about it?'

'Better go.' He kept his voice soft, knowing his sister would love nothing more than having him there with her in Switzerland on her big year-long adventure. 'Love you.'

She'd tutted, teasingly, but conceded she loved her brother too before leaving the call, the screen turning blank.

* * *

Murray wished himself back in his room now that Kurt was hauling open the door to the club. He braced himself for a lot of noise and dry ice clouds.

'Oh!' Kurt had stepped inside then jolted to a stop. 'It is *not* a club night?'

Murray looked around. This was not promising at all. The place was darkened, as usual, with its strings of colour-changing LEDs lining the ceilings, and the lasers were slowly searching the gloom, spinning on their motors up amongst the shadowy pipework of the rafters, but there was no DJ, no shots station, and no crowds of boozed-up winter sports enthusiasts letting loose after a day on the slopes. Everything was... chill.

'We can go...?' Murray was saying, a little relieved at the possibility this date was over before it began.

Kurt, however, was scanning the room, taking in the low sofas that lined the slope viewing point, one vast wall of glass, the floodlights illuminating the snowy pistes beyond it.

Tealight candles twinkled on every table in the place, and laid-back couples in cosy clothing curled up together, the low drone of their conversations mixing with the jangly spa music coming over the speakers.

'*Yoo hoo!*' the bar man called to them. 'Hot glogi? Whisky toddy? Fondue?'

Murray knew this guy, of course. They'd gone to school together. He followed in Kurt's wake, approaching the bar.

'What's all this, Hamish?' Murray indicated his old friend's Scandi jumper and folksy hat. He usually worked in rolled black shirtsleeves.

'We're trying something new. Chilled-out northern lights viewing parties, with a Scandi twist. For the tourists.'

'I *love* it!' declared Kurt, looking with unsuppressed glee at the special menu on the bar. 'We should have the fondue, definitely.'

'I guess we're doing fondue for two,' Murray told Hamish. 'But I'll just have a beer. No hot glogg or whatever you said.'

'Two beers,' Kurt grinned, while for Murray, the reality of a cosy evening's conversation and aurora-gazing sank in.

* * *

'Back home my family make gouda fondue with mustard, but I am sure the Scottish way will be just as good! So long as we're not dipping Mars bar!'

'Hey!' Murray acted offended. 'That's a stereotype, I'll have you know.'

They'd found vacant sofas right in front of the floor-to-ceiling slope-view window, clinked their beer bottles together and Kurt had said '*proost!*' then Murray taught him '*slàinte mhath*' and joked how it was probably the only Scottish Gaelic he knew.

They'd spoken about Murray picking up a smattering of German and French while working in Switzerland (that was all he'd given away about his time there), and Kurt told him he was fluent in English, could read German reasonably well, and of course spoke his native Dutch at home, and this had made Murray feel significantly less impressive than he usually felt when discussing these types of things.

Hamish had tried to be unobtrusive when he set down the fondue with its lit candle on the low table between them, but Murray made a point of asking his old schoolfriend whether he knew if there really were going to be any northern lights tonight.

'Twenty per cent chance, according to my aurora app,' Hamish shrugged, leaving napkins, two long-handled prongs, and all kinds of things to dip in the melted cheese. 'Let me know if the flame dies.'

Kurt had grinned and chucked a large bit of melty sauce with bread into his mouth as if to say there was no chance of the fire dying on this date.

Murray cleared his throat nervously. 'Can we have two more beers, please, Hamish?'

'*Wauw*, this so good!' Kurt said through a mouthful as soon as they were alone again. 'Try the apple slices, honestly. It sounds weird, but you will like it.'

Murray had his eye on the cubes of sourdough bread instead. 'Apple and hot cheese? Really?'

'Of course!' Kurt speared a thick, green-skinned slice and was submerging it under the bubbling surface before making a long, steamy cheese pull which he had to twirl on the prong until it broke. He offered it up to Murray's lips.

There was no elegant way of eating it, so Murray decided just to wolf it. Kurt's blue eyes lit up at the sight.

'Actually, that *is* good.' Murray wiped his lips clean. 'And healthy, because apple,' he joked, and of course Kurt laughed uproariously.

Something like whale song and tinkly bells came

over the speakers and for a beat Murray panicked that they'd already run out of things to say.

'So... do you ski?' he tried.

'Have you *been* to the Netherlands? Our mountains are little hills compared to here. So, no, I never learned how. I did play football and field hockey, and I tried speed skating once. I do a little weights training.' That, thought Murray, remembering glimpsing his thick, corded arms, was an understatement. 'And I like to run, I dance...'

'You dance?'

'Don't you?' Kurt challenged, going in for a slice of smoked sausage.

'I suppose I do.' Murray had learned ceilidh dancing as a kid, like everyone else who ever went to a school Christmas party in Scotland. He resisted the urge to suggest giving him a demo of the Gay Gordons, a pacey couples' dance with lots of spinning and stomping, trying hard not to let the tasty, ice-cold beer that so easily chased down the salty, oily, smoky food go to his head.

'I never learned to ski, either,' Murray said instead. 'Outside of lessons with school, and I didn't love those. I'm just not a very outdoors-in-the-snow sort of person.'

This was safer. Calmer. He had to work with Kurt,

or at least occupy the same repair shed as him, for the next month or two. He couldn't let himself get carried away. But if that was really the case, why had he cared so much about dressing well tonight and making a good impression? He was sending himself seriously mixed messages.

'Can I ask you a question?' Kurt was saying.

Oh no. Here it came. *So why are you single? Have you been in many serious relationships? What is it you're looking for in a guy?* He'd watched enough dating shows to know what was coming. 'Shoot,' he said, as casual as you like.

Kurt looked especially wicked. 'Is that supposed to be a tattoo, or what?'

'Hah! You noticed?'

Hamish set down two more beer bottles and was gone again, giving Murray time to compose himself.

He turned his wrist, pulling back his cuff to reveal the jagged line of black ink. 'It's the peaks of Mount Cairn Dhu. See? Nothing as extensive as yours.'

Kurt was laughing, and not unkindly. 'I think you asked for a proper tattoo but the pain was too much you wussed out, and now you tell people, "Oh, this? It's a mountain."'

'Rude!' Murray couldn't help laughing too. There was a grain of truth in there somewhere. That zigzag line had hurt like hell. 'There's definitely no way I'd get another one.'

He expected a tour of Kurt's arms to follow this, an explanation of the reasons behind each artwork on his skin, but Kurt kept his sleeves rolled down and drank his beer, eyes only on Murray.

'Are you... missing home?' Murray ventured. There had to be more to say. 'It must be hard, working away, especially in the winter.'

'It's OK. I got used to it. I've been eco-build contracting all over Europe for years. But this is my first time in the Highlands.'

'You like it?'

'It's... different.' He chucked another big cube of bread in his mouth with a smile. His lips were glossed from eating. Another layer of Murray's armour dissolved at the sight.

'What *is* this music?' Murray said after a long moment, just as birds began to caw over swirling astral chords.

Kurt had stopped talking completely now and was just watching him, amused and, it appeared, contented. Murray felt a little like a mouse being played with by the Cheshire Cat. The beer made him not mind it all that much.

'I haven't been out for ages,' Murray threw in, before stopping himself confessing to anything more, like the fact he'd been in broken-hearted hiding for months.

He took a long drink from his bottle and looked around at the people coming in. It was getting busier and the sky loomed pitch black outside. It was almost ten o'clock. Why wasn't Kurt talking? He was just sitting there, smiling with his eyes.

'Have you been here before?' Murray asked, temperature rising.

'*Ja*, of course. It's the only place for miles.'

'Course.' Murray nodded, picking at the beer label. He wasn't going to pry into Kurt's social life.

'With the other builders,' Kurt added quickly. 'But they are boring, going home to their wives and kids by nine.'

'Ah.' A tiny hit of relief softened Murray's shoulders. 'They're both Cairngorms guys. I forgot you're the only one who doesn't live here.'

'Yeah, I think they feel sorry for me, alone at the hotel after work.'

Kurt locked eyes with Murray and the atmosphere around them seemed to pulse as though Kurt was emitting his own aurora of charged sun particles.

'I don't think we're going to catch the northern lights from in here, you know?' Kurt said.

Murray looked at the black sky beyond the glass, the glossy white of compacted snow on the floodlit slopes. 'Twenty per cent chance,' Murray said, weighing up more than the possibility of aurora sighting tonight.

Kurt said nothing, letting him deliberate.

'You know...?' Murray ventured at last.

Kurt tipped his head, a blue fire burning behind his eyes.

What did it matter if their spark was more of a happy glow, or their conversation shallower than a paddling pool?

'You might be right,' Murray went on. 'There's too much reflection on the glass in here to catch the northern lights.'

Kurt's smile turned up another notch. 'Take these with us?' he said, standing, holding his half-finished bottle.

Murray threw his beer back in a long swig. When he reached the last drop, he wiped his mouth and sprang to his feet, decision made. 'Let's get some more to carry out.'

* * *

The kiss, when it came, had made something in Murray break loose, like he was going to howl.

On leaving the Ptarmigan, they'd walked along the road lined with streetlights, drinking, laughing at nothing. Kurt kicked his boots on the pavement, his hands shoved deep in his tight jeans pockets. He was acting cute and Murray couldn't help laughing harder.

Then suddenly they were walking faster. Then, after turning the corner into the grounds of the stuffy old Cairn Dhu Hotel, they broke into a run, Kurt grabbing Murray's hand, and they'd thrown their empty beer bottles into the big hotel bins and hurtled into the cold shadow at the back of the building where, in an instant, Kurt had him pushed up against a door and breathing hard. Murray could feel the muscles in Kurt's hard stomach swelling and falling against his soft tummy as they pressed up close, white clouds of breathy vapour in the bitterly cold air around them.

They were in the dank, wintry darkness of the hotel's back yard with its row of pre-fab rooms that the hotel rented out to seasonal workers. The door at Murray's back was a rough, raw wood. Murray let his head loll back against it as Kurt brought his mouth down on his in a kiss.

Warmth. Hops and barley. Soft pillow lips. *Christ!* Murray had needed this more than he'd known.

Kurt said something in Dutch, nestled into his neck, his lips running over tingling goosebumps. Murray didn't care what it meant; it sounded divine.

There was the sound of a key pulled from Kurt's jeans pocket. Then the key was in the lock and Kurt's hands were taking Murray's in his, lacing their fingers, and Murray was absolutely sure he actually whimpered at the shadowy sight of Kurt kissing across their hatched knuckles, the sensations of his nervous system crackling like fireworks almost too much for him and yet... what was that?

Kurt had pulled back too. 'Are you... whining?' Kurt said.

Murray strained his ears. 'I'm sure that wasn't *all* me,' he said, trying to make light of whatever was happening, still drowsy with wanting to kiss again. But something was definitely not right.

'There it is again. Listen!' Kurt untangled his fingers, stepping away, and Murray felt the loss of his warmth like someone had thrown an ice bucket over him.

Yet neither of them could ignore the whimpering sounds coming from the bushes along the hotel's stone boundary wall.

'Foxes?' Kurt guessed.

'Light up your phone.'

Together they approached the sound, shining the phone torch into the low branches of the evergreen hedging.

'Oh my God!' Murray crouched down.

Kurt dropped to his knees and reached a hand into the moving black bundle of sorry little sounds. He lifted out not one, but two shivering, complaining pups, only weeks old by the size of them.

'*Shit!*' Murray's heart sank as his eyes adjusted to the gloom, revealing another, adult, dog deep under-cover. 'The mother? Looks like they've been dumped.'

Behind him, Kurt was already unlocking his door, flipping on lights, carrying the pups, searching for towels to wrap the shivering creatures in.

Murray leaned in closer to the poor, panting dog, already pulling his phone free to ring the twenty-four-hour vet practice in the next big town, half an hour from here.

'Don't worry, mamma,' he told her gently. 'I've got you.'

Murray (admittedly, reluctantly) stripped off his lovely Moncler jacket and draped it over the dog, knowing as well as Kurt (who was clomping around inside his rooms) that the odds of resuming their date tonight had reduced to zero.

19

The twenty-fourth of January and Cary had left the GP's surgery's Saturday morning clinic, relieved not to have bumped into Alice Hargreave. If he had seen her, he'd have had to explain what Dr Millen had just told him (and what Cary had known all along): that there was nothing whatsoever wrong with his heart. The old doctor had found his resting pulse to be just as it ought to be.

It had been Alice's closeness that had set his heart rate spiking that day two weeks ago when she'd visited him at the repair shed with her broken stethoscope, and she hadn't sought him out since.

Cary was a man who knew his own body and his own mind. His judgement was rarely clouded by anything. That's why, even though he'd have loved to pursue what all this might signify with the new doctor, he'd vowed to keep his attraction to himself. She was too distracted, too tired, too busy, to be presented with the inconvenience of some man's feelings.

If, one day, she ever grew happier and appeared to be more settled, not quite so haunted and chased down by some invisible thing that kept her jumpy *and* sleepy-looking at the same time, he might consider confessing. For now, she didn't deserve to hear him say, 'I like you,' as though that were somehow *her* problem. Men did that to uninterested, overburdened women all the time, he'd observed, and that wouldn't be him.

Besides, he was a busy man. Business was booming in Cairn Dhu. The paid carpentry jobs kept coming in. Then there were his Saturday and midweek shifts at the repair shop to do and, added to those, he'd given his up evenings recently to construct the wooden raised growing beds for the social prescribing project.

A few days ago, in the gloaming light, he and Murray (who'd been oddly quiet), along with Sachin Roy and his wife, Aamaya, had followed behind McIntyre's turf-cutting machine which stripped away patches of the mossy old lawn. They'd delved garden spades and forks into the freshly exposed earth, rotating the compacted soil until it was broken up into sods. Within hours they had turned the large patch of lawned nothingness by the side of the big barn into four large rectangular planting beds. Over each bed the crew set down Cary's sturdy frames to create elevated beds, each a foot high, ready to be topped with fresh organic compost. They'd also dug out four deep holes between the beds in which to plant the young Aspen trees, which would be arriving any day now from the Snow Road nursery.

There'd been so many rolled strips of rough turf produced in making way for the beds, Cary had suggested what they needed was a composting system, and even though he had enough on his plate, he'd committed to building that too.

Yesterday he'd completed the giant bottomless crates, so now the project could process its own garden waste and grass cuttings into free, useable compost, and he'd asked for Murray's help in positioning them around the back of the shed where the new glass wall of the extension had been installed. The scaffolding was still in place because the new section of roof still awaited its solar panels.

As they'd wrestled the composting crates off Cary's truck and into position, the Dutch builder,

Kurt, had appeared, offering to help out, but the atmosphere between the two younger guys had been so thick with tension Cary had almost felt himself compelled to make up some small talk to break it. Almost.

Instead they'd worked on, barely speaking. When it was completed, Cary quickly explained how the row of separate bays would work now that they were lined up and ready for use.

The project gardeners would chuck into the first bin any small branches, chipped wood, weeds, torn cardboard, fallen autumn leaves, raw veg scraps and grass clippings, leaving them covered with a tarpaulin until the bay was heaped full. Someone would have the task of turning the rotting material to aid the breakdown of the bigger bits. When there was a good amount of the stuff, it would be turned over into the next bay along, where it would break down further, pulling in the worms and bacteria from the soil beneath, helping speed up the process, and then after a while, the good, brown, sweetly-scented stuff would be transferred into the third and final bay where it could be sieved and used for mulching the growing beds.

'A slow process, but sustainable, and worth it,' Cary had concluded. He had a similar, if much smaller, set-up in his yard at home.

Kurt and Murray had nodded along respectfully, not really paying attention, and their awkwardness had soon sent Cary away, bemused and wanting a cup of tea far from any shed drama that might be simmering.

The atmosphere had been like this ever since the pair of them had found the puppies with their mother and the vet had come for them and it had been decided that, since she was likely a stray, undernourished and with no tag or microchip, she'd spend a few nights at the vet's with her pups.

Sure, there'd been a smattering of thrilled gossip in the shed, in particular from the café corner, about why the two men had been lurking around the back of the hotel late at night to discover the dogs in the first place, but Murray had told everyone to mind their own business and consider themselves lucky anyone had found the pups before the cold got to them, and Kurt had smirked, further fanning the flames of intrigue.

After that, it had somehow been decided – Cary didn't know the finer details – that since the dogs remained unclaimed by anyone after their discovery a week ago, even after the story in the local paper and a big batch of 'found' posters hung up around town, they should come to live at the mill house with the

McIntyres, who, rumour had it, had footed the vet's bill. Roz McIntyre had also coordinated an effort to generate donations, and Cairn Dhu had not let the dogs down. Food, bowls, blankets, towels, beds and squeaky toys had been arriving for days.

Murray, it seemed, had involved himself closely in caring for the pups, and that had generally kept him away from the shed. That and, Cary surmised, trying to put a bit of distance between himself and a certain construction expert.

Kurt too had been keener than usual to volunteer to make the long trips in the builder's van to pick up building supplies and Cary gained the impression that the thing that had been bubbling between the pair all month might well have boiled over and put out their flame. Either way, things had been quieter around the place this week.

Cary, not that he was all that invested, would get an update soon anyway, as he was heading back to the shed, since a busy repair Saturday lay ahead.

There was one job he'd been looking forward to finishing today, and if she'd received his message, Alice Hargreave would soon be on her way too. He only hoped she would take patient confidentiality seriously and not ask him how his follow-up appointment had gone with Dr Millen.

20

Alice was not happy. She'd rocked up at the repair shed doors (not even thinking to take a peek round the side at how the garden landscaping was going), absorbed in the printout she'd read all the way along the high street from her flat.

'Cary! This one's for you,' Sachin announced as soon as she got inside. He'd pointed out she might have a long wait, since it was another 'hoaching' repair Saturday (which is a braw word for when Scottish places are swarmingly crowded).

Cary's head had sprung up over the other clients' when he heard his name called, and Alice made her way through the throng; people queuing for repairs, others huddled in the café chatting and not minding the noise or the heat from all the bodies, and the triage line that just kept growing longer as the doors slid open and shut, open and shut, and everything was tinged in a gaudy pink light from the neon sign on the wall.

She found Cary sitting at an antiquated machine, a wooden frame with what looked like a potter's wheel of stone turned on its side which spun smoothly whenever Cary pressed down on the wooden chock with his foot. A rigged-up black metal bag with a tiny spout dripped water right onto the top of the turning whetstone, and Cary, his eyes fixed on the job of sharpening a full canteen of kitchen knives for a woman wearing a 'Cairn Dhu Hotel and Restaurant' branded shirt, held a blade flat against the stone, razing its edge to surgical sharpness.

The woman must be one of the hotel chefs, thought Alice. She was young and very pretty with long black hair tied in one shiny braid down her back and it was obvious from the way she was trying to entice him to talk that she fancied the vintage pants off Cary Anderson. And why wouldn't she fancy him? Even if she was probably a little too young for dating him.

Assessing his looks now, she guessed Cary was probably in his mid-thirties. Somehow he didn't seem the type for chasing girls fresh out of catering college, although Alice knew it was naïve to make assumptions.

Still, as he worked steadily, rhythmically powering that wheel, face fixed in concentration, peering down the blade, finding just the right angle, she witnessed again the thing she liked about him most: that he seemed to have the manners and composure (not to mention the skills) of a man from an earlier time.

Today he wore a cream-coloured shirt with a collar ever so slightly wider than modern shirts and a well-fitted, buttoned coffee-coloured waistcoat which matched baggy retro trousers with a dark brown belt. The trousers were rolled at the ankles, giving a glimpse of thick woollen boot socks and he had on chunky brown laced boots of buffed and shining leather. The things she really couldn't drag her eyes away from, however, were his hands.

Good strong woodworker's hands with the sheen of lotion and neat nails, telling her he took care of every part of himself. His rolled shirt cuffs revealed a vintage watch worn on his left wrist and there were strappy leather bands on the opposite one. Something in Alice wanted to sigh at the sight.

The chef girl was blethering on at Cary (a phrase Alice had picked up from Gracie at the surgery) telling him he should 'nip in one day' for some of her Cullen skink, which she promised would warm him up after a hard day's work.

'I'll keep that in mind, thanks,' Cary told her, standing up now and bundling her knives safely in their wrap, rolling them up together and fastening the strings. 'Come back when they're dulling again,' he told her across his workbench with a polite, straight-lipped nod.

Possibly to conceal how crestfallen she was at his lack of interest in anything but his work, the woman gave him an unbothered, winning smile before reluctantly leaving.

Cary, however, had a genuine smile to greet Alice, and she was surprised to recognise how rewarded she felt by it. 'Good morning,' he said, his voice cheerful.

'That looked intense,' she said.

'Hmm?'

She pointed to the sharpening wheel and his face showed his sudden understanding, but he clearly didn't feel the need to elaborate on the machine or its use. He only smiled, placidly waiting.

Although this was only their fourth encounter, one thing she was learning about this man was it didn't take too long an absence to make him fall wordless again when next they met, like he reverted to factory settings every few days and forgot they'd spoken before.

'So... I got the message you left at the surgery for me,' she told him by way of a prompt.

'Ah, yes.' He turned to rummage for something on the shelves behind him. 'Did you bring your stethoscope?'

He'd asked her to, so she had. She presented him with it and watched as, without any unnecessary explanation, he swapped the worn-out rubber tubing for a brand-new set, fresh out of the plastic packaging.

It took Cary a while, but when he handed it back she verified it worked by listening to her own chest. He looked away while she did this, and something in the sweet way he averted his eyes made her feel like she was doing something improper. He really was a curious man.

Her heart and lung sounds came through perfectly. 'All working!' she told him. 'How much do I owe you for the replacement tubes?'

'Your donation last time covered it,' he said, with a wave of his hand. '*Umm.*' He seemed to be shuffling his feet, not at all like the softly assured Cary Anderson she was used to.

Without saying more, he presented her with a box, placing it on the workbench between them. It was made of polished wood and was the size of a pencil case with brass hinges for its lid. Something was carved on the top in a smart hand. *Dr A. H.*

'I didn't know if you had any middle names,' he said, his eyes cast down at the object. 'And I wasn't about to ask Gracie at the surgery.'

'What is it?' Her hands fell to the box, smoothing its varnished sides, lifting the lid to reveal nothing at all. 'It's beautiful.'

'You said you'd lost your good stethoscope and the clip it hung from. Now you can keep that one safely on your consulting room desk, if you wanted to.'

'You *made* this?'

He nodded.

'For me?' She hadn't been given a present quite this nice in... well, ever. 'Why would you do that?'

Cary looked a little blank and skittish for a moment, as if he might have made a mistake, before saying, quite plainly, 'Because we're friends.'

A wave of something difficult to pinpoint washed over her. Was it shyness? No, not quite. A feeling of overwhelm? Because someone was being kind and gentle with her? It had made her suddenly shaky and emotional.

She considered hugging him, which is what she really wanted to do, but he was all the way behind his bench and seemed planted there, so instead she demonstrated how her stethoscope fitted perfectly inside the box and closed the lid, turning the gift in her hands, having to hide the burning feeling behind her eyes.

She hadn't actually cried since she got here, not even when things felt very bleak, which they still often did, and she wasn't going to cry now in front of her first and only friend in Cairn Dhu.

'I absolutely love it to bits!' she said, and he seemed very happy with that.

An intrusive little thought piped up. Bastian would hate Cary making her this beautiful, special thing. *Good!* she told it right back.

'Did you get your clock fixed?' she asked, gesturing to the long case that had been pushed against the wall out of the way.

'No.' Cary shook his head sadly. 'Plenty of time, though.' Then he sniffed a laugh at what he'd said. 'It needs some new parts for the mechanism. Dr Bonnet's making them herself. Is it weird to you, hearing her called doctor, when you're an actual doctor?'

Alice thought about this. 'Nope, not really. Doctor isn't solely a medical title. In fact, *Physician* is probably more accurate for me. I'm guessing Dr Bonnet has a doctorate in clocks?'

'Horology, aye.'

'There you go then. She earned the title like anyone else who uses it.'

'Do you want to see her properly?'

'Dr Bonnet?'

Cary laughed, just at the same moment Alice was realising her mistake. He'd meant the clock.

'God, sorry, of course.' If she hadn't become almost immune to mortified feelings during her medical training, she might have wished the ground would open up and swallow her. 'Show me. I'd like that.'

The first thing Alice noticed about the clock was the beautiful simplicity of its case.

'My grandfather was a cabinet maker,' Cary told her as the pair stood before it.

'He built this?' Alice ran a tentative hand down the glossy wood, which had a honey darkness and even darker rings when viewed close up.

'He did, but the dial and mechanism were made in Barbados, we think, where Granny was born. Nobody seems certain how long it was in the family before it came to Scotland in nineteen sixty.'

'She brought it here?'

Cary nodded.

Alice searched her brain, trying to work out what it meant. 'She was part of the Windrush generation?'

'Well, personally she didn't call herself that because she didn't emigrate on that exact ship, the *Empire Windrush*; she travelled overland, through Italy then France, and arrived in England by ferry before the NHS posted her in Scotland. Nursing.'

'With your grandad?'

Cary paused, like he was debating whether to go on.

'It's OK, forget it. I'm just being nosey.'

'No, it's not that. There's a bit of a family legend...' His words trailed away.

Alice decided to be more like Cary and stay silent, letting him decide if he wanted to say more. She deeply hoped he would, even if it only meant she could listen to his lovely voice for just a little longer.

'Granny married twice,' Cary began. 'Her first husband stayed on in Barbados. He was going to follow her later. When she emigrated, she left with her sister. They both ended up working their whole lives at an infirmary in Glasgow.'

'Incredible.' Alice thought of all the nurses she'd met, and the caring and dedication they gave. The love. They didn't do it for the money, that was for sure.

'"You called and we came,"' Cary said. 'That's what

she always said about her decision.' A damp glaze came over his eyes, a quiet pride.

Alice gave him time. She turned the key to open the clock case and the door creaked open.

'We need to work on that too,' he said. 'It's creaky.'

'So would you be if you were... how old?'

'Grandad built the case in nineteen seventy. See?' He pointed to the date engraved on the inside lip of the door casing.

'Your gran's second husband?'

Cary nodded. Alice didn't ask the question aloud, only hoping he could intuit her interest, which, of course, he did. He had a way of reading her that was both alarming and reassuring.

'What happened to her first husband, right?'

'Right,' she said softly.

Cary tapped at the brassy pendulum inside the case and it swung, knocking the chains and ropes, weights and other things Alice didn't know how to interpret.

'They'd only been married for a few months. Never had time to have kids. She emigrated first, he was meant to follow a few months later; he was just waiting for paperwork while Gran had a nursing position all ready. When she arrived here, she and her sister got straight to work and... she never heard from Trevor again.'

'What? No!'

Cary nodded that it was true. 'This clock dial and its mechanism arrived at her door in a crate one day, along with some of their wedding gifts, and there was a note from his mother. He'd passed away shortly after she left.'

Alice felt her heart sink for the woman. 'She must have been devastated. Widowed and in a totally new country.'

Cary let her feel it. She liked that about him. He didn't crowd her feelings out with his. He gave her space and he stayed contained in his space too.

'What were their names again?' she asked.

'Gloria and Trevor,' he said. 'Then she married Grandad Dennis. Glo Glo didn't want us kids to know what had happened. She didn't want us feeling sorry for her, I guess, or she hated the idea of us being sad about Trevor, like she was. So she made up a story...'

Alice had her eyes fixed upon him now. She loved the sound of Gloria, or Glo Glo. She wondered if that had been baby Cary's name for her. Little could she know that pet name had been amongst the first sounds he'd made when he'd begun to find his way to speaking out loud as a seven-year-old.

'She told us kids that she came through the clock,' Cary said.

Alice started in surprise. 'What?'

'She'd have us all crowded around her, me and my little cousins, and she'd tell us how one minute she was in the Barbados sunshine, the next she'd jumped through the clock and appeared in the Scottish rain.'

'Hah!'

'Yeah. And the clock came with her. This was before we understood anything about Grandad Dennis making the case or how tough things had been.'

'You thought your granny was magic!'

'No. We thought *the clock* was magic.' He laughed. 'We just thought Glo Glo was lovely. Anyway, she told us that Grandpa Trevor, who we'd never met, had tried to get here inside the clock too, but it hadn't worked and he'd gone somewhere else, somewhere warm, with turquoise water and lots of colourful fishes.' He wasn't laughing now. He was lost in the memories. 'All so we didn't have to know about things like death, so we could enjoy the magic of being kids for a little longer. That's just what she was like.'

Alice watched him tapping the pendulum, making it rock. 'I wish I could hear this old thing's heartbeat. It would be like having some of the magic back. My childhood with Glo Glo and Grandad Dennis, and my mum.'

'Your mum, she's... um...?' Alice knew she was prying, but she wanted to know this man better, now that he was opening up. She had a horrible feeling this might be the only time this happened, her only chance.

'Mum's in Glasgow still. She's getting older. Doesn't get up here as much. I visit as often as I can. It was her who sent me the clock as soon as I mentioned we had the new horologist coming, to see if it could be mended.'

'So you used to live with her in Glasgow, but you moved here?'

'I did, about ten years ago. Wanted a quiet life.'

'It sounds like you've made a nice life.'

Cary seemed to weigh this up for a second before saying, 'Sometimes I've thought it might be time to go home to Glasgow.'

He fell quiet again and this news passed like a lightning bolt through Alice, who wanted to say, 'Don't do that! I'll lose my only friend,' but she didn't.

'If you swing the pendulum it moves the escapement,' Cary deflected, 'and you can make the clock tick.'

'Escapement?' The word seemed fitting given Cary's grandmother's story.

'That's just one of the moving parts of the clock, it regulates the timekeeping.'

Alice followed his lead, moving closer to the case. Cary pressed his cheek to the dial casing, but she didn't dare get that close to his time machine. It wasn't hers to mess with.

She scrunched her eyes to drown out the intruding hubbub in the repair shed and listened. She felt Cary moving his arm, and the clock made one heavy noise inside. '*Tung!*' it went, woody and echoing, and she heard the accompanying sound of the minute hand progressing before all its sounds resonated away into nothing and the shed was loud again. Too loud.

Cary, who'd been so close she had felt his gentle breath on the top of her head, had moved away once more.

'You don't really want to leave Cairn Dhu?' she said, in a wobbly voice that had come unprompted from nowhere. Why had she asked that?

Cary was staring at her, saying nothing.

A horrible racket started up from somewhere behind the plastic sheeting in the very depths of the shed. A bright light came on back there too, casting shadows on the sheet like a cinema screen. Boots clomped, voices lifted, and silhouetted pulleys hauled something from the ground up into the air. Someone was hammering on something metallic, and then a machine started up, some noisy engine.

Everyone in the repair shop was exclaiming at once at the sound. A toddler started crying.

'What are that lot playin' at?' yelled one of the elder repairers, who marched past in his blue work overalls. From the embroidered name badge across his chest pocket she could tell his name was McIntyre, and had she been thinking straight she might have concluded he was probably Murray's dad. 'Can you curb your din!' the man called in a heavy Highland accent, and was greeted with apologies in English and she thought, maybe, Dutch? The workmens' noises settled back down, while teaspoons clattered and the volume of people talking rose once more, the murmuring voices seeming to bounce off the metal roof above.

Alice's head hurt with the cacophony. It made her rapidly flush with heat. The overalls man apologised to her as he made his way past. 'Sorry, lass, I mean, Doc. They're no' supposed to be working on the build on repair Saturdays. At least, no' on the noisy stuff!'

'No worries,' she tried to say through sudden

dizziness, as the man walked back into the milling crowd.

She hooked a finger inside the collar of her t-shirt which felt suddenly restrictive, and turned back to where Cary had stood seconds before.

He was gone.

She looked around. Still he was gone. The clock case was gaping open like a mouth, the pendulum and ropes swinging.

He's gone through the clock, the troublesome part of her brain told her. *To the time where he's really from.* She knew this was nonsense but she couldn't shake the curious feeling of loss. It winded her.

She put her hands to her knees. *Keep the blood flowing. Take deep breaths.*

The dreamy part of her that couldn't distinguish playful thoughts from nightmarish scenario-making wouldn't shut up now.

Cary Anderson's too gentle to stay here in this noisy, violent, peaceless world, it said, and even though she knew how silly that was, it made perfect sense in that moment as the void inside the clock called to her like the places she went to when she dreamed at night, where nothing could be relied upon, least of all her own brain.

She hauled a breath into tight lungs. It was happening again and she couldn't stop it. The room seemed to rotate around her and all the while the void inside the clock seemed to expand outwards, swallowing everything in darkness.

'Are you all right?' a voice was saying.

Cary?

Suddenly he was beside her.

'Where did you go?' she gasped, gripping at his arms. He was solidly real, and looking at her like she was mad.

Her vision blurred. Cary's face was telescoping close then far away. That's when she understood that it was *her* that was at risk of disappearing, falling back down the rabbit hole.

'Do you need to sit down?' he asked.

Cary guided her across the barn, dodging the too many people standing around like this was a drinks party. Some were laughing. It sounded horrible to her ears. There were no vacant chairs in the café corner.

'Over here,' one of the ladies in aprons was saying, looking at Alice with alarm and producing a chair from behind the café counter. 'Come and sit yourself down.'

The woman cleared a path, shooing people out the way in a not very customer-service-focused manner, and, pushing Alice's shoulders, plonked her down in the seat right in front of the flaming stove fire.

Alice still felt too vague to wonder if she was making a scene or how many people had noticed she was unwell, and in public this time. She'd always been able to save it until she was safely alone and out of sight, but not this time.

She still couldn't seem to hear very clearly; everything had reduced to a buzz of noisy static.

'You too, Cary Anderson,' the woman was saying over the hum, and somehow Cary was shoved into a chair that had also been produced from nowhere.

'You. Drink. Tea?' the woman said close to her face, making big shapes with her mouth, miming drinking from a cup and saucer. She didn't stick around for Alice's answer.

Another woman, smaller, slightly younger, but very much like the first, magicked up a tray in an instant, placing it on the very top of the big stove. Mugs, a teapot, sugar cubes glistening, milk and something that looked a lot like frosted carrot cake.

'Look after her, Cary,' she heard the woman say, putting a gentle pat upon his shoulder.

Cary didn't say anything for a moment, only resigning himself to the impromptu fireside tea party.

He reached for the pot like this was all perfectly normal.

He poured two half-mugs of tea, adding the milk and ignoring the sugar lumps in the bowl. Had he remembered she'd bragged about not eating refined sugar at that meeting?

He turned the handle of her mug so it faced her and lifted his own.

Alice thought vaguely how she had never in her life been around anyone so tranquil. Cary was reaching for his plate and cake fork, observing her in a pleasant, neutral way as though she hadn't just accused him of being pulled into a clock and disappearing.

She scoffed at herself now, but when she glimpsed over the room towards the clock, she shuddered too and had to look away, feeling like a child at their mother's bedside after waking from a nightmare, unsure of what was real any more, the residual bad dream still haunting her.

She made a show of taking a drink, trying to stop her hands shaking. Putting her own plate on her lap, she blew out a deep breath, telling herself she was indeed awake. *Snap out of it, Alice in Wonderland.*

Meanwhile, in the real world, Cary cut a big

wedge with his cake fork and ferried it swiftly into his mouth.

'Is it good?' she asked shakily. Her lips felt tight when she spoke. Her voice sounded unnatural.

He nodded.

She copied him, a big forkful straight in. She closed her eyes to chew.

'I know,' he said, and she wondered if she had exclaimed aloud at how delicious it was. Cary took a slurp of tea.

The act of eating was grounding her, bringing her back to herself. This was no high street coffee chain carrot cake, chilled from the fridge, dense and bland. This was somehow fluffy and light, bursting with spice and zesty citrus, with the sweetest whipped cream cheese topping.

She took bite after bite and the world around her came back into view. Her body regained its gravity and sank heavily in the chair the way it should. Cary must have been able to tell because he asked if she was feeling better now.

'I'm sorry about that,' she said, still not quite over the shaky feeling of wanting to cry.

'Whatever it was, I'd say you can forgive yourself.'

He said it so serenely, so simply, it made her gaze

back at him in wonder. He was happily eating once more.

Neither spoke for a time, and Cary didn't seem to feel the need to fill the silence.

Had Bastian been here, he'd have been loudly proclaiming about the wonders of repair initiatives, how the ethos fitted his own *green agenda*, how it was *simply marvellous* places like this existed and doesn't it just go to show, *someone* must use them.

A small memory of getting ready for a night out together with her old friends early in their dating history, hoping he wouldn't embarrass her, made its way back to Alice now. Maybe her tolerance for being shown up had increased over time and in the end, she hadn't felt it quite so much?

A pang of guilt struck coldly inside her. She had to be misremembering him? Exaggerating his less endearing traits? And yet why had she had so many similar moments since coming to Scotland when she seemed to be able to see her old life in a new light? It made her feel like a traitor to herself.

'Eat up,' Cary was saying, banishing the memories of Bastian's brashness.

Alice tasted the cake again.

'You know,' she told him, feeling a deep need to

reconnect herself to the here and now, to Cary. At her words, his face switched in intensity, gently captivated. 'Back on the wards everyone would bring in their baking and biscuits and big tubs of chocolates. We'd literally live off them on nightshifts. After a while I dreaded going into the staff room, or the nurses' station, even the reception, because there was always something somebody had baked or it was someone's birthday, and you couldn't very well say *no thanks* to whatever they'd brought in. We shared everything we had, if that makes sense? Trying to keep each other going. When I finished with my foundation rotations, I realised the sight of sweets and cakes and biscuits made me feel nauseated. I couldn't eat another one. Is that silly?'

'Course it isn't.' Cary's bright expression told her he wasn't here to judge. He licked his fork and put it down on his empty plate and Alice was surprised to find her own cake gone as well.

'But *that* was amazing, actually,' she said, settling back in the chair with her mug, wanting to close her eyes.

'I think you had a tough time, at work?' Cary said, so softly she might have missed it.

She looked at him, seeing the way he crumpled

his mouth in sympathy. No one else had ever seemed to understand the toll her training had taken on her.

Cary topped up their teas, right to the brim this time.

She could have slept there, even with the background noise and movement, if someone would just put a blanket over her, but a realisation jolted her upright. 'My printout!' she said, looking all around her on the floor and feeling her coat pockets before realising Cary was trying to show her that he had the sheet of paper she'd been carrying when she arrived as well as her stethoscope box. He must have brought them over here with him when she'd turned dizzy.

She sagged with relief. 'Thank you! Carenza would kill me if she knew I hadn't practised this yet.'

'What is it?' Cary asked.

She showed him the printed text. 'This. It makes zero sense, and she wants me to read it at the Burns supper tomorrow night, because *apparently* that's the job of the town doctor.'

'The "Address to the Haggis"?' Cary said. 'We had to learn all about Burns at school, for the Burns competitions? We'd memorise and perform his poems and songs, for prizes.'

'You're all obsessed!' She shook her head in astonishment. 'That would be like us memorising Shake-

speare or Jane Austen and having a little talent show.'
Actually, she thought, that might have been quite nice.

'He's a big deal all over Scotland, even if some of his, *ahem*,' he mock-cleared his throat, 'attitudes and behaviour might irk us now.'

'Well, he irks me, all right. How am I meant to read this out loud in front of a room full of people? I don't understand most of these words. I don't have the right accent, even. I'll balls it up for sure, and everybody's going to think I'm dishonouring their favourite poet on purpose.'

Cary was smiling. 'I'll help you, if you like? Here...' He straightened out the page, running a fingertip along line one.

Alice falteringly read it. '*Fair fa' your honest, sonsie face, Great Chieftain o' the Puddin-race!* I mean, what does that even mean? Somebody's pleased about a pudding?'

Cary laughed. 'Aye. Your job is to praise the massive haggis they're going to pipe in to the supper table. You'll stand over the thing and tell everyone it's the chief of the pudding world, best thing you've ever seen. Then you get to cut it open, spilling out its guts.'

'Oh, God,' she gulped, pulling a queasy face, only partly to make him laugh again, and partly because the idea of haggis made her tummy churn. 'But what does this bit mean?'

'Fair fa'? I think that's just a greeting, a welcome?'

'Oh, all right then, makes sense. *Hello there, haggis!* And what about this bit?'

'Sonsie face?'

'Yeah.'

'Sonsie? It's, uh, bonny. Pretty.' His eyes met hers for a fraction of a second before he whipped them back to the page.

Cary cleared his throat for real this time. They both sipped their tea until whatever that was had passed.

'I'll try to find an annotated version online,' she told him, folding the paper. 'Thanks for trying to help.'

'I'm sure you'll do it brilliantly,' Cary said, and something about his tone told her their tea break was coming to an end.

'Are you going to the Burns supper?' she said, as she placed the stethoscope box in her bag, finding she wanted to detain him a little longer.

'Hadn't planned on it.'

Why had she asked him that? Now he'd think she was angling for him to go with her.

'I'll probably do my party piece then bolt as soon as the food's served,' she quipped.

'I doubt you'd get away with that.'

'Oh, yeah. *Carenza.*'

Cary had said her nemesis's name at exactly the same moment she had. They both smiled at that.

'*Cary?* Repair for you!' came Sachin's voice from the triage desk all the way over by the entrance.

Someone, Alice didn't know who, immediately shushed him and hissed, 'Can you no' see he's busy!'

The spell, however, was broken. Cary's expression had changed. He was brushing away crumbs, making to stand up.

'Are you going to the surgery today?' he asked. 'Sure you're up to the walk back?'

'I might just go home and take a nap. Day off, and all that.'

She was on her feet now too, hating the feeling of leaving the fireside. She could have stayed there all day.

'Good thinking. And you'll be back here at nine tomorrow morning for the tree planting and the garden project launch, right?'

Alice shook away her surprise. 'That's tomorrow? Of course! It had slipped my mind, what with the Burns stuff, and everything.'

There was a pause, during which Alice couldn't remember how you're supposed to act when leaving a friend after they've given you a present and taken you to tea, and you've had a spectacular panic attack right in front of them. '*Cheerio*, then,' she tried, in her best Cairn Dhu accent. Cary's lips spread into another lovely smile.

'We'll make a local of you yet!' came a voice. One of the café ladies was back to clear the tray. She handed Alice a bag. 'Macaroon bar, for later,' the woman said with a conspiratorial air and a pat of Alice's hand.

'Thank you, Ms...'

'Senga Gifford,' the woman said, lifting the tray. 'You looked fit to drop back there for a wee minute. What you need is some home baking and a good night's sleep, by the looks of you.' The woman's appraising eyes took her in from her head to her boots. 'A waif!' she said, not entirely sympathetically. 'Mind you, we're a haven for waifs and strays of all kinds here, aren't we, Cary?'

She didn't give him time to answer, talking over him. 'On that subject, can you not convince yer man here,' she bobbed her head, indicating Cary, 'to take on one of the stray puppies they found last week, down at the hotel?'

Alice had heard all about the pups from Gracie. She wasn't sure how to take the 'your man' thing and didn't think it was polite to protest about Cary being no such thing. Luckily Cary had found his voice.

'Ms Gifford, I already told you, I can't take a dog home. Dinah would go spare. She doesn't like dogs.'

Senga tutted and hobbled away with the tray and Alice suffered a moment's confusion when she could have sworn a stab of jealousy was lodged in her chest at the mention of this Dinah. But why on earth should she mind if her new friend had someone at home, probably a nice homely woman who could have as many of Cary's apples and pretty wood carvings as she wished for? It was definitely none of Alice's business what this man got up to in his private life.

'Dinah's my rescue cat,' came Cary's clear, calm voice, dissolving away her runaway thoughts.

'I guessed that,' she lied, wishing she wasn't like this.

'Did you want to pop in and see the puppies?' Cary said, suddenly. 'They're in the mill house kitchen.'

'Well...' She'd have feigned a glance at her watch if she'd been wearing one. 'Maybe just for a minute,' and she added a nonchalant shrug as if to say she could take puppies or leave them, while deep inside she thought there was nothing else she'd rather do, just so long as the gentle Cary Anderson kept talking to her.

As they left, a muttering line of disappointed locals queuing up at Cary's workstation watched them go.

21

'You called me down to the town early for *this*?' Finlay said. 'You said it was urgent!'

'You were coming down anyway for today's garden project launch, and I thought, what's a few minutes earlier—' Murray began.

'You thought I wanted to rehome a *dug*?' He said it like he was being strongarmed into adopting a rattlesnake.

'Well...' Murray realised he'd made a mistake. 'Aye, I'd hoped you might.'

It had been a tough time for the poor mother dog, a black Labrador, who Livvie's daughter, Shell, had decided to name Nell, and it had stuck. Nell had nursed her pups as well as she could but the vet suspected this wasn't her first litter, or even her fifth, and probably she'd been dumped out of the back of someone's car, an unscrupulous breeder's perhaps, for some nefarious reason they'd likely never understand.

She was underweight and exhausted. The vet had guessed the pups were five or six weeks old and recommended top-ups of doggy formula, so Murray had devoted himself to late nights and early-morning feeds to keep the two pups growing and take the strain off the poor mother.

And growing they were, even accounting for their tough early days. Murray could swear they'd grown a little more each time they woke from a nap.

Murray stayed crouched over their pen in the mill house kitchen, hoping they'd take a little extra breakfast and that might knock them out for another long sleep, letting poor Nell rest and so Murray could get on with the launch of the garden project.

Nell had seen more than enough of motherhood and dragged herself to the spot in front of the Aga for a snooze. Murray wished he could join her. Is this how being a father felt?

Now he knew why his parents stopped at twins. Roz McIntyre always maintained that looking after newborn twins was the hardest thing she'd ever done, but when Murray had made a heartfelt expression of gratitude to his mum and dad over dinner the other night, saying how sorry he was, he'd had no idea what they'd been through until now, they'd looked at each other and burst out laughing.

'Aye, son,' McIntyre had said. 'Two wee pups and two wee babies are just the same thing.'

His sister had told him over the phone this morning that, 'You know, wild dogs raise their pups alone without any human interference, have done for centuries?' and Murray had retorted smugly how Nell's wee doggie paws were useless with ring pulls on the cans of Chum so Ally didn't even know what she was talking about.

'I don't even like dugs,' Finlay said decisively, ready to leave.

'Now, I know that's not true! You loved that old Collie dog at the plant nursery.'

Finlay pulled a 'did *not!*' sulky sort of expression, but he must have known he'd been rumbled.

'I cannae look after a pup up at the cruive,' he protested. 'Think of the dangers! Plus... what kind of dogs are those, even?' He nodded at the tumbling pups, who seemed to be devoted to biting each other's ears.

They had certainly found their barks today too. Not ideal when Murray had their adoptions to arrange. He couldn't help people seeing (and hearing) what a handful they'd been.

'Labrador,' he lied.

Finlay huffed and hawed until Murray had to admit, 'There might be a wee touch of the wandering mutts in there, and so what? Don't be so judgy. Maybe that's why the breeder dumped them? Not much use for selling at a pedigree premium? Anyway, it wasn't the pups I was thinking of for you.'

'*Whit*? The mother! Nae chance. Naw, naw, naw.' He was backing away towards the door.

'Listen.' Murray was on his feet, his hands spread, reasoning. 'She needs a quiet home, somewhere steady and peaceful, where she'll get loads of attention but not be bothered by kids or anything.'

Finlay was looking at the snoring, exhausted mother. Murray gave it his last shot.

'Imagine being all alone in the world. A wee bit gruff and scruffy, aye, but soft as putty underneath. All she needs is a good groom and a few treats, and some long walks, the sky above her, fresh air...'

'No.'

'Please, just think about it? Please.' He'd skirted around the dinner table to where the dog snored, not daring to wake her from her well-deserved sleep but putting his face close to hers. '*Please?*' he said, in a cartoon-dog voice. 'You're my last hope, Finlay Morlich.' He held his paws up, and hung his tongue out. Probably overkill, but maybe Finlay was a sucker for cuteness?

'Are you finished?'

'I am,' Murray said, doing big hopeful eyes.

'The answer's still no. It's bad enough you folk have me down here wasting my Sunday in your garden, upsetting my routine, but now you want me to take a dug?'

Murray nodded like all of that was perfectly reasonable.

'I like things how I like them,' the ranger went on. 'I want peace and to be by myself and not have to bother with anybody, you understand? My life, my cruive, my mountain. Me!' He jabbed hard at his chest.

Murray let his shoulders drop. He'd overestimated Finlay's softer side. Maybe he didn't have one after all? 'All right, fine! But if she ends up sleeping her life away in this kitchen...' he threatened.

'By the looks o' her she'd be very happy with that outcome.'

Finlay didn't excuse himself in any way, didn't take one last, longing glimpse at the puppies like every other caller had these last few days. He merely left, closing the door behind him.

'Well, I think he loved you,' Murray comforted Nell. 'Somewhere deep, *deep* down, he definitely loved you.'

The indifferent dog half-opened one eye as if to tell him even she could see he was deluded and that there was no helping misery-guts Morlich.

Murray put his feet in his wellies and followed the ranger out into the winter morning sun.

'Guard the house, Nell, Babies. Murray's going out to find you a new daddy.'

22

Jolyon Sears was having a lovely day.

There'd been his favourite Greek yoghurt for breakfast and his favourite person in all the world helping him into his coat and gloves. His heart was bursting with love for his mum as she got him in the car, ready for a 'big day out' which sounded very exciting, and things only got better for having his favourite *Batwheels* cartoons on his tablet in the car. And now here he was at a muddy, grassy place and somebody, who he didn't know, but he seemed nice, was giving him an actual proper thingy to dig in the mud with. There were birds making a racket in the big trees on the other side of the big shed, and there was a bright yellow sun in the blue sky, just like the drawings he loved to do, and very, very,

very best of all, Pink Wafer Girl was here, and she had that soft-looking blue blanket with her again, the one he'd have little squeezes of when she wasn't looking, and she was being handed a thingy of her own for digging, and *yes!* she was coming over here to his rectangular box of muck which was just the right height for him to reach in and scoop.

'Hello,' she said in a whispery way, and he beamed back at her, saying his hellos in his very own way. He eyed her hand delving into her pocket, but no, she didn't pull out any biscuits. She retrieved sunny yellow gloves with bumblebees and pulled them on.

'Mum told me we're digging together today,' Shell said, and just because Jolyon didn't *quite* detect the tiny note of consternation in her voice because she'd been paired with a boy not even started school yet, he read her awkward smile as a good sign.

Chirruping with laughter just like the birds, he stuck the thingy into the dirt and flipped a big scoop of soil into the air. It plopped down heavily onto the bare bed.

Pink Wafer Girl watched him for a minute, before her eyes flashed with light, and she did the exact same thing, scooping some mud and sending it flying and whispering a naughty '*fliiiing!*' which made them both giggle. They both did another good fling at the exact same time and not one of the grown-ups seemed to want to stop them, or were even looking their way, apart from their mums and the lady doctor way over there, and they were too busy talking to spoil their fun.

Yes, this was definitely going to be the absolute best day ever.

* * *

'You came!' Alice called, her heart lifting at the sight of Jolyon's mum, Mhairi Sears, standing against the wall where the low winter sun cast a golden glare.

'I thought we had to?'

'What? No.' Alice shook her head. 'Not at all. It's just a bit of fun, a community-building sort of thing.'

'The letter said it was a referral.'

'Oh, well, that's just surgery letters, isn't it.' Alice made a mental note to get that sorted out ASAP. She didn't want to scare patients away with formality before they even got a chance to look at this place.

She'd asked Gracie to send the Sears' letter, and the receptionist had mentioned that little Shell Cooper, who'd been at the meeting that first night at

the surgery, might benefit from an invitation to partic-
ipate too.

'She'll be there anyway, given that she's stuck to
her mother like glue,' Gracie had said. 'But should I
send her one? Make it official?'

Alice hadn't felt so sure about making Shell an
official participant in the scheme, but Gracie had really pressed the point, saying, 'You heard about what
happened with her mother with all those gangland
crooks, didn't you?'

Alice had winced at the indiscretion, but she'd
still asked Gracie to elaborate, and her version of
events, even while taken with a pinch of salt, had been
enough to convince her that Shell and Livvie were
exactly suited to the project's therapeutic benefits.

Alice was so glad to see the mother and daughter
arriving right on time this morning. She wished
everyone had been so willing. She'd had to ring Clyde
Forte on Friday to check if he planned on coming, and
he'd said he'd go if Kellie was going, but then Alice
hadn't heard a peep from her at all and had the
feeling that cajoling her over the phone could easily
go the wrong way, so she'd lied and told Mr Forte she
was certain Kellie was intending to come.

No one else had arrived yet, but Alice knew if they
could just see the place in the low morning sun with

the fresh compost and manure in the bare beds making steam rise in the chilly air, they would think it a good place to spend some time meeting other people and getting some exercise, learning some new skills, even. Granted, the grass around the beds was spongy where it held on to the winter's rain, and there seemed to be a huge amount of work to do, but it would be lovely, come spring. For now, the beds were full of promise, like a new ward opening in a new hospital wing, everything stripped back and spotless.

Her eyes followed Mhairi's darting to a spot across the garden where Jolyon and Shell were playing in the mud with their little trowels.

'Someone's having a good time,' Alice said, though when she looked back at Mhairi there was a touch of concern wrinkling her brow.

'Do you think they're all right? Jolyon's not being too rough?' Mhairi asked Alice.

'They look fine to me.'

Mhairi's face was still clouded with worry.

'What is it?' Alice prompted.

After a heavy sigh, Mhairi told her how sometimes, when they'd been trying out new playgroups or on the rare occasions they got invited to playdates or parties, some of the mums had taken exception to Jolyon's exuberance or the way he might have needed help to read certain situations. It sometimes resulted in other kids getting scared or annoyed, and there'd be tears, and sometimes angry parents, and Mhairi would score another playmate or group off her list of people and places willing to accommodate them.

'I don't want to always be telling him to settle down, not when he's just playing, but it can get too much...' Mhairi was saying when Livvie Cooper joined them, bringing them each a mug of Senga's hot chocolate.

'They look fine to me,' Livvie said, echoing Alice's own words, even though she'd only caught a little of what was being said. 'I thought the point of the garden was to be recuperative? A place for playing.'

'Dr Millen not here?' Mhairi asked, possibly to divert the subject away from her anxieties about how people perceived her parenting.

'Oh, uh, no. I suppose he's given enough to the community over the years?' Alice said with a shrug, not wanting to let anyone know she'd been well and truly lumbered with this project and, as the newbie, she couldn't very well say no to the old doctor.

Livvie and Mhairi didn't say anything but exchanged a quick glance.

'So, do you two know each other?' Alice asked them.

Mhairi went first. 'We've seen each other round the repair shop. I come in for a brew some days.'

'The kids seem to have taken a shine to each other,' Livvie added.

'Jolyon's face lit up when he spotted her just now,' said Alice.

They all watched the children, now being shown how to plant the bareroot rose bushes by Finlay and Murray. Or, at least, Finlay was down on his hands and knees digging while Murray hung back and passed him the twiggy plants from the barrow.

Shell had taken on the foreman role and was re-explaining how it all worked to Jolyon, as though Finlay's explanation was all very well, but the little boy needed to hear it twice as loud.

'Hope he doesn't mind her bossiness,' Livvie said.

'Of course not,' Mhairi said quickly, not seeming to register that she wasn't the only mum worried about how others might respond to their kid's playing style.

'She knows her mind, that's all,' Alice said, before the mums decided they should probably roll their sleeves up and get stuck in.

'I'll catch up with you in a bit,' Alice told them as they joined their children. She stayed by the side of the barn, waiting for her other participants. If they didn't show up it wouldn't be much of a launch event, would it?

She let her eyes travel around the garden, counting off the volunteers, ranger Finlay, the McIntyres, and hoping that no one could guess that she was looking out for a handsome man in vintage gear, hoping she could thank him properly for his kindness yesterday.

* * *

Today there were no clouds, only a little wind, and the mountains lifted like snowy cream-topped desserts up into the cold air. Cairn Dhu resembled a frosty little gingerbread town in its sparkling green valley.

The blue sky had rubbed off on Finlay, who had started his day with a surprising amount of positivity, and he hadn't minded leaving his viewing spot up at the cruive and making his way down to town early, at Murray's request. The place had been quiet, even for a Sunday morning in late January.

Senga Gifford had pulled him aside as soon as he'd hit the gravelled drive of the mill house, telling him she was doing refreshments today and forcing a hot chocolate upon him.

He didn't normally drink the stuff, preferring his

usual coffee, but he'd given it a go just to placate her and he'd found it absolutely delicious, and about fifty per cent melted milk chocolate. The whipped cream and cinnamon sprinkles made it all the sweeter ('the marshmallows are reserved for the bairns,' Senga had told him when he asked for a few) and he'd actually been halfway to a kind of happiness when Murray had dragged him away from the basket of chocolate brownie bites he'd been about to sample, leading him into the kitchen at the mill house, a place he'd never set foot before.

There'd been Murray's parents around the breakfast table, and the place had smelled of toasted bread and coffee and whiffy patchouli candles. They'd greeted him when he arrived the way they probably greeted their own son, all smiles and welcomes.

Murray hadn't waited a second before launching into his, obviously pre-prepared, speech about how Finlay deserved a dog of his own. 'Man's best friend,' he'd said, putting a puppy immediately into his arms.

It had been another ambush, like these Cairn Dhu folk do best. Finlay had placed the thing right down into its playpen.

'Your heart's in the right place, Murs, but mind you listen to Finlay,' his mum had said gently, as she got up from the breakfast table, kissing Murray's cheek, before pulling on a coat from the stand by the door. 'Don't be pushy.'

Murray's dad was up too and lacing his boots, putting on a jacket over his overalls. He'd ruffled his son's hair as he followed his wife to the door.

Finlay was a little shaken to realise his first reaction to the way the parents spoke to Murray was one of revulsion. Imagine having parents all over you like that!

Then he'd checked himself and the reasonable part of his brain pointed out it was wrong to be envious of something someone else had. He heard his own mother's dry voice telling him *covetousness is a sin*. Then, after that, all he could think about was how lucky Murray was. How the man made a lot more sense now, if this was his natural habitat and he'd been raised by folks like this. No wonder he turned out a little bit silly, a little bit assured, and very well loved.

It must be nice, Finlay's heart had said, cracking a little, the way it used to when he was allowed to go to other children's houses and see their toys and eat their meals and watch their tellies. He didn't often get invited back, being an obtuse child who said all the wrong things, but the memories of cosy homes and cuddles and snacks and all the nice belongings other families were used to stuck with him, reinforcing the knowledge that he wasn't like those others.

'You *can* say no to him, you know, Finlay?' Mr McIntyre was saying. 'Don't be letting Murray strongarm you into anything. OK?' He'd addressed this part to Murray. 'Best of luck with the launch th' day, son. I know you can do it!'

He'd spoken to Finlay and Murray just the same, fatherly and soft. Finlay had looked around the room after they'd left, picturing what it must be like living in a big house like this with soft-hearted parents to gently guide you, even when you're an adult yourself.

Murray, however, didn't seem to know how lucky he was – Mrs Morlich would have said how 'spoiled'. Folk never do know.

Murray had launched into his patter about today being Finlay's lucky day, before listing the benefits of dog ownership like he was selling the things for cash.

The whole sales pitch had put him in a dark mood, and Finlay had vowed to get through the tree planting and project launch and return to his cruive as fast as he could, and without a dog, or any other additional responsibilities these pesky townsfolk liked to heap upon him.

23

Alice was astonished to spot Clyde Forte being dropped off from the back of a motorbike in the carpark by a young rider who kept their visor down over their face. She was even more astonished to see him stagger off the seat clutching a spade. He immediately lit a cigarette as he waved his lift away. Alice decided today was probably not the day to give him a lecture about riding pillion while clinging on to a heavy spade, or smoking and stroke recovery. He wouldn't listen anyway.

As he was fending off Senga's insistence that he take one of her hot chocolates and try her brownie bites, Alice swept in to see if Mr Forte needed any help, just as a car pulled up in front of the repair barn.

Both Mr Forte and Alice watched the car turning. There were three people inside.

'That'll be Kellie and her ma and da,' Mr Forte said in a low voice. 'Mind you don't go charging in there.'

Alice had been about to do exactly that, hoping to meet the Timmonys, but she lied and told Mr Forte she'd no intention of interfering, which he scoffed at.

'She's feart of doing things away from her parents. In case it happens again,' he told her, sagely, while blowing smoke right at her.

'Her risk of stroke's not much greater than anyone else's,' Alice said.

'When you've been hit by lightning, you'll always think it could happen again,' he said. 'And it changes a person. You've no idea how much.'

Alice could hear Kellie's mum speaking through the opened car window at her daughter, still in the back seat. 'My phone's on, ring any time, but just try and enjoy it. Half an hour, eh?'

Kellie got out and said something back to her, her hands on the rolled-down passenger side window.

Alice couldn't hear what she was saying, but she could see the way her mum was looking at her, like it was her first day at school and she was putting on a brave face, trying to be encouraging. She thought of her own mum and how she too had often looked at her like that, especially in recent years.

Kellie had straightened up now and watched as her parents' car rolled out of the drive, both of them waving stoically, their smiles overwritten with worry.

When they were out of sight, Kellie's shoulders slumped and she turned, realised Alice and Mr Forte were watching her and trudged slowly towards them.

'I'm staying for thirty minutes,' Kellie said.

'Perfect,' Alice and Mr Forte said together, making them turn and look at one another in surprise.

'Come on then, if we're doing this,' Kellie told them.

* * *

Alice had made all the introductions. Senga had forced hot chocolates into everyone's hands who didn't have one, except for Mr Forte who insisted on finishing his cigarette first.

After a while the kids were finishing planting the roses in rows down the centre of each raised bed with Finlay while Murray gave the orders and kept his hands clean, and Mr Forte, Kellie, Mhairi and Livvie each planted one of the four Aspen trees that had arrived from the nursery with their roots wrapped in cloth.

The plan was they'd finish up getting some of the wildflowers and perennials in the ground, then they'd have their picture taken for the newspaper – the guy was due in twenty minutes – then they'd head inside the shed to discuss future plans for how they'd tend the garden.

So far, things seemed to be going well, thought Alice, even if Cary's absence stung. When her phone rang, she carried it off round the back of the barn, excusing herself.

'Dad?' she answered.

'Ah, good morning, Alice!' he boomed in his affable way.

'Is everything all right?' They hadn't spoken since Boxing Day, and hearing his voice now only reminded her how much she'd missed him.

'Just checking in on my favourite daughter.' His usual joke. She was his only daughter. 'How's the new job going?'

'Fine, thanks,' she replied. In fact, things had been going well in her consulting room of late. It had taken the whole three weeks, but she'd got to grips with the records system, been praised by Dr Millen for exhibiting 'best practice' in a number of areas as he'd completed his first review of her progress on Friday, and she'd caught two cases of pneumonia early, probably preventing hospitalisation. Plus she'd successfully helped launch the area's latest school vaccination programme.

'I'm actually enjoying it,' she told him.

'That's wonderful!' His voice bubbled in his generous, hearty way, and the familiarity warmed Alice from the inside.

'And the community?' he prompted.

'They're...' How to describe the place? 'Interesting. Not quite what I expected.'

'Hah, always expect the unexpected in medicine, eh?'

'Yes.' She laughed too. 'Are you all right?' It felt strange not to be asking how they both were, him *and* Mum.

'Yes, yes, yes, all well,' he said, shutting down that topic. Alice was beginning to wonder if they'd ever be able to talk about the separation or her dad's new girlfriend, who, so far, was a sort of awkward open secret nobody wanted to acknowledge out loud.

'Everything all right with your...' Dad let the sentence finish itself.

What was he referring to? Her daydreaming? The

waking nightmares? The anxiety and panic attacks? 'Yes, fine.' He wasn't the only one who could shut conversations down. She'd learned from the best.

'I'm doing a bit of community work at the moment; a social prescription gardening project. I'm here now, actually.'

'Is that Alice?' came a woman's voice in the background, accompanied by what sounded like the clatter of dishes and cutlery.

'Is Mum with you?' What was going on?

'You know how we like to keep in touch. I've popped round for a visit.'

That explained why Dad had called. It wasn't quite so out of the blue after all. Mum had reminded him to.

'Hold on a minute, she wants to talk to you.'

There was some whispering and a handover. 'Alice, love?'

'Mum? What's Dad doing there?'

'Oh, you know. His Sunday eggs Benedict brunch was always a sort of tradition, and we... kept it going.'

'Right.' Alice sighed. She should be glad they were such good friends. She didn't reckon she'd have it in her to brunch with an ex-husband who'd recently moved in with another woman, but her mum was a better person than she was, obviously. 'Just don't let him take up all your space. That's your house now.'

'I know, I know,' she said in an indulgent way, probably rolling her eyes for Dad's amusement at her fussing.

'Tell your mother about the garden project,' her father called, noisily washing dishes at the sink like his name was still on the deeds. In fact, they probably still were.

Alice explained the nature of the project and how it was actually quite nice to be involved.

'Are you there in an official capacity?' her mum wanted to know.

'I'm workloaded for it. It's OK, I'm being paid.'

This heralded a flurry of questions that made Alice wish she'd kept her big mouth shut.

'But you're not trained for mental-health first-aiding, are you? Isn't there a mental-health nurse there? A community psych? A neurologist stroke specialist, even? Rehab-physio?'

'No, none of them. It's just me here.'

'She's the only medic involved, Cranmer!' her mum relayed.

'What!' Her father commandeered the phone. 'Are you covered for that? Insurance-wise? Seems risky to me.'

'We're fine, we're just pottering in a garden.'

'Were you party to the risk assessment? I'm not sure about all of this, Alice.'

She tried to explain that if they could see how laid back and informal it all was, they wouldn't be so alarmed, but their fretting had set off some feelings of insecurity within her that were glowing like hot embers now. Maybe this *was* risky? What if she did actual harm, instead of helping? There were vulnerable people here who deserved a properly trained therapeutic gardener, not Alice, a newbie GP.

Distraction was her only escape. 'Don't you have afternoon plans?' she said, pinching at her closed eyelids, feeling the tiredness she'd held at bay all morning washing over her.

'We might take a pootle out to Knutsford for supper,' her dad began.

'Who? You and Mum?'

'Yes,' her dad snapped, a warning not to push it.

Alice desperately wanted to ask what his new girlfriend thought about this cosy exes-who-brunch setup they had going on, but she didn't even know the woman's name and the whole situation left her with a queasy seasickness.

'And Bastian's joining us,' he added shiftily.

'What? Why?' She knew Bastian absolutely

idolised her father, but she'd no idea he was involved in their weird games of Happy Families now they'd broken up. This didn't feel right at all.

'He's interviewing for a position with my team soon, joining in my grand rounds in anticipation of the selection process, and doing very well, as it happens. I thought he deserved some fatherly advice...'

'You're not his father.'

Silence filled the space where he might have blurted, 'Well, I almost was!'

'How often do you see him, outside of work, I mean?' Alice asked.

More awkward silence down the line, before the admission, 'He comes to Friday suppers with me and Kimberly.'

So Dad's new girlfriend was called Kimberly? And the three of them shared cosy dinners in the new house she hadn't even set foot inside. It was all a bit sick. She wanted to tell him this wasn't a soap opera. Why couldn't he just leave Bastian out of things?

'The way you and Bastian left things...' her dad began.

'No,' she cautioned, definitely not wanting to talk about this.

'It seems a shame, just because you're there and he's here, temporarily. That's all I'm saying. You know, your mother and I spent a lot of time apart when she was pregnant with you and the hyperemesis gravidarum meant she couldn't work...'

'I know, I know, and you were away doing your stint in that Romanian hospital.' *Like a saint.* She'd heard this story a hundred times and her parents came out of it like a regular Romeo and Juliet, only with more morning sickness, surgical heroics, and lots of late-night Skype calls. They'd stayed together through it all. 'I don't want to talk about Bastian,' she said firmly. 'Please.'

'OK, if that offended you, I apologise.' His voice softened. 'Are you at least socialising up there?'

'Well...' Reluctantly she told him she was attending the Burns supper and ceilidh tonight as a guest of honour. 'They're making me deliver the "Address to the Haggis".'

'Are they now!' His bellowing laugh made her pull the phone from her ear. 'How wonderful!' She listened to him repeating this information to her mother, whose laughter sounded a little less certain.

'Public speaking?' she heard her mother say ominously.

'I've practised. I know what to do,' she told them quickly.

It was true. She'd hit the Burns books last night

with the same amount of dedication she'd expended brushing up on the carpal tunnel injection procedure which she'd performed on Mrs Causwell this week under the watchful eye of Dr Millen.

'My advice to you is—' her father began, loftily.

'Picture the audience naked?' Alice tried, wishing he'd stop. Cranmer Hargreave had been a member of his medical school's amdram group and loved nothing better than the feeling of all eyes upon him and the sound of applause.

'My advice is stand still, legs apart, arms by your sides, go off book, so no reading from the page, and project your voice, really yodel it out to the very back row.'

'Got it, thanks.'

'And pace yourself, don't forget to breathe, or you'll find yourself gulping like a goldfish and fluffing your lines.'

'I'm sure she'll be fine, Cranmer,' her mum said in the background over the sound of the kettle boiling. 'Ask her if she's sleeping any better.'

Always the same question, something her mother had agonised about ever since Alice was tiny and, unlike her sporty, food-shovelling, academic brothers, had proven to be a fitful sleeper. At seven, her mother had shown little Alice a medical textbook that said children her age needed eight to ten hours' sleep every night, and at that point Alice was averaging six. Her mum had kept a chart to prove it.

When Alice had tried to adhere to her new 'sleep hygiene' schedule, this had fallen to five hours a night, and the whole thing ended in a tearful, exhausted Alice begging her mother to drop it and let her close the door to her bedroom in peace, without anyone watching her and worrying. Her mother, realising her mistake, had tried to comfort her, telling her that simply lying in bed resting her body was just as good as being actually asleep, and for all of ten seconds little Alice's heart had lifted. Lying in bed thinking? *That* she could do. She was brilliant at it, in fact, but her dad had overheard and stormed in with his expertise, saying that was "patently untrue", and that his wife knew as well as he that "only full cycles of deep REM sleep contribute to optimal cognitive function and cellular repair. Kindly don't fill the child's head with unscientific bunkum".

'Your mother asks, are you sleeping?' her father parroted down the line.

Ugh! Why hadn't she just sent them a few jolly Highland postcards to keep them at arm's length and stop them feeling the need to ring? She shouldn't have

picked up the call, anyway, not when she was supposed to be working.

Just then, Cary's face appeared around the back of
the shed, searching her out.

'Ah, duty calls,' she said with a flood of relief.
'Better go. Love you,' and she'd hung up before Cary
reached her, but the damage had already been done.

Her head was reeling with their words of warning
about the risk to her professional standing if anything
should go wrong on her watch with this garden
project, or about her chances of fluffing the Burns
supper address under the gaze of the locals and the
scary Carenza McDowell when she was supposed to
be making her very first public appearance as the
(temporary) new town doctor, which called for grav-
itas and dignity, and then there'd been the bombshell
about Bastian still hanging around like they hadn't in
fact split up weeks ago.

'Oh dear,' she couldn't help saying.

'Hey, hello!' Cary greeted her. 'You OK?'

'Absolutely.' She tried to steady her breathing.
She'd promised herself Cary wouldn't see her getting
in a state ever again. 'Is it time to plant the wildflowers
round the trees, then?'

'It is,' he said. 'But before we do, I wanted to give
you something.'

'No more presents, please, Cary, you've already been too kind and... Oh!'

It was just a leaflet.

'I thought this might come in handy,' he said, a little apologetically.

She read the front cover. 'Bonnie Blair, MA, Counsellor, specialist short-term intervention and talking therapies. COSCA accredited.'

'She's setting up an office on the high street. I thought you'd want to know...'

It clicked into place what he was saying. He'd anticipated her very problem, the same one her parents had identified. 'You're right! We *do* need someone like this on board! Thank you! Have you already approached her?'

'Eh?' Cary didn't seem to be keeping up.

'To help with the garden project? I also figured we need a trained counsellor on the team.' He didn't need to know it was her parents' misgivings that had alerted her to this fact. 'What a coincidence.'

'Oh, right.' He had taken a step back, raising a hand to the back of his neck.

Alice turned the leaflet over, reading aloud. 'Deciding to seek counselling after going it alone may feel daunting. I offer a non-judgemental, trusting space where you can share your fears and experiences in order to achieve acceptance, resolution and better peace of mind.'

Cary was looking at her like he was afraid.

A bleak feeling came over her. 'What is this?'

'The other day at the repair shop?' he began.

Alice knew what he was saying. She'd lost it, turned unwell in public. She'd scared him.

'Well,' Cary said, softly. 'Whatever happened, it frightened you, I could see that much. And I got to thinking, when I saw Bonnie putting up her signs today outside her office, I'd bring you one of her leaflets.'

'For talking therapy?'

'Aye.'

'For me to try out? Listen, Cary, I work for the NHS. I can easily find a counsellor if I want to.'

'*Do* you and your doctor friends really make use of counselling services?' He said it so plainly, it rocked her.

'Maybe not as much as we should,' she confessed.

She thought of all the wonderful, conscientious people she'd worked with, who'd done the same training as her, seen the same awful things, held people's hands as they underwent the most traumatic days of their lives, only to go home, eat, shower, nap and come straight back for their next shift. None of them struggled as much as her, she'd concluded. It occurred to her they might be pretending to be fine, too. So many people were pretending out there.

Alice, like all NHS medical staff and students, had access to free and confidential services and information, a round-the-clock counselling line, and a peer-support service. They were even offered a few free sessions of therapy with a counsellor. She'd never made use of any of them. Had her colleagues? Most of them seemed to clear their heads by training for marathons, doing yoga, hillwalking with their partners and dogs, or planning lovely holidays. She had done none of that with Bastian.

'But there never seems to be enough time,' she continued. 'You don't understand. We know our limits, we've been specially trained—'

What happened next winded her: the gentle, soft, wouldn't-say-boo-to-a-goose Cary Anderson interrupted her. 'Listen, Alice. We waited a long time for our new doctor, and now that you're here in Cairn Dhu, we want to look after you. We want you to be happy and well and safe with us.'

She tried to find a suitable reply but all she could do was move her mouth, exasperated. She heard her dad's voice telling her, *don't forget to breathe, or you'll find yourself gulping like a goldfish and fluffing your lines.*

'And do *you* have a therapist?' she said, on the attack and desperate to win this thing.

'I do.'

Alice's bubble burst. 'You do? But you're so... well adjusted.'

Cary let her think about what she'd said. He was kind of infuriating when he was in the right, and so reasonable with it.

'I speak to someone every few months,' he told her. 'Like a wellness MOT. It costs money, but I'm fortunate to have that money, and I see it as an investment in myself.'

She wanted to tell him not to interfere, to say he was being just like her dad, the person who she knew, deep down, she was *actually* angry with, but a little livid streak of indignation was burning within her and she hated that it was Cary Anderson, of all people, who'd stoked the fire, and by being so bloody nice as well.

'Look, I can't get into this now. I have patients to see to and a project to run.' It was haughty. It was childish. But it was the best she could do.

She left Cary standing by the compost bins as she stormed away.

* * *

The photograph, when it appeared in the online newspaper story, captured the whole day perfectly.

Standing around the bare trunk and branches of one of the Aspen trees, boots on spades, were the new doctor, the palest of the lot with a set look of determination on her face, next to the mountain ranger, his hands stained with wet mud, caught scowling towards the grinning Murray McIntyre, spotlessly clean even down to his Hunter wellies, and with a puppy he held close to Finlay's cheek. Kellie (who had outstayed her planned thirty minutes by over two hours) and Mr Forte posed with their spades too but with their arms interlinked in camaraderie. Mhairi Sears and Cary Anderson bookended the group, since Livvie didn't like having her picture taken, so instead stood behind the photographer shouting at Finlay to 'buck up' and to 'fix that torn face'. Mhairi was captured smiling down at Jolly who was very much living up to his name with both hands in the mud at the foot of the tree, happily filthy with streaks of earth over his rosy cheeks, mouth open in a squeal of delight, and hidden behind him, barely visible, was Shell, there but not quite there, the way she liked it, making bunny ears behind Jolly's head, which he thought had to be the wittiest thing anyone had ever done, and *just like* his best friend to think of it, she was so fantastic. Cary maintained a dignified stance on the end, looking down the photographer's lens but not quite able to smile, his look of wistful regret captured forever.

The accompanying headline would read:

Successful Launch for the Cairn Dhu Social Prescribing Garden Scheme: Fun Was Had by All.

24

Burns suppers, for those unversed in these rituals, are a strange mixture of solemnity and sentimentality (things the Scots do very well), with quite a lot of food, whisky and poetry, some staunchly nationalistic, some deeply romantic, and oftentimes a wee bit racy (again, things the Scots excel in).

January the twenty-fifth offers a reprieve from dreich winter nights stuck at home, a few hours' partying, and the opportunity to remember what it means to love this place.

The idea is to celebrate, to toast, to birl and skirl on the dancefloor, to have a good 'greet' if needed (that is, a cathartic sob on a friendly shoulder), and to generally hoot and holler and have a right good hoolie!

Alice, however, was not of the Burns Night persuasion. When she'd felt like celebrating, she'd chosen summer drinks parties in the city, a nice bar or restaurant, all chrome and charcuterie boards, cocktails served by handlebar-moustached hipsters. Nights out for her most definitely didn't involve singing the praises of a haggis.

She'd been known to dance the night away at colleagues' destination weddings, or in big flowery marquees where the women carried their heels and sang along to Ed Sheeran songs and the men grouped around the bar (or someone's phone, if there was footie on).

Royal Jubilees, a coronation, graduations, big birthdays, baby showers, promotions; these were the things she'd celebrated in her lifetime, and not one of them entailed the memorising of over forty lines of complicated poetry or the horrible drone of bagpipe music.

Yet, here she was, standing in front of the big doors of Cairn Dhu Hotel's ballroom with a piper and a drummer in their full tartan regalia and with the whole retinue of kitchen staff lined up behind their head chef (the pretty one who'd had her eye on Cary

Anderson the other day as he sharpened her knives), who was proudly carrying a wooden trencher with an outrageously large steamy haggis on top, all curled up like a sleeping cat, and just as unappetising.

Carenza McDowell had presented Alice with an antiquated knife, which she called a 'dirk' and which Alice was supposed to dramatically plunge into the haggis at the correct moment indicated in the poem. The club president had steeled her with a speech worthy of Burns himself about facing the spotlights and 'jolly well giving it your all', and now there was nothing else to be done but wait for her signal.

Carenza counted down like an instructor prepping them for a four thousand metre skydive. 'Three, two, one!'

The piper blasted an unholy sound in Alice's eardrums, making all her nerves jump at once.

'Go, go, go!' Carenza cried, and the doors were hurled open, revealing a hundred heads turning at once.

'Oh God!' Alice gulped, her copy of the poem screwed tight in her hand. Her feet wouldn't move at first but Carenza gave her a shove and she was over the threshold and trying her best not to grimace.

People were filming the procession on their phones, all of them po-faced like this was a funeral march. She hadn't expected the supper to be quite so formal. Everyone was dressed to the nines. The tables were set with white linen and silverware.

She shuffled on, following the chef and piper, all the way around the room, trying not to trip on her dress, borrowed in a hurry from the kilt hire place. It was a long white thing, not quite like a bride, more like a fifties party hostess, and it had a tartan sash tied at her hip and a plastic thistle pinned to the collar. When the lady in the shop had asked her which clan tartan she wanted, she hadn't had a clue what to say, and as the woman reeled them off to see if any 'rang a bell' somewhere in her family tree, there'd been only one name she'd felt any connection to at all.

'MacLeod? Mackenzie? Douglas? Gordon? Anderson? Mac—'

'Yes!' Alice had blurted, startling even herself, and the woman had retrieved an Anderson tartan sash for her. What a fraud she was, but she hadn't the heart to explain herself, only paying for her rental frock, sash and dancing pumps and getting out of there fast, before she invented any more bogus claims to Scottish lineage.

The piper seemed to have tuned up a bit now and was playing something recognisable as music. Alice carried her knife, feeling like a character in a weird Highland slasher movie.

Out of the corner of her eye she caught the Gifford sisters from the repair shop café. The pipe music was no match for their loud exclamations about how bonny she looked, which was quite nice, really. She gave them a little smile as she passed, knowing one day she'd see them in her surgery and it was probably best to keep on the right side of them.

They'd completed their circuit of the room all too quickly and Alice followed the other dignitaries up the few stairs and onto the raised platform where the top table was set. Her chair was to the left of the middle; the top spot reserved for Carenza as President.

She filed into place only to spot Dr Millen right in the front in black tie and a kilt, enjoying a large glass of whisky with, she presumed, Mrs Millen by his side, and Gracie at the same table.

He toasted Carenza with a wink, and Alice heard her tutting and saying, 'The cheek of that man!'

There was a moment's long droning refrain from the bagpipes as the music faded and suddenly the whole room was on their feet, like this was church.

Alice was in position now, a microphone low on the table before her. The haggis had been set down and the chef and her staff moved off stage to a smat-

tering of restrained applause. The piper stood back.
The room fell quiet.

Carenza, who didn't need a microphone –
everyone in Cairn Dhu would have heard – said a few
words of welcome and a strange prayer about
someone not having any meat or something, and then
she called upon Alice, 'Who will now give Robert
Burns's famous "Address to the Haggis".'

Alice fiddled with the knife, replaying her dad's
words about the importance of going 'off book'. Her
hands shook way too much to unfold the piece of
paper without everyone noticing her nerves, anyway.
She really was going to have to perform the whole
thing from memory.

'Go on,' Carenza hissed as quietly as she could,
which for her meant the tables in the front definitely
heard.

Dr Millen peered at Alice expectantly, brows
knitted.

Alice tried to clear her stiffening throat, the hand
holding the knife feeling oddly limp all of a sudden.
She tried to tighten her grip but her hand was slippery with sweat.

That was all it took to start up the vision.

She pictured the blade slipping from her fingers
and guillotining right down into her dancing shoe.

She heard the screams it would elicit, the gasps of horror. She could see it as though it were happening in real time. She'd probably faint after that. At least that would mean she didn't have to recite the poem.

Oh no, thought Alice, the rabbit hole in her brain gaping, wanting her to fall in, as the room turned hazy and wavy in the steamy reek from the giant haggis.

Not here, she pleaded with herself. *Not now!*

25

Cary Anderson had never been racked with indecision for even one moment in his life, until now.

He'd kept himself busy all afternoon, practising a particularly difficult twisted chrysanthemum joint, the most complicated glue-free joint in cabinetry, and something he usually enjoyed the challenge of, but even that hadn't been enough to distract him.

He should have gone about this morning's conversation with Alice completely differently. He'd taken a liberty, presumed to know her, when in fact they'd spoken only a handful of times before. He'd gone against his instincts and interfered when he should have waited, letting her figure things out for herself. What right did he have to give a woman he'd only just met advice about her own mental health? He'd really blown it.

'Ach!' He stormed into his bedroom in the eaves of his cottage, and back out again, leaning his back on the doorframe, trying to talk some sense into himself. And yet the wardrobe was calling to him. In there were his kilt and jacket, shirt and tie, his ghillie brogues and his woollen knee socks, his sporran and flashes.

He should go to the Burns supper and apologise to her.

He had a ticket. That lassie from the hotel kitchens had been kind enough to drop one through his letterbox with a note thanking him for sharpening her knives, telling him she hoped he'd come. He wasn't green enough to think the chef didn't have designs on him, but he wasn't egotistical enough to think a young woman like her could be happy with an older man like him. Besides, he only pursued someone if he liked them and there was only one person he felt like that about and she hated him right now, probably.

Would he make things worse, bursting in there? Would he risk showing her up when she was, no doubt, already tortured with the fear of performing the poem?

These thoughts churned in his mind as he pulled the wardrobe doors open and ran his hand down the thick pleated Harris kilt with its clean scent from the lavender-oiled cedar wood he'd used to construct his bedroom furniture back when he first bought this place, where he had lived alone, eaten alone, worked alone, and slept alone all these years.

A pining, burning feeling was cast in his stomach at the thought of walking in to that ballroom and asking her to save him a waltz, something that wouldn't make her feel out of place, something you didn't have to know the Scottish secret handshake for.

That woman had arrived here without knowing a soul and thrown herself into community life, *saving* lives. No wonder she was struggling. Cairn Dhu could be an obscure place, its weather as well as its customs not for the faint hearted.

Against his self-control, which had always been so strong until now, he pictured Dr Alice Hargreave in his arms, dancing her around the floor, her cheek against his, moving in rhythm to the ceilidh music. That's when he'd tell her he was sorry. He hadn't meant to spook her. She didn't need saving, and certainly not by him. Quite the contrary, it was him that needed her. *Wanted* her, very much.

That was it. His mind was made up. He yanked his kilt from the hanger, throwing it onto the bed.

He was going after her.

He had to repair what he'd broken.

* * *

The spotlight shone in her eyes, making it impossible to make out faces. Shakily, Alice set the knife down on the linen tablecloth. Carenza's stare burned into the side of her face, but she wasn't going to look round. She took a deep inhalation through her nose, refusing to rush it. When her lungs were full, she let her eyes close and she blew it out, puffing her cheeks. Yes, everyone was watching, but what else was she meant to do?

In through your nose for five, she would tell patients when they hyperventilated. Hold it, then blow out the birthday candle for seven, six, five...

She exhaled hard and long, her eyes still screwed tight. Relax your jaw. Soften those shoulders, and breathe in...

She did it again, but this time she wasn't alone.

Cracking open one eye, she saw Dr Millen up on his feet taking a deep breath too, and moving his arms as though he was conducting the whole audience like an orchestra. When she blew out this time, she heard a gust through the room.

'*And!*' she heard Dr Millen saying, still on his feet, facing the tables at the back, and everyone took a long deep breath in unison. Gracie was on her feet too, looking right at her, nodding encouragement.

The whole thing went on for a good few minutes.

It was ridiculous and lovely and she wanted to cry, but she didn't. She blew out one long, steady lungful after another, accompanied by all the fancy guests, and when the room had stopped spinning, she nodded to Dr Millen that she was getting it together.

The old doctor winked at her as he took his seat again, and Alice unfolded the piece of paper in front of her as a gentle applause broke out across the room.

'You can do it,' Gracie called out.

A few shallower breaths and Alice knew she could get the first words out.

'Fair fa' your honest sonsie face,' she said. *Pretty. That means pretty.*

A quick look towards Carenza – who actually looked quite pleased – told her she was doing all right, and she carried on, giving it her best, the way it was supposed to be said. Not perfect, but with heart.

'Great chieftain of the pudding race!'

Smiles broke out around the room.

She was enjoying this, actually enjoying it! Even if she was shaking all over.

She had the knife in her hand now, provoking a ripple of laughter and a loud, 'Go'an yerself!' from the piper, which she chose to interpret as positive encouragement.

'Aboon them a' ye tak your place!' she cried, whipping herself up into a happy fervour.

She'd made it. She was one of them. Different, but still one of the Cairn Dhu folk.

She opened her mouth for the next line, discarding her paper, knowing that if she could memorise over a hundred medicines, their usages and side effects for that pharmacology exam, she could recall this one poem.

That's when the door burst open with a loud bang.

Everyone tore their eyes from her and stared at the man dashing in, his face overwritten with concern, his chest heaving as though he'd run here, all dressed up for a formal night out.

She faltered, almost dropping the knife for real.

The poetry flew from her brain and all she could do was gasp out his name.

'*Bastian!*'

26

'What are you doing here?' shrieked Alice, as soon as she'd murdered that haggis and got off stage, dragging Bastian into one of the hotel's service corridors under the gossiping gaze of the entire town. Damn right she'd finished her poem, once she'd recovered from the initial shock of seeing the man who, little more than a month ago, hadn't even wanted to speak to her, and now here he was, bursting in on her big moment, just when she'd found her composure.

'Cranmer said he was worried about you, told me you had some big performance tonight and you were terrified. And... I was worried about you too.'

'What did you do? Drive all this way?'

He shrugged it off. 'It's really nothing in the AMG. She ate up those roads.'

'*Ugh!*' Alice winced at his smugness. 'I have to get back in there. I'm the guest of honour.'

After the whole town got behind her when she was struggling with nerves in a sympathetic symphony of soothing breathing, she *really* didn't want to leave the party. Besides, there was going to be more poetry and Carenza was going to sing, and she hadn't even tasted her haggis, neeps and tatties yet.

'I'm sorry you've come all this way, but as you can see, I'm fine.' She turned back for the ballroom.

'Wait, wait, wait.' Bastian manoeuvred in front of her. 'Don't you think we should talk? You owe me that, at least.'

'I owe you? I told you I had a new job, you flipped out and stopped talking to me. End of story. We broke up.'

'Did we? I feel like there was still so much to say.'

'Like what?' she seethed.

'Like I'm sorry. I really am.'

That was unexpected. Bastian rarely apologised for anything.

'I sulked when I should have supported you. I think it's great that you've got your own practice up here.' He looked around the tartan-wallpapered corridor with the antlers mounted on plaques like this was what the whole town must be like. 'No, honestly, I do.'

'It's not *my* practice. I'm only here to complete my training, then I'll find something...' She was going to say 'closer to home', but it struck her that maybe this place had begun to feel like a kind of home. 'I'll find something else,' she said. Though that didn't sit well either.

'I reckon you're turning into a wee Scotch lassie,' he said in a terrible Scottish accent.

Alice had learned enough to know that no one living here would ever call themselves 'Scotch', but she kept that to herself. Bastian had a fingertip on the plastic thistle pinned to her frock and was hungrily taking in her dress, his eyes adazzle. 'It really suits you.'

'Shut up.' She shoved his hand away, wanting not to smile. It shouldn't be that easy. 'You didn't even wish me luck, or wave me off or anything,' she said.

'I know. I had a lot on my mind, trying out for the cardiology programme. Your dad's been coaching me for these interviews coming up, you know?'

'Yeah, I know. He's such a great guy.' She tried to keep the irony out of her voice but it slipped through.

'He really is,' he confirmed, earnestly. 'Listen, Alice, you go do your party. I'll wait out in the Merc. Maybe, if you're not too tired afterwards, we could talk, yeah?'

She looked at him, crumpled and forlorn, obviously frazzled from the dash up the motorway.

'Did you eat?' she huffed in surrender.

'Not one bite since Manchester.'

'Come on then,' she sighed, shaking her head. 'We'll see if Carenza can fit you in at the top table. But then you have to go home.'

'Fine, one wee bitty o' haggis and I'll leave yee in peace.' He was doing the silly accent again.

Alice led the way back to the ballroom, not at all pleased, her arms folded over her dress, wondering what on earth the town were going to make of the new doctor bringing a gatecrasher to their special party.

Bastian skipped to catch up with her, trying to slip an arm around her shoulders which she repeatedly shrugged off, just as the lobby's revolving doors spun and Cary Anderson, dressed head to toe in his Highland outfit and clutching a homemade posy of purple heather, a peace offering for Alice, spilled into the grand hallway, his kilt swinging.

Staggering to a halt, he had to squint to confirm that what he was seeing was real. Alice, beautiful in white, and a guy in tuxedo evening dress slipping his arm around her as they went into the ballroom together.

'Alice,' he breathed in defeat.

He was out of time and out of luck, and he really ought to hurry home and change before anyone spotted him.

27

Bastian had 'accidentally' accepted the offer of a glass of Talisker during the toasts and downed it before he realised his mistake, or that's what he told Alice when they'd eaten the really very delicious food and heard all the toasts and poems and songs, and now it was impossible for him to get behind a wheel safely.

She'd groaned in frustration at his pleading face as he'd said, 'Let me borrow your sofa?' and she'd dragged him out before the dancing began, a real shame because she'd wanted to try this Scottish country dancing that everyone talked about. Gracie had taught her how to do a St Bernard's Waltz one night after clinics, 'just in case', and it hadn't actually been all that hard. Well, *that* had been a waste of time.

She gave Bastian the spare blanket from the cup-board and told him he'd better be gone by morning, and she stomped to her own room and wrestled her-self out of the dress and into her pyjamas, before throwing herself onto the bed, furious with Bastian, her father, and most of all, furious with herself for being far too bloody nice to him.

Maybe it was the whisky's fault – she'd taken one too, and then another – but she was fast asleep by eleven, or was it the having someone else there, making her feel, if not safe, exactly, just *not alone* for the first time in ages?

Whatever it was, sleep claimed her fast, and as she drifted off she dreamed about the steps of the waltz she'd learned, picturing how nice it would have been to move across that ballroom floor once the cranachan desserts were eaten and the lights had been dimmed.

She remembered hearing the local women making wild cries of '*heee-uch!*' as the music started up, just as she was making her way out into the night, picking up a lovely bunch of heather that someone must have dropped on their way to the party and which Bastian almost trod on. The posy was by her bedside now and maybe it was the wild mountain scent making her dream about the music and the lights, filling in with her imagination what she hadn't witnessed with her own eyes, and the whole dream became a vivid cross between a *Bridgerton* ball scene and the wedding ceilidh in *Four Weddings and a Funeral*.

In the dream, she wasn't dancing with Gracie on the Dettolled floors of the surgery's waiting room after hours, and it wasn't Bastian in his tuxedo either.

There was a man taking her hands, Cary Anderson, all dressed in lovely old-fashioned clothes, smelling clean and woody, and he was pressing a flat palm to the base of her spine, turning her around and around like a doll in a jewellery box.

Cary fixed her with his lovely darkest brown eyes and it was so easy to gaze back at him, and they turned and they turned, and everyone stepped aside until they were the only ones on the dancefloor, and the big clock in the corner, Cary's clock, was ticking down to midnight, only they were spinning too fast, and Cary was saying something about it being time to go, he was tired of Highland life, he really should be leaving, and Bastian was there with Mum and Dad and all their friends from her graduation party and they were all pointing at something and shouting, but she couldn't hear them. Suddenly Cary, who had always felt somehow ephemeral to her, unreal, and impermanent, probably because men like him couldn't possibly be true, had danced himself right up into the air, his heels up over his head, and it was all Alice could do to hold onto his hands to stop him flying away entirely. The clock started striking and its case sprang open and even though she'd held on with all her might, Cary was sucked into it, disappearing with a scream of her name. *'Alice!'*

'Alice, wake up, you're having one of your nightmares. Alice.'

She couldn't open her eyes, didn't want to face the night, so she stayed still under the covers, flexing her hands, trying to regain the sensation of dream-Cary's touch.

'Go back to sleep,' said Bastian, climbing onto the bed and lying down beside her. 'It's OK. I've got you.'

* * *

The morning brought a headache the likes of which Alice had never felt before. Whisky, she told herself, was not something she'd acclimatise to, and neither was – she jumped up in the bed – sniffing the air, Bastian's cologne, and, she sniffed again, cooking smells?

Padding to the kitchen, hand shielding her eyes

from even the weak light from the cooker hood, she stopped at the sight.

'You're awake!' he said, smiling brightly.

'You're still here.'

'I didn't want to leave you. You slept so fitfully. I needed to know you were OK.'

There was a pan sizzling on the hob. Bastian, in his baggy designer sweats over his running gear, was frying... something pink and square.

'Lorne sausage,' he told her. 'And get this, the woman in the Post Office shop called these *morning rolls*, not baps, not just rolls, but morning rolls. It's all so wonderfully Scottish.'

'You went out?'

'You didn't have any meat, or anything really, in your fridge. Your freezer's empty too, did you know that?'

'Of course I did.'

'Here.' He'd made coffee and poured her a cup into steamy, frothed milk.

'I have a cafetiere?' Alice opened cupboards, wondering what else was hiding in here that she hadn't discovered yet.

'No, I bought it at the hardware counter in the animal feed store.'

'We have a hardware counter?'

'It's right beside the pig pellets.'

Alice took the coffee and drank. It was perfect.

Bastian served up the flat sausage slice onto the soft white, buttered bread roll and presented it to her alongside a bottle of brown sauce held against his arm like a sommelier presenting the vintage champagne. 'The woman in the shop recommended a bottle of this to accompany our breakfast.'

She shook her head at it, then, thinking again how it might be just the thing to sort her out, took the bottle and splodged a brown blob onto the sausage. The first bite was a sensation. She couldn't help smiling back up at Bastian who was grinning at her as she chewed.

'You look famished,' he said.

'You're not eating?'

Bastian hadn't even tried to sit at the table with her. 'You said I should go first thing, so...' He hiked a thumb over his shoulder to the door.

'Oh, for God's sake, sit down and have some breakfast. It's miles to Manchester.'

'Thanks,' he said, hopping straight into a seat at the little Formica table and assembling his own sandwich.

He looked so contented Alice almost forgave him for storming into her special party.

'After this, you could show me your surgery?' He took a wolfish bite.

'What? Really?'

'I'd love to see where you work. Your dad showed me the picture of you with your name plate on your door. You really deserve it, you know? All this. You worked harder than any of us.' He took another big bite and threw his eyes wide. 'Woah, what do they put in this stuff?'

Alice had to agree, it was delicious.

For a few moments they ate in silence, like old times.

'You see Dad a lot, then?'

Bastian's jaws slowed in their chewing. 'Umm, I wouldn't say *a lot*.'

'What's she like? Kimberly?'

Bastian made a face that asked if she was sure she really wanted to know.

'Tell me.'

'OK. She's super-smart, and destined for the very top.'

'How old is she?'

'I don't know.'

'Bastian.'

'I think she's thirty-seven.'

It wasn't exactly a surprise to know she was only

nine years older than her, but it still felt like a welt rising on her skin as though she'd been struck. 'Ouch,' said Alice.

'I know. I don't get it either.' Bastian topped up her coffee and poured his own, black, no sugar. This all felt comfortingly like things had way back in the beginning.

Alice looked away to where her dress hung in its bag over her bedroom door. Bastian must have picked it up from her bedroom floor while she slept. 'I need to return my frock before work,' she said.

'Do you have to go to work today?'

'I'm a GP, Bastian.' It felt amazing to tell him that. 'But, no, I've no clinic today, only paperwork and the nurse practitioner's weekend lab samples to sort and send away.'

'I wish we could just hang out all day,' he said, unfolding the newspaper he'd bought himself. 'I miss you.'

Instead of replying she drank her coffee.

'Bastian?' she said eventually, trying not to look at his dark lashes framing his pretty blue eyes.

'Yeah?' he said, absently, as he perused the headlines like he was going to make himself comfortable, like this was his place back home where she'd stay over when she wasn't on a run of nights.

'That night, with the thing?' she went on.

'Hmm?'

'You remember the thing that happened?'

He looked squarely at her across the table. 'I remember.'

'You didn't want me to tell anyone about what happened?'

'Do we have to go over this?' He put down the last of his sandwich and stood, leaning against the kitchen drawers.

'I made a terrible mistake that night...' she began.

'Alice, forget about it. I fixed it. Nobody knew. End of.'

'I could have easily filled in a Datix report about it.'

'No.' He folded his arms.

'I could have got in big trouble if anyone found out we covered it up.'

'I was fine,' he said, dismissively.

'No, I said *I* could have got in trouble.'

He looked at her like he wasn't understanding. Alice's brain ticked over, trying to replay how it had all unfolded.

'Hold on, did you stop me reporting myself because of how it might reflect on *you*?'

He shrugged. 'Everyone knows we're a couple. It's

best to appear squeaky clean, you know that. Besides, your dad would never have forgiven me if I'd let you get yourself into trouble. Finish your coffee. Then you can show me your surgery, yeah?'

Alice tipped her head, thinking she couldn't have heard that right. '*Dad* would never forgive *you*? *I* never forgave *myself*! I've been worrying all this time that I'm a danger to my patients. I've been covering up my own concerns, *my* fears! And all you were worried about was staying on Dad's good side and looking squeaky clean?'

'He'll head up my surgical team one day soon, and you know, if you'd just let me look after you, he'll be my father-in-law...'

She stood up so sharply the chair fell back and hit the floor in a crash. 'Dad told you to come and look after me last night? That's what you said, right? That he was worried about me?'

'That's right.' Bastian looked down his body over his crossed arms to his crossed ankles.

'Bastian? Did you tell Dad about what I did at the hospital that night? About you making me hide it all this time?'

He made an attempt at denial, but Alice saw through it. 'Bastian! Why?'

'He needs to know if you're making mistakes, if *a*

Hargreave* is making mistakes! I was protecting his reputation.'

'Oh my God!'

'And yours, of course. Obviously!' He threw his arms in the air. This was the sign she was being unreasonable, her signal she'd gone too far.

She peered at him now, assessing. 'You always do that.'

'What?' he said in a weary way. 'What am I always doing, Alice? Daydreaming? Not looking after myself properly? Hmm? Sleepwalking through my shifts?'

'Shut up!'

'Almost killing a patient?'

'Get out!'

She'd yelled so loudly the whole apartment block must have heard but she didn't care, she was shaking so violently and on the verge of crying. She tried physically shoving him towards the door.

Bastian, barely moving, was looking at her in concern. 'Alice?'

'Why did I let you in here? I was doing fine! I was getting better.'

She was grabbing his coat now, reaching for his bag by the door, his keys and newspaper, piling them up in his arms.

'OK, I'll go. You can call me when you've calmed down,' he told her as she held the door open for him.

'Out!'

She got him into the corridor.

'You have to move on, Alice. You have to let it go,' he said, shoving his face through the gap in the door even as it closed.

She flattened her hand across his face and shoved it. 'And you have to break up with my father, and you have to stop using me to get to him.'

'You're not going to tell him that, are you?' he was saying through the gaps in her fingers.

With one last shove she got rid of him and slammed the door shut, sliding to the floor as soon as the latch clicked.

* * *

An hour before, Cary had been pacing in his woodworking yard at the back of his cottage where the gnarled old apple trees were still bare-branched and the sawdust swirled in the cold, damp breeze, catching in the cobwebby corners. This was where, usually, he'd be contented to work from dawn until dark.

He'd barely slept. He'd phoned his mother. He'd

attempted a cabinetry job but couldn't get the planes right. His eye must be off, his hands too stiff from clenching his fists in frustration.

That's when he'd heard the voices, the guffawing and the gossiping over the other side of the high fence that faced onto the crossroads just off Cairn Dhu high street.

'It's you,' someone was saying. 'Alice's... guest?'

Cary knew it was Gracie from the surgery from the salacious tone in her voice.

'Ah, yes! You were there last night. I never forget a face. I'm Bastian. You work with Alice, don't you? Did you enjoy the party?'

'Gracie, surgery receptionist. Aye, it was certainly interesting,' she replied in a rush. 'Are you, eh, sticking around for a wee while?'

'I think so,' the man was saying, cocksure. Cary hated him even though he'd never hated anyone in his life. 'Spending some quality time with my Alice. In fact, I'm looking for some breakfast bits so I can surprise her, poor girl's barely slept...'

Cary had to listen while Gracie, evidently flustered and a bit giddy, filled him in on every shop in town.

'Has Alice got any days off coming up soon?' Bastian was asking. 'Some leave she needs to take?'

'She's got some Thursdays, here and there, and Saturdays, of course. What have you got in mind?'

He'd reeled Gracie in like a salmon, but it was Cary who felt torn through with a barbed hook.

'I was thinking of whisking her away to a romantic spa retreat. She's exhausted, poor thing. Too much work.'

'Oh, well, you've come to the right place!' Gracie's voice bubbled with excitement. 'There's loads of nice spas round here. Castle McLeod does a couple's retreat with yoga and massages and that kind of thing. That's where I get my nails done.' Cary pictured her displaying her fingers to him.

'Wow!' he was saying, and not all too kindly, Cary thought.

Gracie carried on, oblivious. 'If you tell Sonya on the booking line that Gracie from the surgery sent you, she'll do you a discount.'

'I'll do that. Yep, things are going to change now that I'm around. She's not going to slip back into old habits.'

Cary noted the silent pause, guessed that even in a fit of gossip-gathering excitement Gracie might detect something was seriously off about this guy.

'Right,' she was saying slowly.

'Can't have her burning out up here in the Highlands when, soon enough, she'll be heading back home with me, back to the bosom of her family.'

'In Manchester?' Gracie had definitely got the measure of him now. Cary found her change in tone surprisingly gratifying.

'Yup, when her stint here's finished and we get her back to reality. So!' He clapped his hands. 'This way for the Post Office shop, you said, yeah?'

'Aye. That way.'

And he was off, on his way, the sound of his self-satisfied whistling carrying across town as everyone else slept off their hangovers or nursed their aching feet.

Cary, never one to act on impulse previously, took himself straight into the cottage and up the stairs, hauling his suitcase down from the top of the wardrobe, and without anything else in his head but the vision of Alice with Bastian's arm around her shoulders, he pulled clothes from their hangers and threw them in the case. It was time to go.

28

The postman rarely trekked all the way up to the cruive, tending to dump Finlay's mail at the rangers' station, but today there'd been the matter of a signature and a photograph to acquire; the letter was that important.

He'd found Finlay sitting dejectedly on the snail's shell curve of the stormwall some way down the mountain from his hut, untouched coffee and sweet tablet by his side.

By the time the postie was tramping back down the path, chuckling at the photographic evidence of delivery (a dour, irritated Finlay protesting whether a picture was really necessary), Finlay had the envelope torn open.

He'd been expecting the notice of probate on his mother's estate from the solicitors, Misters Giles and Knox of Edinburgh, and now it was in his hands, and there were some calculations attached which, even now that the solicitors had deducted their fees, made Finlay sweat.

How could the little house he'd been brought up in, with its cabbage-patch garden and creaky floor-boards, have been worth this much?

'People are mad,' he'd exclaimed, looking at the bottom line, his inheritance.

What he hadn't been expecting was a second letter, handwritten on the blue-lined notepaper he recognised so well. Before he unfolded the single page, he brought it to his nose, wondering if it still carried his mum's soap and talcum powder scent. It did not, and he found himself wanting to cry.

She'd been gone for a whole year now, leaving her son the last of the Morlich line. Her influence, however, lived on within him: in his straight spine, 'Good posture is the mark of a good man, Finlay'; in his unheard prayers, 'Every night, without fail, remember'; in his rebellious appetite for confectionary, 'Need I remind you, young man, greed is a sin.'

And yet he missed her.

He opened her letter and read.

Finlay,

I instructed this pair of penny-pinchers and filchers to forward this note to you <u>unopened and unread</u> at the conclusion of all matters concerning your late father's estate, now your estate. I trust that is what has happened, and so I'll be brief.

I'm aware of my shortcomings as a mother and won't go on about them here, but if it aids you, I would be heartsore to leave this earth without letting you know that I am sorry.

Perhaps I could have been more lenient, as your father always wished, but when a mother has a child as obtuse and rigid as I have, it is natural to fear for him and to steer towards <u>discipline</u>, rather than other misguided parents might do and <u>indulge</u> their child.

I spent a good deal of time attempting to shape you into a useful and polite young man. Only you can decide if I ever succeed in that mission, but for what it is worth, as much as I have scolded you, I have also loved you in my own way.

Finlay let his hands fall into his lap. This was his mother to a tee, a bewildering blend of strictness and scripture, faint praise and human frailty, and yet this was the first time she was telling him she loved him at all.

He'd had very little idea of it growing up, when what had mattered most to her was impressing the congregation at the kirk teas and protesting the opening of yet another betting shop, or whatever the bee in her Sunday best bunnet was that week.

Yet she'd fed him (sensibly), clothed him (respectably), and taught him about living in moderation (fiercely), and his father, a rational, good-hearted man (weak-hearted, it had turned out, when he died all too early), had made sure he knew the name of every moth and beetle in the kirkyard. It had been an education.

Finlay hadn't thought to complain about any of it. It was simply the way things were. Nothing much changed when he told them at twenty-three that he liked men. They received the news of his sexuality with the same weary acceptance with which they accepted his school report cards and the rejected job applications or in the way they let him grow wildflower cuttings and tiny saplings in jars all along every windowsill in the house.

'She loved me, in her own way,' he told himself, not sure if it really mattered any more. He'd believed he'd made his peace with her influence over his life, and *not* at that maudlin funeral service on the out-skirts of Edinburgh, but out here on the hills.

Now there was this trouble with probate con-cluding and him having a vast deal of money to dis-tribute. Mountain rescue helicopters always need money. Then there were the Highland rewilding projects he took an interest in. They'd be glad of a chunk, surely.

He bit at a big square of tablet and braced himself for more of his mother's words.

> *You have today come into your money, Finlay, and I am pleased for you, as your father would be. Now that I'm with him, I have one last wish for you.*
> *Do not dispose of this money.*
> *I may not understand you, but I <u>know</u> you. You'll baulk at the amount and want to give it away as fast as you can, thinking yourself 'rich enough', as you've been telling me ever since you took that job in the Highlands, but this is your opportunity to make a <u>real life</u> for yourself; a meaningful, connected life.*
> *Now, I'm not telling you to store up your treasures. Only, spend them wisely on <u>some-</u>*

thing that will see you bloom, and so you may enjoy long life on the earth.
This is my very last wish for you,
Mum

Finlay's coffee went cold in its cup that day as he sat out on the stormwall, letting his mother's words sink in then blow away again on the chill wind.

He was still here, he told himself, looking for comfort. *He* still had his mountain dominion.

As if to remind him this didn't come without its downsides, a party of hillwalkers approached his coffee spot and hailed him for a chat.

They seemed sensible enough, experienced with their map and compass (he made them demonstrate as much, and whether this had offended them or not wasn't any of his concern). They told him they'd walked this route many times, and so he'd allowed them to go on without even parting with one of his leaflets, only warning them to be safely inside their bivvy by six tonight because there was freezing fog forecast and that would mean sharply falling temperatures and low cloud that could sit over the range well into tomorrow afternoon, maybe even for days if they were unlucky. The party went on their way and he watched them go until they were colourful dots, like pins on a map, in the far distance.

His mother's letter was folded in his pocket and, with it being ten o'clock, he figured he'd better begin his morning rounds on the community paths, picking up rubbish and stopping *heid-the-baw* hikers (which is as unflattering a nickname as it sounds) arriving with neither map, provisions or a plan, so he could send them back down to sea level where they belonged. That's just what he needed, he thought. A good chance at a roaring out. That'd help.

Speaking of life down there... He lifted his binoculars once he hit the well-trodden heath path near the rangers' station, and scanned the town below, with its roof tiles gleaming in the low winter morning light.

The library was opening. A good reminder he had books to return, and there'd be new releases to browse. The chimney was smoking at the police station. The bank was of course shut. And the repair shed, not that he was all that interested, was... hold on!

Finlay adjusted the focusing ring, pulling into sharper view Murray McIntyre, it had to be him, turning out from the gap in the mill house wall and making for the high street. Who else wore white trousers and a cream jumper with a long cream puffa coat while out walking a big silly old black Labrador – currently spinning round and round on her lead like a pup?

He shouldn't look. There was Gillie Fell still to sweep for litter, and that steep section of path by the bins where everyone *must insist* on slipping that still needed salting because the temperature was unlikely to rise all day, what with that white haze of icy cloud cover sinking lower over the snowy tops of the mountains on either side of the valley.

One last glance and, painfully inevitably, there was that young builder, a bright-orange stick figure from up here, bounding towards Murray, fussing with the mutt. The builder was opening his arms, gesturing for Murray to step in for a hug.

Finlay let the binoculars drop, turning away.

Do something that will see you bloom and enjoy long life on the earth. His mother's words resounded like the old kirkyard bell in his head.

'I'll *bloom* right here where I'm planted, thanks very much!' he huffed. 'All by my bloomin' self!' and he hiked off along the path.

29

Kurt hugging him had recalled everything about their date that had come so very close to being perfect, and even now, after ten days, Murray regretted their evening being interrupted.

Though, if it hadn't been, he wouldn't have the pups. Maybe it was for the best.

'You are walking the dog,' Kurt pointed out, needlessly.

'I am,' Murray confirmed, also pointlessly.

'I have been thinking, Murray, about you and me...'

Everything about Kurt's lovely mouth, his lovely accent, his personality, it was all so nice and so appealing, but Murray couldn't deny something had come between them since the date, something that made him hope Kurt wasn't about to suggest they try going out again.

'I like you a lot...' Kurt was saying, his smile breaking sweetly, all his emotions on show and nothing hidden. All the qualities Murray had shied away from in the past.

He'd been afraid of keen men. But Kurt liked him, plain and simple, and had Murray run a mile in the opposite direction? No. He'd tried finding out if there was something more between them, other than fancying him a ridiculous amount. In the last few days, when he allowed himself to be honest, it wasn't Kurt's generous feelings and easy manner that put him off attempting a second date; it was simply that they weren't all that well suited.

'Listen, Kurt,' Murray interrupted, 'I like you too, a lot, you're gorgeous, actually, but...'

'I think we should be friends,' both men said at the same time.

'What?' Kurt laughed. 'You're passing up on this?'

This sent Murray into a fit of throaty laughter, which, were a particularly sensitive person straining their ears for it, might be heard resonating across the mountain range.

'*Hey!* You were giving me the brush off too!'

Murray said, landing a friendly fist on Kurt's arm. Murray ignored the accompanying intrusive memory of the inked skin and taut muscle hidden away under Kurt's padded winter layers.

'Oh, well,' Kurt said laughingly. 'Friends is good.'

They'd stayed like this for a while, chatting about the dogs, and the builders' progress on the extension, how the scaffolding was coming down soon, and Kurt's plans to leave in a few days. His next posting would be in a villa complex in Andalucía.

'Sounds terrible,' Murray mugged. 'Won't you miss all this?' He was pointing to the low clouds rolling in, but Kurt was gazing right into his eyes, making a small bite on his bottom lip.

'I'll miss it,' Kurt said, before stepping close and delivering a kiss to Murray's mouth, lingering the teensiest millisecond longer than was strictly friendly, and then he was off, on his way to the construction site, leaving Murray glad they'd talked and (because he's not made of wood) a tiny bit giddy from the kiss.

However, the light-headedness from Kurt's goodbye was obliterated almost immediately by a text message making his phone ping. It was from Ally.

> Incoming in about 10 seconds.
> Barbara is on her way to her office
> to phone you! We just had the
> morning huddle and your name
> might have been brought up to take
> on some upcoming freelance jobs.

Murray's instincts were to immediately swipe his phone off, but she'd anticipated this.

> PICK UP! And say YES to anything
> she offers you. P.S. You owe me big
> time!!! This is your return ticket
> back into the world!

He didn't have time to reply, because sure enough his phone was ringing with Barbara Huber's name on the screen next to the descriptor 'Big Boss'.

'Y'ello!' he answered, stupidly. *Since when did he answer calls like that?*

'Murray? It's Barbara, but I suspect you knew that,' said a sharp, smart woman with a sharp, smart German accent, 'since your sister has forgotten the office walls are made of glass and I can see her texting you.'

'Oh!'

'And now she's staring in at me through the glass,

and now I'm waving, and... yup, there she goes, back to work.'

Part of Murray cringed for his interfering twin, because she did *not* want to piss off Huber, but part of him loved her all the more for trying to wangle whatever this was about to be.

'Yeah, Ally mentioned something about freelance work,' Murray confessed, gritting his teeth as Nell decided now was the time and this was the high street lamppost to do her morning wee against.

Barbara didn't mince her words.

There were three contracts on the table. Future Proof Planet needed overseers for transferring funds from Switzerland to new community projects in various spots around the globe, and all of them required an experienced person to accompany them and get the projects' initial phases off the ground.

This had been one of Murray's favourite perks of the job: travelling all over the place, meeting people, seeing the world, learning new sustainability strategies.

'I know you made it clear you were never coming back to HQ...'

'That's right, I can't,' he said.

'You were always competent, Murray. A safe pair of hands. A people person. *That's* why we hired you.'

He heard that change in intonation. She was telling him he hadn't been brought in as a mere perk of the job for Andreas.

'And you know,' Barbara went on, confidingly, 'Andreas Favre won't be with the charity for much longer.'

'Really? Why?'

'Strictly between ourselves? He's been head-hunted by David's company.'

Her tone conveyed her feelings about that. She'd lost her right-hand man to Andreas's billionaire boyfriend, David Zoros, and his space tourism firm.

Murray let that sink in. David had been a major supporter of Future Proof Planet for a long time, appeasing his conscience (and avoiding the taxman), by giving millions in donations to the charity. Ultimately, Andreas Favre had sold out and turned corporate for a rich old space junk salesman. Maybe every eco-warrior CEO has their price, thought Murray, but it would never be him sleeping with (and in the pay of) one of the biggest polluters on earth.

'You don't have to agree now, but I hope I can tempt you by saying the first posting is to an ocean-cleaning co-op on the beaches of Bali.'

Murray would be mad not to accept right away. Nell, however, had her lead tangled around the lamppost and was now bouncing for joy at the sight of Cary's wandering cat, Dinah, over the road, as much of a fluffball as it was mean and hissing. He struggled to keep the phone to his ear while untangling the barking dog.

At that moment Cary's truck pulled up alongside the cat and Murray only half-observed the carpenter getting the feline into the passenger seat beside him and driving off at speed towards the town limits.

'I'll think about it.'

'I will need a decision for HR in the next fortnight. I'll send over the project files for you to look over. And Murray?'

He straightened up, holding tight to the lead.

'Your sister fought hard for you in today's meeting. I won't keep these avenues open for you forever.'

'Got it. I appreciate you...'

Barbara had hung up the call.

'Bali?' Murray mused out loud, not that Nell was listening. 'What would I do with you and the puppers if I was sent to Bali?'

Nell didn't have an answer for that, but she did reckon searching for that disappearing cat along the high street was a good idea. Murray braced tight on her lead to control her.

'What you need, Nell, is a good, long, calming...'

Murray scanned the town and the mountain vista beyond, his eyes lighting on the boulder pass that led to Finlay's cottage, '...walkies?'

Nell, in her heartfelt agreement, dragged him off the pavement, into the slow-moving traffic and right across the street. A hill walk was what they both needed.

* * *

Up on the pass, minding his business, through binoculars, Finlay hadn't caught Kurt's kiss goodbye, but he had clocked the determined strides Murray was making, right this second, up the hill path towards him with that besom of a dog, and they were already drawing level with the rangers' station carpark.

There was only one reason Murray would be marching that daft mutt up the mountain, and Finlay had no intention of being found when he came knocking, looking for an adoptive dog-dad.

He zipped his coat and hightailed it for the line of low cloud now sitting down fully over the upper slopes and obscuring everything there with freezing droplets of fog. He'd hide out until his mountain was his own again.

Finlay didn't have the presence of mind to stop and examine any other reasons he feared being in Murray's presence, but if he'd taken his time, his concerns would be numbered: one, Murray was infuriating; two, Murray was excessively braw to look at and very intriguing; and three, Murray wasn't interested in him one iota, and that stung quite a lot.

In his haste to do a runner, Finlay didn't entertain any of this stuff and, just as fatefully, the fleeing Finlay didn't witness Nell slipping her collar and bounding like a seal on legs, her hindquarters undulating with excitement as she broke away, her tail helicoptering with the sheer joy of being free, an itinerant dog once more. He also didn't see poor Murray, not a natural hillwalker by any stretch of the imagination, trudging exhaustedly behind, wheezing the wayward mutt's name (and a number of other more colourful names as well), just as the clouds were sinking down further over the hills with the weight of their freezing raindrops.

30

Somehow Alice had made it to work, and somehow she'd dodged Gracie, who'd looked positively bursting to talk with her when she'd pushed through the doors and headed straight to the sample-sorting bench in the nurse practitioner's room.

All she had to do was put the different patient sample tubes in the correct envelopes and posting bags for the collection driver who'd be here at one, and in order to do that she had to *not* think about Bastian, or the fact he'd told her own father the thing she was most ashamed of in the whole world, her biggest secret. Their big secret. The terrible thing Bastian had told her never to tell anyone, and now her father knew, and he'd sent Bastian up here to check she wasn't losing her mind. And she couldn't truthfully say that she wasn't.

She sorted through the sample bottles, organising them by sticker colours, checking the attached docket matched the name on the stickers. The nurse's handwriting was clear but still, Alice had a hard time focusing.

How could he? And he'd smarmed his way back in and slept in her bed last night! Thank God nothing happened. But, Alice dreaded to think what could have happened if he had not made the mistake of banging on about his special relationship with her dad, and all his ambitions to be part of the family. Maybe they'd have had a good day? Maybe he'd have wheedled his way into staying another night?

'Ugh!' She brought a bottle closer to her eyes. 'Is that McDonagh or McDonald?' She couldn't tell. 'Come on, Alice,' she told herself. 'Red goes in the white bag, orange ones go in individual white envelopes, or is it the blue bag...?' She didn't seem to know, even though she'd done this task last Monday and she hadn't made any mistakes then, or had she?

The tubes on the table before her seemed to lose their shape, and she felt the pins and needles feeling at the back of her neck, the one that made it difficult to hold her head straight. 'Oh.' She bent double, head to her knees. 'I was getting better,' she told no one at all, her chest tightening.

The knock at the door brought her round and she found herself on her knees on the floor. 'I'm fine, Gracie. Let me concentrate on this...'

'It's me,' tolled Dr Millen, as he opened the door. 'Now, are we going to talk about all of this, or am I sending you home on leave?'

Alice looked at him through teary eyes and he locked the door and came to sit cross-legged before her. '*Ooft*, my knees! Well, now we're both down here, and there's very little chance of me getting back up any time soon, you'd better start explaining why my new doctor is crying on the floor, surrounded by poo, blood and wee samples.'

* * *

Alice's words, once unstoppered, came out in a gush, and since she was ending her career, she figured she might as well unburden herself fully.

'It was about,' she stopped to think, 'about nine months ago now. I was in General, and a patient who'd come back in for wound care after surgery suddenly turned morbidly unwell in Bastian's clinic.'

'Bastian was the fellow that turned up last night at the Burns Supper?' the old doctor confirmed.

'That's right. Well, this patient, it turned out they were having a major internal haemorrhage and needed theatre right away. Me and Bastian were supposed to be clocking off, but of course he scrubbed in immediately and headed in to support the surgeon and I stupidly offered to assist and observe, even though I was tired. We both were. The surgeon asked me to start the major haemorrhage protocol...'

'Preparing for a transfusion?'

'That's right. I had the patient's blood tested for a match with the donor blood, and I was bringing the bags down myself to hand over but I... I don't know how it happened...'

Dr Millen wasn't saying a word, only listening like she was a patient in his office and this was a normal consultation.

'I get... caught up in these dreams. I get distracted, or confused. And before I knew it, I wasn't coming down the stairs from the blood bank, I was in theatre scrubbed in and in charge of the instruments, counting them in and out and imagining myself miscounting and how awful it would be to leave a clip in the patient's stomach and how it would be all my fault, and... I was still daydreaming about how I'd break it to the family, telling them that I shouldn't even have been assisting, I wasn't qualified, and that's when I realised I was just standing there being shouted at by Bastian, outside the theatre, and he was dragging me into the scrubs room and barking at me, showing me the labels on the blood as if I was crazy, which I... I really think I must have been, because I was about to give A plus to an O minus patient and in the state they were in...'

'A haemolytic transfusion reaction could have killed them,' Dr Millen finished her sentence gravely.

Alice swallowed hard. 'Yes.' Now she knew how criminals felt when they turned themselves in at the police station after years on the run because they'd been unable to keep their secrets any longer.

'That's a Never Event,' she told him, pleadingly, hoping he'd berate her, as if his censure might set her free from the guilt. 'Something that should never, *ever* happen.'

'But... it didn't happen,' the old doctor said.

'And we have a duty of candour to tell the patient about the mistake, to confess. I didn't fill in a Datix report. I was a coward...'

'Woah, hold your horses! Was anyone hurt?'

He didn't seem to understand what she was telling him. 'Well, no, but...'

'Did anything actually happen that you needed to report to the patient or to officially log?'

'I shouldn't have got so far as bringing that blood to the theatre door. Bastian sent me home, and he sorted out the mess.'

'And yet you learned from it?'

'I don't know, I never went on a blood run again to find out.'

Millen was fixing her with an impatient stare that said she knew what he meant.

'I've tried to catch myself when it's happening, the daydreaming. Sometimes it works...'

'And is this something you're concerned about happening here? Is that what happened last night before the Address? Is that why you are on the floor in here?'

She let her head hang. It told him all he needed to know.

'Are you concerned enough about it to allow me to mentor you with this in mind?' he said. 'A weekly check-in, daily, if you like, logging when it has happened, and what triggered it? Maybe it happens at times you feel especially pressured? We could ascertain what tasks or conditions are associated with it, try to get to the root of it...'

'I've daydreamed all my life,' she confessed. 'I

should never have gone into medicine, but it was expected of me and...'

'But the catastrophising? The panic? Did that happen to you as a child as well?'

She shook her head. 'It started when I began my training. And it just got worse.'

'And now? Since you came here?' Millen asked.

'It's been less, much less, since I got here, but it's not gone away.'

'OK, well, now we have a baseline to work from. Let's see what observations we can record, what diagnoses, and what improvements we can make.'

Alice couldn't believe what she was hearing.

'You're not going to report me? Fire me?'

'Caring about your mistakes makes you a good doctor,' he said simply.

'But hiding them?' she said, tears rolling down her cheeks now the words were out.

'I wonder if you were *persuaded* into hiding what happened, against your better judgement? However, we must remember no one was harmed. You caught it before anything happened.'

'Bastian did.'

'Who is this fellow anyway?'

'He was my boyfriend back home. He's in wound

care. He wants to be a consultant in post-cardiothoracic surgical wound care, and I'm sure he will be.'

'Well, he sounds like a very helpful person to have in your corner. You're very fortunate to have him.'

Alice was about to exclaim how she didn't have him but Millen was still talking, telling her about his supportive wife and how she would be waiting at home for him come seven o'clock with his casserole and whisky ready.

'Fine woman. I'd be lost without her,' he went on. 'We must look after the ones who look after us. A doctor's life is no' easy, but it would be damn near impossible without our special people supporting us, eh? You cannot do this job for another thirty or forty years without a strong network of support.'

Instead of thinking of Bastian, or her parents, or any of her colleagues or mentors, she thought of one person only, Cary Anderson, and how all she really wanted to do now, after a long sleep and a shower maybe, was fall into his arms and tell him how much she valued him.

'Dr Hargreave, you need to put this behind you, and you must remember this, above all else you've learned in your training; our motto *do no harm* must also be extended to ourselves. Please take care of yourself, Alice. Starting now. I'm dismissing you for the rest of the day. Go get a proper lunch and a good sleep. I'll finish these samples off, and I won't be saying a word to Gracie about any of it.'

His expression was so kindly and his words so sincere, Alice thought she might cry again.

'Now, help me up off this hard floor before I have to be stretchered out of my own surgery.'

31

After a hasty dash uphill, Finlay was dismayed to learn, as he hid behind a rock only a few feet inside the thick Arctic mist, he still had a phone signal, and he knew just who it would be ringing him, but since he was still on shift, he had a duty to pick it up.

'Finlay?' came Murray's voice.

'I'm no' wantin' your dug!'

Murray wasn't playing around, however. He was shouting down the line. 'Nell's slipped her lead and raced off up the boulder pass. I couldn't keep up. I think she's half whippet after all!'

Some of Finlay's rescuer instincts kicked in. 'And where are you?'

'I don't know, somewhere up past your cruive and in between a rocky, thin bit?'

'A rocky, thin bit? Are you meaning the Gillie Fell walls? Did you pass through a wide crevasse onto the upper trail?'

There was silence. Of course, the townie had no idea what any of that meant. 'What can you see?' Finlay yelled.

'Just... cloud.'

'Start making your way down.' Finlay was already heading in Murray's direction, only a matter of thirty minutes downhill then west up the fell trail. If indeed that's where he was.

'But what about Nell? I have to find her, it's freezing up here!'

Finlay could already hear Murray's teeth chittering.

'She's covered in fur and, from the looks of her, she'll come down herself when she smells the town cookin' their dinners.'

This clearly didn't quell Murray's panic. 'No, I think I'll look for her a bit longer. Nell! *Nell!*'

Pulling the phone from his ear, Finlay felt his nervous system shift gears from fraught to frantic.

'I'm telling you, Murray McIntyre, to retrace your steps and *get back down.*'

Finlay moved swiftly. He'd always been nimble like a mountain buck, and he was now deftly covering the distance between his hiding place (*what a bloody stupid thing to do*, he berated himself, *hiding from a man and his dog!*) and Murray's location. Or at least, the place he *hoped* Murray might be, given the fool's scant description of his route.

He muttered all the way, thinking how, when he reached him, Murray wouldn't just be on the receiving end of a safety leaflet and a lecture; this fellow was getting a clip around the ear and roared out for endangering himself, coming up here dressed in stupid white town gear, *and* bothering wildlife with that out-of-control mutt of his.

Before that could happen, he'd have to locate him.

As Finlay descended, expecting to come out of the clouds at any moment, consulting his watch altimeter, he swallowed a hard gulp. He'd come down a good hundred yards and the hill was still engulfed in white fog, and not only that, but freezing, sun-glaring fog too, the likes of which every hillwalker should fear for their lives in.

He knew the drill for when this happened. *Stop in a sheltered place. Report your location to your contact down on the ground. Bivvy up, stove on, sleeping bag if you have one, and sit it out safely.* Because Murray, always underprepared and flighty, wasn't equipped to do *any* of that, Finlay wasn't wasting any time.

'Murray!' he yelled, marching on, leaving behind the ice-scoured rock underfoot and hitting slippery, grassy earth, thin over smoothed rock, knowing that ridiculous man would be well out of his hearing if he really was up in Gillie Fell, but still responding to the deep need within him to yell his name anyway.

'Murray!'

He heard a loud bark somewhere way up behind him where the white was thickest, its echo dampened by the wet air.

'Dammit!'

He had his radio in his hands and the call connected in seconds.

'Scramble A-Team from Cairn Dhu station. There's one man off the paths and in cloud somewhere near Gillie Fell, possibly. Visibility for me is at two metres. Over.'

'A-Team preparing to move out, Finlay. We'll just need the go-ahead from mountain rescue re visibility,' came Jemmy's crackling reply. 'I've no sign of you on our GPS, by the way. Have you yer tracker on? Over.'

'I'll do it now,' said Finlay, still walking fast, consulting his compass in the haze of the low morning sun at his back which shone diffuse through the

cloud, turning the fog into a glaring cottonwool
soup.

However, walking while hurriedly attempting to
stow away his compass in his backpack, and with his
thick gloves on, combined with the difficulty of
keeping hold of his radio and his mobile phone,
proved too much at once and before he knew it, Finlay's phone had dropped to the rocks at his feet. He
lunged for it as it tumbled over wet ground, then
without knowing how, his boots were suddenly out
from under him, his right shoulder hitting the rough
terrain, his face in damp grass, a glove somehow gone,
his hand stung on something and with grit in his
teeth.

He was sliding downhill, something hideous
crunching at his collarbone when he tried to stop
himself. Ten or fifteen feet of ground covered in a
downward slide, he estimated, still unable to stop
himself, and then suddenly his legs were unsup-
ported by the earth, and now his back too.

Out over a precipice he went, and no matter how
he clawed with his fingernails he couldn't prevent
himself going over the drop and into the air, cas-
cading into white nothingness, bracing himself for a
hard landing he didn't know where.

32

Down in the town that morning, the only person known to be missing so far was Cary Anderson, though Senga Gifford had it on good authority he'd left town in a hurry. She'd heard via Tony from the hop-on, hop-off tourist buses, who'd told his cousin, Jean, who'd told her that Cary had loaded up his truck with suitcases this morning, and that he'd mentioned to the lassie at the petrol station in the Garten valley that he was filling up for a long drive, *and* he'd had his little cat with him on the passenger seat.

Alice, who'd left the surgery, instructed by Dr Millen, and decided to take herself out for lunch at the repair shop, received this gossip with dismay as she waited for her coffee at the café counter.

'Bannock?' Rhona asked.

'Lost my appetite,' Alice said, even though a moment ago they'd looked delicious.

'He'll be visiting his mother,' Sachin put in, also at the counter and buttering a toasted bannock for his second breakfast. Mrs Roy, he'd told the little group, had served up his favourite salmon scramble only an hour ago, so no one was to go grassing him up for snacking now.

The repair shop was empty but for some of the volunteers. On Mondays the shed hosted McIntyre's vehicle maintenance and repair sessions out on the gravel drive, and although they were still sparsely attended, being new, the shed still opened to serve food and catch any general repair clients who might happen to call by.

Mortified, Alice had to ask, 'Did Cary say when he was coming back?'

Riled she didn't have this knowledge to impart, Senga made a big deal of pronouncing, 'That's none of our business!' The absolute gall of the woman.

'You'd think he'd have mentioned travel plans to someone at the Burns supper,' put in Rhona innocently.

All eyes turned upon her, and she flinched as

though suddenly found guilty of withholding in-triguing information.

'What?' Rhona protested. 'I only saw him through the window. He was coming runnin' up the drive of the hotel in his kilt. Didn't anybody else see him?'

'And *when* was this?' Senga seemed not to believe her sister, having not witnessed the sight herself.

Rhona shrugged like she wanted everyone's eyes off her, but even Livvie, Roz and McIntyre were crowding round now, to hear more about their loyal repairer.

'When *exactly*?' Alice couldn't help herself, a feeling of sickly dread sliding down her insides. 'Do you remember?'

'I'd say it was just before they served the dinner,' Rhona told her, but glancing between the others. 'He was all dressed in his tartan, and he had a braw posy of purple heathers with him, but, come to think of it...' She paused. 'I never saw him inside.' She looked to her sister. 'Did you?'

'No,' said Alice, answering for everyone, heaviness settling deep in her core. 'I didn't see him.'

Something told her, however, that Cary had seen her, and Bastian too, most likely, and that might have had something to do with the abandoned heather she'd found on the hotel steps.

Alice slipped off the café stool and carried her mug to the quiet spot by the fire where no one could see her absorbing this news. The fire's glow failed to warm her today.

Was it conceited of her to think he'd been coming to the supper for her? Because she'd asked him if he was coming, hinting that she wanted him there? And he'd made the effort because he was the rare sort of man who'd turn up just to support her? A man who couldn't be more unlike Bastian who'd gatecrashed her big moment expecting to see her failing, and to reclaim her like lost luggage.

Had Cary really come for her and left disappointed? Or was that just another of her wild fantasies? A daydream?

God knows she'd thought about him often enough since the last time she saw him. She'd wished they could have the conversation about the therapist all over again, and this time she'd be kinder, and she certainly wouldn't fly off the handle when he told her in that gentle way of his, that he might have an idea to help her feel better.

She still carried the leaflet for that counsellor in her coat pocket. It called to her almost as loudly as her heart was right now asking her where Cary had gone.

She sat with her head in her hands. Why had she snapped at him and scared him off? And why, *why* hadn't she been on her guard when Bastian blind-sided her? She should have pushed him straight out of the hotel's revolving doors on sight, putting him into his precious Merc and slamming the door.

Instead she'd been weak, like her mother allowing her dad to call the shots about their separation, making sure to keep one foot in his familiar, comfortable old life while he had the other in his new life with his young girlfriend.

Just like her mum must have found, Alice had been momentarily overwhelmed by the comfort of Bastian's familiarity, as well as his confidence and brazen charm.

As soon as Alice had left work after her confession to Dr Millen and she'd found that the sky *hadn't* fallen in and the world hadn't stopped turning now that her secret was out, she'd gone looking for Cary's house, not hard when everyone in town knew the man and were only too willing to give her directions, but when she'd banged on his door there'd been no answer. When she'd walked down the vennel to his yard and peered through a gap in the fence, the place was shut up and in darkness. She wasn't sure why she'd done it other than knowing she needed to apologise as soon as possible for the leaflet thing. That, and her growing sense of unease, as though her happiness here in this town was somehow tethered to him.

Sachin's radio, set to the local station, interrupted the non-stop music hour to warn of sudden freezing fog descending over the valley, meaning low visibility for driving, advising residents to 'stay home and enjoy the tunes', before a Proclaimers song resumed, blaring about walking a thousand miles to be with a loved one.

Alice sat very still, wishing Cary safe and warm somewhere, hopefully with his mother, enjoying a short visit home, and *not* putting into motion his idea of going back to Glasgow for good, like he'd mentioned.

The repair shop felt oddly deadened without hope of seeing Cary at his workbench, and so she gathered her things to leave.

'He'll be back soon enough,' came a voice behind her as she made for the door.

Alice turned to find Livvie Cooper fixing her with her ice blue eyes. 'Like you, he belongs in Cairn Dhu.'

Alice had the tiniest inclination to protest that she hadn't the foggiest idea what the woman was on about, but she gave up trying to keep her private hopes private any longer and only smiled sadly, jamming her recently purchased Fair Isle bobble hat down over her ears and making her way out into the cold, thinking how she probably did look very much like a local now.

The radio presenter had been right enough; the whole high street was obscured in thin, shifting bands of white, and it was absolutely freezing. Alice drew her coat closed across her chest and started to hurry towards her flat. The streetlights were blinking into life as she ran, even though it was only a few minutes before noon. Their white glow, diffused through icy particles in the fog, made the ground under her feet shimmer with frosty glitter.

She should buy some fresh cartons of soup at the Post Office shop, she thought, and more of those nice morning rolls. She should change her sheets; even though nothing had happened, they'd still smell of Bastian. She should call her mother and talk with her about healthy boundary-setting with their exes. She should probably try to sleep for a while. Her head buzzed with all the *shoulds*, as always, and it took a while to realise her feet were slowing, and just as she was wondering why on earth she was almost at a standstill, lingering on the street corner in miserable weather such as this, the mists cleared to reveal a door and a sign that read:

Bonnie Blair, Counsellor

Through the window, she could see a woman behind a reception desk working on a computer and there was a sign that seemed to shout out to her.

APPOINTMENTS AVAILABLE

The desk was positioned right by the window in a waiting room set up to resemble a cosy lounge with two white sofas with plump scatter cushions, empty mugs on a tray upon a coffee table, a very prominent box of tissues, leaflets in racks and tasteful artwork with inspirational quotes on the walls.

A sign by the stairs in the depths of the room said in large letters:

Consulting Room Upstairs

The woman, who'd been typing, lifted her head. She wore her hair in a bun and big square, arty specs. She looked back at Alice through the glass and smiled in an open, easy way, as if she somehow knew the reason why a tired-looking Englishwoman would find her feet stuck to the pavement right outside her door.

Without having to think, Alice walked right inside.

33

'Morlich, come in? Morlich? We lost you there, pal. Over.'

It was Jemmy's crackling voice over the radio receiver which lay probably only a few feet from where Finlay lay on the hard ground. The radio may as well have been a hundred miles away for all Finlay could move to go feeling for it in the fog.

'We tried your mobile and you've lost signal on that too. Over.'

His phone? That must be another thing thrown from his hands as he fell.

Finlay raised a shaky hand to his shoulder, gingerly feeling the horrible mass where he knew his arm was out of its socket and he whispered some curse words that would have made Mrs Morlich spin in her grave, God rest her.

He managed to unzip his jacket and reach into his fleece's inside pocket, wondering if he could locate his compass. Then he remembered, he'd had that in his hands as well. It was gone now too, and somehow that was worse than being out of reach of his phone or the radio.

He touched his head where his hat had somehow been taken off. A bit of blood, superficial, so nothing to worry about, but there was a spongy, swollen lump at the back of his skull. That was a little more worrying.

How long had he been out cold? His clothes were covered in a frosty white glitter, though he couldn't see all the way down to his feet, the fog was so thick.

A horrible thought occurred to him. He hadn't told the station that the lost man he'd been in search of was Murray McIntyre. Was it possible Murray might somehow have made it down by himself? He was certain Murray wouldn't abandon that dog on the mountain. Could he have got himself into the same mess as Finlay now found himself in? Murray's life was a great deal more significant than his own, so his rescue should be prioritised. Not that anyone was out looking for Finlay.

That lot down at the shed, the McIntyres, he thought, were utterly devoted to their son. He'd witnessed it with his own eyes just yesterday, in their kitchen with all the dogs and the warmth from the Aga. The memory made him wince in pain, setting off a dreadful piercing sensation in his mangled shoulder.

He should be thinking of saving himself. He should be crawling all over this area to locate the radio, and his backpack with his sweets in, but his body was as heavy as the granite bed he was sprawled out on. He pictured how he must look from way up above, through white cloud: spreadeagled, twisted, over-glittered with sparkling frost.

He had absolutely no notion where on the slope he could be, only that he was somewhere between the snow line above and the dense green line of what mountaineers called the *ffridd* below.

The air was so thick with glaring white moisture it dampened all scent, so he couldn't even, like the stag, sniff out what vegetation he was near.

In better visibility he'd be able to detect the patches of squat conifers and scrubby yew. He'd know if he lay amongst the broadleaf plants that had evolved over millennia to survive up here on the margins between the human world and the heavens. But he didn't have a clue.

He knew one thing, however. If indeed he was going to die of exposure and respiratory or pulmonary difficulties brought about by inhaling what were essentially ice crystals, Finlay was glad it was going to happen out here, surrounded by the plants, rocks and trees he felt himself bound to like brothers.

He calculated that, having taken in absolutely nothing since his morning coffee and sweet treats, it would likely take less than five, maybe six hours before he'd fall into a hypothermic sleep and then he'd know nothing after that.

His body vibrated with shivers he couldn't control.

Bloom, his mother had written. He was supposed to bloom and live a long life on earth, and yet here he was, willingly giving himself to the cold ground. While he still had air in his lungs he should at least try to shout, but when he opened his mouth, he found only one word would do.

'*Murray!*'

The pain in his shoulder bit hard with the effort, and the white blanket over the range absorbed the sound as soon as it formed, yet he called on, into the fog.

'*Murray!* I'm here!'

34

'There has to be something more you can do!' Roz begged, while her husband held her by her shoulders. 'Heat detection cameras? Rescue dogs?'

Jemmy opened his mouth to speak but Kirsten Holmberg, the chief mountain rescue officer for the area, answered in her Scottish-Scandi accent. 'We can't launch the helicopter in zero visibility. Likewise, a hill party wouldn't be able to see the ground in front of them. We have to wait until it starts to clear.'

Everyone assembled at the mountain rescue office (little more than an equipment store and comms room at the back of the police station) looked to the window where, beyond, there was nothing but white.

'And how long's that going to be?' asked McIntyre,

his voice cracking. 'It's been two hours since Murray rang us to say he was stranded up there.'

'Weather reports say at least another six hours, less if the winds pick up and move the cloud, but it's as still as unstirred Scotch broth out there.' This was Jemmy, all in mountain ranger green, trying to keep a lid on his worst fears. 'Soon as it thins, we'll have every unit up there searching.'

The call had gone out to all rescue units across the region to be on standby for a Cairn Dhu recovery mission, but half of them had reported their own stranded walkers hunkered down somewhere up in the clouds, and who knew how many of them were getting into difficulties and would need carrying down or airlifting out of their positions when the weather allowed?

'We'll do everything we can,' Kirsten said, standing over the map across the office tabletop. 'Finlay Morlich reported Murray was between the rocks of Gillie Fell at precisely eleven zero one this morning.'

'Aye, that's where Murray *thought* he might be when he phoned us too, but...' Roz hesitated, not wanting to criticise her son's geography skills, 'but he isn't all that familiar with the mountain.'

'But he did say he'd been walking towards Finlay's

cruive when the fog swallowed him and the dog ran off?' Kirsten said, pinpointing the little cottage. 'That means that, even if he's continued to attempt to travel on foot, he can't be anywhere outside of this perimeter.' She drew a reassuringly small circle on the map with her finger.

'I think he has the good sense to stay still and await rescue,' put in Jamie Beaton, the local police officer who'd come in early for his shift as soon as he'd heard about the missing men.

Roz and McIntyre exchanged glances.

'Not necessarily,' said McIntyre, blanching.

'There's a good chance he'd keep going, trying to find Nell,' Roz said, ready to weep.

'He doesn't know Finlay is now considered lost on the mountain, right?' asked Jamie.

'I imagine he'd have tried phoning him again, after he spoke with me, but...' Roz shrugged, 'did he get through? We don't know.'

'Could he have realised, in the same way we've lost touch with him, that Finlay could be in danger, and put two and two together? Could he have tried to go looking for him, as well as looking for the dog?'

'That's an unknown,' Kirsten concluded coolly. 'Let's work with what we do know, yes? Two men, one a skilled mountain ranger, probably dressed for the weather, who could, if required, navigate the mountain even in lower visibility...'

'If he isn't injured,' Jemmy put in, his face sickly green. 'And now he's out of communication, making no traceable signals.'

'And there's one man, dressed in...' Kirsten paused to check her notes, 'white casualwear, possibly a cream cashmere jumper, with zero survival experience and also now with no signal from his phone.'

Roz threw a hand to her mouth to stifle the sob. McIntyre crumpled around her in a clinging hug. 'They'll be all right,' he told his wife. 'It's just a wee spot o' fog.'

Now it was Kirsten and Jemmy's turn to exchange doubtful glances, before the whole lot of them fixed their eyes on the slowly shifting candyfloss white beyond the pane.

Kirsten lifted the radio to her lips. 'This is Cairn Dhu mountain rescue centre. Over. Do you read us, Ranger Morlich? Over.'

Nothing but a static buzz came over the open channel.

McIntyre clung to his wife all the tighter.

35

Finlay's mouth was the only dry thing about him. His clothes clung to his damp and clammy skin beneath his waterproof coat. The fog had seeped in between every layer.

In a dim spot at the back of his brain he pondered how it was possible he could hate clouds now when they'd always been a source of intense interest for him.

He'd already categorised his life up until this moment as The Time Before. Now he was in the ethereal In Between and even that was loosening its tenuous grasp upon him.

His pain had gone, leaving a drowsy numbness in his entire body. He wasn't even cold now. His body still draped, shaping itself like a wet ribbon over the contours of the rock.

His gloveless hand lay in contact with the ancient granite, the thing that had been his touchstone in the last years of his life. Stone that the last ice age had scoured of soil like his mother's bubbly washing-up sponge cutting through grease as she did the dishes.

There she was, before him at the sink in some sort of nineties camcorder home movie, projected on the white cloud, looking like the prim lady in the washing-up adverts when he was wee. *Cuts through even tough grease at low temperatures.* A TV jingle played in his brain. He smiled weakly at it, closing his eyes, seeing his mother's tight perm and even tighter smile. She turned to look at him with despairing eyes, as though choosing words designed to wipe away his stains. The kitchen faded. His mother slowly vanished until she was just a voice. *Can't you at least try? Look at all the other boys, out playing football together. You can't hide in your room forever. What am I going to do with you, Finlay Morlich?* He'd heard it all, even though she accused him of never listening. The main thing he'd learned was that he was easy to dislike and very, very hard to love.

Were these going to be his last thoughts? That didn't seem right.

How was it he'd fled here and found his Eden, some place that loved him back, cosseted him in beautiful green nature, and yet he'd spent his time here terrified that one day he'd stumble across a body lost in the snow or at the foot of a landslide? And now *he* was that body! He'd become the thing he feared most.

A thought for Jemmy arose. Would he be distraught to find him here in a day or two, mottled and moulded to the rock like... like... Finlay couldn't even remember the name for the Cairngorm rock lichens he loved so much, the ones that looked like weather-bleached flesh stretched over stone... He was forgetting himself.

His head bobbed with each shallow, laboured wheeze.

The winter sun was about to set, he knew that much. He could detect the sudden change in light, even through shuttered eyelids. He prised them open to catch the last glow lighting the clouds as the sun sank beneath the unseen horizon.

On any other day, he'd be able to remember the sunset times. It didn't matter now. With the loss of the sun, the temperature would plummet in seconds, drawing him down with it. But he wanted to see the spectacle for himself. Mother Nature, innocuous, harmless, his true mother, not minding him dying. He opened his eyes as wide as he could.

The mass of white before his eyes had thinned, he realised, allowing hazy fingers of his last day's last light to penetrate the gloaming. He couldn't even tell where the sun was in relation to him.

A thought struck him. He wanted to say farewell to this last light before he became rock and lichen and dew and dark sky.

Inhaling as deeply as he could in order to power the necessary movement, he fought against gravity and his rubber legs to draw himself to a crumpled kneeling position. The strain made him wail out in pain. It was worth it to look at the golden blaze through the fog.

'Ah!' Finlay gasped at the sight of his own ghostly shadow on the glowing cloud-screen before him as it flushed a rosy peach. It was his own Brocken spectre coming for him, his own sorry shape projected onto the cloud by the low sun at his back. So he knew he was facing east. He was orientated on the earth, at last. This was good.

He raised a hand to welcome his shadow, and it too lifted a hand, waving goodbye. The effort of holding up his body was too much and he slumped forward, his shoulder jarring as his hands hit hard stone. He heard sinew crunching in his neck in a burst of sickening pain.

Still he raised his one good hand again as his shadow drew nearer, but this time the Brocken spectre didn't lift its arm.

His shadow must be broken, Finlay concluded. It was detaching itself from his body, the way Peter Pan's shadow could come loose and get lost.

This was it. The parting with his body.

He turned his lips to the earth and whispered into it the only Gaelic he could now remember, taking leave of his friends, his mountains.

'*Mar sin leibh, Am Monadh Ruadh.*'

He kept his hand raised, watching his ghost shadow looming larger, just the way mountaineers had for centuries described the optical illusion. Finlay Morlich, in the end, was nothing but a short-lived trick of the light. He rolled forward, face against hard rock, eyes still fixed on the spectre.

His shadow, however, refused to kneel. It kept coming for him.

Through barely opened eyes, and accompanied by the sound of laboured breathing not his own, he watched the grey figure loom larger out of the glowing fog, now not like a shadow at all, but like a human taking its angel form.

It drew nearer still, seemed almost to bring with it the sound of heavy footsteps reverberating through the rocks against Finlay's skull. It brought panting breaths, too. There was no heavenly music playing, no harps like his kirk minister father had foretold, but the shadow angel held out its hand to him, revealing a silver glinting disc.

Finlay closed his eyes, exhausted.

'Thank God!' came a voice, breaking free of the mists, but Finlay was insensible to it now. He didn't know the figure wasn't his own shadow and it wasn't an angel either. It was a pink-cheeked, pale and puffing man, and the glint in his hand was Finlay's grandfather's compass, picked up only a few feet away, and arriving by his side now was Nell the Labrador, the dog that had led Murray McIntyre all the way here through the dense fog.

'Finlay!' Murray called, shaking him by his coat, finding him unresponsive.

* * *

'This is Mountain Rescue,' a radio crackled. Murray turned all around him, frantic, catching sight of a tiny red light blinking just out of arm's reach of where Finlay lay. He grabbed for it, barely able to make out the buttons as the last light faded on the mountainside.

'I'm with Finlay now!' Murray shouted into the receiver, not even knowing how to operate the thing, having to heave air into his fog-soaked lungs. Why couldn't they hear him down there? What was he doing wrong?

He pressed every button and twirled every knob. 'We need help!' he yelled.

Nell had already decided the best course of action was to throw herself down bodily upon the comfy bed that was the unmoving Finlay.

Something caught Murray's eye as the bands of fog thinned further. A backpack, lying only a little way off. He'd retrieved it in seconds, struggling with frozen fingers to undo the zippers, and inside, seen through tears of absolute relief, he found something he *did* know how to work.

* * *

Down in the town, where everyone had long held a collective breath, standing sentry at their windows or in their gardens or in the street, wrapped in layers, radios to their ears, keeping their eyes fixed on the white mist that hid the mountain behind the magician's cloak they hoped at any moment would be whipped away, every last person saw the firework emerge from the gloom, casting a diffuse red light over the western slope: a bright red flare signalling that at least someone was alive up there.

36

It was probably for the best that Finlay didn't know a thing about what had happened next: the whole team arriving with helmet torches flashing, the stretcher rescue – since the helicopter still couldn't fly – and the jolting march back to the cruive where Doctors Hargreave and Millen stripped and warmed him, re-setting his shoulder under the single bare light bulb, the sedation making no difference to him, he was so lost in the In Between.

There'd been a mask over his face and gas and air, a bleeping monitor on his finger, a drip in his arm, a cold stethoscope pressed repeatedly to his chest in front of his fire which had never been so stoked with logs as it was that night.

It had gone eight in the morning when he'd finally opened his eyes, and although he was dimly aware of a vast assembly of figures crowded in his little cottage, the first sight that greeted him was the face of Murray McIntyre leaning over him in amazement, and by his side loomed the long, pink, disgusting tongue of a big, black, ridiculous dog with a smiling, drooling mouth.

'He's awake!' Murray said, visibly drooping with relief.

With a sense of floating lightness that Finlay had never experienced in all the years before he nearly died on his mountain, he let his eyes close and he drifted off into peaceful sleep once more while Murray tightly held his hand over the covers.

* * *

'Don't worry, I'll look after him, and as you said yourself, it's just for a few days, until he's fully on his feet,' Murray was saying at the cruive door as Dr Hargreave took her leave.

'You can call me at the surgery or on my mobile, any time,' she said, before taking one last look at her patient, reclined under blankets on the sofa in front of the crackling hearth.

'I've got this,' Murray reassured her, and Finlay

wondered how the decision had been made that it was to be Murray, of all people, who hung around to nurse him.

There was a lot of stuff his memory was hazy on. Finlay's rational brain knew that there had passed one whole week since he'd awakened – Murray had confirmed it – a week of his lying prone by his fireside, submitting to being monitored and jabbed, weighed and washed, alongside all the fuss of people bringing up supplies and dropping in to 'check on the patient', but it had all merged together into a strange, drowsy blur.

Now all of that was over and he was to be left alone again. He'd continue to allow Murray to stay, if he really must. That dog, though? That was another matter.

Nell snored on the hearthrug as Alice stepped out into the bright early-February noon light.

'Stick to the community path!' Finlay shouted after her from his sick-sofa, and she waved away his concern as the door closed. She'd made the trek up and down from the surgery so many times in the last week, she knew the route all too well.

Murray stood on the doormat, his fists bunched at his hips. He was giving Finlay a funny look.

'What?' Finlay wanted to know.

'Nothing. It's just strange, everyone leaving at last.'

'*Hmph*,' Finlay grunted. 'Thought they'd never leave me in peace.'

'*They* saved your life.'

The fire crackled in the silence as Murray let that sink in for him, but Finlay had heard enough about what happened to know it had, in fact, been Murray who'd saved his life. Though Murray had deflected that it was 'all Nell'. According to him, it had taken hours to reunite man and dog on the mountainside, but once Nell was safely back on her lead, she'd been the one who had scented Finlay and dragged Murray the hundred yards to where he'd fallen. 'Clever girl,' Murray had repeatedly called the dog over the intervening days, while feeding her bits of the cold chicken and pork pies that the town folks had sent up.

It turned out Finlay had fallen only a couple of metres off a stony outcrop, but it had been enough to knock him out, dislocate his shoulder, crack some ribs, and send all his belongings flying.

'Hungry?' Murray said now, still standing awkwardly by the door.

Finlay took pity on him. 'You don't have to stay, you know. Don't you have a job to go to?'

Murray seemed to consider this. 'Not immediately, no.'

'What does that mean?'

'You should eat something,' Murray said, ignoring the question, and picking up a chart the doctor had left for him. 'Every four hours.'

'Like a baby.' Finlay harrumphed.

'I draw the line at night feeds.'

Murray, it turned out, made a pretty decent nurse. He'd helped change the bandages on Finlay's fingers and over his scraped ribcage the day before, bathing the scratches in antiseptic before applying clean gauze and the big sticking plasters, all with Alice showing him how.

Now Murray was making his way down through hatch doors in the floor in the corner of the cruive and rummaging around in the sunken coldstore that passed for Finlay's refrigerator, accessed by a few steps. Finlay called it his 'scullery'.

Murray's head popped out from the room, the glow from the scullery lamp lighting his face from beneath like a ghost in a play coming through a trap-door. Finlay determined not to laugh at the sight of him.

'There's bacon, sausages, and a tonne of new potatoes,' Murray relayed. 'Dropped off from Laura at the deli. No charge, she said, not for her *favourite* customer.' Murray's eyes gleamed with delight. So the man still enjoyed taunting him, even now?

'Pass,' Finlay grumped, unable to prevent his own smile forming.

'Let's see. What else? Chutneys, cheddar and some nice crackers from the library staff.'

Now that was a surprise. Finlay really hadn't expected them to care in the slightest.

'Didn't know you had so many fans,' Murray said, as though in agreement, his head disappearing once more.

'Makes two of us,' Finlay said, unsure if Murray could hear him.

In fact, he'd been astonished at the response to the news of his rescue. There'd been a flower delivery from the garden project people. Not project-grown stuff, of course (there'd still be nothing to show for the season's growth down there), but a big blousy bunch of early daffodils and tulips, probably sent in an aeroplane all the way from Holland, but he'd forgive them the emissions just this once, since they looked so bright in the sink and they scented the place with springtime.

There'd been a hundredweight of sugared almonds, gummy bears, chocolate bars and lollipops. Kids' stuff, brought by Jemmy and his team. Murray had been trying to ration them out to him, but he was easy to get around, if Finlay complained hard enough.

Murray had already let him have all the tablet Senga had made the postman drop off no sooner than the fog had cleared.

'Oh, and there was this from Gracie at the doctor's surgery,' said Murray, still peeping out from the scullery hatch, giving the misshapen ceramic vase he was holding a dubious look.

'Looks handmade,' said Finlay, not knowing what else to say about it.

'Looks rubbish,' said Murray.

Nevertheless, he quickly escaped the hatch, filled it up from the tap and, confident it wasn't leaky, plonked the spring flowers in it and set it on the mantel.

'That's no' half bad,' Finlay had to admit, prepared to forgive Gracie perhaps a small amount for all her prying and gossiping.

Back down the steps he went once more. 'The police station sent this,' Murray was saying, emerging after a moment holding a big colourful box.

'What is it?' Finlay asked, craning his neck to get a look.

'Chocolate cake.'

'That's dinner sorted, then,' concluded Finlay, another wave of lightness passing through him, an increasingly regular occurrence since the rescue.

Murray dropped the scullery hatch closed behind him and Finlay's heart sank when he saw he was bringing with him *not* the double chocolate gateau he'd hankered after, but a big cellophane-wrapped fruit basket with a Brazilian pineapple peeping out of the top.

'Before you start grumbling about air miles,' Murray stopped him, 'you need some vitamins before you can stuff yourself with any more cakes. Let's start with a tropical fruit salad.'

Finlay conceded with a big sigh. 'Who sent the fruit basket?' he asked, letting Murray drop it in his lap so he could pull at the red ribbon ties with his free arm – his other arm was still wrapped in its sling.

'I did, as it happens. My get well soon present,' Murray told him as he rummaged in the kitchen drawer for a knife, before bringing over two bowls, two spoons and, Finlay was pleased to note, a big pot of cream.

With some effort, Finlay shifted his still stiff legs to make room for him, and Murray perched on the end of his sofa.

'I didn't know so many people cared,' Finlay said

gruffly as Murray chopped a papaya, sticking its 'Mexico' label on Finlay's knee, just to annoy him.

'They don't,' Murray said with a sly grin, eyes fixed on his task. 'They're taking pity on me stuck up here with you. That chocolate cake's meant for me.'

'Commiseration cake?'

'Exactly. I'll let you have a wee slice. Maybe. But only after you eat your...' Murray pulled a fiery pink and green fruit from the cellophane. 'Uh?'

'Go on,' taunted Finlay, sure Murray had no idea that was a dragon fruit.

'Spikey devil pear?' Murray smirked, before cutting the thing open and gasping at the seedy white flesh inside.

'Aye, spikey devil pear,' Finlay said in a voice that couldn't disguise its fondness. 'That's exactly what that is.'

As Murray filled the bowls with glossy, sweet-smelling fruits, he would glance now and again at the fire and the shelves, and the kitchen corner.

'What is it?' Finlay asked.

'I'm just thinking it's quite nice up here.'

Finlay tried to sit himself up a little more so he could look around too, trying to see the place through Murray's eyes. 'It was little more than a stall for ani-

mals at one time. My late mother,' Finlay felt the need
to clarify, 'she's gone now, called it a hovel.'

Murray kept cutting, meeting his eyes only to say,
'I'm sorry to hear about your mother. But she was
wrong, this is no hovel. This is off-grid living.'

'Oh, here we go.' Finlay made a show of rolling his
eyes but he couldn't help the warm feeling inside him.

'How do you charge your phone?' Murray wanted
to know.

'Down at the rangers' station, and I have a couple
of rechargeable power banks to top it up with. I'm no'
quite the Luddite you think I am.'

'I honestly didn't think that at all,' Murray said,
standing to dump all the fruit peelings into the compost crock by Finlay's sink, near enough filling the
thing. Noticing the power bank on the little windowsill, he quickly slipped his phone, perilously low
on battery, into it.

'I think,' Murray went on, turning to him like a
detective in a movie about to reveal whodunit. 'It
might be *you* that has all these critical words in your
head. I've never heard anyone call you anything other
than Finlay the ranger.'

'Doubtful,' scowled Finlay.

'Actually...' Murray was on his way back, settling
down properly onto the sofa this time, handing Finlay

his bowl. 'Senga and Rhona Gifford might have even called you *sweet* every now and again.'

Finlay narrowed his eyes.

'Well.' Murray crumbled. 'Maybe what they said was, you could occasionally be a bit of a *nippy sweetie.*'

'No' quite the same thing, is it?' Finlay took his spoon in his hand, wondering where that tub of cream had got to.

'Just look at all those cards,' Murray reminded him, indicating the colourful row along the mantel. 'Plenty folk like you fine.'

For the first time in his life, Finlay felt his cheeks warming in a blush. 'Where are you hiding that cream?' he complained.

Murray smirked in a knowing way that told him he could see straight through all his mumping and moaning, and he pulled the top from the carton, drowning their fruit salads in the stuff.

They talked and they ate while Finlay explained how everything worked up at the cruive, from rain-water harvesting to the multi-fuel stove and the solar panel that powered the lights, and how in the summer his shower was just water scooped from the barrel round the back.

'What? In the nuddy outside?' Murray laughed.

'It's just the squirrels watchin', and the occasional sparrow.'

'And the postman!' Murray howled with laughter in their cosy corner of the room as the afternoon wore gently on and the chimney smoked.

All through the evening, as Murray attempted to master brewing tea with the big black kettle that swung over the fire on its hook and as they made short work of the chocolate cake and the last of the cream, Finlay caught himself just before he accidentally remarked aloud how he could get used to this, because that was precisely the one thing he dared not do.

37

Murray woke in the half-light of the mountain dawn to the sound of metal and tin clattering.

He sprang from the bed that Finlay had insisted he take, since the ranger didn't want to move from the sofa, to find Finlay by a fire newly swept and re-lit, attempting to get the lid off the kettle so he could fill it up.

'What are you doing?' said Murray, his feet hitting the cold stone floor.

Startled, Finlay said in dismay, 'I wanted to make us coffee.'

Murray was by his side in an instant, wrestling the kettle and coffee canister from him. 'That's why I'm here! Shift over. Let me.'

Finlay moved reluctantly away. 'You've already done so much.'

Murray looked him up and down from where he crouched before the flames and couldn't help laughing.

'Whit!' Finlay protested.

He'd managed to change into a new pair of pyjama bottoms, heavy green flannel ones, at that, but his feet were bare and there was a woollen jumper pulled over his head and over one arm but ridiculously bunched up above his bad shoulder in its sling, the sleeve inside out. 'I wanted to wash and dress myself. I've been wearing the same thing since that first night...'

There was a smear of toothpaste at one corner of his mouth, and his hair and face were, Murray noticed, damp, and droplets of water clung to the ends of Finlay's scruffy waves. Murray looked around at the evidence. There was plenty of water on the floor in front of the kitchen sink and a damp towel in a bundle on the countertop.

'Come here,' Murray told him, and Finlay obeyed, but not without a lot of grumbling and muttering, which he ignored.

'Can I?' Murray asked, before pulling the wrinkled

woollen down over Finlay's bandaged arm, leaving the sleeve inside out.

'Did you take your painkillers?' he asked, and Finlay snapped that of course he had.

Murray now took the towel and rubbed it gently and thoroughly all over Finlay's damp locks. 'I could have washed your hair, you should have waited till I woke up.'

'I managed,' came the reply.

Murray took the opportunity to wipe away the toothpaste from his mouth. 'Sure you did. Now, where are your fresh socks, hmm?'

Finlay looked forlornly behind him at the clean, balled woollen socks by the sofa. 'It's easier getting them off than putting them on again,' he admitted, his voice smaller than Murray had ever heard it.

'It's OK. Just sit.'

Finlay looked like he was ready to protest again.

'Sit!'

Over by the door, where Nell had been waiting patiently for her morning walk, the dog put her bottom on the floor, wagging her tail to show what a good girl she was being.

The men had to laugh, and Murray helped Finlay lower himself onto the sofa, trying to resist the wicked urge to flex his bicep where Finlay gripped him for support.

'Daft dug,' Finlay said, but his tone sounded more like praise than an insult.

'Did you feed Nell?' said Murray, kneeling at Finlay's feet, unballing the socks.

'Just a bit of jellied chicken from a jar,' Finlay said.

Murray shuddered. 'Good, because, *ugh*! I wasn't eating that!'

'One of Laura Mercer's presents,' Finlay said, trying to keep the small talk going as Murray decided not to put the socks straight onto his feet but to apply some of the medicated cream the doctor had prescribed for the sore skin around his ankles where the frost had bitten him.

Murray found he welcomed the distraction because Finlay Morlich, it turned out, had seriously nice feet, and his ankles were really kind of devastating when viewed up close and held between two lotioned hands. He gulped. 'You never, uh, fancied Laura, or anything?'

'Uh, yeah, no,' Finlay replied. 'Obviously not.'

Murray didn't lift his eyes, rubbing the last of the lotion in before pulling the fresh socks into place, making sure to give Finlay's wool-clad feet another rub over just to warm them.

'There,' he said. 'Now where's your comb?'

'Eh?'

'Or do you use a brush?' Murray looked around the room, spotting the shampoo bar on the side of the sink, and the toothbrush and paste, but nothing else in the way of personal grooming stuff.

Finlay shrugged. 'I've never really bothered combing my hair.'

Murray resisted the urge to interrogate him about how that was possible, but something within him told him Finlay might have had enough of being questioned and picked at for one lifetime, so instead he kneeled up higher and reached his hands up to the ranger's damp hair.

Finlay flinched, pulling back. 'What you doing?'

'Sorting your hair. Is that not OK? I won't, if you don't want me to.'

'No, I do,' Finlay said. 'Startled me, that's all.'

Murray took this as a sign to move slowly around him, and he let his hands reach into the thick light-brown waves of Finlay's hair at a snail's pace.

'Hmm.' The sound came from Finlay at the first touch of his scalp.

Seeing that the ranger had his eyes closed and his lips parted like this was all new to him, Murray stroked his fingertips through his damp hair all the way to the nape of his neck, before pulling them free and starting again from his hairline, raking through the coconut-scented waves. He really must ask where he'd bought that shampoo bar, but for now he stayed focused on the sensation of running his hands through Finlay's hair, listening out for the gruff, approving sounds that told him he liked this as much as Murray did.

There came a point when the two had shifted so close together that Finlay's damp, bobbing head was in danger of coming to rest upon Murray's chest. Murray pictured himself pulling Finlay that little bit nearer until he leaned on his sweatshirt and how he'd hold him there, stroking him back to sleep. Murray had been just about to enact his plan, when a notification pinged on his phone.

The pair jumped apart, and Murray stood on wobbly legs, making his way to where his phone sat forgotten on the counter. This last week had to be the longest he'd gone without taking the slightest interest in his phone and the wider world. He hadn't missed it once.

What he found was a message from Barbara Huber, reminding him she needed a decision by tomorrow. 'Shit!' Murray ran a hand over his unshaven face.

'Problem?' Finlay asked from the sofa.

When Murray returned with the phone to show him, Finlay had rearranged his face from the dreamy surrender of a moment ago to something he probably hoped resembled casual interest. In fact, his cheeks were flushed and his pupils were still tiny pinpoints.

'It's, uh, it's this job offer I was supposed to be thinking about. My old boss, in Switzerland, emailed me some potential postings I was supposed to be considering.'

'Postings?' Finlay handed back the phone, having examined the message.

'Contracts overseas. I've got until tomorrow to decide which ones I want, if any.'

'Right.' Finlay shifted back against the cushions where he sat looking uncomfortable. 'Where might they send you?'

'The last one they arranged was to Mali,' Murray said, suddenly unsure why the idea didn't appeal to him as much as it once had when he'd been over-looked for the Mali trip after causing a scene at a big charity donors' gala event, when he'd caught Andreas arm in arm with billionaire David. 'I know one contract's for an ocean-cleaning thing off a Balinese beach.'

'Well then,' said Finlay, as though that must be Murray's mind made up. 'Congratulations are in order, I suppose.'

'That's the thing, you see?' Murray dropped onto the sofa beside him. 'With all this happening, I haven't had a chance to even open her email and find out what these contracts will involve. They could be days, they could be months long. I've been avoiding opening that email, to be honest, up here with you, and I didn't get the chance to...'

'You should go home.'

'What? No, I...'

'I'm better, honestly.'

Murray didn't believe that for a second. 'I've got until tomorrow to decide.'

'So...' Finlay's eyes had turned puppy-dog wide. 'You can stay for breakfast, or breakfast *and* lunch?'

The hope reflecting back at him made Murray's heart swell. 'And after that, afternoon tea?' Murray teased, unable to hold back his smile.

Nell's ears had pricked up at all this talk of food and she peeped her head around the arm of the sofa.

'You can have some too, Mutt,' Finlay said, putting his hand out to her so that she transformed into a bouncing, tail-swinging lump of pure energy once more.

Murray shoved his phone between the sofa cushions and joined in with the dog pats, and the pair let themselves forget about the world outside once more, just for a little while longer.

38

The thing about the Highland winter weather that people down south neglect to mention is how some of the finest, brightest, crispest days of the year can come in February, surprising everyone with their chilly beauty.

Today, Wednesday the fourth of February, was one such day, though it only went a small way to mending the longing ache in Alice's heart. She'd tried to fill it, of course, with her therapy and her work, and with treating Finlay Morlich without the need for a hospital admission, something everyone, especially Finlay, had agreed was for the best, given his attitude to busy institutions and, well, people. Then of course, there'd been last Saturday, the very last day of January, which she'd spent away from Cairn Dhu in a wonderful old castle with its own spa and pool, and a series of group talks and activities arranged by Bonnie, the counsellor, for lots of her women clients who battled with anxiety and trauma, and the whole thing had been eye-opening and challenging, as well as freeing and restful.

For some reason, everyone in town had wanted to want to pick her for details about it. She couldn't understand why it was anyone else's business and she'd explained to no one, not even to the overly invested Gracie, what exactly she'd done on her precious spa day.

There was one person she'd have liked to tell all about it, but he still hadn't returned to town and Alice had begun to accept that, horribly, he was never coming back.

She'd needed him too, on Sunday, when no one was around to help with the garden project because Finlay and Murray were recovering at the cruive, and so she'd had to muddle through the planting of some winter pansies and the turning of the compost heap all by herself until, much to her surprise, the whole gang had arrived; Mr Forte, Kellie Timmony, Livvie and Shell, Mhairi and Jolyon, and they'd all stuck it out for at least twenty minutes before they'd fled inside the warmth of the shed and demolished Senga's big cairn of chocolate-dipped rock cakes in front of the fire.

Even though everyone had been chattering away, getting to know one another better, and the two kids seemed to be happily sharing Jolyon's tablet to watch cartoons, Alice hadn't been able to join in with their talk with quite the same enthusiasm as she might have had Cary been sitting next to her taking a deep interest in her life, the way he used to.

She'd noticed Kellie being quiet too, hanging back from the conversation, until Roz had come in bringing the two puppies and asking if anyone wanted to help walk them. Kellie had been the first to volunteer and she'd gone out on her own with both of them, walking the tumbling, squabbling little dogs in slow laps around the repair shed and the new garden so many times Kellie said she'd lost count, but the whole time she'd been smiling more broadly than Alice had ever seen. When her parents had picked her up, Kellie had a hard time saying goodbye, not to the rest of the group, but to the dogs. Alice had already asked Roz if Murray would mind her incorporating the pups into all the garden project Sunday activities until such a time as they were rehomed, to help Kellie's recovery, and Roz had, without even checking with Murray up at the cruive, said that would be more than OK.

On her lunch break today, which Dr Millen was insisting she take away from her desk, Alice arrived at the repair shed and took her customary peep inside, just to check. Cary's workbench was still piled with new repair jobs – she wasn't the only one hoping for his return – and behind it stood his grandfather clock under a dust sheet, all fully repaired, according to Dr Bonnet, who was making herself at home in her designated corner of the shed which was already cluttered with her tools and with umpteen ticking clocks on the wall.

Alice had ordered and eaten a toastie with salad and crisps, and a slice of fruity flapjack with green tea, then she'd sought out the other thing she had come here for. There was the small matter of the garden project participants' feedback forms to attend to and, as patient liaison, that was her job.

She reached for the little box on the café counter, hand crafted by, of course, Cary. It put her in mind of the polling station boxes where she'd slip her voting papers back home. He'd made it knowing they needed a way for folks referred to the garden project to anonymously report on their experiences of it, and this was Alice's first time emptying the thing.

She tried to put from her mind the knowledge that Cary's hands had cut and hammered, sanded and painted it – in a gaudy pink to match the shed's neon logo on the wall – and she turned the catch to release the door on the back.

Inside were three folded papers. She sat at one of the café chairs to read them, since there was nobody in here this morning, except Rhona pottering behind her counter, and McIntyre washing oil from his hands with stinky Swarfega.

The first paper showed a stick-figure drawing in crayon of a boy with a red curving smile and a girl holding his hand with what looked like a blue blanket in her free hand, standing under a spiked yellow sun. She turned the paper over to find in an adult hand the words in Biro:

Thank you. We are enjoying meeting new people.

Mhairi and Jolyon Sears, thought Alice. It had to be.

A second paper displayed the shaky whispery ink of someone trying hard to control the pen.

Too cold for gardening. What kind of eejit starts an outdoor project in January? Enjoyed meeting new folk, even if it is freezin. Come summer, mind, I might feel up to a wee bit of weeding. We'll see.

Alice was sure this was Mr Forte who had spent a good amount of the last session complaining that it just 'wasnae the weather for pottering aboot outside'. She hoped the project wasn't already at risk of losing its first participant, put off by the elements. Maybe she'd put him on seed-sowing duty inside the shed, if he came back.

A third paper was filled in with bullet-pointed notes in a youthful script. Kellie's, for sure.

- *Friendly* ✓
- *Cold* ☹
- *Well organised* ✓
- *Bonus puppies* ☺
- *Kind of a weird atmosphere between some of the project facilitators (do they fancy each other or hate each other, or what?!?)*

Alice hoped this last point referred to Murray and Finlay who, no one could have failed to notice, didn't always get on. It was, however, just as possible Kellie meant Cary and her. The thought made her shrink with shame. She was supposed to be the medical professional at the heart of the project. Had the patients seen through her disguise to the messy reality beneath?

Something Bonnie, her therapist, had spent a long time unpacking with Alice, both at the therapeutic spa escape and in her consulting room over the high street, was exactly what Alice thought she had gained from hiding her difficulties from the world. Alice had to conclude that not one positive benefit had come from acting like she was coping when she wasn't.

Just saying out loud how unbelievably hard it had all been for her – the awful things she'd seen in training, the parental pressure to excel when she'd have been happy just coasting along, had she been allowed, and then everything with Bastian and how, deep down, she'd known she was dating him to make her dad happy, while letting her own needs go unmet – every word of it, when said out loud in front of a trained listener and knowledgeable advisor, had felt like weights lifted one after another from her soul.

'Penny for them?' came a woman's voice.

Livvie Cooper was by her side in the café.

'Oh, just...' She'd been about to lie. 'Thinking how far I've come.'

Livvie smiled like this was something she'd been waiting to hear. 'Good for you, Doc.'

Little Shell emerged from behind her mum's back, fixing those startled wide eyes on her.

'You OK, Shell? Why aren't you at school?' Alice asked in her softest voice. Still, the girl withdrew like a snail being eyed by a hungry bird, pulling back its horns.

'The primary school kids can go home for lunch if they want,' said Livvie, though Alice had never heard of such a thing happening in England. 'I pick her up and bring her here to eat with me. She was hoping to see Jolyon, I think.'

'He's a nice boy,' Alice said, careful not to pose this as a demand for Shell's agreement.

The little girl nodded almost indiscernibly. 'He's all right,' she said. 'I wish he'd keep his hands off my blanket.'

Alice laughed but when she noticed Livvie pointedly *not* laughing, she straightened her face. The girl clearly objected to this infringement, and who was Alice to say that was unreasonable? It was her security blanket, after all. Alice, of all people, having sent Bastian packing all too late, should know how frustrating it was when a boy insisted on pushing a boundary.

'Here,' Alice said, sorting the letters in her hand, figuring it couldn't do any harm. 'He drew a picture of you both.'

Shell took it wordlessly in her hand and looked it over, a smile sneaking over her lips. In an instant she was gone, digging for her paper and crayons in her backpack over by the beanbags.

Livvie and Alice watched her settle down to draw.

'She'll be making him a picture,' Livvie told her, coming closer, deciding to sit, but only perching on the edge of a café chair. 'When the police moved us out of town, we weren't allowed anything from the house, just had to go in the clothes we stood in. But Shell happened to have that doll's blanket with her. She grew right out of baby dolls while we were away.' Guilt and worry creased her face as she spoke. 'But she kept hold of the blanket.'

'I get it,' Alice said. 'You know, if there's anything else we can do, at the surgery... or if there's anything I can do, you will just ask?'

Livvie smiled, as much as she'd ever seen her smile. 'You're doing enough, just being here in the town,' and that, coming from the measured Livvie Cooper felt like the best appraisal Alice had ever had.

'I'd better head back to work then, now I've col-
lected these,' Alice told her, folding the feedback
forms up to take with her, and letting her eyes for the
briefest moment flit to Cary's side of the shed and his
vacant spot by the sharpening wheel.

'Do you still think he's coming back?' Alice said.
'It's been ten days.'

Livvie tried to soften her shrug of uncertainty with
another smile.

39

After a leisurely breakfast of streaky smoked bacon fried on the skillet over the fire, Murray had insisted on washing up and, after that, he'd insisted Finlay go and have a proper sleep in his own bed.

'I've been fine on the sofa,' he'd said.

Murray hadn't listened to a word of it and made him climb onto the bed, tucking him under the sheets, fluffing the pillow at his back, telling him to take a nap, but Finlay was fighting the tiredness brought about by his painkillers, not wanting to waste a moment of Murray's last morning at the cruive.

Murray handed him the tin mug of tea he'd asked for at breakfast but hadn't drunk yet.

'No biscuits?'

'No biscuits,' Murray lied.

Finlay sipped his tea like a sulky child.

'What is it about sweeties that you love so much?' said Murray, perching on the bed with his own tea.

'Dunno.' Finlay turned even sleepier with the warm drink in his hand. 'Suppose I was never allowed them when I was wee, except on Sundays when the Sunday School tuck shop was on.'

'Oh yeah?' Murray listened, fixing a smile on his face, but deep down he could feel a sadness in Finlay as he reminisced.

'That's when I got my pocket money and I loaded up on cola bottles, strawberry bootlaces... fudge... peanut brittle...'

'All right, all right, you're just listing confectionary now.' Murray left the bed for a moment and headed for the small cupboard where he'd hidden the treats. 'Kit Kat?'

Finlay didn't need asking twice and they split it between them, making it disappear in two bites each.

'I know it's no good for me,' Finlay said, washing the chocolate away with a drink of his tea. 'But I know folks that drink a bottle of wine every night, or scroll for hours until they nod off and their phone falls on their face. We all have our thing.'

This hit Murray harder than he'd have liked. He

clasped the tin mug in both hands, shifting on the bed until he was leaning against the rough stone wall.

'What's yours?' Finlay was asking.

'I suppose...' Murray searched himself, wanting to strike upon the truth, thinking Finlay deserved it after sharing so much of his life with him. 'Hitchin' myself to unavailable, cold men?'

Finlay was looking at him with questioning eyes.

'That and electronics, new clothes, shoes?' he threw in. 'I guess we all self-medicate in our own ways.'

'My treats don't seem so bad now,' Finlay was saying. Murray read it as a way of lightening the mood, so he smiled, but there was a sorry little flickering in his brain, something not quite happy.

'That builder doesn't seem unavailable or cold,' Finlay said out of nowhere.

'The builder? You mean Kurt?'

'Aye, your... boyfriend, I think?' Finlay was looking down at the sheets.

'No, not my boyfriend. No.' Murray turned bodily on the bed, folding his legs beneath him. 'We tried a date but it was a bit of a flop.'

'Why? He seemed that keen.' Finlay looked as though he wasn't buying any of this.

'I don't like keen men, usually. And at first that's

what put me off about him, but then we had our date and it turns out he's really nice, perfect, in fact, but I still couldn't let myself go, because... because it didn't feel...' Murray stopped there. *Like this*, he wanted to say. *It hadn't felt like this.* He shrugged instead of finishing his sentence. Finlay had been thinking he was with Kurt all this time. Why did that thought make him giddy? 'So,' Murray said sneakily. 'I'm not seeing anybody.'

'Right,' Finlay said. 'Probably for the best, with you leaving soon? Off to Mali or Bali? Somewhere braw.'

If he hadn't got used to Finlay's ways, that would have felt jarring.

'Somewhere braw,' Murray echoed with a smile.

Finlay understood too that a job was a job and of course he was going to take the contracts.

'I'm running out of money, if I'm honest,' Murray told him.

But Finlay was thinking. A crinkle had formed between his brows. Murray let him formulate the question he knew was coming.

'What were you even doing back here, when you could have stayed in Switzerland?' he asked at last.

Bingo! The big question. One he needed to answer truthfully.

'My unavailable, cold boss boyfriend dumped me, and I ran back home, leaving my job behind, trying to save face.'

Finlay was looking at him still. 'I'm sorry about that,' he said. 'But if you dinnae mind me saying so, he sounds like a right balloon.'

The laugh this provoked in Murray set off the feeling of wanting to cry, somehow. 'He *so* was. An *absolute* balloon.'

'Unavailable men'll get you like that,' Finlay added, and Murray felt the crack at the floodgate.

'I wasn't always icked by keen men. I...' He'd got this far, he had to say the rest. 'I had a boyfriend in college. Wulf.'

He lifted his eyes to check Finlay was still with him, and not passed out asleep.

'Good name, Wulf,' Finlay said, his mug now empty in his hand.

Murray reached for it and put it with his own – still full – mug on the little stand by the bedside.

'I was head over heels. He used to run the campus sandwich bar. Beautiful he was, sheeny blond hair, the lot. I still can't look at a prawn marie rose baguette without thinking of him.'

'Be serious,' Finlay said, delivering a kick through the blanket aimed at Murray's thigh.

'OK, OK. I brought him home to meet my family, came out because of him, spent every second with him, and then, after a semester in his bed, just when I was planning our next steps, he told me he wasn't interested in me like that, and he never meant it to be a serious thing, and he...'

'Broke your heart,' Finlay said.

'Aye. And you know, I was only twenty-one at the time, and you'd think I'd have got over it sooner, but it stuck with me. I wanted him back. I'd see him around, watch him at parties getting off with someone else, phone him up, tell him I'd be happy just being friends, a total lie, of course.'

'Of course,' Finlay said softly.

'Some nights he'd turn up at my dorm, when he'd missed his last bus or had too much to drink and we'd be back together again for a couple of days, and it took me ages to realise the thing that we used to have was dead and I was beginning to hate myself for loving him the way I did, but I *really* did.' Murray glanced at Finlay's face, open, listening, commiserating. 'Anyway, after that, I wasn't going to fall head over heels for anyone. I was Mr Detached, zero feelings, no commitment.'

'And how did that work out for you?'

Murray snorted a laugh. 'Terrible.'

'You cannae help liking someone, if you like them,' Finlay concluded.

Murray made the obligatory half-arsed joke about having t-shirts printed with that on, and then there was nothing left to say.

'You're meant to be having a nap,' he told Finlay.

Finlay patted the pillow next to his, and without another word, Murray shifted himself into the space beside him, curling on his side, and he listened until Finlay's breathing pattern changed, before letting himself close his eyes too.

40

Finlay was hiding in the bathroom, looking at his grizzled face in the rusted old mirror that had been hanging on the wall when he moved in, like most of the furnishings had just been here too.

He needed a few minutes to compose himself. He had to figure out what it all meant: the electric buzz at his scalp this morning when Murray had run his fingers through his hair; the way he had practically begged the man to stay a little longer; how he'd managed to put up with his annoying dog around the place. And now he'd let Murray nap on his bed.

He hadn't been about to deny his guest the only home comfort he had to offer him.

Murray probably had such a nice room down in

the mill house. He tried not to picture himself sleeping there, and how that would feel. It was probably all white and soft and carpeted and warm and clean. The idea made him sigh and shudder too.

What was he torturing himself like this for? Murray had a life of his own that he couldn't ever hope to fit into. He had contracts to look at, options for travel and sunshine and adventure, and there was his puppies to get back to, and the repair shop.

'You OK in there?' Murray called, with a rap at the door.

They'd both woken up from their nap at the same time, just a few moments ago.

'I'll be oot in a minute,' Finlay shouted back, far too gruffly. He pictured Murray drawing his neck back, affronted, walking away, shaking his head at Finlay's rough manners after he'd opened up to him earlier.

He'd always been like this though. No good in company. No good with men. He shook his head at his reflection and attempted, one handed, to apply the lip salve and moisturiser that Murray had forced upon him. Who carried these things around with them except Murray McIntyre?

He smoothed the cocoa butter goop over his weather-roughened lips. It turned out he'd do anything Murray told him to, not something he'd have done for any other man, not that he knew many other men these days.

He'd spent time with men, of course. Back when he lived down at sea level, when he'd been in the city, before he knew the perfect solitude of the hills. He'd even been on the apps, scrolled profiles, chatted some, reached out, responded. Back then, he would shower and dress as well as he could – for a man disinterested in fashion – and he'd go out to meet braw-looking men in bars or at their front doors, and sometimes he'd let them drag him inside their flat and they'd kiss and conspire and give away little bits and pieces about themselves until the night buses were running and it was time to go home.

The thought of those nights dizzied him now. The way he'd been accepted, desired, cared for. Yes, Finlay had known a lot of good men, but that had been a long time ago.

He examined his jawline, patted his tummy, dismayed with himself. What was he doing, keeping Murray here like this?

He swiped some of the honey butter stuff over his face, surprised at it melting in so quickly, and he tried the door. The handle wouldn't turn.

'Murray? The handle's slipping with this stuff on my hand. Can you...?'

Murray pulled the door open, a towel over his arm, gesturing for him to step into the kitchen where he'd set a table for lunch.

'Welcome, sir,' he was saying, bowing like a maître d'.

Finlay stepped into the room, his reservations from a moment ago dissolving all over again. Murray was one big salve, one huge soothing presence. Finlay had never been so hungry for more of something in his life.

Murray flapped a napkin, which turned out to be a tea towel, and placed it over Finlay's lap as he sat at the low table right before the fireplace.

'That's one of my emergency candles,' Finlay told him, seeing the fresh white taper flickering in the middle of the small table.

Murray ignored him, whisking around the room, presenting him with a steaming dish. 'Soup d'tomate,' he said.

'What language is that?'

'French?' Murray tried, not giving a monkey's. 'And there's salad de canned tuna and boildy œufs for mains.'

'Oh aye, boildy's just how I like them.' Smiling,

Finlay lifted his spoon, mirroring Murray, now seated opposite.

'None of your cutlery matches,' Murray told him.

'Does it need to?' Finlay tasted the soup.

Murray seemed to accept this answer, and he tried the soup too.

There were big wedges of bread which Murray was about to reach for when Finlay stopped him. 'Hold on,' he said, pointing to the toasting fork hanging on its fireside hook. 'It'll want freshening up a bit.'

Murray got the message, spearing two of the thickest slices on the prongs and holding them close to the fire.

'You look like a garden gnome with his fishing rod, sittin' like that,' Finlay told him, from behind their low table out of scale with the two mismatched dining chairs, decades old and creaky.

Murray laughed and turned the fork near the flames.

Their lunch passed in companionable, happy ease until all the bread was toasted, slathered with good Scottish butter, dunked and devoured, and the tuna and egg salad was gone too. Finlay had taken pains to make sure Nell was slipped as many scraps as he could manage without Murray telling him he was spoiling her.

After the dishes were washed, not easy with one arm in a sling, but still Finlay did his best to help, and Murray had swept up the crumbs and stood the broom back in the corner, the inevitable moment came.

Frantic, Finlay thought of ways to detain him.

'Do you think you could return my books, please?' he asked, pointing to the book tote hanging on the hook on the back of the door.

'Oh, aye,' Murray said, bubbling with intrigue. 'To your pals down at the library?'

'I dinnae like getting a fine.'

'Do you want me to pick you up any new books?' The question was innocent enough.

Finlay considered this. 'Judy knows the kind of books I like. She said she'd put aside a few for me, actually. You could bring those, if you like?'

He tried to say it like it was no big deal, but there were two or three volumes he'd been looking forward to ever since Judy had described them to him.

'I'll do it,' said Murray, reaching for the book bag. He looked inside, just as Finlay had feared.

'*An Unmannerly Affair*? *In Love With His Mistress's Master*? You read *romances*?'

'Aye.' Finlay raised his jaw. 'And what of it?'

'Well, nothing really. It's just surprising, that's all.' Murray's eyes had a wicked gleam. 'What's this one? *Catch and Release*?'

'That's about a pair of fishermen who... look, what does it matter? I enjoy them, OK?' Finlay snapped, snatching the book from his hand and shoving it back into the tote.

'You are nothing like I thought you'd be.' Murray grinned, observing him. 'I mean that in the nicest possible way.'

Finlay let the mocking wash over him. Insult or compliment, it didn't really matter because they'd shared these last twenty-four hours of solitude and it had been wonderful.

'Where's your library card?' Murray was asking.

'You don't need it to return books,' Finlay snapped. 'And Judy can issue the new ones to me on her computer.'

Murray's eyes gleamed at this. 'Is there something you don't want me to see?'

'*Och!*' Finlay reached for his wallet by the door and, struggling with only one working arm, freed the card and handed it over. 'Satisfied?'

Murray's laugh made the air crackle. 'Finlay *Way-*

ward Morlich? You're joking! Your parents named you Finlay Wayward?'

Finlay snatched the card back. 'Aye, well, naebody needs to know.'

Murray straightened his face. 'Right enough, let's keep it between us and Highland library services.'

'The name was supposed to be a reminder,' Finlay went on, smiling in spite of the smarting embarrassment.

'Of what?'

'To be good, I suppose.' Finlay forgot his injury and tried to shrug, flinching when the pain shot like a thunderbolt through him. '*Jeez-o!*' He sucked air sharply through his teeth, and Murray stopped his teasing to steady him, two warm hands clasping his arms.

'Careful, careful,' he warned. 'Your shoulder.'

The two stayed like this for a beat, adjusting to the closeness. No one felt much like laughing all of a sudden.

'Well,' Murray said, bringing his forehead down to rest on Finlay's, which felt as miraculous as it did natural. 'I'll stick to calling you Finlay, if you don't mind? There's nothing that seems wayward or even the tiniest bit bad about you, to me.'

Finlay heard Murray swallow through the thrum of tension between them.

'Will you visit again soon?' Finlay said, his eyelids growing heavy, wanting to close them.

'I will. How about next week? By the time I sort out these contracts, and my travel and accommodation arrangements, visas, maybe? And there's the pups to look after. I've really left Mum and Dad to deal with them, and there's the adoptions to sort out, and there'll be repair Saturday to endure, and the garden project on Sunday, I suppose?'

'Lots to do,' Finlay said.

'Lots.'

Finlay nodded, letting his forehead rub against Murray's, still neither of them wanting to pull apart.

He risked moving his arm to Murray's waist, before spreading his palm flat against the shallow of his spine.

Murray's breathing faltered.

Finlay pressed all the firmer and Murray closed the gap between their bodies.

'I'll bring you back some sweets,' Murray promised on an outward breath.

Finlay summoned all his courage to look into Murray's eyes, finding them heavy-lidded and soft. 'You don't need to. I'm feeling sweet enough,' he replied, barely thinking what he was saying, and with one shared breath between them, their lips met in the softest way possible.

Once Finlay got the message that this was all right, he kissed a little harder, a creature sound escaping from his chest.

Murray scooped his arm around his back, holding him fast, the other, above Finlay's bruised shoulder, cupped his face; a sensation Finlay had thought he'd never experience again in his lifetime.

A thumb brushed at his cheekbone as Murray kissed into him, deeper, better, all thoughts suspended until they were breathless and gaping at one another, open-eyed on the doormat, wondering at what had just happened.

'Are you OK?' Murray was asking through the fog.

'You kissed me,' Finlay told him stupidly.

Murray's mouth, still so close, broke into a hazy smile. 'And I'll come back and kiss you again, if you'll let me.'

Finlay nodded, stepping reluctantly away, keeping Murray's hand in his until the last moment, when the bolt was slipped, the door prised open, and the pair of them stood blinking at the early-afternoon light, amazed there was still a world outside their bubble.

Murray shouldered Finlay's book bag. 'See you after the weekend, yeah?'

Finlay could only nod, speechless. He watched as Murray walked down the little path to the gap in the low stone wall, turning right for the long path to town.

Suddenly, Murray stopped and looked back with a huge grin.

The muscles in Finlay's core ached at the sight, hoping he'd come running back, changing his mind, shouting to hell with town.

Murray whistled once, and Nell, who'd been sleeping on the hearthrug, sprang up and ran out of the door after her master.

Every fibre in Finlay's body had answered that whistle too, like iron filings yanked to attention by the magnetic Murray McIntyre, and yet he closed the door, having watched the two head down the path together.

He took himself back to the table where they'd eaten lunch, astonished at how a tiny cottage cruive, barely bigger than a shepherd's hut, could suddenly feel so utterly vast and empty.

41

There was trouble at the repair shed this lunch time, and it was all Jolyon's fault. Or that's what Shell was maintaining as she cried in her mum's arms out on the gravel drive.

'But he brought you a packet of pink wafers today,' Livvie was saying. 'And he's missed playing with you so much. Don't you think you can forgive him?'

Shell, with tears welling in the way they only can for tiny aggrieved girls who have been done a massive injustice, shook her bunches.

'We were doing the Stickle Bricks,' she said, 'which I don't mind because he's littler,' another big breath and a sob, 'and I told him he could sit on my blanket if he really wanted to...'

'That was nice of you,' said Livvie, wiping away her daughter's tears only for more to fall.

'And the next thing, he's walking around with it, cuddling it!'

'Oh, Shell.' Her mum pulled her closer. 'I think we might have to leave blankie at home, if this is going to keep happening?'

'No! I can't!'

Now it really was serious. Shell was gasping for air.

'OK, OK, we'll think of something,' Livvie soothed. 'Do you maybe want to... not see Jolyon for a wee while?'

'No!' Shell howled. 'He's my friend.'

'OK, got it,' said Livvie, glancing across the carpark to where a similar scene was playing out between Jolyon and Mhairi, and there was only a few minutes left of Shell's school lunch break to sort it all out. She'd have to get her back there before the bell rang at one.

Only Mhairi, who hadn't heard Shell defending her fledgling friendship, wasn't feeling quite so hopeful as Livvie that they could find a way around this problem. In fact, she was ready to get Jolly back in the car and leave.

This morning, they'd gone along to the first of the

long-awaited referrals, made by Dr Hargreave for Jolyon, and Mhairi had watched as the occupational therapist, who had been lovely – though that hadn't made Jolly's long appointment any less gruelling for him – put him through test after test, watching him play and do puzzles and hold a pen and make marks, and asking him to move around the room in certain ways, making him lie down and manipulating his joints this way and that.

Mhairi had found it tough, and she was only watching. So when it was all over she'd thought it might be nice to pop in to the repair shop and see if there was anyone around to play with on a Wednesday afternoon, underestimating how dysregu-lated and tired her son was, and the unexpected sight of his best friend in all the world had resulted in a great burst of enthusiasm, followed by a fast decline into sleepiness and so, when he'd innocently reached, yet again, for the blanket that was so precious to poor little Shell, the result had been one big crying match, and now this.

It was bringing back all those times a kid had read Jolly wrong, or there'd been parents grumbling about him not responding to friendly prompts the way *their* child would have. Yet she refused to explain herself or how her family worked, just like she refused to stop reminding other parents that 'be kind' was more than just a hashtag they stuck in their social media bios. It was a hard and fast rule for life in the Sears household, and what it meant was, don't judge, forgive easily, and keep your opinions to yourself.

Jolyon clung to his mother's neck, sobbing.

'What shall we do, eh, Jolly? Shall we go home? Maybe Daddy will be finishing work early? We could all cuddle up and watch *Bluey*, hmm?'

Jolly didn't loosen his grip.

'Or do you want to stay here and try to have a milkshake with Shell?' This wouldn't have been Mhairi's first choice.

Jolyon nodded against her neck and pulled back, his face streaked with tears and his eyes red.

'I promise you, I will look high and low for a blue blanket, just as soft and squishable, OK?'

And she meant it. She'd even considered asking Livvie if she could take a photo of the blasted thing so she could post it on Facebook with an appeal to find her son one exactly the same, because he'd formed an attachment to it in a way that was making things tricky with his new buddy.

With a sigh, Mhairi prepared herself to face Livvie

Cooper, another mother who must, by now, be beginning to think there was some kind of discipline issue that wasn't being kept on top of.

Mhairi raised a tentative hand to wave to Livvie across the carpark to signal they'd be over in a minute, but she wasn't looking.

Shell was busy whispering something in her mother's ear, which turned into both of them glancing across in Mhairi's direction as Mhairi quickly whipped her hand to her side. Then mother and daughter went off to find Roz who'd just come out of the mill house and the three of them fell into what appeared to be a very serious conversation about Mhairi and her son, if the troubled glances in their direction were anything to go by.

This signalled the end of her visits to the repair shed café, thought Mhairi, and more than likely it was the end of the gardening project for her and Jolyon too. The Coopers were no doubt, right this second, asking Roz to have them removed for disruptive behaviour and for repeatedly causing problems like this.

Maybe they aren't our friends after all, Mhairi said to herself, pre-emptively processing the rejection that was to come.

They didn't have to come back here if people weren't going to accept them. They could find another group to go to, though Mhairi was running out of options and she'd really, really liked it here, and more importantly, so had Jolly.

With a heavy sigh, she got up, zipped Jolyon's coat and made sure he still had his wellies on the correct feet before, resolutely, bundling him into his car seat, leaving Jolyon distraught and wondering where his friend and the promised milkshakes had got to.

Roz, Shell and Livvie remained in their secretive little whispering huddle as the three of them headed inside the repair shed together, forgetting entirely to wave goodbye in their direction.

'Oh, well.' Mhairi sighed as she clipped the seat belt. 'It was nice while it lasted.'

* * *

Murray had been amazed to find, as he made his way down the path to town, that the first signs of spring had arrived. Snowdrops bloomed in the hedgerows and the verges were alive with yellow crocuses. When had that happened? How could so much transformation take place in so few days?

He'd taken a last look up towards the cruive as he'd hit the turning for town and found it was only a little brown speck up there on the hillside. Even that made him smile.

Nell had hung back and had to be recalled many times as she'd tried to sneak back to Finlay and his scullery store of delicious food, but as soon as they drew near the mill house she'd broken into a run, remembering her pups.

Murray, not wanting to see anyone else quite yet, not until he'd tidied himself up a bit, had tiptoed across the drive and into the house, only to be met by a wild, yapping tumble of puppies who had grown a colossal amount in the days since he'd last seen them. Nell was happy to be reunited with her daughters, for a brief while, but by the time Murray had showered and shaved, she was back in her spot sleeping by the Aga, ignoring their antics.

This was a good sign, he thought. It was time to let the pups go. They didn't need her and she didn't mind being away from them, just so long as she got lots of love, food and naps.

'It'll be hard saying goodbye to you wee ones,' he told one of the pups, eye to eye. She stretched her tongue to lick the end of his nose.

'OK,' he said. 'I have emails to read.'

He set up his tablet on the wide expanse of his parents' kitchen table, thinking how echoing everything seemed in here after the cramped cosiness of the cruive. He had to stop himself daydreaming about that place, and about Finlay, and that kiss, or he'd never be able to stop the words swimming around on the screen in front of him.

'Contracts attached, for your consideration,' it read, and Murray forced himself to concentrate.

42

Another garden project Sunday came around and Alice had a lot to prove. First of all, she was going to demonstrate her professionalism, easier said than done since her helper, Murray, couldn't take his face out of his phone where he was booking flights, and sending messages, and who knew what else. She'd as good as written him off as a project participant now he was occupied planning for his new jobs.

Kellie was the only volunteer to turn up so far, though she had come with her mum and dad today, and they were all showing a lot more interest in the puppies than in sowing the two big bags of seed potatoes, and who could blame them, honestly?

'And how do we plant these?' asked Livvie, lifting a tuber and inspecting it.

'Umm.' Alice hadn't a clue. How she wished Finlay Morlich was recovered. He was the one who knew all about this stuff, not her.

Car doors banged out on the drive and Alice tried not to look too hopefully in their direction as three new garden project recruits made their way towards her. All of them had been invited to join the project following recent appointments at the surgery, and all were looking around, unsure what exactly was going to happen.

A motorbike engine roared then cut out on the drive and, to her surprise, Clyde Forte, not without some difficulty, clambered off, swinging his leg over the machine, straightening himself up on the gravel.

He'd biked himself here today, and even if it was only a short distance from his home, this clearly signified that he'd smashed his goal of getting back on his motorcycle. So in spite of all his grumbling, recovery was coming withing reach. She thought how she would buy an extra big pack of custard creams for this month's stroke clinic in celebration. He removed his helmet and Alice caught the gleam of pride in his eyes. He was also, she noticed, excessively bundled up in layer upon layer of woollens.

'No chance of getting cold today, then?' she said as he made a beeline for the tea urn, remembering how he'd told her not to go rushing in, gushing, over Kellie's achievement of getting to the project on that first day. She held back now just as she had then. He would already know that she was delighted for him, and that was enough for now. Besides, her heart wasn't too busy swelling with happiness for Clyde to forget it was still hoping for the arrival of someone else.

In the two weeks since he'd gone she'd thought of Cary every time she safely stowed away her stethoscope in its box on her consulting room desk, and more than once she'd sighed and caressed its smooth polished planes and wished for him to be back in the repair shed the very next time she called in. She'd become an even more frequent visitor these last few days, sampling almost everything in Senga's admittedly delicious baking repertoire, but he was never there.

At least McIntyre was here to help, and now he was calling the little gathering together out by the raised beds.

Senga was of course here too, striding around offering everyone a slice of chocolate orange brownie, one of Alice's absolute favourites in recent weeks.

Jolyon Sears made his way through the forest of adults' legs to get to the front and claim a chocolatey slice, sitting on the edge of a raised bed to eat it, leaving his mum at the very back of the group. He'd made it very clear where he wanted to be this Sunday morning, and his mum's offers, meant as a distraction, of visits to the wildlife park or the reindeer visitor centre, or tubing on the baby slopes, had all been refused. He wanted his wellies on and his garden trowel. So, resignedly, and braced for trouble, she'd brought him to the garden project.

Sure enough, trouble was still brewing. No sooner had Livvie pulled up in her car, she and Shell had hopped out and streaked across the driveway grabbing a flustered Roz on the way, and all three of them had dived into the shed, conspiring together, just as they had the other day.

'No Livvie and Roz? What about Shell?' McIntyre was asking now over the heads. Mhairi didn't say anything about how they were busy plotting against her and her son, although Jolly pointed through the wall of the repair shed, indicating he'd noticed them going inside.

'You take over now, Doctor,' McIntyre said, and he took a respectful step away.

'Oh, right.' Alice awkwardly held her half-eaten

brownie slice as she addressed the group. 'As you know, today is our very first day of sowing our potatoes and planting out our woody herbs, and there's tomatoes to sow too, apparently. Now that the weather's taken a turn for the drier.'

'Thank goodness!' Mr Forte chimed in. He was drinking his tea and had a cigarette tucked behind his ear.

'It couldnae have got any wetter, that's for sure!' Senga chipped in.

Alice wondered at how calm she felt in front of the big group, even with the threat of an occasional heckle. Maybe her experience addressing the haggis so successfully had helped her get over some of her nerves in situations like this, or maybe it was something to do with Bonnie and all the hours they'd spent in her cosy consulting room? Or was it the way Dr Millen had helped her manage her anxieties at work by charting and identifying the pressure points throughout her day and how she responded to them, making plans to lessen the pressure next time around with practical adaptations to their working routines and systems, helping each other with the harder tasks, always talking through what went well and what needed tweaking for next time.

'Quite,' agreed Alice. 'It's been a tough winter, but

now there's some warmth in the February sunshine, sort of, and we've lots of things to put in the earth, and since our experts aren't all here, I suggest we just try to work it out for ourselves. Herbs go in that one.' She pointed to the bed behind her to her left. 'Potato seeds in one end of that bed, and there's seeds to sow, if you can make out the small print on the packets, and they'll go in trays in front of the big glass windows at the back of the repair shed café, now the building materials have almost all gone from inside. Oh, and people working outside, be careful not to tread on any of the wildflowers that we planted around the aspen trees last month. How does all of that sound?'

Surprisingly, no one seemed fazed, and one of the new recruits, Miss Sylvia Wilson, a keen knitter in her early seventies with a blood pressure problem, was rolling up her sleeves and asking Mr Forte if he wanted to team up, since she hadn't her glasses with her to read the instructions on the seed packets.

He'd waggled his readers at her in a jolly sort of way, and the pair had headed inside to where Alice has set up a sowing station by the fire, with tomato seeds and compost and little coir pots at the ready. From the sprightly way Mr Forte accompanied the smiling Miss Wilson into the shed, Alice had a feeling she might have inadvertently struck upon another way of increasing the appeal of the garden project for him.

'Shall we?' McIntyre said, appearing by Alice's side, handing her a trowel.

'Right you are,' she replied and she made for the herb bed, ready to muck in.

* * *

Alice had been up to her wrists in crumbly compost when she realised the low winter sunshine she'd been enjoying had gone.

Looking up, expecting to find a cloud blocking out the sun, she instead saw a pair of dapper, belted trousers, a tidy waistcoat and a shirt, complete with a tweedy tie and, above that, a really very endearing, if a little anxious, smile.

'Cary!' She was on her feet in an instant, wondering if ever, in the history of anything, a person had been so glad to see another.

* * *

Finlay couldn't get his coat on properly, but that hadn't stopped him trying and, with it draped over his shoulders he limped out to the stormwall with his rations tin.

The binoculars felt too heavy in his hand, so he'd left them in the cruive.

It was a beautiful day with a smell of the first shoots of wild garlic in the air, so early this year. The spotty fronds of tough little ferns were unfurling from gaps in the stone wall. Spring was showing itself, even up here amongst the rocks. Finlay inhaled it deeply.

His hand reached reflexively for his tin, but when he flipped the lid open to survey his goodies, he was surprised to find not one of them tempted him. Not even the tablet.

He scratched his head and thought very hard.

The cruive stood behind him, the door open, awaiting his return. The chimney gave off a thin curl of smoke as the hearth died down.

There was something not right, not right at all. Was he ill? Sleepy? Hungry? No, it was none of those things. What was this?

Murray was down there in the town. He'd promised him he'd be back to see him next week, and it was Sunday now. Finlay was already driving himself wild with waiting. Murray had sent him a text every morning and every night, and there'd been rather too many photos of puppy dogs, and not enough messages about where exactly the pair of them stood now. Neither had there been any mention of those contracts Murray had either signed or shredded. Finlay had a good idea which it was, and guessed Murray was holding off on telling him the bad news until they were face to face. There was also the small matter of his library holds, another thing Murray had proven not very forthcoming in detailing. Had he got the new KJ Charles or not? A man needed to know these things, but most of all he needed to know if Murray was burning for him like he was for Murray.

'Dammit! This is insufferable!' he shouted, scaring his sparrow friends away.

He stomped his way back to the cruive and pulled the door hard behind him, not thinking once how he'd left his precious rations tin out on the wall for the crows to find.

He was going to have to go down to town himself.

43

There hadn't really been time to talk, what with her new recruits to see to around the garden, helping them settle in. Cary had simply told Alice he was glad to see her looking so well and then headed inside the repair shop, followed by Senga Gifford, hot for some gossip.

So Alice had done her job, chatting with the participants and their families, asking about their current prescriptions or their physio regimes, and answering their questions about how she was finding the town, now she was settling in.

She'd helped Jolyon plant a long row of seed potatoes, noting how withdrawn he and his mother were today and finding that nothing she said seemed to cheer them up. Soon they were out of seeds and glad of the excuse to follow Cary indoors, she excused herself and made her way into the shed. As she entered, Livvie, Roz and Shell were on their way out, and the little girl was giggling about something. She'd have thought more of all this if she wasn't determined to see Cary.

He was at his workbench where he had been deep in conversation with Senga or, more likely, she had been filling him in on Finlay getting lost in the fog and Murray and Nell's rescue mission. Yes, that would be it. There was so much he'd missed.

'I'll leave you two to catch up,' Senga said upon seeing Alice standing there, and with a look so indiscreet she'd actually wanted to laugh, but Cary didn't look like he was in the mood for laughter.

'So, you're back,' she told him.

He nodded.

She took her time building up to her next utterance. 'And... do you think you're staying?'

'I don't know yet.'

This jolted her. 'Is it me?' she demanded. 'Because if it is, I'm sorry. I know you came to the Burns supper that night, Rhona told me she saw you...'

Cary's face fell.

'It *is* me, then!' she cried. 'You know I sent Bastian packing, right?'

Cary looked wary.

'He stayed the night and made you breakfast,' he said, 'and he was on about whisking you away for a spa break and how things were going to be different with him around, and then Senga was just telling me about how you *have* been off on a spa break, which of course is none of my business, but...'

'A spa break?' She breathed deep to stop the dizziness striking, just like she'd mastered, working with Bonnie. 'I was away for one day at a lovely castle, and I suppose, yes, technically it was a spa, but it was a women's wellness retreat.'

Cary blinked.

'And I went on my own, or rather, I went with a load of other women and Bonnie was there too.'

'Bonnie?'

'The counsellor I've been seeing. The one you recommended?'

Cary took a deep breath as light dawned. 'You weren't away with your Manchester doctor boyfriend, then?'

'God, no!'

'Not that I'd have any right to any kind of opinion about that.'

'Is Bastian why you've been away for so long?'

He shook his head as though not understanding. 'Oh, no, well, only partially. I went to see Mum. She was moving into sheltered accommodation and I decided to go and help. And yes, it was prompted by your boyfriend coming to get you, but there was also a lot of things of Mum's to pack and to sort through. It was a lot of work, moving her from a big house into a small one.'

'Oh!' Alice dropped her heels to the floor. She hadn't realised she'd been on the balls of her feet until now. 'Is she OK? Your mum?'

'She is, thanks.'

'And that was why you were gone for so long, without telling anyone?' *Without telling me*, she thought.

'I needed to get away from it all, to clear my head for a while. Sometimes even I need to get away, to think. I'm not as self-contained as folks might think, just because I'm quieter than most. And this place can get on a person's wick, with all its gossiping and never being able to get away from folk.'

'You wanted to get away from me.'

'I needed some time not seeing you, and I wasn't that keen on seeing you with him. It's true. Sorry.'

'Don't apologise.' Alice thought of all the noise

Bastian had made, coming into town that night, thinking himself a knight in shining armour, all the disruption he'd caused.

A silence bloomed between them. The shed grew warmer.

'So you're seeing a counsellor?' he said at last. 'I'm glad for you, but I shouldn't have interfered like that.'

'No, no, I'm glad you did. It was the push I needed. And you going away showed me I had to rely on myself, first and foremost, but I also had to learn to ask for help, and to say out loud when I was struggling... So that's what I've been doing.'

'And?'

'And it's been great, and hard, and scary, and there's a long way to go but... overall it's been good.'

Alice didn't tell him how she and Bonnie had been working on separating out her anxiety, which kickstarted her frightening visions and catastrophising, from her good dreams, the ones that pointed her in the direction of the things she needed. Things like a home and a community and her work, and Cary, if he'd ever have her.

'It took me a few goes to find the right counsellor for me, the right fit,' Cary said.

'Me and Bonnie just clicked.' Alice beamed.

Cary smiled back before asking, 'Are we friends again?'

'Should we get back out to the garden?' she asked, not knowing how to reply to that.

Cary crooked his arm, and she looped her hand through it, and they walked out into the darkening February afternoon just as the floodlight was coming on, drenching the whole place in a golden glow like a summer's day.

44

All the potatoes and herbs were in the ground now, and it was time for a celebratory mug of tea. Murray was about to take his parents aside to show them the congratulatory email that had just come from his boss in Switzerland, now that she had his signed contracts on her desk. There'd be the small matter of telling his sister, Ally, that he'd be seeing her soon too, albeit briefly, over there.

He didn't want to think about what all this meant for his nursing of a certain mountain man back to full health, and he wondered if he could wait until tomorrow to go racing back up there to the cruive to find out.

As he was approaching his parents, a woman

made her way up to Murray, tapping him on the elbow.

'Kellie, right?' he asked her.

'That's right,' she said, a little awkwardly. 'There was something I wanted to ask you, and I'm not sure how you're going to feel about it.'

Her mum and dad had come to stand on either side of their daughter and Murray listened as she explained how much she'd enjoyed the garden project, and it wasn't that she was ungrateful or anything, but the thing she'd look forward to most about her visits was the chance to see the puppies again, and in particular one of the pups, the smallest.

'You want to adopt her?' Murray said, not quite sure how to feel.

'We've seen the improvement in her, day by day, just from being around Poppet,' her father said.

'I'm sorry, who?' It took Murray a moment to register it, but then the pup tumbled up to Kellie's feet and he watched as she scooped her up into her arms.

'Poppet, eh?' said Murray, grinning.

It didn't long to sort it all out. Poppet was old enough to leave with the Timmony family today, if they wanted, and Kellie said she'd hoped he was going to say that because they'd already bought her some stuff from the big pet store out of town.

Murray had only just finished waving the family and their new dog away in their car, with Kellie beaming with joy in the back seat holding her little Poppet, when two things happened at once.

Firstly, Murray felt himself wanting to cry, thinking he couldn't give a second puppy away, determining that even if she had to stay here with Nell, who no one seemed to want to adopt anyway, and be a repair shop dog forever, he'd see to it that happened. And secondly, a lurching, limping figure in a coat with the sleeves flapping like wings behind him was stumbling through the gap in the wall.

Murray scrunched his eyes and blinked in disbelief, then flew into a panic, because what on earth was he doing in town?

'Finlay Morlich! Have you hiked yourself all the way down that hill, in your condition?' But he was smiling, just like Finlay was, even if the ranger looked fit to pass out.

'Get inside here, you silly, silly person!' Murray marched the breathless man into the mill house kitchen and made him sit at the table.

Murray was busy pouring him a glass of water when they heard scratching at the door and he had to go and let Nell in too.

The ranger tried to drink his water while Nell

shoved at his legs and bounded in leaps of happiness at seeing her friend again. Finlay had to put his glass down to pet the dog.

'Are you going to explain to me what all of this is in aid of?' Murray demanded.

'It's just that I...' Finlay paused, suddenly unsure of himself. 'It's just I... I missed... this stupid big dug, and I thought to myself, I wanted to see her. So, I got my boots on...' Murray's eyes fell to his unlaced hiking boots, the tongues lost inside. 'And I came down to see you, I mean Nell. I came down the mountain to see Nell.'

Murray's smile broadened. 'I see. And had you any plans beyond that?'

Finlay shook his head. 'Well, not really. Only, I actually did miss the mutt and wondered if the offer still stands to... take her off your hands? Do you a favour, like.'

'Ah, a favour to me? Right.' Murray nodded. 'I think that could be arranged.'

For the first time in a very, very long time, at sea level, Finlay smiled too, and he patted the dog's head. 'Daft creature,' he told her.

'Yes, you are,' agreed Murray, talking directly to Finlay. 'So, is that it? You've done everything you came to do?' He folded his arms, standing over the mountain man and his newly adopted best friend.

Finlay gulped and with some effort, got to his feet, before sitting sharply back down again. 'Actually, can you give me a hand getting these boots off? My feet are killing me.'

Murray kneeled before him, making quick work of it, and once his boots were off, staying down there to rub the places his feet must hurt. 'You were about to say...?'

'I was about to say,' Finlay began, 'that maybe it wasn't just the dog I was missing.'

Murray stifled a laugh. 'I'd only been gone three days.'

'Four whole nights, actually,' Finlay corrected. 'And I was thinking how, it doesn't matter where in the world your job is posting you to, I'll be here waiting for you when you get back.'

'You will?'

'I will,' Finlay said simply. 'But I'd still like to know, pretty sharpish, where in the world you're planning on going. I'm assuming you do know by now?'

Murray abandoned Finlay's feet and stood before him. 'I *am* going to Bali, as it happens, for three months starting in September, though I've said no to the Texas job.'

'Why?'

'Too far from you, I suppose.' Murray shrugged. 'And the other contract, I accepted as well.' He could tell Finlay was putting on a brave face, preparing for worse news. 'It's in Ballater.'

'Ballater? Ballater as in, an hour down the road, Ballater?'

Murray nodded. 'Overseeing community heat sink projects. Three months, starting at the end of February. Home in the evenings.'

Finlay Morlich looked as though he was about to pass out, so Murray reached for him, and with steady hands lifted him to his feet.

'So I'll be seeing you,' Murray told him, and he kissed him on the lips, to make sure he understood. 'A lot. If that's what you want?'

Finlay dropped his head to Murray's shoulder with a laugh of relief and the three of them, two people newly in love and the ranger's delighted, bouncing dog, hugged in the warmth of the mill house kitchen.

45

Cary knew that they were supposed to wait for the big reveal, like McIntyre enjoyed, and Dr Bonnet probably wanted, so that the horologist could talk at length at him about the minutiae of her repair work, but that didn't appeal quite so much as sneaking away now to take a peek at the restored clock with Alice.

So as the first of the gardeners were taking their leave for the day, and the afternoon was turning cold, he held her hand and led her into the repair shed.

'Do you want to do the honours?' Alice asked, and Cary shook his head. No, he wanted her to pull the cloth.

As the material fell away, Cary felt all words leave

him, and he stepped towards the clock, Alice's eyes fixed upon him.

He put his head to the case where inside the pendulum was swinging, *tick tock*, in a deep tenor that carried him right back to his childhood in Glo Glo's house. Never a man afraid of his feelings, he let his eyes fill with tears and spill over.

The wood, the stain, the metal, the glass, everything looked and smelled just as it had done when the clock had overseen every family party he had known. He had his old friend back.

'Look,' he said. 'Mum gave me this.' He drew a photograph from his pocket and handed it over.

Smiling children surrounded an elderly couple at the centre of the picture and in the background stood the clock, looking much as it did now. 'And that's me,' he said with a laugh in his voice, pointing to a very dapper little boy in a suit amidst all the others in jeans and t-shirts.

'I'd have guessed,' Alice told him, with a fond look at the child he once was. 'There's something I have to tell you,' she said. 'And it might sound strange, but hear me out, yeah?'

Cary was sure it couldn't be that bad, so he waited for her to be ready.

'You see, the thing is...' She swallowed hard.

'When you told me you might be going back to Glasgow for good' – Cary resisted the urge to interrupt – 'and you told me your Glo Glo's story about the clock and how it was magic, and... well...'

He nodded his encouragement. 'It's OK. Go on.'

'I was so afraid you were planning on leaving. I couldn't stop thinking about it. I kept dreaming about you going away, and it all sort of got mashed up in my head with your story about the clock, and I'd daydream about how it was going to carry you away, out of this time and place, which I know is silly, but...'

'I used to imagine the same things exactly,' he told her. 'When I was a kid. It is, after all, a very magic clock.' He was smiling, wanting her to see it was all right, but she wasn't done yet.

She nodded as she spoke. 'But it was *me* who was in danger of slipping away, because I needed to take better care of myself. I needed to ask for help. Do you get it?'

'Of course I do.'

'And talking about all of this with my counsellor and in my mentoring sessions with Dr Millen, and really *actually* taking care of myself, and dealing with Bastian at long last, and being here, and working in the garden, and *all* of it... made me even more sure that I liked you, very much. And I don't want you to go back to Glasgow, not because I need you, but because I want you, and because I'm planning on staying here. For good.'

The words made his heart chime like the bells inside the clock case.

'And not that I can make you stay or anything,' she went on. 'But I wish you would. So, there! That's what I had to say.'

It was so beautiful he wished she'd say it all over again, but instead he reached for her hand. 'I'm glad to hear it.'

'Are you?'

'Of course. I don't want to be anywhere you aren't.'

'But, Cary...' She hesitated. 'You... you're so quiet, it's hard to know what you're thinking.'

'Well then,' Cary smiled, his heart swelling with pride to be the one who got to tell her this. 'Let me be perfectly loud and clear. Dr Alice Hargreave, I have been at your service since the day we met outside the bank. I've *liked* you since that meeting at the surgery when you looked fit to drop with exhaustion and sadness. I've been *devoted* to you since you fell ill here in the repair shop and we sat by the fire together, and I had to go to war against all my instincts in case I told you how I felt, there and then. And, God knows, I've *wanted* you since you listened to my heart beating through my shirt that day, and you sent my pulse sky high with the need to hold you, and from that day my heart's beaten *only* for you.'

He stopped, letting her think.

'Is this clear enough?' he asked.

'So, we're not going anywhere?' she asked. 'Neither of us?'

'We're staying right here,' he said, and not able to hold back a moment longer, he stepped closer so they could kiss, and they stayed like that in each other's arms until the clock had struck the hour, and the next one too, because Alice Hargreave was, at last, exactly in the spot where she needed to be.

46

Mhairi had made it to the car and Jolyon was safely strapped in his seat, exhausted from a long day's gardening. She wished she could say she'd enjoyed it as much as him, even if Shell seemed to have forgiven her son enough to come and plant a few potatoes and herbs alongside him, but Mhairi had been unable to shake the feeling of eyes upon her, of being judged. But soon they'd be home and out of sight of everyone. What a relief that always was.

'Mrs Sears,' a voice called. 'Can I have a word?'

Mhairi froze. That phrase, whether it was said with a beckoning finger at nursery pick-up, or by a health visitor at her doorstep, was enough to strike her frozen with fear.

She turned slowly on her heel, taking the time to rearrange her face, but on their way across the floodlit carpark towards her at quite a pace were Livvie and Roz and Shell, and they looked like they meant business. She took a deep breath.

'Look, I know you want us gone from the project,' Mhairi pre-empted.

'Before you go, we wanted to show you something,' Livvie was saying over her, 'because I think we might have been getting ourselves in a pickle unnecessarily.'

'Oh?' Mhairi said, wincing and wishing herself miles away.

Jolyon, however, was chuckling from his car seat, waving at his friend.

'Show them, Shell,' said Livvie, and from behind her back the little girl produced her precious blue blanket.

Jolyon's eyes lit up at the sight of it and he reached out a hand.

'Oh, you can't be handing that over, Shell. Isn't that your special blankie?' Mhairi said, looking between the girl and her mum.

Shell, however, seemed resolute and, stepping closer to the little boy, she pulled her hands apart to reveal the blanket was somehow cut into two halves.

Mhairi's chest sank with a heavy weight of emotion. 'You split it?' she said.

'*She* did,' said Shell, tipping her head towards Roz, 'but it was *my* idea.'

'I may have hemmed it in blue satin all the way round so it won't fray, and there's a wee bit of embroidery too,' said Roz.

Shell sorted the two pieces, showing Jolyon his name stitched in sunshine yellow on his half. 'And my half says Shell.'

'You weren't cross with us?' Mhairi asked, her mind racing. 'This was what you were doing when you all disappeared together into the repair shop?'

Jolyon had the blanket in his hands and against his cheek in seconds, and Livvie steadied an emotional Mhairi with a hand at her arm.

'Of course we weren't cross,' said Livvie like it was obvious. 'What's there to be cross about amongst friends?'

Jolyon, once unstrapped from his car seat, joined in the game of giving out hugs, stretching his arms especially wide for Shell. The little girl laughed at this and held her friend tight, and no one had to say another thing because, as the bairns had proven, sometimes love needs no words at all.

EPILOGUE

Alice Hargreave was daydreaming again.

Cary's woodworking yard was leafy and bright under the late-March sunshine. She was in her favourite place, under a blanket with her coffee, watching Cary working on his latest cabinetry commission. He stopped for a moment to wipe a hand across his brow, smiling for her, and she smiled back.

Even though it was only early spring, she was dreaming already of the sunny season here and in the gardens at the repair shop, which were already sprouting with fresh green life, and the aspen trees had budded heavily, ready to put out their leaves.

She dreamed also of how lovely the blossom would be on the apple trees all around Cary's lovely yard, and she dreamed of her mother coming to stay for Easter, alone, now that she'd followed her daughter's lead, with a fair bit of talking over the phone, and she'd put some gentle boundaries in place for her erstwhile husband.

Alice was dreaming too of the town's Beltane bonfire celebration that she'd heard all about from Gracie, knowing it involved wine and wild dancing until deep into May Day morning.

She sighed and sipped her coffee, drawing Cary's attention, summoning him as if by witchcraft to wander over and take a sip from her cup, before he kissed the top of her head and went back to his work.

She dreamed of getting better, and the long lifetime of self-care she had ahead of her in that regard, but she was prepared for it, and prepared to continue reaping its benefits too.

A sound broke through her peaceful reverie, a voice, growing louder.

Cary lifted his head and mouthed in silent terror the name, 'Carenza!' before gritting his teeth in fear, making her laugh.

Sure enough, on the other side of the fence, passing down the wide path that separated Cary's workshop cottage from the other houses, was Carenza

McDowell in full property-mogul sail, and behind her trotted Murray, Finlay and Nell.

'Now that Finlay's coming down from the mountain,' Carenza was saying, 'this kind of pied-à-terre is just the sort of home two modern men about town need.'

Cary abandoned his work and crept over the yard to his girlfriend, taking her hand as she shucked off the blanket, tiptoeing and giggling as they made their way inside to avoid catching Carenza's eye through the gaps in the fence. Who knew what plans she had up her sleeve for the town's newest doctor since she'd found her so accommodating with the Burns supper? Alice didn't want to be caught by her and find out.

Alice shut the pair of them safely inside the cottage and, finding herself face to face with Cary, who she hadn't grown remotely tired of kissing, stretched her arms around his neck in a languorous way, and he whipped her up into his arms, carrying her out of sight of the glass door as she laughed and sighed in perfect contentment.

Outside, Finlay was pretending to listen to Carenza as she jangled a huge bunch of keys and led them up a garden path to a slim cottage with a garden bursting with spring bulbs. He didn't really mind what kind of property his money went on, so long as Murray and Nell liked it.

It hadn't taken him long to make his decision to leave his little cruive, not when it had begun to feel lonely up there, especially when Murray was working away and it was just him and the dog – who he was now utterly devoted to, even if he did complain about her behaviour and call her a 'daft creature' every day. Nell loved him back ten thousandfold and really seemed to be *trying* not to bolt off any more, even though sometimes she'd get an idea, or a whiff of squirrel, and there could be found a Nell-shaped gap in the cruive hedges (why use an open gate when you can escape through the bushes?) She'd be discovered down at the mill house visiting Wayward, the remaining puppy (and named as Murray's idea of a joke), or Poppet (who Kellie still brought back to visit Mr Forte and the others on garden project Sundays).

Murray's absences while he was working away from Cairn Dhu on long days were something they'd both borne well, mainly because it meant romantic reunions come seven o'clock and having it re-confirmed every evening that the two of them were unshakeably drawn to one another like magnets.

Carenza was opening the door and stepping inside the really very lovely old building, the perfume of the little courtyard's daffodils in the warming air.

Finlay's mother hadn't been right about many things, but she had known her son was waiting for his moment to bloom, and that moment was now, and every other moment he had Murray's hand clasped in his, and Nell's lead in the other.

'Now, I think you'll like this one, Mr Morlich,' Carenza was announcing, so loud the whole street could hear. 'This one used to be the town sweetshop!'

'Oh, now,' said Murray, about to follow her through the door, 'that sounds right up Fin's street.'

Finlay, however, pulled at Murray's hand to delay him in following Carenza inside. He glanced up at the mellow old stone and the roses already in glossy green leaf all around the charming yellow sunburst door.

Murray followed his gaze up over the sash windows with their window boxes planted with colourful violas, and up to the swallows' nests in the eaves and the black mountain slates on the roof.

'What's wrong?' Murray asked.

'You don't think all this,' Finlay looked longingly at the welcome mat and the pots of tulips on the worn stone step, 'is too much? Too... nice?'

'No,' Murray told him, confidently, pulling him

close for a kiss and not letting him go. 'Just because you don't require much doesn't mean you only deserve the bare minimum, remember?' He kissed him again for good measure, knowing it would turn Finlay soft-hearted and starry-eyed all over again. It was his favourite thing to do.

'I'm learning to remember,' Finlay replied, and before Carenza could yell at them to come and admire the country cottage with its open fireplaces, spiral staircase and lion's claw bath, Finlay led his boyfriend, and their spoiled, happy dog, inside their sweet little house and closed the door softly behind them.

* * *

MORE FROM KILEY DUNBAR

Another book from Kiley Dunbar, is available to order now here:
https://mybook.to/SparksBackAd

SENGA GIFFORD'S CHOCOLATE DIGESTIVE SQUARES

This recipe is my mum's. She always made these tasty, moreish, deliciously sweet bites for every birthday or Hogmanay party we ever hosted and, not really knowing what to call it, we always just referred to it as 'chocolate stuff'. It is the stuff of family legend and no 'do' is complete without it. What do you call it where you're from?

2 tablespoons Golden Syrup
100g Salted Butter
1 tin Sweetened Condensed Milk (I use Carnation's 397g tin)
2 tablespoons Soft Brown Sugar

400g Crushed Digestive Biscuits – with extra on hand in case they're needed
(or, at a push, the same amount in Abernethy Biscuits or Graham Crackers)
1 large bar Milk Chocolate

First, crush the biscuits into fine crumbs in a large mixing bowl.

Heat the butter, sugar, condensed milk and syrup in a heavy bottomed pan, stirring all the time to dissolve the sugar, bringing the mixture up briefly to a bubbling boil. 5-10 minutes on the hob should be enough all together and the mixture will turn a little bit thicker and more caramel coloured.

Pour the hot mixture into the biscuit crumbs and mix together very well until every crumb is coated. It should be dry rather than runny, so add extra crushed biscuits if it feels too wet to get a good set.

Press the mixture into a lined 10-inch tray or tin making a solid layer around 1 to 2 inches thick.

Refrigerate until set firm and very cool.

Then break up your milk chocolate, heat in 30 second blasts in the microwave until melted (careful not to let it burn!) and then pour over the chilled biscuit and put back in the fridge until this too has set.

Cut into squares while still setting and store in an airtight container.

Lasts up to a week in the fridge, or the length of one terribly serious work meeting you want lightening.

Enjoy!

JOLYON SEARS'S FAVOURITE ICED BISCUITS

Here's a quick and easy 'no cook' treat to make with kids.

You only need ten minutes to assemble these tasty treats which should be eaten on the same day, after allowing the icing to set fully (but if you can't wait and it's still a wee bit gooey, I'm not going to judge).

Abernethy Biscuits (a Scottish favourite, similar-ish to Digestives or Graham Crackers, which you can also try, or use any kind of homemade shortcake biscuit, but that's more of a faff.)
Strawberry Jam
Powdered Icing Sugar

Water, and a few drops of lemon juice (if you want)
Half Glace Cherries or Jelly Shapes (or what-ever you desire) to decorate

Stick two Abernethy biscuits together with a thorough slathering of strawberry jam. Do this as many times as required. Don't mind any sticky messes.

Following the instructions on the packet, mix up as much icing sugar as you will need to top each biscuit sandwich, using a few drops of cold water at a time (and lemon juice for flavour, if you wish) until you have a stirrable but firm consistency. You don't want your icing running off your biscuits!

Ice the top of your biscuit sandwiches, then decorate with your chosen sweeties or half cherries.

Pop in the fridge until the icing sets, then eat them all up, quick!

ACKNOWLEDGEMENTS

Hello! You're reading my second Highland Repair Shop book? I'm glad to hear it! Thank you so much for picking it up. It comes with one caveat and a lot of thanks.

Number one, thank you to all the GP receptionists, especially Auntie Catherine, who was the very best in that job. I know that no one like Gracie could possibly work in our wonderful NHS, but a sensible, discreet person in this role would interfere with a jolly story, so I hope you'll indulge Gracie's nosey nonsense. That was the caveat.

My thanks go to everyone at Boldwood Books, especially Francesca. It is lovely making books with you. Thank you so much to Cecily Blench for my copy edits and helping me wrangle the timelines until they behaved themselves. Thank you Rose Fox for your excellent proof reading.

Thank you, Nic, R, I, and Mouse. Thank you, wee Mossy, too. Thank you, Dream Team, big and less big.

Thank you, Claire H (and your Gaelic teacher!), Kirsty B, Lizzie F, MJ, Vicky, and Imogen. You're all lovely.

I have had amazing writing inspiration and support from the LWS this year, so thank you to everyone there.

Most importantly, thank you for being here to read my story and witness me bringing my thirteenth book into the world and proving that even imperfect things can be joyful in the making and the sharing. Thank you for supporting me all this while.

I'll be back with the *Highland Repair Shop* book three before you can say 'Summer 2026'.

Until then, happy reading and repairing,

Love, Kiley, x

ABOUT THE AUTHOR

Kiley Dunbar has been telling romantic stories since 2019, including her bestselling Borrow a Bookshop series. She lives in the north of England with her partner, her two lovely Dunbar babies and a beloved Bedlington Terrier, Amos. When Kiley's not writing cosy love stories she is a senior lecturer at The Manchester Writing School.

Download your exclusive bonus content from Kiley Dunbar here:

Visit Kiley's website: www.kileydunbar.co.uk

Follow Kiley on social media here:

instagram.com/kileydunbarauthor

facebook.com/KileyDunbarAuthor

ALSO BY KILEY DUNBAR

The Highland Repair Shop

Fixing a Broken Heart at the Highland Repair Shop

Mending Lost Dreams at the Highland Repair Shop

Making Sparks Fly at the Highland Repair Shop

BECOME A MEMBER OF

THE
SHELF
CARE
CLUB

The home of Boldwood's
book club reads.

Find uplifting reads,
sunny escapes, cosy romances,
family dramas and more!

Sign up to the newsletter
https://bit.ly/theshelfcareclub

Boldwood

Boldwood Books is an award-winning fiction publishing company seeking out the best stories from around the world.

Find out more at www.boldwoodbooks.com

Join our reader community for brilliant books, competitions and offers!

Follow us
@BoldwoodBooks
@TheBoldBookClub

Sign up to our weekly deals newsletter

https://bit.ly/BoldwoodBNewsletter